The
DIRTIES

Daniel H. Gottlieb

Canopy Publishing
Post Office Box 1645
Lake Oswego, Oregon
97035
www.canopypublishing.com
www.climatebull.com

Library of Congress Control Number: 2011909458
ISBN 97809753655-5-7
Printed in the United States of America

The
DIRTIES

Daniel H. Gottlieb

CANOPY PUBLISHING
Oregon   2011

Books by Daniel H. GOTTLIEB

The Galileo Syndrome, *2004*
The Fires of Home, *2010*
The Dialogues of Sancho and Quixote, Mythical Debates
      on Global Warming: 1997-2010, *2010*
The Dirties, *2011*

For La

"Patriotism is supporting your country all the time, and your government when it deserves it."

Mark Twain

PREAMBLE

For two-hundred years, the infighting, the petty jealousy, the salve of love, a manufactured need for more goods, the media blur, the curse of alcohol, and the joy of drugs had all worked together to form an impenetrable barrier of consumer lust keeping society ordered and safe. This first Wall, better known as the middle class, remained an effective barrier between the elite and the have-nots until the mid-twentieth century when the lust began to spin out of control. Information and capital gushed out of the corporate structure like a planetary arterial wound. By the mid 1990's, the cannibalizing of the middle class went viral.

Fully seasoned by the beginning of the 21st century, the social contract of nations became myth and avarice superseded it as the de facto community configuration of industrial society. The barrier of consumerism collapsed as lobbying efforts hauled government functionaries through obscene political maneuvers, like swine on a rope. Information became the enemy of civilized society as morality was remodeled into a decor and the battle for power between nations and the corporate states took center stage.

The middle class shriveled in the developed nations and

erupted like a cancer in the developing nations. Dilettantes declared it a healthy economic cycle and media support held it as truth. In this rush of madness, the dysfunctional social ethic of leadership without responsibility grew--was exported to country after country--and the vast economic benefits of iniquity became an objective. Nepotism and greed aborted governmental oversight in the guise of freedom.

Smelling blood, the abortionists, the multinational power junkies, fanned mantras targeting children through the media. Dad was duped and mom was a bitch. Like dominos--societies fell as the family structures withered. Consumerism flourished briefly in each new market, Japan, China, India, Brazil, the corporate tit engorged, and the resulting wealth crushed a withering national self-image through myths of excessive control. That banished the last of government oversight in the developing nations. The national state became an endangered species and the expectation of responsibility by leadership faded away with each new generation.

With the demise of the middle class in the third decade of the 21st century, chaos spread swiftly as poverty and disease grew. The corporate tit turned away from the masses, then evaporated. Anger erupted and cities burned. Another barrier was required. This barrier would need to have no political ambitions, no will, and no voice. The lesson of the well-educated Baby-boomers demanding rights and basic human freedom remained a fresh wound in the gut of an emerging world order. The power elite, dedicated to self-gratification through control initiated a worldwide competition among colleges and universities to seek a solution to chaos.

The Redding Wall rises three-hundred feet from the ground. The barricade in Northern California near the Oregon border uses the remains of the consumer barricade to protect those that brought down civilized society. Brownish gray in color with black shadows and bloody pink stains from its rain of weapons. An odor of filth radiates from the Wall. A ghostly extension of its immense core. Made of debris and crushed autos, the Wall gift-wrapped the raped social contract of 18th century philosophers and statesmen, Then it displayed the bastardized ideals as a barrier of trash.

Completed almost a decade ago, the Wall has codified caste.

Outside the Wall, the poor--and the family of the poor--dies a medieval death from sores, rotting teeth, starvation, torture by an angry mob, a cold snowy end freezing for lack of warmth, or a thousand other once-purged horrors. The Monopoly-game-winners behind the Wall retain the best goods six-thousand years of progress can produce--because there is so much available behind the Wall. The remains of the service class, almost one-hundred and seventy-million strong, live behind the Wall--and they know how to serve. In return they seek only peace and security.

With a base as wide as it is tall, the pyramid-shaped Wall wears a flat top of weapons and protruding perches for armaments, surveillance, and assault countermeasures--as well as air conditioned spaces containing black glass sport courts, swimming pools, and bicycle trails running along the peak. The guard outlooks, with their unbreakable glass behind steel netting are constructed of the same material as the rest of the Wall: trash. The perches run the entire length of the Wall's peak from the Pacific Ocean to the Sierra Nevada Mountains. And the outlooks are alive. They observe in the dark, in the fog, in the most blustery of west coast storms. The men and women who work in the outlooks see themselves as all knowing--and all powerful--ready to kill any threat to peace and security.

The rectangular snouts of the guard outlooks and their cannons, missiles, flame throwers, and Gatling guns could probably have guarded hell from God's avenging angels. And the Dirties never stop trying. But the resourcefulness of the hoards is regularly analyzed by a set of ten supercomputers running simulations, gathering data on the Wall's assailants, and recommending countermeasures. The Dirties often say the devil himself has built the Wall. Small wonder the guards, and everyone on the north side of the Wall, wears the moniker of Demon to those tying to get around, over, through, or under the Wall.

In the first days of the Wall's construction, many families hated the sight of the Wall and had fought their way south just to be away from the abomination. It was agreed by the Patricians that this symbol of strength should be hated by the Dirties to reinforce the differences of their lives: an ordered and safe society versus a chaotic, deadly society. The computers declared the Wall would have to be an incredibly effective psychological deterrent--in both form and intent.

Drawing on propaganda films and TV programs from the early 21st century that pronounced above all else that: Resistance is futile, the Wall is meant to be a focus for, and to defuse, the anger of the masses. By declaring assaults acts of folly, this monument rising to the sky, running horizon to horizon, bright in the night, buckled into the ground, and deadly to all says: "Submit--or be buried in my shadow."

Initially this was so; between the smell and the ferociously effective armaments hidden in the Wall's skin, no one from the other side, the so-called Dirties, ever made it passed the Wall. More importantly, the Wall guards knew their lives depended on protecting the winners ingesting the last resources of a battered planet. The Wall security guards sees the Dirties for who they are: less fortunate versions of themselves.

Oddly, security guards promoted from the ranks are the most lethal officers. They are sure the horror that they see every day could be theirs. Glad to be on this side of the Wall, they protect the behemoth with an unreasonable ferocity. There is no court martial or rule of law inside the Wall. Those accused of pity or mercy are drugged. Rolled down the Wall to the other side and left to fend for themselves, if they survive the broken bones and the angry crowds.

The stories of mobs torturing the disgraced grow worse every year. While rumors of cannibalism continue as well. This serves the purpose of terrorizing the guards. It also helps explain why the food hasn't run out for the Dirties. So while Wall security believes their brothers and sisters live on the other side of the Wall, they remain faithful to the core myth of their culture: Survival--without cost--is the win.

Not surprisingly, the Redding Wall has become the focus of anger for billions of people around the planet. Millions arrive on the American shores every month. In an ironic parody of the American dream of centuries past. They come not to enjoy the gift of wealth, but to destroy it. Everyone wants a piece of the American Nightmare--the Wall--to annihilate the madness that has taken over a once great dream of freedom and human dignity. Nonetheless, after ten years, the Redding Wall still stands as a tribute to technology and engineering.

But like an old headstone, it is scared by time.

Once, four-hundred feet was about as close as one could get to the base before becoming violently sick from the odors. Initially, baking soda catapults were launched against the Wall day and night. The effect was minimal. The odor became bearable as close as two -hundred feet. This facilitated the first effective defenses against the odious Wall: Gardens began to bloom near the wide base.

Dandelions, roses, azaleas, lilacs, poppies, cypress, and fruit trees now run in long perpendicular stripes to the Wall. Thousands of gardeners have died violent deaths trying to add more beauty or plant flowers. It has taken the gardens six years from the first orange-yellow stripe of California Poppies along old US 5 to the brightly colored stripes that now run at the abomination along its entire length.

The architects of the gardens would have laughed had they known the gardens terrified the leadership. The highest levels of Wall security characterize the plots as: "The most brilliant piece of psychological warfare ever conceived." Teams from Psy/Ops continually study ways to kill the gardens and their gardeners, but the fields always come back. Often at the cost of lives. If the Gatling guns rake the crops and those tending the plants die, new gardeners appear, using the dead as compost. Regardless of weapons and budgets, the plants flourish.

The Flowers of the Dead--as the Dirties call the gardens--was not initially meant as an offensive action. The gardeners had hoped the plants would be a way to breach the smell and reach out to the Wall guards appealing to their humanity. As well as grow food for the hungry masses, but it did not develop that way. The gardens were deemed an assault on civilization, constantly vilified by the think-tanks. Even though no one speaks out-of-turn or contradicts a superior. It is a time of horror and myth for both sides.

The growth of the gardens has also led to rumors of civilization south of the Wall. Small pockets of civilization have emerged for the Dirties. Once they grow large enough, the settlements, worldwide, are smart-bombed out of existence. The Patrician Order thrives on the belief that outside of their munificence, only hopelessness should exist.

Other core myths of the Patrician Order say that the guards

have better weapons and smarter commanders. That economics will stand its ground against the onslaught of the angry, unwashed, masses until the stored food and the planetary resources become used up. That the chemicals and machines that fed so many from corporate farms are the keys to life, and that the scorched earth policy employed by the retreating order is a gospel of goodness. Regardless of the widespread death and anger among the crowds outside the Wall.

So with their guards at the ready, the Patricians snack on civilization, thinking their economic omnipotence--and someone else's barbarism--will control the future. Sure that the Dirties are a bump in the economic road, and that anger will lead to a slaughter for the last morsels of food, the Patricians have declared that disease and suffering are the convenience of a civilized society.

This last myth is the Patrician's fatal mistake: The enemy of avarice isn't self-directed anger. Once the rabid propaganda machine ceases. The enemy of avarice is truth, honor, and a social contract of responsibility that grows because of shared need. Ethics emerge again as a survival system for society. A focus develops.

The masses hate the Redding Wall as evil in solid form. So it has become a tool for rebuilding civilized society. People have reversed their exodus away from the Wall and have begun crowding up against the length of the Wall. The attacks have intensified.

The strategists inside the Wall see the change and report it saying they already knew it was coming. More importantly, the computers already knew: "The Dirties consider the Wall odious, uncaring, murderous, and vindictive." All is well.

The absurdity of this viewpoint is also the spawn of fear since corrupt power is never completely blind. And while it abhors intelligence above all else. Processing is left to computers and their handlers--those in power can see a problem is forming. As the attacks intensify and incursions multiply, an increased effort is undertaken to minimize the flow of information on the battle and maximize pop culture behind the Wall. Triviality blooms once again for the masses. Media removes relevant information and instead focuses on convincing the service and support sector inside the Wall that the end is near for the Dirties. Otherwise, the plan remains the same: Any data that isn't in support of an approved commercial interest is made inaccessible to the population.

Only a few engineers and historians whose primary job is to separate truth from myth appear concerned. They wait to speak. They know the ground is the Wall's real enemy. And like the nuclear scientists of the Nazi regime a century before, the engineers and historians have said nothing about the real danger that faces their masters. As a result, no effective defense is put in place to counter the threat of the Dirties digging deeper and deeper, undermining the Wall's foundation.

When the first truck-sized tunnels reach daylight on the inside of the Wall's perimeter--six years after the Wall's completion--the computer models update themselves and come back with predictions of disaster: If forty-five million miners are employed to tunnel under the Wall, there is no way to stop them from breaching the structure-- undermining it and eventually overrunning the lands behind it. Initial estimates say that sixty-eight million able-bodied Dirties are within a hundred miles of the Redding Wall.

An elite tank corps, the SWATs are formed to take on the task of attacking and containing the Dirties as they emerge from the tunnels on the inside of the Wall. Helicopter gunships are converted from defense of the Wall, to offense inside its perimeter. The strategy of tunneling under the Wall becomes a media joke. Numerous late night TV shows make jokes of a failed strategy employed by stupid people.

On many levels though, it isn't a joke: Initially, the average life expectancy for those emerging on the inside of the Wall was measured in minutes. Incredibly effective weapons' systems come on line against them within months shortening that to seconds. That doesn't matter though, many just want to breach the atrocity and give as good as they had gotten. Blind unreasoning hatred mixes with hope and drives suicide forward. Soon everyone south of the Wall knows someone who has been killed either inside the tunnels or emerging from the tunnels. Then, in an insight of genius, the tunnel designers' begin to branch out laterally along the Wall's foundation. Some break out into the daylight but many remain underground. Their purpose, undermine the Wall above.

This year, the eleventh anniversary of the Wall's completion, the computers estimate that ninety-million miners are at work undermining the Redding Wall--all along its length. The demise of the Redding Wall is now an incontrovertible future occurrence.

Construction of a new Wall has been underway for almost four years.

ARTICLES

CHAPTER ONE

This is a retreat. There is no other word for it. Why burn the bodies so the grunts don't know about the increase in incursions? Everyone knows the Dirties are not starving. The one-armed Colonel struts across the room to the next contractor.

"...So all this means your clean-up crews will become cost effective. A good thing since we're expecting a spike in deaths. And as I have said, not only are our ovens mobile, they can handle double the load--with a simple field add-on. They are clean-burning, reliable, with almost no carbon dioxide output, and the human remains are recyclable."

Colonel August Cavanaugh interrupts the two Generals who are seeking a retreat from the hawker's barrage about efficiency in burning bodies. "Porter, we are interested in real solutions. Like a soundproofing system for the outlooks--not ovens. We need to defeat the echoes from the hoards banging their rocks together. Or tanks, I can't get any new tanks. Can you help me with that?" The two Generals walk away. Auggie Cavanaugh is a smart soldier.

"Colonel, the SWAT tanks come from Lippman or Feiss, not us. But for the soundproofing, I can help you. As you know the reliability of Wall guards is our best defense against the Dirties and our vigilance increases by more than double through Porter Industries' improved soundproofing techniques. Thereby decreasing the incursions and making us all safer." The contractor, Jack Porter, stops at the buffet table and picks up a meatball. "This means the cost of the soundproofing is paid for by a decrease in medical leave and psychiatric services. Which we estimate will be reduced by almost forty-five per cent giving you an ROI of six months per cube. Colonel, silence is our best friend--but soundproofing isn't the only answer. We need to have an efficient system for removing the dead." The meatball disappears behind a bright smile.

One of the other vendors emits a polite cough. Jack Porter winks at the man and then ignores him. "At some point we have to stop asking for handouts to protect ourselves. We need to cut costs by using more efficient systems. That makes sense doesn't it, Colonel Cavanaugh?"

The Colonel nods to the man in the dark blue suit. "Gotta' drain the snake." He takes his leave.

Jack Porter looks for, and finds his wife, Susan. The lithe beauty breaks free of the three men who are surrounding her with compliments. Putting his drink down, he strolls over, waving at other tuxedo-clad men. "Are your stooges as dull and stupid as my officers and contractors?"

"These men and women who manage the Wall might be stupid, or maybe the are just tired. Regardless, they are defending us against the incursions until the new Wall is complete. For that they deserve our gratitude and our respect, Jack." He looks away scanning the buffet. Jack Porter no longer cares about her disinterest in his world. He believes the end of time rushes towards him.

A large opulent cafeteria with its salad bar and round tables juts out over a large pond. A waterfall emerges from under the platform cascading down into the water-garden. Rock stairs and flaming torches define the paths leading to the orchards. Tanned by the evening shadows, twenty botanists tend the plants.

Sitting around tables, the remaining soldiers of a Fort 54 are eating dinner and chatting among themselves about how they are getting screwed, again. Specifically, how all of their tanks are mash-ups now and how their families have been sent upstate to Portland. Fort 54 is no longer considered safe for family. The soldiers will see their loved ones once a month now, instead of every day. Of course that will change when the expected destruction of the Redding Wall takes place. No one mentions that. The losses will be devastating and no one wants to curse a comrade.

Even so, once the Wall is breached, the soldiers and their families all expect to be moved across the Columbia River where--they are told--life will become easier. Their common knowledge: "There is no way the Dirties can safely dig under the river."

Meanwhile, the soldiers sit on leather chairs eating their steaks and drinking beer. These men and women are well fed, well clothed, and attended to at every turn with portable shopping trailers, posh apartments, and unlimited video. They are the remnants of the consumer society, soldiers sacrificed to maintain a system they can never enjoy. Knowing this, and knowing they are caught in the middle, these men and women fight to keep themselves and their children from falling into the abyss. At all costs, they must fight against the horrors of the Dirties and keep that misery outside the Wall. This is also the underlying message of every bit of media they ingest. A new movie will premier tonight after dinner. Called "The Cannibal Express," the film's star used to be the President.

Some of the men and women around the tables have been passing on the first run films for weeks now. They are tired from battle and weary of propaganda. Everyone could use a rest. Unfortunately the new Wall on the banks of the Columbia River isn't quite complete yet and so these soldiers, while they have every reason to reunite with their families, will fight to the death buying time for the construction battalions to finish their work. The men and women who fight from these tanks have strong family ties. It is one of the chief reasons many of them have been chosen for their task. The SWAT tanks are both the first line of defense, and the rear guard in a retreat.

The incursions by the Dirties increase daily--their penetrations closer and closer to the military facility that sits on a grassy hilltop. The mushroom-shaped structure dominates the surrounding valleys. Inside the mushroom cap, cylindrical cones house the sensors. Nothing moves in the valleys without the eyes and ears of this facility detecting it. Once this facility was a military rest area, considered safe from the mayhem of the Dirties. When the Redding Wall became more porous, the facility was upgraded to a fort. Now meant to house the defenders of civilization and fight the stream of angry former citizens determined to reach those who cursed them, and pay back an ever increasing debt of anger. Fort 54 is one of ten remaining forts in the state of California. All the rest have been relocated to Washington State.

Glowing in the dusk--the pale green glass sitting like a crown over the matt black structure below--the Fort has become an island of desperation in a sea of chaos. A cluster of smaller buildings sit huddled together under the mushroom cap, inside the razor wire, behind the poison gas, well back from the mines. Fort 54 also contains a gym and apartments, a mess hall, a shopping center and a media/entertainment center, as well as an unused visitor's center.

The visitor's center recently functioned as a school for the children of the tankers and their support teams. Now, many of the other buildings are deserted and the visitor's center has been converted into a motor pool that rebuilds tanks. The Wall is twenty miles south of this facility putting it within a day's run of the tunnels.

Off in the corner of the Fort, by the dump, surrounded by mud and tree stumps, sits a scrap yard of SWAT tank parts. Five soldiers perch on flattened fenders, having finished their meal an hour ago.

Overhead, flood lights hide their glow with cowlings. The bulbs buzz and hiss. A keg of beer sits in a cooler full of ice. Cigars smolder in the ash trays. It's poker night. "You're bluffing, Rader," says one of the five men. "So I call. No way you filled the inside straight." These men are the veterans of battle. The survivors of bloodshed, a rare and highly prized group, any of them can turn the tide of battle. They will be the last group out in the event of a major breach. Though none of them chooses to believe that is a possibility. They think their dedication and worth will keep them safe when things get bad.

"Screw, you." Ewalt Rader tosses his cards into the center. He is a horrible poker player but no one calls him on that. He is a dangerous man. "Damn it," Rader says, watching the other players show their cards. The holder of three kings rakes in the pot of gold squares.

The soldiers find gold everywhere. The yellow metal had been hoarded by the retreating masses as their world fell apart. When buyers found almost no market outside of its hype, the value of gold collapsed. "I am going to figure this game out sooner or later," says Commander Ewalt Rader.

"Sure you will," says lanky man raking in the chips. His name is Miller Huggins. He is Ewalt's driver. The current value of gold is under five dollars an ounce--if these soldiers cash it in at the commissary. They would be surprised to know for civilians, its value is almost zero. For their generation, the metal d'amour, is copper.

Commerce is based on power. The money means nothing-- just a way to keep order and facilitate the accounting. These soldiers do not know that. Relevant information, any relevant information on economics, is far above their pay grade. They are paid to kill.

A horn bellows.

Ewalt and the man who has just called his bluff jump up first. Miller Huggins, sprints across the field ahead of the others. Other soldiers emerge from bunkers checking into their defense posts. Commander Rader follows his driver into the covered staging area of the new motor pool. Miller Huggins is barely twenty-six years old. Ewalt Rader is forty--and considered a legend. Though certainly not because of his poker skills. Because of two other attributes: One, his longevity, and two, his insistence on going into battle without joy juice. The narcotic that is pumped into the tanker's helmets. With joy juice the horrors of battle disappear--in a fog of focused inebriation. Once gassed, the tankers can kill like machines, but do little else. It is the main reason why most tankers die if their tanks are hit and they are tossed out onto the battlefield.

Not many will say it to Ewalt, but most tankers believe him to be a homicidal maniac. A madmen who enjoys the kill so much he refuses to use gas to blunt the horrors.

When a tank is terminally damaged and the tankers must exit the tank, it takes two minutes for soldiers to figure out where they are and what to do because to the gas. That's about one-hundred seconds too long for survival in a battle. This is Ewalt's reason for turning the gas off in his helmet. His superiors, while they admire Ewalt's wisdom, know others do not have his strength. As a result, it is they who began a whispering campaign about Ewalt years ago, claiming his refusal to use the gas was madness. These days his homicidal tendencies are considered a fact of life. Ewalt has given up trying to find the source of the slander.

It is never mentioned that an increasing number of tank crews never return from battle due to the inebriation. Commander Rader has lost three tanks in the last six months, half of the average. Most importantly, he and his driver still live.

A little over six feet tall, broad chested, with a constant black/gray stubble covering his sharp jaw, his blue green eyes charm the pants off women. He views himself handsome. A message delivered by a crowd of lovers in his younger days--and that is the end of it. Short hair flows back from a wide forehead while the lines of age seem only appropriate. When he angers, his features turn stone-like. As his breath shortens, Ewalt's gaze narrows. That focus then flows throughout his being making him a superior gunner and brilliant tank commander. Ewalt Rader is no maniac. He seeks levers in battle, not the kill because Commander Rader takes his responsibilities seriously. Ewalt is a family man. He is unmarried but takes care of his father. A man who has stuck close despite Ewalt's many mistakes of judgement.

Inside the staging area, a showers of sparks spew from tools. Welders seek to repair and replace various parts of the tanks. Overhead, one dark green gantry holds a tank undercarriage. A second gantry holds a mangled drive section. The repair crews are taking two terminally wounded tanks and making a third battle-ready vehicle. A fourth battle-scared Eisenhower 501 magnetic track Special Weapons and Assault Turbine tank waits at the far end of the building. Ewalt hurries to it passing three bodies lying under greasy tarps. Trying not think that any of those dead men could have been him, he climbs in the rear hatch slamming the door to seal the SWAT.

"Come on Miller, get this beast moving. I've got a party to crash." Ewalt no longer refers to the pitched battles as firefights. Too many friends have died in this losing war. The incursions by the Dirties have quadrupled in the last month making the carnage of the last few weeks unequaled here at the Wall. Tens of thousands have died. He assumes that a full breach of the Redding Wall will be any day. Believing his turn to leave will happen soon, if he does his job right, Commander Rader checks messages and continues to talk to officers.

Ewalt engages the loading system for all cannons. Miller starts the compressors and runs the computer check on the engines. "Commander, they didn't repair the back-up turbine."

Ewalt speaks into his helmet microphone. "Maintenance, this Rader. What happened to my turbine?"

"This is Maintenance. You find us one that works and we'll put it in. We should have a spare one later tonight when the junk haulers come back from the battle near Whiskytown. Or you can bring one to us. Carry it on your back, Ewalt. You're on your way to Whiskytown right now. Maintenance out."

"You catch that, Huggins?" Rader says out loud. "How the hell did they get so far north without detection?"

"That's peachy." Miller stares at the side wall of the tank. "Commander, TopCat says because of the turbine we can stand down--considering we are one of six units attending. I think going into battle without a redundant turbine is an unnecessary risk." He doesn't wait for an answer. Miller knows that Ewalt believes that dedication to task will save his life. Miller considers Ewalt's views a sad joke and continues to search for his own way out of the expected slaughter. He begins strapping himself in for battle.

"The Wallys are practically useless and sooner or later we are going to bug-out, asses north and guns south. Let's just keep these slimy little bastards from getting to Portland before us, okay? Besides, what's a few thousand to one odds, anyway? Unnecessary risk, are you kidding? Just how would you define unnecessary risk, Huggins?"

"Trying to fill an inside straight?"

"Fuck you. Okay we're loaded," Ewalt calls out. "Get going."

Miller engages both tracks. The sudden change in momentum throws Ewalt back against his seat.

"Hey, Miller. What the hell?"

"Sorry Commander," Miller says, with a hidden grin. "It got stuck--only one turbine, remember?"

The tank exits the compound, meets up with the other SWATS that form its platoon, and speeds up rolling down the hill to an old freeway on-ramp. The tanks accelerates onto the main artery, treads tearing up what is left of old US 5.

The back of the bar glows red from an overhead neon sign as rain falls from the thunderstorm. The bar is called Purgatorio. The steel door bangs open and a pair of helicopter pilots stumble out into the alleyway. The female falls to the muddy ground and immediately pops back up not wanting to show any weakness to her copilot. He leans against the wall laughing at her. "You know. If I ever see your dad again I am going to tell him he raised one screwed up kid. I am so sick of rescuing you. What the heck is wrong with you? All the money in the world and you wallow in the dung with the rest of us."

"Us? Oh you poor, poor boy." Amanda Feiss wobbles from the quad package of boiler-makers she has imbibed in the last hour. Trying to focus her green eyes on Thomas Jefferson Lippman, her copilot, she hears a flight of jets overhead. With their rumbling, she looks for lightning, laughs, then tries to shake the confusion from her skull.

"Where are the fly boys off to now I wonder?" Asks her copilot.

"The jets are a show for the soon to be ravaged city of Portland," she mumbles under the downpour. The rain falls in sheets.

"Nah, they are going to carpet-bombing the crap out of some Dirties." TJ Lippman laughs stumbling over to Amanda Feiss. They begin to walk back to their base. He yells skyward. "Keep it up gents.

I've got a trust fund to fatten up."

Amanda feels the rain. Her head clears. "They've got bullets thanks to your dad. They've got jets, fuel, and drugs thanks to my dad. Damn--we are great--not." They laugh.

"Let's get back to base. Morose is no fun at dawn." TJ Lippman leads Amanda Feiss along the brick facade of the bar. Thunder rumbles as a glare of white light fills the city. The storm is upon them.

CHAPTER TWO

"ELENA ETU. ELENA AND YOU! SHOP WITH ME!"

It was the most successful media campaign in the history of advertising--said the Wiki. For almost a decade, the super model Elena Etu had graced every major net site, newspaper, blog, and TV channel on the planet. Smooth chocolate skin, light brown eyes and a sensuous voice, Elena had the ardor of every man, and the envy of most women. Long legged, thin and graceful, she wore her fame like royalty-- speaking in soft tones and adding her voice to causes that claimed the high ground on overpopulation. With tan hair sometimes worn tight, or flowing out over soft bared shoulders to an ample bosom; her best feature was that smile. Open and ingratiating, those soft sensuous lips sent a perfect glow to her admirers. Elena sparkled when she laughed, owning any venue with a warm open tenor.

Her graciousness--the CEO of Feiss Industries once said--saved civilization. Elena had been the spokesperson for Feiss Industries, the builders of the Redding Wall as well as the world's largest munitions and drug company. A modern day Kate Smith, Elena Etu attracted billions in Wall Construction Bonds. Her appearances at bond drives doubled the pledges and ensured payment. No one wanted to disappoint the woman they love.

Then, according to urban myth: At the height of her career, she left the glamour and wealth. Elena Etu disappeared from advertisements making her way to San Francisco to help her ailing mother. Just before the city fell to the insurgents. A national day of mourning is remembered every year. Various news organizations still search for her image in the monthly reconnaissance photos of that city's devastation.

Elena, myth said, watched the city that her mother loved turn into a mad house. The fires, the attacking soldiers, the gangs, the hunger, the religions of terror, suicides, until finally despair swamped her city and destroyed it. Some say Elena stood before the hopeless along the Pacific Ocean between the Great Highway and the sandy beach, and fed thousands--just before the end. It is also said a dying Elena Etu claimed she would rebuild San Francisco, even as it burned. History says the model died defending the life of her mother against the Dirties--a martyr to her family and her beliefs in America.

The myth of her heroism was a major motion picture this past year. Put out just in time for the Christmas shopping rush, it won eleven Academy Awards. Hailed by the critics as "...A magnificent tragedy of foolish heroism..." The media reported the film grossed over a billion dollars.

Of course, the makers of myth would not be surprised to find her alive. Even though those inside of the Wall believed her efforts were putting off the inevitable: The Dirties could only own a short ugly period of the city's life.

But aside from the myths...She had a mission to complete.

Elena Etu brought her wisdom about people to a doomed city. Tenacity and dedication kept her alive. Then it fed her dominion of the ruined metropolis. Having grown up in New York City, she knew chaos better than most.

After arriving in the city under armed guard, Elena, her lover Baylor Grandel, and thirty specially picked soldiers hid in the reinforced basement of a department store waiting for the city to fall and the anger to quell. Three weeks after the city fell, she intertwined some stranded silver necklaces into her long sable hair, stepped into her silvered shoes, and exited the store on Union Square one foggy San Francisco morning to began her journey of dominion.

It started as a trek west to Land's End. Her lover at her side, the guards assigned to her accompanying her through the chaos. They had armaments enough to quell a small riot. Everywhere they saw hungry, desperate people. Disease and pain seemed to pause when the starving citizens of the city saw the well-known vision of beauty that is Elena Etu. So the people followed her. That was step one.

The guards wearing torn and smelly clothes over body armor, blended into the crowds telling everyone they passed that this really was Elena Etu and that she was their savior. Passing fires and mobs, soldiers and overturned cars, burning buildings and dead bodies, they marched out along Geary Street heading to the Pacific. No one was able to stand in her way--the story goes--not the warlords, the cannibals, or the crazed. Her lover and the soldiers made sure of her safety.

By the time she reached the end of Geary Street, the number of people following her to the Great Highway numbered in the thousands. Thundering against the rocks, battering remains of the Cliff House, the Pacific mesmerized the crowd as they questioned what was next.

When her supporters began crossing the Great Highway to the sandy beach she could see no end to them. The soon-to-be setting sun painted her in exquisite reddish tones. Her back to the ocean, silver strands in her hair giving her a most stunning glow, Elena Etu had begun to chant. Her melodious voice was truly a gift from the divine. It rang out strong, and courageous, full of hope and pain.

The sandy beach grew longer with the lowering tide, others begins sharing their songs. The guards had backpacks full of disinfectant swabs. People tended each other's wounds and sang into the night. Between songs, Elena talked about the coming changes and how there was no food and that she would solve that. Fires were lit burning the remains of civilization to keep them warm. The crowd continued to grow as the huge fires attracted scavengers and the hopeless. The fires could also be seen far out to sea.

Only one song was known by all of them: "San Francisco," a song made famous by a thorny-voiced woman who sang it over a hundred years before in the early part of the twentieth century. Hundreds of people sang it in falsetto, then thousands, all laughing at themselves, staring out over the water. Every single cold, starving, person had become lost in the revelries. Then many cried at the moment of sunrise. The crowd agreed among themselves that Elena Etu was their holy priestess, and their savior. She was after all--still beautiful. For these sick hungry people beauty was hope.

Elena represented a hidden magic that would rescue them. They believed in beauty because they knew there was truth in beauty and that truth was good. No one recalled that specific message about beauty had been repeated over and over for the previous months throughout the Bay Area on TV and net stations. Commercials said it. Sunday morning pastors said it. The news media said it: "There was only one truth and that truth is beauty. It has to be trusted." Many secretly pledged themselves to her protection--and all this before the great miracle!

That morning, soon after the dawn, thousands of dead fish lie waiting as a feast. The people on the shore were certain Elena Etu had brought forth the food. They silently thanked her as they gathered up the fish. The hungry feasted all day. The supply seemed unending, a second tide bringing in another bounty. Desperate people in search of food arrived. They were fed as well. The sea continued to feed them on every tide.

Sadly, that first night, many weakened by disease died from the same toxins that had killed the fish. Many more people lived. The people sang and loved. More fish washed on shore the next day. Finally, their hunger sated, the city dwellers began salting and storing the fish. Attracted by the voices in song and oily torch fires that now lined the sea, more people arrived, ate, and worked. The survivors began to believe that here was more than hope. There was Elena Etu.

When the moon rose that third night, Elena Etu was officially ordained as the goddess of the city by the sea. Fifteen of her guards were dead by then. Many had died killing those who challenged her imminent dominion. Baylor, protecting his woman, had killed well over twenty people. As she accepted the tributes and pledged her support for the people of the city, Baylor wandered among the crowds looking for malcontents. He killed one man and took another's Bowie knife. That knife became his symbol of fear.

That next morning, with the Priestess Elena Etu leading the crowd, they walked away from the sea into the humid sweat-smelling canyons of the ruined city. Baylor took up his position alongside her, a fresh scalp on his belt.

Elena has never forgotten that moment when his eyes began darting about like angry crows. Madness didn't own Baylor yet. Anger was his current savior--but it was his undoing. On the road back others decided to try and claim the riches of the sea or try to take the role of city leader from the model. The rest of her guards died on the trip back making Baylor a killing machine. He had become her last line of defense.

She had pleaded with him not to come with her on this assignment. He would have none of it. When they rested that night, her lover ate cat food and laughed maniacally. Elena Etu cried quietly. She never considered that a brave man might be too brave for his own good because Elena Etu was a survivor. Regardless, Baylor had said one way or the other he would protect her. So she had relented knowing the idealistic man had made the choice of any free man: how he wanted to die. That mistake still haunts her. Worse, behind her guilt, she secretly sees his insanity as cowardice.

The Priestess and her supporters flowed throughout the old department store finding and distributing the hidden store rooms full of supplies. Within a month, other buildings in Union Square filled with her worshippers, architects of change, and her defenders. If she mentioned the need to share food and spoke of a hoarder on a Monday, by the end of the week those that were hoarding food were located and given the option of altruism or death. Quickly, people learned to make do and traces of order returned. The concept of binary law: cooperate or die, made sense to these people. Soon, the city-wide riots were quelled.

Myth in San Francisco now says that a heavenly creature had appeared from above and having descended among the people, was there to lead them to a better life. It is also said the Priestess Elena Etu is guarded by the divine. The story neglects mention that her lover had been equipped with a pair of Tommy guns and that scalps of every color graced his belt in time. Her lover had worn the face of fierce determination in those early days. Six months later, he would wear the face of madness.

Three months after the fall of the city, and one month after the last soldier made safe haven behind the Redding Wall, the city by the bay had a tenuous grip on peace. Her rule grew. Despite the nightly bombing missions taking place around the Bay Area, destroying infrastructure and industry. Elena Etu had now completed the second step of her assignment. She had set up a theocracy in San Francisco.

The following June, a man by the name of Doctor Joseph Vaz presented himself at her Union Square headquarters. Requesting an audience with the Priestess Elena Etu, he waited three days for her to see him. During their discussions, he claimed he could feed the masses. He asked her help to make that happen.

That was nine years ago.

Elena opens her almond eyes just enough to spy on the male child. He chews a food cake standing in the empty concrete bowl of the rooftop pool. With great dirty deadlocks reaching passed his shoulders, feral eyes that dart every way, and blackened teeth--he stops eating and stares at her--seemingly aware of her gaze. A scars runs along his cheek. Watching him, she wonders how he slipped past her guards. *That isn't good,* she says to herself, *even a child knows how to kill.* She senses this boy is just hungry--no threat to her. Elena also guesses his age to be around ten or eleven.

Rising from the old chaise, she startles the skinny boy. Not so much by her movement but by her lack of clothes; she wears a black bikini. Black hides the dirt. The young boy looks away, while trying to keep on eye on the potential threat. Grinning at the Victorian morality that grips the masses these days, Elena speaks while covering her body with a stained towel. "Come here, boy."

The filthy child emerges from the empty pool shell and slowly approaches her; he stops just outside her reach. *The child's eyes look older than the dust. His gut is not distended and the muscles of his arms look strong,* she says to herself. "There's more Kandy." The children of this city call Dr. Vaz's food, Kandy. "You can have as much as you want. Would you like some for your family?" She tilts her head to one side while flashing a bright smile. She notes he stares in wonderment at her white teeth. *That's good.*

"What happened to your arm?" The boy asks, pointing to an ugly scar that runs down Elena's right arm from shoulder to elbow. He cannot see the scar on her leg.

She watches the child's mouth as he chews the small food cake. *All those rotten teeth. He knows nothing of civilization.* "How old are you?"

"I was born before the city died. Mother told me that's all that matters. I am twelve years old."

She notes the children are healthier but shorter. To her, that balance seems fair. "Don't lie to me. I said how old are you?"

"I will be fourteen in the fall. Pretty ugly slash," he says still chewing his food. "Someone get though to you?" He will not be dissuaded from his tasks

"About a year before you were born, two men broke into my home and tried to rob me. They cut my arm and my leg before they were killed."

"Did you kill them?" He asks, enthralled by a story.

"No." Looking passed the child, to the flowers that grow in a concrete planter, she wonders where Baylor is right now.

"That's it? No blood? No gore? You tell a lousy story, Priestess. I didn't see a cut on your leg. Can I see your leg?" The child asks.

Elena extends a long graceful leg and shows him the ugly scar that runs up her calf.

"Brutal, no hair either. Must be cold in the winter," says the boy. "Grown ups don't heal as quickly as kids. Did it happen here?"

"No. I was in another city--where I worked. My job was to be beautiful. The wounds made me less than beautiful. So I was given this job here in San Francisco."

"What's San Francisco?"

"That what this place used to be called." The western sky holds thick puffy clouds rolling east.

The boy seems to finally notice her beauty. He colors in blush. "What job did they give you?"

"Priestess."

"I see." He takes another bite of the red cake that he holds in both hands.

Elena notices his thumb tips are missing and sighs. "What happened to your thumbs?"

"Matt, my new daddy belongs to the New England Patriots. To join his religion they cut the tips of my fingers off. That way when I die, Saint George Washington will know I'm an American. Not one of those Stinkos from the south," the boy holds his thumbs up to her. "They don't hurt," he says kindly. "Can you feel anything through your scars?"

"Some." Elena hates the mad religions that have cropped up. "Turn away, please." She reaches for a pile of brownish silk veils stacked on a metal table streaked with rust. Dropping the towel, she drapes the smelly veils around her in a drab sarong while stepping into torn silver slippers. "Okay." The Priestess Elena Etu walks to table admiring the purple knots of azalea flowers in bloom this morning. Pulling a small silver tray of red and blue cakes from underneath a soiled table cloth, she hands him the entire silver plate.

"Mother said Kandy comes from the city of plenty--by way of the Food Man. That he comes from the land of Disney. Is that true?"

The insane question sends a shiver up her back. Based on valued images and corrupted memories that have taken the place of thought, the allusion is typical. "Eat your Kandy. When you leave, take some with you for your mother. I know you're strong enough to carry all this. Share them with your mom."

"I can't give my mother any. She's dead. So is my father. I'm glad I finally got here. I have got to ask you that question of hers. It took me a month to get in here to see you. But I had to do it. I promised." The child watches her, a brief tear in his eye. "How soon before we march into the promised land?"

The Priestess shakes her head slowly. "Wouldn't you rather we build paradise on this side of the Wall?"

"It will never be as good," he says. "When can we go through the Wall. I want to see Disney. When will it be?"

"Sooner than you think, but not as soon as you wish." She watches the child as he tries to measure the truth of her words. "Did you know I'm going to see the Wall soon? Is that why you picked today to show yourself to me?"

"You're leaving tomorrow morning," he says completing her thought. "Yes, I want to go with you."

"To fight?" Elena wonders if she should change the route. "Do a lot of people know I am going?"

"I spy on your guards. That's how I know. I didn't say anything."

"And how did you get up here?" She asks noting he hasn't taken any of the cakes. She puts the tray back on the table.

"The two guards that watch the back stairs mate at this time." Now he takes another cake.

"What's your name?"

"My name is Russell," he says.

"I am the Priestess Elena Etu."

He nods. "I know." He reaches over for more cakes, quickly filling a dirty plastic garbage bag that appears from his pocket. The silver platter empties rapidly. "My friends likes the white ones and my sister likes the blue ones. I like the blue ones also. I eat the red ones so they can be happy. My sister is such a fussy eater. My friends said I'd never get in here. This will send them crazy."

She reaches out for the boy. He steps back. "Sorry. How can you come with me when I go north and still get the Kandy to your sister?"

"You don't want me to go with you. Okay. How do I get out of here now without getting spanked by your guards? But if I am back in time, can I go? This Kandy will feed them for days. And your trips take only a day."

"How did you get so smart?" She asks.

"I remember the gunfights, the blood, and all the burning," he says quietly. "I don't want to die before I see the promised land on the other side of the Wall. That means I need to be smart and work with my friends. Everyone who was alone is dead. I am not stupid."

"Why do you want to see the Wall?"

"To burn it down," he says, taking a bite of a blue cake. "I just want to be sure of how to get there."

What will they do when I tell them everyone talks like this child? That there is no rhyme or reason for it all. That they just want to eliminate the Demons on the other side of the Wall. My failure will be complete at that point. Did I make a mistake by allowing the food factory? Did I just delay their suffering? Does it matter?

"I'll command the guards to help you get home." She pulls a small whistle out and blows into it.

A male and female guard quickly appear from the other side of the Azaleas. They stuff their stained tee shirts into dirty shorts. Each has a shoulder holster and a small club. "Murphy," she says to one of the guards, "help this child. Get him home and make sure his people know how to get food. Tend to his family. See if someone will watch over them. Then arrange for him to accompany me north. If he wishes. He wants to see the Wall." Elena smiles at the female guard. She nods her apology and Elena turns to the boy. "Go with them. It's important you listen to them." She cups his ears with both hands and whispers a silent prayer.

The boy considers the two guards as she straightens up. "I see. So what's the scam?"

The guards smile at him. "What is your name?" The female guard asks. She is a mother to six orphans and believes she knows how to set a child at ease.

The child glares at her, then faces the Priestess. "You didn't have to lie to me. I see they are not going to help me get back in time to go with you. But, we'll see about that." He hoists the plastic bag of food over his shoulder. "Where should I meet you?" He asks the Priestess.

Elena smiles at the guards and nods. "In the square, we are leaving at dawn."

"You saw the large round moon last night? When it returns to ground, I'll be back." He says, cocksure of his skills

"It will take you that long?" She says.

"Funny." The child stares at her arm, at her scar. "You're a good liar. I'm just a better one. If I want to go there is no way you can stop me." The child bows briefly and the guards take him away.

CHAPTER THREE

Jack Porter brushes back blond hair and adjusts his black bow tie. Scanning the room, he watches the senior executives cruise the Northwest Back and White Ball seeking more leverage. These executive know the key to staying on top of the spittoon--so they work themselves into a froth making sure everyone likes them. As a tier one supplier, Porter Industries is a key partner to Feiss. As the CEO of Porter Industries, Jack's presence at the party is not optional. Even so Jack Porter has plans. He has begun to see the expected breach in the Wall as an opportunity.

Nonetheless, it has been a tough week. After touring the forts and supply depots, determining what to save and what to leave, the meetings on the soundproofing and the cremation systems contracts, Jack Porter just wants to sleep. He is exhausted but the continued insurgency strikes are moving closer and closer to the Oregon border and the intelligence on their undermining of the Wall is getting sketchy. He wonders how much the Feiss people really know about the Redding Wall's longevity. He expects that tonight the military people in the room will either verify, or expand, on the Feiss Industry briefings that his company receives every morning. Those briefings say the Wall has six to twelve more months of usable life. Jack figures a month at the outside.

While he was touring the forts, ostensibly to design a plan for spare parts removal, he saw defeat everywhere. His Vice President of Operations is still down south--designing the destruction of the anchored resources. *The breach will be ugly--and dangerous.* Porter Industries has already begun buying up resources from other companies so he can move them out of Portland. Porter Industries moved all of its essential people and process out of the city weeks ago.

Walking around the displays looking again for that one-armed Colonel Cavanaugh, he smiles as he examines the showcase of weapons used by the soldiers who will be manning the Columbia Wall. The systems for destruction of the expected flotilla of barges appear more than enough to handle the problem. He remembers thinking that same thing about the Eisenhower 501 SWAT tanks. Jack Porter has become a man impressed with the resourcefulness of the Dirties. He spends every day working on his exit strategy, believing that no matter what is done, the Columbia Wall will fail as well. He has come across credible reports of food factories feeding the Dirties.

With one hand holding a champagne flute, and in the other a blini with salmon, he begins to make his way through the crowd. Behind him, out in the verdant central garden of the Fort Lewis Museum, a salon orchestra plays Strauss. A handful of couples waltz in the warm moonlit night. The Black and White Ball has shrunk over the years. This year the ball is small enough to hold at the Museum. Jack estimates the number at fifteen-thousand or so. Well below the fifty-thousand that had swamped downtown Seattle the first time he had attended, twelve years ago. He wonders where everyone has gone.

"Something wrong?" It is his wife, Susan. Shimmering diamond earrings light the deep blue of her eyes. Then there is that smug grin he has come to detest. She dismisses the idea that the Dirties will ever be a problem. Susan believes that Elena Etu is still alive and that she will decide to just make peace. They argue about it often. Jack makes jokes about Elena Etu and Elvis shacking up. Rather than laughing, her smug smile blooms. "I told you so" forms on the bright red tattoo of her lips. He hates her smile because she is so sure she is right. No matter how many times he asks her why. The response is always the same. She just knows.

Susan has a lover in the Seattle area. Jack has a detective and an attorney working the problem, but so far he sees no reason to pursue the issue. Especially since the lover, a woman, pilots one of the Porter Industries jets. Jack is not a vengeful man. He is a practical, sometimes belligerent man. Once he has the appropriate leverage he will turn the lover against Susan or terminate her employment and foul her record. Like most families these days, the Jack Porter family is a collection of non-combatants: a husband, a wife and two daughters. All of whom seek nothing from the others except convenience, title, and perqs. "You look tired, Jack. Fix your tie."

He adjusts it, scanning the room for his girlfriend. Her attendance keeps these boring events interesting for him. His mistress' escort tonight is Jack's chief of security. So far he cannot find him either. Jack does see Colonel Cavanaugh. "And there is the ever effervescent Colonel Cavanaugh, half a league, half a league, half a league onward." He faces his wife. "I'd say we have another couple of hours here." He winks at her putting on his most confident smile, and walks towards the crusty soldier. Glad to be away from his wife, Jack un-adjusts his tie.

The white-haired Colonel stops in front of a life-sized manikin dressed in torn clothes. A skirt of human scalps flank the manikin's waist. The filthy looking manikin has wide insane eyes and a fearsome frozen scream behind rotted black teeth. Open sores cover the face and lips. Both arms are up, like an attacking bear. One hand holds an assault rifle above his head. The other hand holds the blood-spattered helmet of a United States soldier. Strips of jerky hang like a necklace. It is not clear if they are supposed to be human meat or not. Staring at the figure, Colonel August Cavanaugh cannot believe the people that this manikin represents might win this war.

The Colonel moves on to stare at one of the original renditions of the Redding Wall. Jack immediately recalls this Colonel painted the picture and swoops in. "It looks majestic against a morning sky." He is sincere. As a young man this old soldier had real talent. Now he has one glass eye, one arm, and an addiction to pain medicine.

"Hello, Porter," says Colonel Cavanaugh. His thin chest and drawn face seem lost in his uniform. Needle-like white hair still covers his head. "The best part of this painting is the sky. I really got that perfect." Leaning forward on the black railing, the Colonel pushes a red button mounted in front of his painting. He doesn't care about the words. He is still measuring the vendor, Jack Porter. It is part of his job.

The salon orchestra adds musical irony. It plays Aaron Copeland: "Fanfare for the Common Man." The Feiss senior executives have just joined the party

A recording begins and Jack ignores a bitter smile on his potential benefactor. "This world famous painting called Eden depicts our bulwark against the hordes of desperate, hungry people searching for a way through the tragedy of our time: Overpopulation. Still flooding across the South Atlantic, the insurgents have currently been halted by American military might at the Redding Wall. A Wall which would have been useless without the commitment to duty of America's soldiers..."

Bored, Jack's gaze wanders to his reflection in the glass covering the painting: a casual portrait of wealth. He admires his well-trimmed blond mustache feeling it gives him a scholarly air and a perfect counterpoint to his shrewd bright blue eyes. A black tuxedo covering his lean middle-aged body typifies hope for the future. He is the only one among his contemporaries who is really prospering. Despite the enormous wealth brought north by the Californians. Feiss Industries runs the show and Jack Porter understands power. The others merely admire it. He uses his clarity to make bits of progress with the CEO of Feiss Industries and his wife.

As a result of those connections, Jack also knows wealth is no defense against the insanity of the Dirties. Only the Wall matters. When the Redding Wall falls, the Columbia River and the new Wall along the Washington State shore only holds the hope of more time to escape the coming slaughter. Jack Porter, unlike many others in the room, thinks he knows why the Dirties have not starved to death. He wants that leverage in his pocket.

"The Dirties are growing in numbers, Porter."

"I know."

"Why don't you and your friends find out where their food comes from? You do that and you have my business. Don't do it and it won't matter. With an increasing population, the Dirties will win--sooner or later." Porter brushes a piece of lint from the arm of his jacket astounded at the comment.

"We're working on that, sir." Jack Porter watches the old soldier as he admires his painting.

In the event of a total breach, Jack Porter believes making and keeping close contacts with the soldiers will be his last line of defense. It is another reason he had personally visited those forts this week. Jack Porter is assembling a dossier on soldiers, seeking the ones he knew in the past, and finding new allies. He now wonders if he has been under surveillance.

The painting's narration continues: "...By the time construction started on the Redding Wall, Europe, Asia, and Australia had been in ruins for years. Africa looked like an escape route to the new world; a funnel for the hordes that trekked across Asia and Europe to get to the Americas--the twin continents of blessed abundance.

"Brazil and the United States took on the task of guarding the important conduits of the South Atlantic and the Bering Strait. Both countries sure that if the insurgents gained a foothold in the Americas, there would be no stopping them. Of course as we know, the prowess of the American soldier was underestimated."

Jack Porter glances at the Colonel. He appears entrenched in an audio that he no doubt has heard more than once. Jack readjusts his stance knowing he is stuck playing the Colonel's game.

"...For three years, two mighty navies spent every moment of every day battling ships, airplanes, sail boats, and barges--sending them into oblivion. Yet the insurgents kept coming.

"In the fourth year of Operation Seawall, the South American satellite eyes began to fail. Brazil was blinded. Its navies were unable to track the thousands of vessels approaching its shores. The tiny wooden-hulled crafts crammed with people soon began to land in South America and the sabotage inside Brazilian Navy facilities took its toll."

"Those weren't your satellites that failed were they, Porter?"

"No sir. We are not in that business." Jack Porter sees a wry smile in the eyes of the old soldier and wonders what he knows. *Or is he just being an asshole?*

"...The South Atlantic became a freeway filled with boats and people, most of them mad with hunger and more than happy to kill themselves while doing as much damage as possible to some great warship. Stories spread to India and Australia. Heroes were sinking great naval vessels, and people were gorging themselves on the plenty of South America. The tales spurred a new migration to Africa. In retaliation, bombing missions were conducted on the African coast.

"In contrast to Brazil's failure, the American defense perimeter in Alaska held--and even strengthened. Plans were enhanced for a Northwest Keep and stockpiles of nuclear poison began to be deployed along the Eastern border of British Columbia, Washington, and Oregon, to dove tail into the Redding Wall.

"When the Brazilian weapons stores became depleted and raw materials for their replacement were exhausted, the South American tide of battle turned. Even though the population of Dirties was decreasing by hundreds of thousands every month due to starvation and the amazing skills of the American Navy.

"Sadly, six months after the Brazilian satellites became blind, the remnants of the Brazilian Navy and the South Atlantic US carrier battle groups moved north to defend Central America. Leaving the task of defending our southern neighbors to the Brazilian foot soldier. Their courage will be long remembered by all.

"With the remains of the United States and Brazilian carrier groups now defending Panama and the Caribbean Island chain, the defense plans for the Northwest went into full gear. South America and Central America became little more than a killing field guarding a heroic retreat.

"The Bering Sea area, on the other hand, held back the onslaught. Assisted by the cold, and other factors, it became a secure back door for America, freeing resources for enhanced defense of the homeland. To this day the stalemate in the Bering Sea continues..."

The old soldier laughs as he walks away. "You get us that information on their food, Porter, and we can turn this bitch around. I wonder who is leading them?"

Jack Porter just follows the man to another tableau--under glass--of rioters sacking Rio de Janeiro. Below the display, the floor contains red tiles arranged in swirls. In the exact design of the famous promenade near Copacabana Beach in Rio. The soldier presses the button to listen. Jack wonders why this man is so morose tonight. It worries him. "Poor Rio, a million died the day the city fell. Too late governments realized every ghetto and favela saw the battle of the Dirties as a jihad: A holy war against the greed of the rich. Negotiations proved fruitless as older generations told younger generations of the duplicity of the elite. As a result, the ever-increasing guerilla war gained an unending supply of saboteurs. All determined to settle the score with the well-to-do for deserting the poor decades before and supposedly gobbling up precious resources for their pleasure. The favelas had become a cauldron of hatred. Fed by a three-hundred-year store of anger. Soldiers, who were trapped behind enemy lines, died a hero's death defending liberty and truth in the streets of Rio."

The Colonel leans over to Jack. "Did you know that when the Dirties pushed forward and the defending military forces were cut off--the defenders found themselves treated like the enemy and attacked. That was the result of corporate policy defining government strategy. We could have saved thousands of our troops. The effort was considered too costly. And after all--the problem is overpopulation--right? Was your company paying those lobbyists, Porter?"

"No sir. We are a tier one supplier. There are rules against us lobbying Congress. Only the big boys get to lobby. This is America."

Cavanaugh snorts. "Truth is the Brazilian soldiers shed their loyalty like smelly coats. Once they found out they were to be betrayed. We could have that same situation in Oregon within a few weeks."

"American soldiers will never do that," Jack Porter says, knowing there has been ample proof of American forces being left behind the Wall and attacked as they tried to make their way back.

"Seems some industrialists in Sao Paulo made deals with the soldiers. If they were ever caught behind the lines they could all work together to make an escape. I wonder if it worked. Is that what you were doing at my forts, Mr. Porter?"

"Colonel, the rape of South America was completed within eight months because the population of South America swelled to six-hundred-million angry people. The soldiers showed them where to find the military stores making the whole thing worse. We can't afford to take any chances like that. I was at the forts to make sure our stores will be safe or destroyed."

"I thought you said our soldiers would never turn," says the older man. He doesn't wait for the answer. "The jungles were a sieve." He points to another of his paintings: It shows a set of simultaneous nuclear explosions. "Did you know the effort I show here in my 'Burning of Africa' painting used almost eighty per cent of the United States' functioning nuclear capability? Or that we incinerated the Caribbean Islands into a chemical hell because there was a sale on poison? It all made no difference. Nothing stopped them once they got pissed at us." The Colonel's eyes close from a jolt of pain in his side. He turns away and takes a pill. A moment later his eyes glaze over. Then they seem to refocus on the conversation but he is dazed. Colonel Cavanaugh is a junkie.

During the battle for San Luis he saved his platoon from a suicide bomber. The effort took his arm, his eye, a kidney, and a lung. The addiction is caused by a tablet he takes. It is a concentrated version of the calming gas used by the troops after battle. It is now available to anyone in the military for free.

Jack tries for an opening knowing the first few seconds of the pills are disorienting. "All the reports say San Francisco is the main source of the food. They say Elena Etu is behind it."

The soldier looks at Jack understanding the point of the probe. "Of course she is. But intel says she didn't have the training to make it happen. Who did?"

Jack stares at him, unmoving, shocked at the confirmation. He considers just what this tactician might want from him.

"Why do you want my money for your sound proofing, Porter? Are you mad? Solve the real problem. Those people down south want your blood." The man's droopy eyes then seem ready to melt from his sockets.

Hoping to keep a good face on the interaction. Jack points to this Colonel's most famous painting: Eve. "Colonel, look at this," says Jack. "You painted that."

An exhausted woman covered with blood rests her head on a machine gun. Her flinty eyes peer out at the viewer. A broken wooden sign behind her points off to the left. The sign originally had said San Luis. Scrawled in blood under the original writing are the words: The Buck Stops Here.

"I know we can't give up. But you know the battle works both ways for the companies. The only people losing here are the people who believe in the puppet government. My company can't help fund efforts for change. We have no charter to engage in defense of our facilities. We tried that years ago. Then Congress eliminated that option for suppliers. If I can find Elena Etu, will you help my company with defense, in Washington State?"

The old man sighs seeing the eyes of a trader. Jack Porter has no loyalty beyond his own skin. "I can provide funding for solutions through the Corporate Council for worthwhile research projects." The old man looks at his painting. "I was in San Luis, Porter. Where were you?" He walks away.

South of Yuma, and just north of where the Colorado River empties into the Gulf of California, the insurgents had butted up against the United States' military might in the battle of San Luis. Forty square miles of the Southwest became the center of death on Earth. In a battle that turned the Colorado River red and the beaches of Baja pink, the engagement pitted astonishingly efficient killing systems against an unending tsunami of angry, desperate people. Wave attacks, suicide attacks, guerilla warfare, madness on a titanic scale; it was unending bloodshed. The well-disciplined US military fought valiantly, standing its ground against 1000 to 1 odds for two-hundred days. Them the costs of battle became too much and the troops were pulled back. Through California and eventually behind to the Redding Wall, the retreat was rapid and painless. The Wall and the irradiated zone to its east now defines the United States of America: Northern California, Oregon, Washington, British Columbia and Alaska.

Oddly, the immense wealth in California was like liquor to the mad human horde. It stunned them. They paused for almost three months gorging on every found resource. The radiation belts of Idaho were finished and the front door to civilization was completed and slammed shut at the Redding Wall.

Jack follows the Colonel, thinking this old man is doing more than bellowing out concerns. He is suggesting a strategy for Jack Porter and his company. Walking with the old soldier, Jack mentally kicks himself for being so dull to the hints these last few months. "Colonel, those animals devoured the entire planet. We have to be strong as a nation to defeat them. They burn and loot without mercy." He watches to see if his speech has any affect.

"Porter, don't give me any of your bullshit. You rich scum-buckets devoured the resources of this planet in the name of economic growth, your economic growth. I grant you at one point it appeared that your economics could work. When you bastards saw the path was wrong--rather than correcting the problem--you just took more. Thinking you could starve the rest of humanity to death and ride the crest of desperation into an ordered empire based on Patrician control." He glares at Jack. "Those animals on the other side of the Wall are us. That means they are smart. That's why we are losing this battle. But make no mistake they aren't the locusts. We are. The Dirties are reclaiming the planet from the real locusts like Feiss. And since my job is to protect our country..." He stops, staring at Porter. "And you don't care." The Colonel has said too much.

Jack Porter sees a lever point regarding Feiss Industries. Colonel Cavanaugh is at war with Feiss. Recovering, the older man looks around and sees that this conversation is being ignored by the Feiss Executives. The Colonel, so far as Feiss Industries is concerned, is a non-event. So he is declaring himself an ally--in Jack's eyes. "Sir, I do not want to be cannibal meat. I am sure you don't want to be either." Jack takes a step backwards.

"It's not cannibalism that feeds them, Porter." The Colonel curses the reasons people like this have come to control his country.

Jack continues, "If you are right then I would have to agree with you. We will not be safe until we obliterate their food supply Or bring their numbers down to a manageable level. Why are you allowing me this data?"

The Colonel smiles. Sure this man is a pirate at heart. "The Corporate Council has refused to consider my plans for incursions into the land of the Dirties. I don't know why. I know they should support it. I am guessing the problem is Feiss Industries. They are readying their own teams. I also know you are not inner circle. Here is a chance to get some leverage. Get me some intelligence from the other side of the Wall. I'll get funding for your teams." The old man's eyes seem bright for just a moment.

"Jack, dear?" Susan slides her hand along his back. "Excuse me Colonel, I need to borrow my husband for a dance in the garden."

"You get back to me on that issue, Porter," says the Colonel. "If you address that concern of mine then you have those contracts you want."

She has been listening to their interaction. Susan leads her husband to the dance floor, watching the reactions of the other executives around the room. The jokes about her husband cut into her like a knife. Other comments about the battle in California are worse.

They begin to waltz and she leans closer. "Jack, is it true the Dirties are taking prisoners--trying to learn our weaknesses?"

"Just gossip." He holds his wife a little closer. "I'd like you and the girls to go to that cabin you hate near Vancouver and stay there. So far as I can tell the battle for Portland is about to begin. I don't want to take any chances with your safety."

She leans back in his arms to look at him. "That's sweet of you." Susan will allow herself to be a little closer to her husband tonight. Tomorrow she will leave him, and move to Seattle. Susan had seen Jack's mistress with his chief of security. Just before she asked him to dance. "How bad do you think it could be, Jack? Are we really in danger this far north? Will they really roll up the state and get to Portland that quickly?"

He sweeps her around the dance floor, smiling and winking at the other executives, nodding at his chief of security. "It's anyone's guess what will happen next. I don't want to take any chances. Do you remember Ewalt Rader?"

For the first time in years, Susan Porter fears the future. "Too well. He was so drunk at our wedding, I doubt that he remembers me. What do you want with him?"

"I think he may be of some help to us--out in the future." Jack holds her a bit closer.

"Jack, I can think of no good reason for you to contact that homicidal maniac, Ewalt Rader." She leans up and kisses him again, the smile less smug a minute ago. "The girls and I will leave tomorrow morning."

CHAPTER FOUR

The old man wears a dirty canvas caftan over rubber-tire sandals. Phillip Stein leads twenty prisoners along Taylor Street crossing California Street. His long beard is braided and his white hair is tied in a knot giving him the look of a modern day Moses. He limps and slowly steps around rubble. The prisoners and their guards make allowances. Phillip, or Whitebeard--as he is known--is a close advisor to the Priestess Elena Etu. The men and women in chains look around the city as they walk. Each of them fear death is at hand. All of them are surprised at the squalor. While the city's people note order and peace.

These are special prisoners. All of them are officers, captured on the other side of the Wall by specially trained incursion squads. The vast network of tunnels now in place has made it possible to inject three or four people behind the Wall at will. As long as they are sent during a battle that kills hundreds, sometimes thousands. Nonetheless, the benefits of capturing officers with strategic knowledge of the defenses behind the Wall have made those efforts worth the insane losses. The breach of the Wall is now in sight. So getting a sizeable force to Portland quickly has become paramount. Some say there is a second Wall.

The old man, Phillip Stein, is a brilliant strategist--with an angry temperament and a myopic focus--to breach the Patrician's keep. He walks paying minimal attention to the prisoners. Baylor follows the prisoners hoping one will try to escape. The scalps on his belt have dried in the hot sun and Baylor likes the dripping blood on his sandals. It keeps his feet moist. No one will escape or cause a problem.

Up ahead, an old cathedral sits in ruins. As do most of the buildings on Nob Hill. This place more than any in San Francisco received the core of the crowds' fury. It was seen as the home of Patrician interests. Nob Hill paid for that perception in blood and fire. Only the cathedral remains a recognizable structure. The steel and glass apartments, the chic restaurants, and the condominiums were razed the first week. In their place, shacks and farm plots greet the sun.

Phillip whistles while the prisoners make their way over the two metal tracks embedded in the roadway and the twin iron bars between them. The space between the bars, where the cable had run, has filled with debris. Oddly, the rails and bars of the ancient cable car system still glisten. There is some pitting; but for the most part, the tracks look as though they have been used recently. The curiosity of this has taken the attention of every prisoner--as planned.

Around the corner, a group of old men and women sit on the cobblestones polishing the rails with rags soaked in water and dipped in sand. They lookup and smile, then anger as they see the prisoners. The guards form a tighter knot around the men and women steering them off the rails and out towards the sidewalk. As they pass, a flood of four letter invectives pour out from the men and women. One prisoner stops, staring at an older women with deep sores on her arms.

The woman stands up and spits on the ground. She turns her back and walks into a nearby building. The man is shaking with pain moving like the walking dead--to stunned to speak. The guards push him along. Phillip grins to himself, pleased that his intelligence reports were correct about this mother.

Phillip then begins whistling a new tune that most of the group remembers as "Comin' 'Round the Mountain." Many of them haven't heard it since childhood. The old man's rendition is far better than anyone might have expected. He punctuates the tune with pops and ticks from his tongue. Every so often he clicks his lips to simulate a horse trot. They all laugh. Phillip believes that these men and women will speak to an old man they do not fear.

He is correct; the prisoners smile at the canvas-frocked old man with his white braided beard and macrame purse wondering how they might use him. Being polite, they will not ask about his past. Asking about his past would also have been considered consorting with the enemy. In contrast to the prisoners' false smiles, the people who stare out their windows grin, understanding the absurdity of this parade. The question in their minds is why the Priestess' trusted minister, Whitebeard, leads the entourage acting like a clown.

"Why are they polishing those rails?" One of the women finally asks. She has short brown hair that frizzes out around sad eyes and a bloody mouth.

"For the same reason they hate you. We are rebuilding the city after the Patricians and their greed destroyed it." Phillip says. "Fixing the cable cars is a mania for some. Surprised at the civilization?"

The man who had seen his mother hesitates, then speaks. "Yes." He has already decided to do whatever is necessary to see her and take care of her. The hate in his mother's eyes was too much for him. The other officers pity him. It will be their task to kill the traitor as soon as possible--regardless of the cost. None of them can see the glee on Baylor's face.

"Have you been enjoying our walk?" Phillip doesn't wait for an answer. "Good. You won't soon. I am sorry to be your teacher." Phillip returns to his whistling. All of these soldiers have important strategic information. It is why they were abducted.

After a few more blocks, they reach the remains of Chinatown. It is an abyss spanning a four block area. Sewer pipes, long useless wires, an old cable car, and a taxi cab all sit in a huge crater. A concrete tunnel frame hangs out into the crater. A set of twisted rails glisten from the tunnel's mouth. Pieces of cable project out of the tunnel's ragged jaw. As they get closer, the prisoners see that one piece of rail, the center piece, has been bent down. A notch is cut into it, a watercourse, flowing onto a copper stone. The water then leaves the stone and flows into a small pool at the deepest part of the crater. Bright pink water lilies float in the pond.

"Do you know what made this crater?" Phillip asks, standing on the edge.

The others gather around him. "Looks like an explosion," one of the women says measuring their options for escape. When she sees the look in Baylor's eyes she decides there is no chance at this point.

"This was part of the rapid transit system, the Third Street Extension." Phillip says.

"The old rapid transit system for San Francisco," says a silver-haired man in the group of prisoners.

"Are you from here?" Phillip asks politely.

The man says nothing pretending to stare at the huge crater.

"Sorry, didn't mean to put you in a bind." Phillip throws a small rock at the pond. It falls short. "After the battle of San Luis, the government began running drills for public safety in San Francisco." Phillip speaks with a distant, remote tone. As if he were describing a favorite dream. "The drills included sending people down into the underground shelters. They said they wanted to see how many people could safely be put in the shelters. After the first drill it was clear the underground had more than enough room. The drills continued in an ever-widening circle. First San Francisco, then Oakland and Berkeley, and so on. More and more people crowded into the shelters." Phillip laughs. "This same thing is going on in Portland and Salem as we speak. But you already know that." There is no reaction from the prisoners. "Then, as time went by, certain people were told they were needed above ground during the drills, and not to bother."

"Like you?" Someone says.

"Exactly. I was an executive for an intelligence contractor working out of downtown and over at the Colma facility." He watches them look at each other. No one wants to believe him.

He continues. "When I was young I knew many professionals--just like you. Hell, I was like you. We'd go to work, make fat salaries, live in nice homes and drive expensive cars. It wasn't that we were stupid. Any information that filtered into us that contradicted our luxury was simply ignored. We were all well-educated, like you. We refused to consider anything that threatened our little cubbies. We knew it was an evil world. We knew we were a part of an evil team. We tried not to be part of it. We saw those who fought the system get ground into dust. So we supported the graft and corruption by looking the other way. We didn't understand the cost. I think we thought we were invulnerable. So long as we followed the rules set forth by the corporate fathers and mothers. And now we have this. Crazy isn't it?" He shakes his head. "We didn't recognize that the profit motive made a poor protector of a citizen's rights. When things started collapsing around us, we closed our eyes until it was time to become cost. Three weeks after LA fell, the alarms sounded here in the Bay Area. People were sent into the shelters--trained like lab rats. They were told it was for their own safety. Many knew it was a lie. They missed the truth that said we were the enemy."

"Yeah, so?" Says a short paunchy man. "You were a fool. It doesn't mean we are."

The old man pauses. His tired eyes drift down to the crater. "During that drill, the shelters were sealed and the vents were shut." He stares at the group. "I have friends who heard the screaming coming up through the ground."

A man directly in front of Phillip is apparently horrified that soldiers might have hurt the civilian population. He had heard rumors of this after LA. The man hadn't believed it.

Phillip now counts three officers that he believes will give him information. The old man grins and points to the man's neck. "You hide your shock well. But your carotid artery makes a liar out of your eyes. It's bouncing about your neck like a rubber ball." He looks at the guards to point out another who should be treated well. Then his gaze returns to the other prisoners. "The soldiers plundered the city, loaded up transports and left. Then the hordes came from the south and raped the city's corpse. During that time I was making my way here."

"Where were you when it started?" Someone asks.

"I was in the south. At the Hunts Point Hotel in a meeting with Feiss Industries."

"You are full of it. There were never meetings for Feiss at the Hunt's Point Hotel. It was off limits to Feiss employees. And there was no plundering when I was here, and the population was fine." One woman says, regretting her words the second after she has said them.

"Had Los Angeles fallen when you were here?" Phillip asks with suspicion.

"Yes." She thinks quickly back to the week she had spent in the city and decides on a lie.

"What were you doing here?" Phillip asks, his eyes narrowing to slits.

"I can't say."

The other prisoners notice the four guards are no longer disinterested watchdogs, but lean in like hunting hawks. Phillip's eyes seem to glaze over until he blinks them shut. "Perhaps you were in the battle to save the city?"

"I was unloading a ship full of supplies at the Embarcadero when the battle started."

"What was the name of that ship?"

She sighs, then speaks: "The, ah, Cheney."

One of the guards, a black man with dreadlocks and huge shoulders walks over. He cuts the rope that ties the women to the chain of prisoners. Baylor grabs the stub and drags the women off. Her screams die in a flood of blood.

Phillip continues speaking. "After they locked the population below ground and looted the city, criminals like her headed east to loot Sacramento. The Cheney was a barge on the river that carried the loot."

"Those were brave men and women who went to meet the enemy and fight for your country," one man says angrily. "I bet you weren't even one of those who donned the yellow jump suits issued to the population to fight the hoards of Dirties. You were probably already a spy for them."

"Oh you mean the survival suits?"

"What, you have a problem with survival too?" Says the man.

"I do," says Phillip quietly.

"The yellow jump suits were issued to everyone so the soldiers could tell who is a friendly and who is the enemy. Hell they just issued them to my family in Portland."

"Do they still have that screwed-up neck where the string doesn't cover the opening but goes around the shoulders?"

"Yup," says the man, looking around the crater. "It's a wonder anything works. You conspiracy nuts take mistakes and turn them into evil when it's really just stupidity."

"How absurd." Philip holds his scarred hand in front of him as if admiring a manicure. "All of my comrades who were not in these shelters wore the yellow jump suits. They were slaughtered as a diversion. During a counter attack to retrieve some digging machines."

"Nice story," one man says with false bravado.

The guard who cuts the ropes steps forward again. "Colonel Desmond Franks, Special Forces EOD. That's Explosives Ordinance

Division, Bordo." Bordo is the derogatory term used by the other services for the Border Patrol. "And you better listen up, soldier. I saw our soldiers slaughtered. It happened. While you were sailing away on the Swanee River, chump, our men and women were being murdered. They were extra baggage--yellow fucking jump suits or not." The man steps back and folds his arms, his angry eyes boring into the officer's face.

The prisoner nods to Phillip. "I'm supposed to believe what?" He asks, mocking his captors.

"I stood where you stand," says Franks quietly. "You'll see."

Phillip continues: "Anyway, some people didn't follow the rules and they refused go into the shelter. Many of them died protecting their property. Others just hid out. After the looters left for Sacramento, some tried to get people out of the tunnels. It took days to figure out how impossible that might be. This is only shelter where some of the people survived." He points to the center of the crater.

"You planted an explosive ahead of time?" The man who had seen his mother asks in astonishment.

"In the basement of a building that had stood here--to make sure they could get out. Just in case. Only about a hundred thousand people came out alive. Almost five times that were in this section."

"War is hell. So what? What does all this mean to me?" Someone says immediately.

Phillip nods. "Glad you asked."

The guards produce a rope ladder knotted with cross ties that forms rungs. The tight-lipped guards do not look at each other. No one likes going into this crater.

"You were all soldiers?" Someone asks.

"We were indeed, Bordo," says Franks.

"Then why didn't you make your way back to our lines?" Asks another man.

"General Order 22--you know that one, Bordo?"

"Assume that those coming at you are the enemy." The order suddenly takes on a new meaning for these men and women. "I thought there were arrangements made, transponders, passage codes, safe zones for pickup--"

"All ignored--unless you have a league three or higher corporate code." Franks looks at the prisoners. "I lost sixteen men and women as I watched five executives practically waltz through a firefight."

"What about your country?" Says a defeated voice. Phillip counts four sources of information.

"I am defending my country, Bordo. You're defending the Fortune 500."

Baylor reappears. No one misses the long-hair scalp added to his hip.

Moments later, the rope ladder is lowered and the group descends to the ledge formed by the railway tunnel. A few minutes later they are inside the maw. At a cave-in that blocks the rail tunnel, they enter a dark hole on their right. Under torchlight, Phillip speaks to the prisoners. "It is sad when someone learns that they have been fighting for the wrong side. It is even sadder to learn this way. Everyone on this journey is guilty of that sin."

They enter a long room. As the group begins to walk, the concrete walls start to show signs of white tiles. "The first canto is not so interesting," Phillip says. The flickering yellow light of the torches gives a fluid look to the stained tiles encircling them. The cold earth seizes the prisoners. The damp walls have an acrid smell. They come upon a round metal door that looks as if it had come from a submarine. Phillip turns the handle, pulling it open and crosses through. On the other side, he descends a cold metal ladder. He waits until all the prisoners are present: "The first rescuers never knew there was a ladder there. They had to climb over the dead bodies. In fact, they had to pull the bodies out piece by piece." The old man looks down a wide hallway that still smells of dry blood and death. "This way."

They reenter the railway tunnel. The circular walls are covered with the remnants of advertisements long ago shredded by frantic fingernails. A prisoner trips on the train tracks and falls onto a thick bluish mold covering the floor.

Ahead, the rest see the sleek snout of a rail car poking from the tunnel. The car is covered with stains and dust; scratched into the front glass is the word: "God."

"Come on. We haven't got all day."

The prisoner stands. They rest are pushed to the train's open side doors. "See this?" The old man asks, thrusting his torch into the flank of a train. Thousands of human bones cover the floor. "They used a special poison on the trains so that when the owners came back--all that would be left would be the bones. Also the residue from the poison kills any creatures that comes and feeds on the interior materials. A maintenance crew with a good quality pressure washer will have this train back in service within a week."

"Are you trying to tell me the government not only put poison in this train to kill the occupants but it was planned to the point that they thought about pests and clean up?" Says one man.

"Don't you get it yet? There is no government involvement in this. There is no government. This is the result of corporate planing for asset storage. We have economic vassals who had agreed there are too many people costing too much money. So they had to be eliminated. First by economic evisceration, then by rapidly rising health costs, stock market crashes, housing crashes, a lack of work, bad food, bad water, a poisoned environment--but we kept thriving. Then their control systems crashed from that economic evisceration before they could reduce the population to controllable levels."

"Our government would never--"

"It isn't our government. There hasn't been a functioning government since the oil wars at the end of the twentieth century. Don't you think it's a little odd that we have jets buzzing us all the time, yet you didn't know Elena Etu was alive or that we have food? One economic fiefdom doesn't tell the other economic fiefdom anything that might lessen its power. That's not government. That's management by objective and the objective is power."

"You're insane," says one man as the others nod. "I don't know what this is--but I do know you're propagandistic lunatic."

"Really? Look at what's left of these people. There is no meat left and there are also no bugs. Nothing grows in the train, not like out there. Not like the mold you fell upon. Look at the walls inside the train. There is nothing growing there either. You can feel the dampness. Do you think that nature for some reason said: 'Nope. I won't let any mold or mildew grow on those trains. They're just too damn pretty." The old man spits on the floor. "Open your eyes." No one says anything. Phillip can see at least half of them believe him. He has planned this tour for weeks. "Come on, last stop."

After a short walk through the tunnel, they enter another station. The floors are covered with the same thick mat of mold. A walkway has been cleared. As if the mold and compost were shoveled snow. "What is this mold?" A woman asks as they follow the path. "Why'd they let that grow?"

Phillip points to a large sign that leans against a round pole. The sign says. "Evacuation Safety Zone". He picks up the sign and scrapes aside the mold on the floor beside him. Revealing a rich black compost, small pieces of human bone can still be seen. The rich soil has a sweet smell. He scrapes lower and comes up with just black compost. "What do you think of this?"

"It looks like dirt," someone says. "It also seems to me this is just a bunch of BS dreamed up to confuse us."

Phillip speaks: "It's very rich dirt, covering hundreds of miles of tunnels, stairs, and platforms. It is made up entirely of human remains and vermin." He replaces the sign, leaning it against the pole. "I do this tour about once a week now." He is lying. "When I return in a week, the area will be flat again. Isn't it oddly convenient that after these people starve to death their remains will morph into this organic material to use as either biofuel or fertilizer?"

One of the men digs his hand against the pole beside him, his hand sinks into mold. He pulls it back quickly, his hand full of rich compost. "Not bad. I bet someone got a big bonus for this bit of chemistry."

"That was a person," Phillip says angrily looking at Baylor.

"Not anymore. This stuff is really valuable. Can we go now?"

Baylor grabs the man and drags him off--like some wild animal that has made a kill. They disappear into the shadows. The others look around, fear in their eyes. "And you hate us for our brutality?" Says one woman.

"Yes." He shakes his head looking at the gouge in the mold. "The mold on these poles is there because they strapped young children to the poles to keep them safe in the dark." A couple of the prisoners vomit. "It's about damned time. Come on."

"How'd you know to set up the explosives?" Someone asks.

"I had seen a demonstration of a chemical agent designed to keep coal mines clear. I saw the same containers during the practice evacuations. My wife was told not to come down here. She did anyway. I still don't know why."

The men and women follow him up a wide set of stairs reading the epitaphs scratched into the metal handrail.

"God help us."

"Steven says: I told you so, Owen!"

"Last stop."

"We gave our lives for our portfolio."

"Simon says, die."

"Long live America."

"It's getting dark."

"I am dead."

"Curse you who reads this."

Some of the words are written in blood. One of the prisoners stops. He is the same man who saw his mother. He is practically crying. "How come there is no mold on the words?"

The people who wrote these epitaphs already knew the poison in the train inhibited the growth of the mold. They spread it on the metal banister as a memorial to themselves. They would die about an hour later. Still, many people got out when my little explosion went off. If that helps. But there was mass suicide before I got here."

"How could they know anyone would rescue them?" Someone asks. "Of course they'd take the easy way out."

"Worse than that. The mold started forming within twenty-four hours of being isolated from external air. These people were here for almost a week. By the way, that tightness you feel in your lungs will get worse. By midnight it'll hurt like hell. It'll be gone in the morning. Your exposure here will be too brief for it to linger. That takes three days. Ever wonder why there was that manufacturing flaw in the survival jumpsuits? The one where the hood's string goes around the neck instead of the hood's opening?"

At the top of the stairs, Phillip yanks on a cord that hangs from the ceiling. A moment later a gasoline motor catches and the area fills with noise and fumes. A wide shopping promenade leaps into view, lit by red and green Christmas lights.

Hanging every few feet from every beam, like trees in an upside-down forest, are human beings. Most of the figures are elongated into a bulb shape. They are stretched from their own weight. All intact. "Before the rescuers could get to them, many people decided that there wasn't enough food or water down here for everyone. So the brave ones--or the cowards, depending on your perspective--hung themselves. Others just waited to die. That manufacturing flaw I spoke of makes the perfect hangman's tool. Odd, isn't it, that anyone who wore those yellow jumpsuits remains intact? Unlike the other poor souls strewn on the floor. The jumpsuits are impervious to the mold's corrosive action. So here they hang. Bags ready to be loaded onto a truck. There are places like this throughout the evacuation system. You asked me before about my problem with the yellow jumpsuits. The jumpsuits are compost bags."

The men and women are speechless.

Phillip speaks again: "If people hadn't sacrificed themselves--I doubt a single person could have gotten out alive. Can any of you still recognize heroism?" Phillip wanders through the forest of hanging bodies and enters a storefront that announces: "Rebecca's Sourdough Croissants." The men and women follow him, passing baking ovens, into a long room.

A single shiny wire, newly strung since the disaster, crisscrosses in front of a doorway. Phillip leans over and throws a small knife switch. The lights come on.

In front of them is a long narrow room filled with pumps and thousands of canisters that look like old time milk containers. They line the walls far into the darkness. "This is how the mold is introduced. It is a fully automated system that senses external airflow. The spores come from a mutated yeast that was sold to bakers in the city in the months before it was abandoned. Pumps sucked the spores in and the machinery incubated the spores placing them in these containers, in stasis, until they were needed. Once the shelter is sealed, the canisters are activated. Then they release the mold into the underground."

"This incubated the spores?" One man asks, his blood boiling with rage. A former worker in the national labs he knows the truth. These canisters are his design. He will say nothing about that--but he will be the only person to speak of the Columbia Wall. The others will deny it exists. He will also explain how to render the spore systems useless. After, he will sacrifice his life as a decoy on the battlefield.

"Another system took the mold spores and processed them to make the poison. Whomever put this program together knew they wouldn't be back for a while. So they opted for starvation, disease, and desperation to kill these people. After all, there was no place the people down here could go. The food would run out. The water would run out. Power ceased almost immediately. There was no question of the eventual result."

"Other than compost," says one man. No one laughs.

"These people were condemned to a hellish death," Phillip says astounded by the response.

"They took the economical path of letting them kill themselves," a man says. "Nothing personal."

"Premeditated murder," one of the former prisoner's mumble.

"Killing them would have been murder," someone else says. "They did this to themselves."

"Because they believed in what they were told," Phillip says.

"These people killed themselves. They should never have trusted the powers that be."

Stunned, Phillip cannot speak for a moment. "So you soldiers are looking at assets, not people."

"What do you want from us?" Asks a man. The others do not condemn him for speaking. There is confusion among their ranks.

"Help us. You will be working for the citizens of this country. All we ask of you is to do your best to defend the people of the United States of America. Tell us what's taking place on the other side of the Wall. Breach their wall of secrets."

"Kill me," says a thin man with black mustache. Baylor has not yet returned and none of the other guards will act on the request. They will pass the words onto Baylor. The man will die after his throat is cut.

Phillip cannot bear the courage of the young man. "Follow me." The old man stops in front of a particularly wide hanging figure. The men and women circle around him and stare. Then they see this is a woman with two children strapped to her chest. "This is my wife and our children. She left a note saying she could take no more of it. Our children died from the mold. They had asthma." He looks up at the body.

"In her presence, I tell you this: Do what the Priestess asks. She is the country you believe in. Not the nonsense pushed by those dirty bastards who run your life behind the Wall." He faces the body of his wife and lights his hand along the remains of a shoulder.

"You forgot to mention that those nice cakes you eat are made from these poor dead souls," says a woman. "Hypocrisy obviously didn't die here with the building of the Wall."

Phillip spins to face her. The speed of his pivot surprises the others. "We do not eat our own people, dead, or alive. Every single one of these hell holes--throughout the world--are kept in tact. Every body is kept in memorial. And so far as I know, not one body has been removed or altered. Unless the immediate family has done so for religious reasons. You find it so easy to believe in our cannibalism because that is way of your leadership. They eat the weak: economically, spiritually, physically. Preying on the defenseless is the core of--and the reason for--the rot that consumes your society. Welcome to the party, ladies and gentlemen. The choice is yours: Continue as a Demon or try to become a human again."

.

CHAPTER FIVE

He bellows his orders across the flight operations room with the authority of office. "And I'll repeat it again. No more wild shots near my SWAT tanks." Colonel Cavanaugh's voice is hoarse from the alcohol of last night's party. "We need those tanks, now more than ever." A black lectern supports his hangover. Behind him, on the wall, is the air-wing's emblem: twin angry black eagles holding bunched arrows in their talons. "The tanks are charged with covering our strategic pullback to the Columbia Wall--should that occur. We need them. We aren't getting anymore. Do you pilots hear me?"

"You mean those funny metal boxes that roll around the ground are ours?" Someone calls out.

"Yeah, they're ours. And you're supposed to be working hand and hand with them. So no more wasting ammo to try and realign their movements--understand--Captain Feiss?"

Amanda Feiss, who had been staring at her nails, looks up. She runs one hand through her short auburn hair and winks. Pondering what Cavanaugh would do if he knew that she had just been bored. "I am all yours, Colonel." She believes the Colonel is touched by her beauty: high cheek bones, warm eyes, small mouth and sensual smile.

Her eyes scream "Sex" to everyone including him. "Oh I mean I am all ears. Like them?" She takes her hand and pushes the earlobe out. Her skin color is the same shade as a mountain cougar. Amanda smirks at those around her so they all know who really runs this base. Beauty, power, wealth, and the promise of safety have their rewards in the remains of a republic.

Cavanaugh snarls at Amanda Feiss. Though he doesn't desire her, he would like to paint her nude. To expose her beauty for what it is: the heartless veneer of nihilist philistine. But her father is Lucien Feiss of Feiss Industries. Cavanaugh never bites the hand that feeds his troops. He is a patriot of his time: ruthless, calculating, and without an ounce of caring. Holding the ideal of nation in his heart, expecting to die that way, the Colonel wants his piece of truth on the table before the whole program falls to ruin. He detests Amanda Feiss.

Amanda Feiss grins at him. She has a video-game attitude to life having lived a younger life without consequence. Which is why she is a pilot: Life and death have meaning on the battlefield. This desire for meaning is typical for children from the ruling class. Almost all of the pilots who fly the helicopter gunships these days come from that caste. Their privileges appear unending to many. Of course, compared to Amanda Feiss, the other pilots are paupers. Even so, the sense of morass that seems to permeate every other soldier bypasses these graced pilots. Their parents tend them well.

The pilots no longer view their tour of duty as a diversion from a long, boring party--though they still carry the attitude. Rumors of an impending breach have made an impact on them. Therefore the pilots believe it is only a matter of time before the insurgents also breach the Oregon keep. They also believe the nuclear option will be employed in Oregon, ending human civilization for twenty miles outside the Columbia Wall. Their myth is fed at every turn by parents who cannot bear to convey failure, and their fear that the retreat to the Columbia Wall is the beginning of the end. The nuclear arsenal of the United States is a fairy tale. Were it not, the north-south dead zone that runs down the Washington and Oregon border would have already made a hard right turn and irradiated everything for twenty miles south of the Redding Wall.

That had been the original plan. Until the six ships carrying the weapons slated for the task sunk west of Hawaii, when a weapon exploded. It is a story of sabotage that is known only at the highest levels. For the rest of the population, the story says the ships are docked in Bremerton and the weapons are waiting in reserve.

The briefing continues as Cavanaugh watches the men and women flirt with each other. He watches Amanda Feiss disrespect him. Along with her beauty and perceptive capabilities, Amanda Feiss, has another quality; she is the best pilot in the group. Her natural instincts are quick and decisive, beyond compare. But the recognition of her position matters more to her. Cavanaugh often wonders if she knows she has small chance of taking on the role of power baron like her father. It makes working with her much easier. So he smiles at her and Amanda goes back to her nails.

He finishes the briefing. "We will also need to conserve SWAT ammunition as their supplies are going north soon." Colonel Cavanaugh remains reasonably sure the new order for him to take command of air/land tactics is her father's doing. Cavanaugh has a first class record for keeping his people alive. In return he will be allowed to protect the historical tableaus he has painted. He has lost over a dozen pieces of work so far. Some to mysterious circumstances and always after a serious altercation with Amanda Feiss. "Supplies for everything will shorten soon."

"Nonsense. I'll get us what we need. Just let me know what items the tankers need and I will take care of it." The audience laughs. "I mean no disrespect. Sir, you need to understand that this is just a hunting trip. Paid for by Uncle Sam--with expendable humans as the targets. If it gets too tough we'll nuke them. It's a fun job but someone has to do it."

At sixty, he think he knows better than to let any of this get under his skin. *She is insane.* Colonel Cavanaugh sighs. *God, what have we done to ourselves?* His fury boils out of him. "Those are people down there."

Captain Feiss looks up at him. "I think socialist rhetoric like that is the real cause of our problems. We owe the unwashed nothing but the opportunity to get ahead. They didn't take that path so that's that." She glares at him.

"I am sure Daddy will appreciate your support." The room fills with giggles and cat calls. "Gotchya' Manda." Captain Feiss ignores the comments.

"All right." Colonel Cavanaugh places his one arm behind his back spreading his feet shoulder width apart. "Regarding suppression tactics, the Dirties are not the same rag-tag enemy we had been facing even two months ago. Their weapons technology is improving with every day. Word is they are developing heat seeking missile technology and even aircraft. Also, WeatherEye has informed us that there will be no more patterned assaults--we're losing too many tanks. That makes your Rapiers too easy of a target for the missiles. So you will go back to sweeping the hillsides first. The kill ratios will go down but we will retain more aircraft. Next, the Wallys say all of our remote sensing systems south of the Wall are a write off. Lastly, we received proof this morning of incursions as far north as Ashland. Make sure your transponders are functioning. We wouldn't want to mistake you for one of the great unwashed."

The room fills with short angry coughing sounds that have the distinct sound of "Up yours."

"That's enough." The room quiets down. "And remember, the Wallys don't like to be called Bordo. So if you see them, they are to be called Special Forces, Wall Security Detachment, or Black Berets. Remember that. Lastly, you're here to support my SWATs so you defend them like your mother was in those tanks. She may need one to get across the Columbia River."

"What if we get another breakthrough like last week?" A new female pilot with blond hair and a monocle asks. "What if we have to make a choice between staying with the stinking SWATs or closing another bigger hole in the damn Wall?" Her words are slurred and guttural from drugs.

"Good question, Thompson. When you find a new hole contact WeatherEye with the data. Then they'll tell you what to do next. In the mean time, you and the tanks will follow SOP. You sweep back to the hole you are assigned. We'll bring in a Hercules to close it down. When that is done you work on the second hole if necessary. But remember, until your break is buried, under no circumstance are you to leave the assigned tunnel. Even my tanks are secondary."

A pilot named Tubbs with glossy white teeth under a furry red mustache raises his hand. "Ah, what if the Wall collapses?"

Only a few of people laugh, mostly the new kids.

"You stay with you're assigned tanks, period. Reserve SWATs will blunt anything that gets out of the Redding valleys. You'll hear a code red if there is a breach. Also you will need to conserve fuel so you can get up to Medford. Keep your speed blades on low in the event of a retreat. My tanks will not be able to baby sit you if you are on the ground. Any other questions?"

Amanda raises her hand. "When are the Dirties going to give up?" The room breaks into more laughter. Everyone wants to curry her favor. She will get out in time.

The Air Officer speaks: "Soon, Captain Feiss. The check is in the mail. Dis-missed."

The chairs scrape on the concrete floor and the pilots hurry out into the cool morning. Amanda looks up at the cloudy sky. "I like Cavanaugh more and more. At least now I know he really hates me and not just because of my father. I feel so special. " She speaks to Tubbs, the pilot with the furry red mustache. He jogs beside her as they each head towards a different aircraft.

"Ah, yes, Manda, sure Manda. Ah, anything you say, Manda." Tubbs slaps her on the back. They have known each other since prep school in Hawaii.

"I like you too, Tubbs." Amanda sprints away, down the flight line towards her gunship.

The AH-150, as the Tenark Rapier is officially called, carries forty air-to-ground missiles mounted in twin hard points hanging from the short wings. Further out on the wing tips are six 20 mm cannons. Twin Gatling guns and three sets of machine guns points forward toward the earth. Twin rotors mounted above the stubby wings provide lift and a mini-rotor speed system mounted on the stern provides the three-hundred mile an hour top end--even though most of the engines' torque goes to just lifting the massive amount of ammunition.

The "Egg," as the pilots call their helicopter gunship, has an oviod-shaped black cabin that holds a pilot, a copilot, and a gunner. The pilot doubles as a long-range gunner, the copilot doubles as electronic weapons and missile suppression officer. The SGR, Short-range Gunner, Rotary just kills people. The SGR, pronounced sugar, is suspended by a body harness that has rigid arm rests and twin joy-sticks. Hung in a large clear plastic bowl below the cabin's bulletproof bottom framing, the SGR has an unobstructed view of the ground. Controlling weapons and coordinating battle tactics with the SWAT, the SGR breathes in pure euphoria while listening to music chosen from a list of tunes supplied by the Feiss marketing team. It all adds an eerie isolation from the death below. Of the three, the SGR is the only one constantly gassed on joy juice during battle. Their life expectancy is about a third of the other crew members. From the outside, the gunner appears to be floating in the bottom of the helicopter. The Dirties call the SGR, the Angel of Death. SGRs are the number one target in any battle.

Amanda's copilot appears alongside her as she circles her gunship. "Three more tunnels just opened, Heaven on Earth for the downtrodden."

Thomas Jefferson Lippman, Lipps is a well-to-do young man who often makes jokes about the defunct middle class as if it had been a table scrap. Decency is not a requirement for his job. His father's company, Lippman Industries, runs the largest munitions factory in Portland. Born in Boca Raton, Florida, he loves the excitement of battle--because it scares him silly. Tall, handsome, brown-haired, and a devil on the piano, he inherited a fortune at the age of twelve from his grandmother, then joined the military at twenty.

He and Amanda have flown together for years. They are close, but the loss of his mother and the distance of TJ's father has taught TJ to fend off relationships with elusive charm and bright chatter. It makes for a good working relationship with Amanda Feiss. He plans to marry her, but everyone knows that trying to get close to Amanda is like trying to hug the Wall. There is just too much of her. Then there is the Ewalt Rader problem.

He circles the gunship in the opposite direction and waves at their gunner who continues checking instruments and weapons. The SGR, Ernst Craster--is called Crackers--for no other reason than he always used to correct Amanda and Lipps when they didn't pronounce his name right. And even though he had been hardly middle class--he is an immigrant--and that is enough to make him the brunt of every class joke. Born in Latvia, Crackers had fought his way out to Calais just as the European continent drowned in a flood of hungry desperate people. Swimming three miles out into the channel before being picked up, this son of large-scale farmer had ten million dollars in diamonds sewn into his wet suit. That got him across the Atlantic and into the military. Crackers loves his job of killing the Dirties up close. Most gunners do.

"All right, lets go kill some wet and smellies."

Flashes of fire and smoke light the moonscape that was once the Shasta National forest. Captain Feiss banks her helicopter towards the once-green hills.

"We've have three tanks in trouble over the next hill," Lipps says. "WeatherEye says one has a minor hit and it is leaking coolant. Another one has lost most of its weapons system." Lipps studies a screen above his head. The third one has a turbine problem. Some idiot went into battle with only one turbine." Lipps scans the bright yellow dots showing Dirties on the ravine's steep sides and notes the ID of the tank. Unknown to Amanda he frowns. "The Dirties look to be flanking the tanks--one tank has a damaged weapons systems leaving a gap. The enemy is reforming to exploit the gap."

"That's our target." Amanda speaks her crew, as well as the other two ships in formation behind her.

"Those tanks are assigned to another tunnel," Lipps says.

"Roger that," Amanda says. "We're going in. Crackers, you're up. Bring those tanks into your com line."

"Roger Captain. This Ernst, for all you rich fuckers out there in death-land. I'll be handling the information relay to the SWAT tankers on the ground once we begin the sweep. We have most of the enemy on the hills, probably only a thousand in the flat keeping the sick tanks busy. We're switching over to WeatherEye Command in three, two, one, mark."

Amanda looks over to Lipps and smiles. "WeatherEye this is Warbird One with a flock of two. Permission to engage in support of three SWATs our location." Captain Feiss says.

"Granted," comes the response on her headset.

"Do any rules apply to you?" Lipps says.

"Nope." Amanda directs the flight over the hillside. The valley below is chaos. Smoke and munitions light off as tanks fire ribbons of flames and tracers. "Alright Crackers. Hit it."

Ernst begins speaking. He is all business: "Rabbits, this is Warbird One. I show two steel curls of four tons each about a klick in front of you. One is a fake that's why you're in the shit. Also, the Dirties on the ground are flanking at your six. They are forming up to run you into a meat grinder--by the time you turn they'll have the mines and mortars in place behind you."

"Where's the hole? That's our objective." Comes the response from a tank.

"Easy, Cowboy, first things first," Ernst says. He continues: "There is a deep ravine ahead with some scrap steel in it. WeatherEye says they used that to confuse your detection systems which is why the damage has been so bad. It's doing the same to ours. So you'll have to wait until we defeat it. Our best guess is there is a hole near it with lots of magnets."

"So kill it, Crackers. We're going in," comes the response from the SWAT. Ernst, now sure of the voice, frowns as well. "Crap." He switches frequencies to speak to Amanda. "Captain, they're going in parallel with our attack."

"Drugged out lunatics," Amanda mumbles. She scans the tank IDs, but doesn't see Ewalt's ID. Amanda speaks into the microphone: "Crackers, send the data on these dumb tankers to WeatherEye. Ask them to advise on a probable evac chopper for the idiots in the tanks. Make sure you tell them the tankers will be going in wounded and stupid. Warbird One to team: Okay, team, lets' go in and sweep those hills. The boneheads in the tanks are doing a gung-ho." She banks the chopper to give her computer a final chance to draw up a killing model. As soon as she hears a beep, the music from the gunner begins and the gun-smoke appears, drawn up through the blades.

Small arms fire and bright red tracers whiz by. Nothing pings the cabin. "Captain, this is TJ. WeatherEye has confirmed our attack pattern including that magnetic curl. They concur it is masking the likely target. We've been ordered to take out that signature then close the hole."

"Warbird Three you will fly cover over us and Two is on our wing."

Lipps confirms the six missiles already selected by the CPU. The HUD lights drawing three different yellow-lined maps of the engagement area. One display for each member of the crew. "Got it?"

"I copy," says Lipps. "Okay."

"I copy," says Crackers. "Okay."

Amanda engages the battle computers and checks the small projection on the monocle by her right eye. She fires the six missiles in sequence. The pile of metal explodes in a hundred different directions. The magnetic signature disappears. There are three holes, not one. "Flight, this is Warbird One. Next stop the hills. Then we'll mop towards the tanks. Warbird Three, you are on back-track."

"Roger," comes the response.

"Warbird Flight we have located the holes," comes the message from the tanks. Crackers relays this to WeatherEye and to his Captain. He continues to isolate Captain Feiss from their communications.

"WeatherEye, this is Warbird leader confirming tank telemetry that we have three holes and six class eight trucks with launch capability. A few thousand individuals scaling the hillsides--likely each hole is a size three opening. All data good."

"This is WeatherEye. We confirm that a leak is full open and the SWATs are going in to plug it. Continue to work the hillside after you remove the trucks. A Hercules will assist you to seal the holes. WeatherEye out."

"We copy that," Amanda replies. The three gunships intensify their attack. Amanda's ship and another Rapier begin to rake the top of the hills, swooping in wide clockwise circles above the bowl of the valley while the other gunship loops counter-clockwise. TJ watches her work wondering if she knows who is in the lead tank. Amanda is all business.

Six plumes rise burning bright yellow for just a moment. "Alert, six high," Lipps calls out. "I've got truck locations."

As missile suppression officer--Lipps immediately lets loose air-to-air chafe and smaller interceptors. He takes out three missiles with the rocket propelled drones.

Surprisingly, their wing-man, attacking the western hill, turns directly into the path of the fourth missile. "Pull hard, Thompson," Amanda screams.

The pilot pulls the ship into a tight turn, but the missile, instead of whizzing past, also makes a turn. In a short second, the missile dives down on the craft and spears it. A pause, then the inevitable fireball.

"WeatherEye this is Warbird One. We have one down. I repeat, one down--and by a smart missile." Amanda's board lights up with launch locations. Moments later Crackers and the computer controlled weapons pepper the trucks.

Amanda watches as the tanks reform up in a line to cross the valley. "That means they'll take damage." Ernst says.

She clenches her jaw and speeds forward as the tanks fire on the mob defending the holes in the valley floor. "Warbird Three scour the hillside." She sees two impacts on a SWAT. Amanda checks and sees it isn't the one with the compressor damage. "That tanker with the single compressor slides past munitions like a greased monkey. Tom, is that Rader?"

"Wrong ID, Cap."

She glances at him, then turns back to the battle.

"Warbird One, this WeatherEye. Can you confirm curls, launch sites and kills?"

"Roger that, WeatherEye. Still two trucks moving."

"And you say one missile was smart?"

"Roger that, WeatherEye. Where's that Hercules?"

"She's coming from the north. Switch over in five."

Amanda glances back for any sight of the large helicopter. A moment later it comes out of the sun. An evil-looking craft, the Sikorsky Hercules looks like a witch with twin broomsticks in back. It has none of the grace of the Rapiers. It is a death machine, incapable of defending itself, but easily capable of slaughtering a hundred thousand people and moving tons of earth with its missiles. The Hercules is sometimes called "The Mop." Anything below it will be swept away.

"Warbird One, this is Duster Five. Good day, Kiddies. I show a triple breakthrough and idiot tankers."

"Duster. We have tanks--all wounded. We have ground fire and suppression to the sky as well as trucks moving. Do you copy?"

"Got it."

"This is confirmation of three holes at location nine-delta-whisky."

"Roger that, WeatherEye. Duster Five to TopCat. Tell your tanks to back off. We are going in to secure the position and we're coming in hard."

"This is TopCat. We copy that. Out."

"Warbird One, this is Duster Five. We have another appointment so we are going to do this the sloppy way. Crap, it looks like World War Three out there. Shit. One SWAT just blew itself to scrap. I see a second one beside it in deep hurt and they may need evacuation. Can you help, Warbird One?"

Below them, the two remaining SWAT crews are pouring out death, fighting for their lives against the tide of people rushing toward them from a new hole not fifty yards away. If they are overrun, they will be dead in seconds. Worse than that, standing orders say no tank may fall into the hands of the Dirties. Amanda looks over to Lipps. "What does WeatherEye say about the battle down there?"

"We have at least 500 a minute pouring through the new hole. The Wet and Smellies might take those tanks home if the hole is left open." Lipps watches the tanks.

"We both know they'll never get those tanks," Amanda says as she banks toward the hole.

The Hercules comes in on their tail. The smaller Rapier helicopter pulls up tight in front of the large Hercules for missile defense by flying just below it. The Hercules' distinctive tail fans out. It carries fourteen high velocity Gatling guns. As they swoop over the tanks, the fourteen Gatling guns begin firing. Their fountain of death turns the ground red. "All right Warbird, try and keep up. Let's go get this done." The Hercules begins sealing the leaks by killing everything in a half-mile wide swath.

Amanda banks the Rapier, to allow her gunship to fire at those coming at the tanks from the hills. Lipps speaks: "Amanda, we're supposed to ignore the tanks," he pauses. "Fuck it." He pulls two ancillary machine guns from Cracker's control and begins putting out a murderous barrage. The tanks dance back destroying missile locations in the hills while keeping just behind of the munitions flowing from the Hercules.

"Crackers, start a sweep back as soon as Duster Five shuts that hole. Tom, confirm zero launch capability. I don't need a missile enema today." She watches the ground battle. "Boy can that guy can sure gun. Gee, I wonder who it is?" Amanda says sarcastically.

Crackers spins backward and concentrates part of the Rapier's fire on buried trucks that might have launch capability. A few seconds later they are destroyed.

Amanda glances back at the Hercules to make sure it is positioned right. Missiles fired from the Hercules could upend a Rapier. A salvo of rockets from the Hercules collapses the hillsides in an arc. The battle ends as the outflow of people and trucks from the holes are cut off. Thirty seconds later, the ravine flowing with blood, the Hercules retracts its Gatling gun arms. "Duster, we confirm a full seal. WeatherEye, this is Warbird One. Holes shut. Intruders suppressed. Hercules returning. We need an evac and some assistance for the bug crews. WeatherEye, do you copy?"

"Warbird One, this is WeatherEye. All units are detained. SWAT self-destruct is now armed. Destroy remaining insurgents then return to base. We'll do what we can to evacuate the personnel in the SWATs as soon as we can."

"Mr. Lippman, that crazy SOB with a single compressor is the only thing moving, protecting the other tanker. What an animal." This class of gossip is an after-effect of the narcotics the gunners breathe. "Who is that guy?" Crackers says. "Shit." Ernst thinks he has given it away.

Lipps knows better than to speak, watching the SWAT as it maintains cover fire, providing life support for the other tank. He knows who is running that SWAT. Amanda knows as well. She shuts off her microphone. "How many missiles are left?" She asks Lipps.

"Just one. Don't do this, Captain. All Cavanaugh needs is an excuse to ground you. Amanda!" She fires the remaining missile into the burning hulk of the downed Rapier and turns her microphone back on. "WeatherEye, Warbird Two shows movement."

"Roger that Hawk. Evac and Ops on the way."

She turns off her microphone looking over to Lipps. "That SOB, Rader, changed the ID on his tank and you knew about it."

"Whom are you referring to?" Lipps says with a smile.

"Jerk." Amanda, switches on her microphone."Crackers keep an eye on those tanks. We have evac coming over the hill."

TJ Lippman watches the battle wind down. An evacuation helicopter arrives with a security team. Tasked with destroying the Rapier helicopter and looking for its survivors, they check the destroyed helicopter then move towards the tanks. This ensures the tanks will be obliterated and the tankers will get to go home. Amanda banks the helicopter north.

Tom Lippman again wonders why people love the way they do.

CHAPTER SIX

The smell of mint permeates the locker room. In a few seconds, the mint-scented euphoria fills their minds. The rush of battle and the chill of fear fades into the steam. The quiet from lost friends disappears and the voices of boisterous soldiers fill the shower stalls. "...And was she something."

"...So this guy follows me into the ladies room and says, 'Hey baby, I like you.' So I finish my business and kick 'em in the short-leg. Wham. Hell, if I'd known he was a Wally, I would have broken both his knees also."

"Oh, bullshit. Tell the truth..."

The mist is like a sledge hammer on every neuron in his body; Ewalt finds he can barely stand. Yellow and red lights pop bright in front of his eyes. He gives himself into the drug and begins to clean his hair. The warm water is ecstasy. Comrades joking is the sound of heaven. "You know. I was reading that more than seventy-one percent of the adult population in the US support the borders of the current United States. But I think that number is low. From everything I've read, every man, woman, and child has been fighting the crushing vise of overpopulation in one way or another for a long time. But of course what choice do we have? We are doing the work of angels." He rinses the soap from his graying hair. Laughter fills the room.

"You know, Commander," Miller says taunting Ewalt. "You always sound like a recruiting advertisement when you take a shower. Why is that?" Miller Huggins, the lanky country boy named after the famous baseball player of the twentieth century, loves teasing his Commander. "Support the Wealthy. Kill the poor. Hate your neighbor. The troubled masses are idiots. Blah blah. Oh and then Ewalt's all time favorite: It's good business--so it's good for the US. By the way, sorry about all the economic screw-ups. We didn't really mean to screw you guys over. We'll do better. Just trust us. Fuck me, Ewalt. You're stoned." The room erupts in retorts.

"You're already fucked," comes a comment from down the way.

"Ah the voice of experience," comes Miller's response.

"She's right, Huggins. You are fucked."

"Wait. Let's all listen to the man who likes to kill straight and dour. The grim reaper of the Shasta Forest, the Boy Scout Cutter, Mister Death himself, Ewalt Rader."

"That doesn't sound like our boy, Ewalt," someone says. "Rader's a church mouse."

"With a barbed wire heart--sorry girls--and enough guy steroids to kill a moose with his teeth."

"You still got any teeth, old man?" Wham, a wet towel hits Huggins in the face.

"That's our boy." The room fills with laughter.

At this moment, Miller Huggins believes his crew commander fights stone sober because he loves it. The narcotic fed to the tankers during battle has the side effect of making them mean-spirited and angry for twenty-four hours. That is why the tankers are kept apart from the rest of the troops. They are deadly 24/7. For the tankers, if something goes awry, it is often the fault of the Wallys. The tankers trust each other and no one else. Of course Ewalt is a bit different because he avoids the battle drugs. He is just angry.

The helicopter pilots, on the other hand, are fed a narcotic that leads to an easy humor. They rarely get along with the tankers. The Wall guards are fed a drug that keeps them calm, but vigilant. As a result, the three legs of the country's defense each see the other as either, evil, nihilistic, or stupid. And that's not a coincident side effect; no one in command wants these three groups to form an alliance. If something were to go wrong.

"Who's up for a trip to the mall?" Huggins says while rinsing the last of an apple-smelling soap from his body. "That doesn't include you, Commander Rader. You just need a place to hide from that woman who keeps you here on the front lines so she can mess with you. So don't make it easy by showing up at a Feiss-run commissary. She is sure to gun you down. Or bitch-slap you the next time she sees you." Sometimes the drugs are a little too much for the tankers. They speak too many words.

"Hallelujah," comes the cry from one of the adjoining showers. The only time someone says hallelujah is after a bonehead statement or bad mistake. "From the mouth of babes, Ewalt. He nailed you. Duck kid. Here it comes."

Miller readies himself for a fist. For a moment, only the sounds of the hot water splashing on the tiles fills the large shower area.

"Corporal Huggins," Rader growls.

"Ho' Lord."

"Better piss 'cause he ain't gonna' miss."

Miller peers through the mist.

"I hide from nothing. That's why I fight sober. I never run from anything, or anyone."

"He can't be talking about a certain Amanda Feiss?" Someone says loudly.

"Nah, couldn't be. No wait. Is this the Amanda Feiss? The one that punked his girl. So she could take him home instead and tone his bone?" An evil sounding cackle comes from a distant stall.

"Yeah, that's her. Too bad Rader, took offense at a Feiss killing his girl. Now instead of getting screwed, he's getting fucked."

Miller can barely believe what someone has just done to him. In the shadow of laughter and hurrah, Miller waits in a paranoid's nightmare. There is no escape. A moment later, he is on the floor, his right side a flare of pain. The others shut off their showers and walk by. "Ah, he was easy on you." The men and women in the shower hoot at him. "You'll walk again." Miller Huggins finds wet towels and soap bars raining on top him. The tankers begin making rooster sounds.

"The last guy that blew Ewalt's cover has a wheel chair."

Ewalt growls a return to that comment. "I'll do whatever I need to do to settle the score with that bitch, Feiss. Whether that includes dealing out death, keeping a low profile when that lunatic bitch comes swooping down, or kicking your ass."

Miller lies on the floor, unable to get up or speak. "Someone broke someone's heart." A tall female medic leans over Miller to check his side. "Learn to keep your mouth shut, kid. You don't know dicky about love." When he reaches up for her bare breast, she gets up leaving him on the floor.

"He's okay," says the medic. "And you, Ewalt, don't need to be sensitive because a certain rich chopper pilot's daddy owns everything that hasn't been eaten by Dirties. Don't you know his dumb daughter doesn't know what the hell she is doing. She loves you and she hates you. You just don't know when what will be where. But you know, if you get contrite enough. You could go talk to that certain Rapier pilot. I am sure she'd be happy to make amends. You could apologize. Right, Ewalt?"

"Me apologize? She's a murderer."

"Fuck you--so are you." The room fills with laughter. Ewalt towels off. "Well, if she ever takes out my tank I'll make sure to save enough energy to toss Miller's sorry ass over the Wall and let the

Dirties cook him for brunch."

These tankers know nothing about the food cakes that feed the Dirties and support their assaults.

"Cook me? Screw you, Ewalt."

"Too much, juice, Huggins. Button it up," the medic says. The others take their leave to the lockers.

A buzzer pierces the mist three times. "Not again. Are the guards opening the holes in the Wall themselves?"

"This is happening way too often," Ewalt says.

"You've been saying that for months. It's getting to be suicide out there." Another set of three buzzes.

"Crap--two breaches?"

A bass voice calls from somewhere outside of the locker room. "Third and forth of the 54th, we're off to plug a couple of leaks."

In seconds, the changing area fills with soldiers getting dressed. "We're not supposed to be back on for thirty-six hours," Huggins says. Ewalt helps him get to his feet. Lugging Huggins to the lockers, he drops him on the bench. There is no way Miller will win the sprint to the tank this time.

Ewalt walks away drying his thumb to place it on the small indentation in the center of his locker door. The door snaps open about an inch. Rader pulls it open. A note falls to the floor. He stares at the name wondering what Jack Porter wants with him--after three years of silence. Ewalt decides the increased incursions are tied to the note. Wondering if this may lead to an assignment away from the Wall, he wears a full-on grin.

Miller Huggins speaks: "Sorry Commander--it was the juice." The gas inside the room has changed. He opens his locker without looking at Rader. "We were damn lucky that missile of hers went wild." Miller pulls out the plastic shrapnel-resistant material of his under-suit and puts it on.

"It's getting to the short strokes," Rader says. "She's just crazy." Still, he wonders why Amanda buried a missile in the Rapier instead of his tank. She had him dead.

Neither man speaks further as they strap on leggings, a sleeveless vest, and the green fire-retardant jump suit. Black gauntlets and helmets complete the uniform. The tankers hurry down a covered ramp to the tanks.

Sixteen-feet high and thirty-feet square, when parked, the Eisenhower 501 tank looks deceptively blank. With only a driver's blister in front and back, an elongated half-bubble on the top, the vehicle looks like a cardboard box with a vitamin E tablet stuck to the top. Gatling guns, machine guns, cannons, a flame thrower, and small rockets hide behind the tank's black skin. Magnetic treads that pull the vehicle around the battlefield like a race car lie snug under a side-skirt of Kevlar.

When civilians, not insurgents, first see a SWAT tank with its ports open and the guns exposed, they often comment that it looks like a porcupine. Veterans like Ewalt consider it a rolling ammunition dump. Designed to kill as many as possible before it finally explodes in some battle. Regardless, Commander Ewalt Rader loves these tanks as if they were his mother. He is a born-warrior.

Ewalt places his palm on a silvered square next to the back of the 501. A ramp drops down revealing a Spartan interior. Ewalt enters the tank followed by Huggins who limps in and sits. Filled with gauges and joysticks for the weapons, the tank smells of sweat and strawberries--the joy juice. Rader climbs up the driver's ladder-back seat to a small shelf that runs forward. He crawls quickly to a recumbent saddle under the clear dome. Miller shuts the hatch. Moments later the SWAT's interior lights. The blue screens begin to glow. "Commander, we have a second turbine in this baby."

"I'll be damned." Rader straps himself in with shoulder belts that cross at the sternum. He begins flicking a series of switches built into either side of the cockpit, then sends a thumbs up to one of the technicians who watches the start up. The woman smiles at him. He misses it. Ewalt has had her and he wants no part of her desires for a family. As a younger man he was always a short step away from being considered a womanizer. Now there is nothing for Ewalt Rader but the battle. The concepts of betrayal and treachery have become real to him.

Amanda Feiss showed Ewalt the error of dancing with hearts. Truth is, as young man, he considered women as fun partners but little else. Until Amanda Feiss murdered a woman he loved. Among the other ramifications, it taught Ewalt not to toy with a woman's heart. Or to become the toy of a woman's desire to win. The low hum of the motors fills the cab then the turbines begin moving liquid nitrogen that will keep the treads running aloft with almost zero friction.

Rader grabs his helmet, switches off the gas, and plugs into a set of three video monitors. The three video screens in front of him come to life. The one on the far right says "Navigation." The one in the center says "Weapons." The one on the far left says "Communications." In front of the driver, three monitors glow with a similar trio of information, except the one in the center console says "Vehicle Operations," instead of "Weapons."

"Rabbit One, this is TopCat. Are your hares all set?"

Rader checks the readout on the other two SWATs in his team. Both show green lights. "TopCat, this is Rabbit One. We're a go."

"Proceed to interdiction point at flank speed. You've got a leak to fill. Luckily it's the easy one. When you're done relaxing, you'll go help the boys doing the heavy lifting at the second leak."

"We're screwed. And you're a lying sack of shit, TopCat. Copy that. Switching to WeatherEye in 3,2,1." A map appears on the console showing a blinking yellow star near a thick black line that represents the Wall. The armaments of the insurgents as well as their locations download from the battle management system, WeatherEye. Ewalt watches the tally rise.

"Miller, Rabbits Two and Three, this is One. You seeing this? I am getting thirty-thousand on the ground and two clustered steel signatures of three trucks each."

"This is Rabbit Three, copy that, Commander. We're in crap this time."

"This is Two. Looks like the Dirties have figured out how to get around a recent tunnel closure. Carpet team was just there."

"This is Rabbit One. They've cleaned a hole from this morning?"

"It looks like a side tunnel. The Dirties planned for it before they broke through."

"What the hell is going on?" Miller curses.

"They're sending though recon teams again, I bet," Ewalt says. "All we need to do is stay alive a little longer. Then we pull back. Keep that in mind."

Huggins speaks as the tanks lurches forward. "MI says the huge network of tunnels under the Wall will soon cause the Wall to buckle. I wish I knew when."

"WeatherEye, this is Rabbit One. How big is the clustered steel? I am now counting eight trucks."

"This is WeatherEye. We've got vehicles pouring through both tunnels. We are up to twelve. Good luck, Rabbit One. Keep those beacons on. We don't want those choppers mistaking you for an ore truck full of Dirties and start blasting." This is the warning that Amanda Feiss will be flying the mission as well.

"Copy that. Rabbit One out." The SWAT continues rolling forward. Commander Rader checks the beacon identifying his tank as a friendly. As soon as they leave the compound, he changes the signature to reflect a tank call-sign that is different from his. He used to think this is how he kept his former lover from turning his tank into burning hell. That missile in the downed-Rapier contradicts that theory. The reasons bothers him.

He speculates again about her apparent mercy, Ewalt cannot understand why she did it. He is a man lost in clarity.

CHAPTER SEVEN

Firing weapons and spreading death like demons, the three SWATs roll forward through the valley. Estimates from WeatherEye are ten-thousand dead so far. The main force of the Dirties is still two thousand yard in front of them.

The strategy to this point has been simple: The SWATs penetrate to the center of the mob, then kill everything on three sides with the Rapiers supporting that effort killing everything on the hillsides. Then the tanks widen their line and lasso the rest moving forward in a frontal assault working the Dirties back towards the holes.

The weapons systems of the Dirties remains comparatively primitive and their missile systems, though more effective than they used to be, are in short supply and reserved for the helicopters--at least it has been that way in the past. Of course, an eighteen wheeler filled with rocks hitting a tank at thirty miles an hour will crush an Eisenhower 501. Or send it bouncing side over side so it can be overrun, or crushed against a rock outcropping.

Unknown to the tankers going into battle, the trucks have instituted a new strategy: tandem attacks teamed with missiles that sacrifice the first truck allowing the second truck to emerge from the smoke and kill a SWAT. Fourteen tanks have been destroyed today. The average had been less than two tanks per day.

The three tanks move forward into small arms fire from Dirties hidden in the bare trees. Bullets ping off the clear bubble top. A small explosion tosses Ewalt from side to side as a brown soot covers the right side of the bubble. Blinding the gunners is another of their effective strategies. "C'mon Miller, what the hell was that all about? Did you forget your training wheels?" Checking the hills for the launcher, Ewalt scans the mangled bodies hanging from a pair of a huge dump trucks on his left. The front cabs of twisted metal, burns wildly sparking munitions. Overhead, a pair of Rapiers assault six missile launchers dug into the hillsides. The remaining trees spark to fire from munitions.

A thud hits the tank and a small crack appears over his head. The tank groans and slows. "That's a missile. What the fuck, Miller? They got our vector." He releases twin shrouds of Kevlar that quickly cover the bubble like twin eyelids. A fluid flows sealing the crack and a quick wash of water cleans the bubble. The whole process takes less than half a second. Ewalt again scouts for targets, setting the guns on them. As they fire he continues checking the screen that computes the direction and elevation of the enemy's effective rounds. He then scans the temperature of the 20 mm cannons that poke like porcupine bristles from the skin of the tank making sure the compressors are functioning.

The computer beeps calling out three possible locations as new launch points. Ewalt knows two are fake locations--the Dirties have lit fires and heated metal to simulate a concentration of bodies--another lesson learned over the years.

He switches one cannon to manual knowing somewhere on those scarred hills a second anti-armor missile is being readied against them. Guessing which elevation is optimal, Ewalt quickly scans that part of the hillside and finds a pile of dead bodies. Three rapid shots ping the turret one after the other. He sees the flashes. "That's ranging for us too chum, thanks." He reprograms two 20 mm cannons to follow his trace to the launch site while he begins firing into the stacked bodies revealing a hillside position.

"C'mon Miller, get this bug moving. They're targeting us and Rabbit Three."

Another set of three rounds ping on the other side: He programs three weapons on that side to track and commence firing based on computer analysis. Ewalt just wants to keep them busy. "They've got us targeted from two sides. Here they come from the back to distract us." He sets the rear gun on automatic and he continues to fire at the first target. Theoretically, the weapons systems are supposed to set out a curtain of lead and depleted uranium, keeping the enemy away. Unfortunately that evaluation was based on an enemy that wants to live. All around them bodies pile up--getting closer to the tank by the second.

"Okay, coordinates are set, Commander." The vehicle lurches to the right in an evasive maneuver. Rader's guns cuts through the bodies. A single missiles immediately flies out from the tank and explodes in the hillside. Ewalt counts the secondary explosions. There are five of them. A year ago he was surprised to see even one secondary explosion from an emplacement. "There goes their launch site. We got 'em." He rotates to the left, spinning the blister fast, like an amusement ride. Planning to take out the launch site on the other side, instead he sees an approaching motorcycle. Ewalt jams down on the blister's foot brake and spins it back, releasing a flame. The explosion shakes the tank. Suicide riders have been common from the beginning.

Ewalt spins back to the far hillside as a small missile appears. "Again? Miller, kick it." His fire trails the plume as the tank lurches forward. The missile explodes fifteen feet behind them. The driver had lurched the tank forward just in time. With these new missile attacks, this is an essential skill for survival these days. Helicopters engage the last launch sites.

The cannons cease when they find no more large metal signatures. Body count is well over twenty-six- thousand for the three tanks and their helicopter escort. Rader begins to sweep the flats with the Gatling guns, chewing up bodies like a chain saw through brush.

Once they are sure they have removed the last anti-helicopter missiles, the tanks will begin to widen out in a line. A scout helicopter will come in and confirm the results. A Hercules helicopter will follow to seal the hole.

Shrapnel cuts into the lighter armor on the back blowing out a red ID light. A high pitched alarm begins to warble: "Huggins, what the hell?"

"I'm checking the coolers," Miller says, as he examines the displays. Then, all six screens in the tank blink bright red. One of the other SWATs has just been killed. "What the hell happened? Did you see it, Commander?" He asks. "How many holes are there?"

"WeatherEye this is Rabbit One. Their ordinance now includes enough missiles for the tanks. I repeat the tanks are now rocket fodder as well. Rabbit One out. "Huggins, what's with the cooler?"

"Another damn hose went on a turbine. It's on back up. We still have two turbines. We're still good. For now."

Rader puts the guns on automatic sweep, waiting for the last telemetry data from the dead tank to feed into his computers. It's last output of data should pinpoint the kind of missile and its source. In the mean time, the tanks are in an evasive pattern throwing their occupants around in their seats.

"Commander, I have a picture of an ore truck filled with Dirties about a mile up on the right. According to the WeatherEye it showed up as a stationary supply site. The launch information from Rabbit Three now confirms it is the launch site."

"That's where we go. Burn it up, Miller. We're heading into a trap. Rabbit Two, evasive Delta Charlie."

"How do you know?" Miller had been already slowing down to

protect the compressor. He engages full throttle.

"It's what I'd do. Rabbit Two, did you get the spike data for Rabbit Three, over?"

"We copy, Rabbit One. We're coming up and will be with you in about 3,2,1, cover. We're here. Your SWAT is pushing smoke from a hit just below the left engine. Rabbit One, spin so we can see your back." Miller puts the tank in a quick pirouette so the other tank can do a visual inspection. "You've lost a vent line--nothing serious."

"Copy that. Rabbit Three, you okay?"

"The Commander is dead," comes the response. "You're running our guns now. Don't fuck it up, Ewalt."

"Copy that. Guns engaged." Ewalt speaks: "WeatherEye, we're on the road to the hole. We have one gone and two fires. Rabbit Two is down one man. We are on single control of guns. We could use some high support from the Eggs."

"Rabbit One, this is WeatherEye. We copy that. Rapiers still engaged clearing those hillsides."

Ewalt curses. "Copy that. Okay, Miller, bring us up the roadway as fast as you can manage it. Stay behind the low rise. Rabbit Two you follow and I will cover. I am guessing two more launch sites along with the one that killed Rabbit Three."

"Roger that." Turning the corner, the valley floor fills with dust and debris. Vision becomes almost nil. Ewalt switches to a secondary observation systems. He sees more than he did before but less than his own sight. The eerie blue and gold images bother his eyes.

As the two SWATs accelerate up the valley floor, Ewalt, syncs a pair of machine guns to each driver. "If you see anything kill it. Forget about overlapping targets." Rader begins to fire weapons as soon as the twin tanks round the corner. The drivers begins spraying the near trees with bullets. The targeting telemetry from the second SWAT begins adjusting the 20 mm cannons. Ten rockets from the two tanks launch at once at what appear to be large concentrations of refined metal. The tanks are now ghosts due to the launch plumes. Both drivers cut left to miss any possible approaching fire. Ewalt watches the set of explosions. Three sites are hit and they all have secondary explosions. "The launch sites are out. Keep an eye out for more trucks. We still have open holes." The two tanks begins picking off targets on the hillside. Only one in five rounds do not hit flesh.

"Rabbit One this is WeatherEye--confirming the Rapiers are inbound for a sweep with the Hercules."

Then Ewalt sees it: Two dump trucks loaded with Dirties carrying armor piercing weapons are racing toward the tanks from a third hole.

The tankers move to adjust fire but the blood and the mud makes them slip and respond slowly. Both drivers quickly adjust their treads to the slippery terrain--unfortunately the new program takes a large amount of computing power and the guns will be a little bit slower to respond. Ewalt takes control of the forward weapons putting them in manual mode. He can only control his tank's weapons this way. He primes the flame throwers getting them ready for their bursts of terror.

"Fuck. Here's that damn trap. WeatherEye, we got four more trucks with thorns coming out of the hole. Rabbit Two, I got this, you take the road and keep that hole in the hillside quiet. I'll keep your starboard guns. You take port. That's where they are going next." Ewalt starts firing at the trucks. Bodies fly apart as the vehicles start to disintegrate. He launches a missile that detonates over the top of a logging truck The rain of metal kills all as the truck veers sideways into a rock outcropping and explodes. A second truck following close behind keeps coming towards the SWAT. Ewalt blows the truck apart. "WeatherEye, this is Rabbit One. The insurgents are sacrificing their trucks with a tandem ramming strategy. One truck follows the other."

"Copy that Rabbit One."

A third truck careens off to the side. Ewalt spins the blister as Miller spins the tank in the same direction. Within a half second, he faces the truck. Its front grill hurtling straight at them. He fires all the front weapons at once. The vehicles disappears from earth in a shower of flame and sparks.

"Here comes more of them."

Miller gnashes his teeth and checks the gages that surround him like a cocoon. They are going to destroy another turbine, but he knows better than to mention it. At least Ewalt will get them home alive--if he can. The small space around him begins to heat. Miller's leg throbs as it controls the throttle while both hands begins wrestling with gears. Sweat pours down his face.

Rader scans the telemetry. "Rapiers inbound."

Miller speaks: "The breaks are half a click up on the right side. Let's go."

The tank stops moving.

"The hose..." A thud strikes the side of the tank. Miller's stomach knots. The dark space lights bright blue. Hot metal lances into the vehicle. "We're hit. Four 20's out," Miller calls. "Telemetry reads launch at eighty-six-dec-fifty. Where the hell did they get all these missiles?"

Smoke fills the vehicle. The Gatling guns fires automatically as Ewalt adjusts half the remaining 20 mm cannons at another ore truck.

"What the heck is this, Miller? Use the methane."

"Maniac." Miller pushed the metal "T" switch down. The SWAT pauses for just a minute, as if it had forgotten what to do, then bolts off down the road. "They're going to tow us in again."

"If we're alive. Then we can apologize."

Rader spins around firing a missile that tears off the top of another truck. The Gatling guns fire as a smaller truck appears. Sparks fly off the back bed of the truck. Then from the hole, six modified SUVs charge them. "What the hell--now we have a fourth hole?" Ewalt uses the flame throwers to burn the SUVs to useless. He fires the machine guns but the semi keeps coming. "WeatherEye this Rabbit One, we have a truck that's got padding." He continues firing. "It's headed straight for us. Rabbit Two break off." He sees a woman stand up from the truck. A tube pointed at them, Rader cuts her in half before she fires.

"Miller, hard left." Miller tugs on the gears, sending the SWAT left as another missile flies passed them. Amazingly, the red tail of the rocket suddenly shoots straight up, takes a crazy left hand turn and drives itself into the hill, just beside them, exploding with a bright flash. "WeatherEye, they have homing on the missiles as well. They suck at delivery but they will get there soon." The tanks stops again. "Miller, what the fuck?"

"Copy that, Rabbit One."

Rader fires a missile obliterating the truck. He checks munitions as the helicopters being spraying the hillsides and sweeping the Dirties back to the break. Miller struggles with the controls--then the tank begins to move again. It's a footrace now between the wounded tanks and any trucks bearing down on them. Smoke fills the interior. "We got to get out of here. We're overheating and that last round took out my screens," Miller yells. "That fucker is going to ram us."

"Not yet." Rader directs two missiles amidships of a truck. A moment later the semi truck explodes in a storm of fire. Hell-fire from the destroyed trucks rains all around them. Through the smoke they cannot see a second truck that had been hiding behind it, now racing towards them

Miller speaks: "We're gone, partner. And we're home free. WeatherEye this Rabbit One. We're 54, copy." Miller turns the fire suppression on and the tank fills with a yellowish gas. It smells like chocolate. A second later the blowers evacuate the smoke from the tank. "The fires are out. Heading north. Gear down." Miller slows the vehicle.

"No. Kick it. We got another," yells Ewalt, firing the remaining weapons. The truck roars out of the smoke barreling towards them. A missile rips into the truck, destroying the engine and the cab. It impacts the tank anyway sending it over on its side. Sparks fly and smoke fills the area as the SWAT comes to rest on its side.

Rader pulls the wires that connect his helmet to the vehicle and slides down the gunner's ladder. He lands hard on his side. Commander Rader kicks the self-destruct switch as he grabs Miller. Miller stares at him stoned unable to fathom what has happened. Ewalt blows the bolts on the back hatch and both men tumbled out. Miller rolls onto fire. His tunic is ablaze. Ewalt jumps on top of him smothering the fire. Miller grunts as he takes a bullet in his side. Ewalt pulls him away from the tank.

A small truck careens around the corner heading towards the tank. "Ice cream, hot damn," Miller says, still a little stoned. Ewalt pulls out his pistol and fires killing the driver. The truck smashes into the tank just as the self-destruct system engages, sending an orange flame skyward and debris everywhere else.

Ewalt pulls his driver into a ditch. He applies a dressing and morphine from the uniform pocket. Miller sags out of reality. The ground around Rader begins to spew mud from bullets aimed at then. A truck heading towards them erupts in flames, but still heads directly on from momentum. Inexplicably, it then seems to lift itself into the air and split open like nut, coming to rest in burning pieces all around them.

Rader tries to lift Miller but falls. Blood pours from a wound in his calf. A Hercules helicopter dives at the hole and a loud thump shakes the earth. Then a Rapier gunship descends firing weapons. *Who is that crazy bastard? They're going to attempt an evacuation.*

The black gunship hovers quickly then lands. Painted on the side are five aces of spades. Ewalt's eyes narrow as he reads the markings. The words underneath read: Dealin' Death. "No, fucking way," he mumbles. "Twice in one day? She hunts me, then finds me, then misses with a missile, then she saves me? What the fuck?" He pulls his driver towards the helicopter. As the driver's brain clears, Miller's eyes open. He sees the rescue helicopter's markings. "That's Feiss's chopper. There is no way we're gonna' get away with it twice in one day. Commander, we're dead. Don't do this. I don't want to die."

The guns from the Rapier fire in rotating circles as Ewalt pulls Miller along the ground. Twin slings appear on either side the gunner's blister. Tossing Miller in a sling, Ewalt circles around keeping his face hidden. He dives into the other evacuation sling. Only the metal skirt that extends out around the pilots' section of the Rapier, protecting the pilots from ground fire, keeps him hidden. Tapping the blister, he nods to Crackers with a wide smile giving him two thumbs up. The man, despite the drugs, stares open-mouthed. Ewalt punches the bubble and Ernst opens a small side port giving Ewalt command of two ancillary machine guns. The Rapier takes off. Jerking to the side and almost tossing him out. He looks up and sees a fist. A middle finger extends out, waving back and forth.

Amanda Feiss laughs. She begins an attack run keeping Ewalt's side of the gunship furthest from the ground fire. Ewalt can feel the impact of weapons fire against the far side of the Rapier's bullet proof shell. The slings are nylon. After a few more seconds she levels the helicopter. Ewalt is no longer looking the cloudy sky. Cursing Amanda Feiss, he fires below defending himself and the Rapier against enemy weapons fire--knowing Miller Huggins hangs lifeless in the other sling.

The helicopter bounces up and down tossing him around the sling. He grabs on to keep from being thrown out onto the ground below. She is playing with him. Then the bouncing stops and he sees why. A pair of Hercules helicopters have taken up position above them. They are approaching the three remaining holes quickly. He curls up in a ball exposing only his back to the expected heat. The rockets light off from the Hercules. Their heat is incredible. Because of his battle coverings only an exposed part of his ankles are seared. Even so the superheated plastic of his suit partially melts onto his skin. Against his will, he passes out.

CHAPTER EIGHT

The pilots' favorite play station in Portland, the Hollywood Bowl, is a rave of despair. Every pilot in the huge bowling alley knows the battle for Oregon is lost. Today thirty Rapiers and three Hercules helicopters were destroyed. Of the three-hundred SWAT tanks that went into battle, only thirty returned intact and four-hundred crew remain unaccounted for. Many of living are in the hospital. Battle teams from the Dirties inserted all along the Wall guided today's battles. Estimates put their numbers at over one-hundred teams. The pilots know that when the Wall is finally undermined, the death toll today will seem minor and the road to Portland undeniable.

As another volley of bowling balls smashes into the pins. Their thunder also crashes into her skull. Captain Amanda Feiss, her head tilted back looking up at the skylights, raises her head from the wooden railing behind her. She hates bowling alleys, but she cannot sleep. Of all the people in this room, her astonishment at the tide of battle is unequaled. It is a personal defeat for her family at the hands of the masses. Her view: Barbarism will soon blot out the peace and security brought forth by her family. She broods wondering how her dad could have possibly let this happen.

Another fusillade of bowling bowls releases from a team of six. The balls smash into the sixty pins at the end of the alley. Only her copilot's sector of the alley has any pins standing. Everyone hoots his name and thanks Lipps for the next round of beer. Amanda wonders how he can continue to bowl. He is so poor at it. She normally appreciates TJ's drive, but unnecessary derision on days like today seem pure madness. She has a boatload of confusion inside her skull, undeterred by the alcohol. Number two on the list is Ewalt Rader.

TJ gives her a thumbs up and checks her out. This last flight scared them both. He wonders about her ability to make decisions. There will be an inquiry about the dead SWAT driver. A tank on the ground captured her deliberate act of homicide. She banked the Rapier to expose his sling to ground fire and protect Commander Rader. Rules are the pilots are to ignore those in the slings and complete the mission. The tank's frantic call to WeatherEye has prompted tomorrow's court of inquiry. TJ doesn't worry about that. He ponders her motives. Thomas Lippman had hoped that Ewalt Rader was a fading memory. When she landed, Amanda inexplicably tasered Ewalt--telling him he needed to keep his mouth shut about his driver. He was already swimming in pain and TJ doubts he understood a word of what she said. He watches her stare at the skylights.

I should have dropped that bastard Rader to the ground. If he testifies against me I will kill him. Amanda Feiss is losing touch with reality--driven this time by the booze. Tom bounces up the three small stairs to where Amanda sits. "Want to bowl my last frame?"

"Not on your life." Amanda and TJ Lippman started flying together just before the evacuation of Northern Idaho. She likes him. Tonight she knows he looks at her with a stink-eye. Unsure of why, Amanda stares at his bright pink tee-shirt. It says: "Hire the handicapped, give a Wally a job." Amanda shakes her head. "Sooner or later a General is going to see that and chew you a new orifice."

"Right. So you are here telling me how to keep out of trouble?" He winks. "Talking about that, Cavanaugh is getting bumped over to the JAG office. He's a stockade warden now. Someone else will be running the inquiry tomorrow. I hear it's the purchasing Colonel who handles Feiss Industries."

Amanda rocks forward. "Thank you, Dad." Her mood brightens for the moment. "I'm glad to get rid of him. Is Ewalt going to be called as a witness?"

"Text says, the prosecutor has concluded Commander Rader was probably too stoned on juice to know what was happening. He is considered an impeachable witness. Rader will be ignored. He'll also remain in hospital. Cavanaugh raised a stink. So they made him a warden."

"Serves him right. Whenever I watch Cavanaugh pacing back and forth on those stubby legs, his torso bent over. His hand behind his back. He reminds me of that old Jew comedian, Groucho Marx. All I can think of is him pulling out a cigar and talking about a sanity clause.

Lipps let an embarrassed chuckle. "You know you are a bigot." Lipps generally avoids the topic of ethnicity with her when he can. Tonight he is drunk and angry. He has never learned to deal with a real threat to his world.

"And you like to fuck Asian ethnics--as a rule." She smirks. Amanda Feiss knows the corporate fathers want Tom and her to wed. She still refuses. "You know what that cretin Cavanaugh did the other day?" Without waiting for an answer, she sticks her chin into her chest to form a triple chin, and clears her throat. "Say Amanda," she says mimicking Cavanaugh's deep voice. "How about you and I having a nice dinner in Portland? I'd like to paint you." Her head bounces from side to side. In an almost perfect imitation of the officer's nervous habit.

TJ is indeed surprised. "Are you kidding? Captain America asked you out for dinner? I don't believe it." He pauses a second and watches her eyes. They dart right, then left. She is lying about this invitation. He tries to figure why she'd bother to even mention the topic, let alone lie about an invitation. "Maybe he just wanted to paint you. On the other hand if he paints you, I'm sure that it will screw you."

"He is pretty good at painting," she says. "A lousy officer, but a good painter."

TJ, previously unable to figure out why Amanda continually made up these stories about the other officers, now thinks he knows why. He believes she is looking for scapegoats for the failed Wall strategy. At least he hopes that's it. "So," he says. "Are you going to go grease his gears?" TJ is a survivor. His frat-boy demeanor has gotten him the side seat with the best pilot in the squadron.

Amanda rolls her eyes. "Groucho would have a better chance. Besides, my new sweetheart might get a bit upset."

Lipps nods. "So when am I going to meet this guy?" Ewalt Rader has left a lasting scar on an already wounded heart.

"Soon, TJ."

"Ewalt Rader is the only confirmed kill of your love. By the way, I am impressed that you worked so hard to keep him alive. He may still hate you given what happened in Idaho. Why risk a court martial to protect him?"

"With WeatherEye squawking in my helmet, what choice did I have?" Amanda's eyes dart right and left.

He pauses, then decides to go for it. "You had him as good as dead as soon as he was in the evac sling. All you had to do was bank right and go in low. But you didn't. I don't think you ever really wanted to kill him," Lipps says. "Maybe it's time to make up with him?"

"Groucho would have a better chance." Again they both laugh.

"C'mon Tom. Lets get it going," someone shouts.

She looks at TJ, appreciating his comments. "Ewalt will stew over the death of his driver. That's enough pain for him today. I prefer to take him apart piece by piece."

"Ah, the lessons learned from our parents' joy," Lipps says as he strolls back to get his ball. Amanda saving Ewalt Rader then killing his driver is a tough one to fathom. So far as Lipps could see there was no reason to kill the driver. The attack computers took into account the two evacuations and the vectors looked safe for both men.

As TJ Lippman hefts his bowling ball, ready to toss it down the alley, he ponders his options. If Amanda has started going off the deep side, his efforts at control of Feiss Industries may be curtailed before he even gets a chance to step up to the plate. TJ releases the ball and walks back to the smile of his team mates. It's a strike.

He decides that any hint of compassion from Amanda screams danger. Lipps saw what happened in Idaho. He was there. And then after all that, Ewalt left her cold one day, and never contacted her again. *But that was years ago.* TJ thought their love had become a blood feud between warriors but somehow Amanda Feiss has softened. *Ewalt Rader was supposed to be a failed asset. How could love erupt at this point? Is it a mask for her desperation?*

Twenty minutes later Amanda and Lipps leave the bowling alley. A money game is about to begin and TJ is persona non gratia when there is pay at stake. They walk along the night-deserted street passing an old gas station that functions as a cat-house. The side streets are a mash-up of cock-fight parlors, bars, movie theaters, restaurants, and bordellos. Bare buzzing bulbs light the buildings around them. Turning the corner onto Broadway, the odor of fish sauce permeates the area. Restaurants line the street, per military order. Every color of the rainbow beats down to the puddled roadway. From the glowing bulbs overhead, it hardly seems night on planet Earth. The civic leaders will have no blackouts in Portland. Myth is the city is invulnerable.

"Hungry?" Lipps asks as he stops at a Thai restaurant.

"It's three-thirty in the morning."

"I didn't get any dinner," says Lipps, already reading the menu in the window.

"Tom, that waitress has gone home. She will never bed you." Opening the plywood door and ringing the chimes, they enter the recycled Starbucks. An older woman stirs with the sound of the door chimes. Soon, no longer sitting on a chair, having called out into the kitchen, she approaches them. Greeting the pilots with a bow, she motions for them to take any table, then returns with tea and spoons. White table-cloths cover each of the ten round tables. In the middle, a metal fountain spouts green water in a single stream that falls on itself. Overhead, on the ceiling, a picture of the Wall glows in iridescent reds and bright blues.

They sit beneath another picture, taken from an aircraft, that shows the black Wall running perpendicular to the remains of US-5. All four lanes stop at the Wall. Trash and encampments cover the southern side. A pristine green veldt covers the other side dotted with farms. The picture is over nine years old. There is no hint of the fields of flowers on the southern side of the Wall. Smart money says the eventual collapse of the Wall from tunneling should be right at its intersection with I-5. The roadway facilitates the delivery of tools and equipment for digging.

The last picture on the ceiling is that of the Buddah in red and silver. It hangs above the projected pictures of food, over the front door.

Lipps hands Amanda a menu wrapped in yellowed plastic.

Amanda shakes her head no. He looks over the menu then says to the waitress. "Mee-krob and eggplant," he says, handing the waitress back the menu. She disappears into the kitchen. A second later, a loud screech and the sounds of a pan hitting the floor startles them.

"I guess the cook was still asleep," Amanda says. "I wish I could sleep like that."

The mirth wanders from the copilot's face. "We don't fly until two. You'll sleep."

Amanda stares at the table. "I have this new dream. I am at the base trying to get away. I am with some guy. I don't remember who it was. We are in charge of opening and closing the gates to the field. Anyway we are out by the old passenger terminal. There is a rocket attack. We start running toward the front gate. The guy keeps screaming that he doesn't know where the gate is. He keeps begging me to help him find it. I tell him. I'll handle it. We begin weaving and dodging the rockets. The rockets are the ones with the red glowing tips."

Lipps pours them both tea. "They don't glow, Amanda."

She ignores his comment. "Anyway, we run right into a group of Dirties, all females, about sixteen or seventeen years old. They pull out knives and start to cut us. Damn, I can still feel the knives cutting me apart. Then they break my arms and kill me." She looks at him. "God, I hate that bastard, Rader. I didn't know she was his squeeze."

He sips his tea, astounded at the comment. He was there. "That was years ago. I thought you'd forgotten him."

She looks out the window. "Company," she sips her tea.

"Hey, Feiss, ah guess what?" The door bursts open and their bowling buddies file in.

"You guys finished cheating already?" Lipps asks. The waitress brings out the fried eggplant and hands out menus. Moments later she walks away with a dozen orders for food.

"Someone torched a generator. We figured it was you, Lipps." Tubbs leans over and smells TJ for gasoline. "Guess not. Oh, I just read a text from our friends at the JAG about the bug-jockies you evacuated by Whiskeytown. Ready?" Says Tubbs. His big grin stretches to include everyone at the table.

"Sure," Amanda responds. "I know this will not be pretty. You all are having too much fun." She glances at the others. Everyone waits for the punch line.

"Ah, the court of inquiry has been cancelled."

Amanda takes a quick sip of dandelion tea, holding the white cup in her hands afterward.

"Amanda, don't try to hide your joy," Tubbs says as the waitress drops off a round of beers. "But you know you'll feel better if you tell your old buddies the truth. What really happened with you two that turned you into a medal winner?"

"A medal?" Lipps asks. "Instead of a court martial? Too funny."

"As I hear it. Now what happened?" Tubbs asks. "Is it true you and Commander Rader once made poets blush?"

"Where is he? Is he still at Fort Shasta Medical?" Amanda asks. Another container of warm tea arrives at the table.

Tubbs puts his hands up. "Forget it. We all heard Cavanaugh, No pot-shots at the tanks. That goes for hospitals too. Our lips are sealed. Unless you care to make a trade, information for information. You tell us what happened--oh so long ago in Idaho. We might give you our best information on where he is. I'll tell you this: He's no longer at Shasta." Tubbs waits for a response.

"Is he okay?' Lipps asks.

"Ah, some burns and a flesh wound. They're sending him north for rehab at the burn unit in Chehalis. Damn, now how'd that leak out?" He laughs. "Please Massa' Feiss, ah, don't nuke the hospital. Just to display your rendition of heart."

Amanda picks up a beer. Everyone at the table hears her foot tapping on the floor. "Maybe I'll just ask the medics to put you there first, Tubbs."

Tubbs laughs. "Ah, no one's going to do diddly. You dodged a big bullet today, Ms. Feiss. Ah, but even though you are invulnerable, do us a favor. Don't wander around Portland machine gunning the streets because you're pissed some dumb grunt had the balls to say fuck you."

"That will be the day, Tubbs," Amanda says with a demure smile on her face. The people around the table break into nervous laughter. Amazed that Tubbs would be so direct, Amanda takes a baby carrot from Lipps' plate and puts it in her mouth. The waitress arrives with more food. Most of it is beef or pork practically black on the outside.

"You know, Tubbs. Maybe she's just putting you on about hating this guy," Lipps proposes, with a scholarly air. "Maybe she cares about him and that's why she did the evacuation."

Amanda shoots him a withering stare. The nine people around the table nod while they chew.

"Never," Tubbs stuffs food in his mouth after seeing her blistering continence. "The Dirties will die off and we'll all go home before that happens. I've known Amanda since we were at Punahau. Amanda Feiss never lets a vendetta drop. Death before forgiveness. There aren't many things important to Amanda. At the top of that list is hunting down Ewalt Rader and making him suffer for tossing her out of the sack like she was some bimbo. Frankly I think he was nuts to do that. You are one major hottie, Captain Mandy. So, why did you dust the driver and save him? Ah, I ran the vectors. You were clear."

Amanda smiles.

"Hate. It keeps them both alive," someone says.

"You mean Feiss and Rader? Their hate for each other?" Tubbs says. "On second thought that is nonsense. He could give a damn about her. That's the real issue. Everyone is supposed to care about the Feiss family. Those are the rules. And I tell you that was okay with me. When Feiss had things under control. Ladies and gentlemen things are no longer under control. So the hell with Feiss. Ah, say I." The table goes quiet. Drunk Captain Tubbs receives a hard kick under the table. He quickly adds, "Ah, maybe it's like us and the Dirties. We hate them, but respect them." Tubbs sticks a slice of meat into his mouth. "I suppose, if we admit we hate each other then we lose our edge. Nah, I don't buy it. She loves him. And I think that's because he doesn't give a shit about her. Oh the pangs of this mortal coil."

A cold chill rolls through Amanda Feiss. She is unused to this kind of grilling and decides it is time to change the subject. "We saw some better technology today," she says, finishing her bottle of beer. The advances by the Dirties are always the conversation of prime interest. "I saw a missile fired at the tankers change course."

"The tankers reported that as well," TJ says.

"Why hasn't disease gotten them, or hunger?" Someone says, with a full mouth of food.

"They say there must be a billion of them at the Wall," says another of the pilots.

"Ah, they're cannibals," Tubbs says, sipping tea. "They grow some percentage of their children as food. They slaughter the young and eat them." He laughs.

"You don't really believe that do you?" Lipps asks. He can't help but look down at the pieces of pig and cow flesh on the plates around him.

"There's no other explanation. One of the tactical liaison officers says that there's no sign of cultivated fields anywhere in the state. But the Dirties are fatter than they used to be. You figure it out."

"Someone is manufacturing food for them," Amanda says.

"Oh bullshit," says Tubbs. "They're animals. Or is that us?"

"Well they can't grow crops," one of the other female pilots interjects. "We made sure of that."

Amanda will have no more this. "How do you explain their weapons and health?" Amanda says. "They have a food source. I am sure." The table quiets hearing the voice of power.

"Fuck you, Amanda. You don't know everything," Tubbs says. He wipes his chin with a brown cloth napkin. "All they know is fighting. There is no difference between us and them. Nothing matters to them except getting to the top."

Everyone watches Amanda examine Captain Tubbs. No one doubts what is to come.

"Well if they are cannibals, then you'll make a very tasty treat, Mr. Tubbs," Amanda replies with a smile.

By tomorrow afternoon he will be reassigned to reconnaissance duty along the Willamette River. He will be dead within the week when the aircraft he is flying is shot down. The cause of death for Captain Tubbs will be determined at a hearing. The official conclusion will be human error. The conclusion will be reached right after Tubb's maintenance mechanic is found dead in her bunk from an overdose of Roadies.

CHAPTER NINE

Dr. Joseph Vaz carries a torch. There is not enough oil to run the ancillary generators. The refinery in Richmond was bombed into rubble a few weeks ago.

He moves carefully inside the dark hallway. The damp railing feels slimy and cold. The furnaces are on low as well. Stepping slowly, partially because of the dark, partially because of a hip wound that has ruined his gait, he negotiates the slippery metal floor of the catwalk. The near fatal attempts on his life not withstanding--Joe Vaz is a prudent man. The feel of the rail gives way to a series of bumps. Joe reads a Braille message taped to the railing. The fuel supplies are delayed. "Bastards," he says to the dark.

Brilliant, and idealistic, his former university students used to call him Don Quixote--and not just because of is thin frame. Joe guards his idealism with a ferociousness that surprises many because his appearance gives just the opposite impression, that of a beaten man.

Thin, and physically disproportionate, as if someone had stitched together a body from excess human parts, his arms are crooked and his legs are too long. His head seems skewed; Joe's eyes do not line up straight. A large head, with a pug nose stuck on a gaunt face, a graying brown mustache, his short goatee of dense coarse hair, and deep set brown eyes--they all form an odd face. Even so, some say he is handsome when he laughs, a serene figure in a dirty green cloak and torn jeans. That stoop to his shoulders though, that seems a testament to his imminent destruction.

It all passes away when he works. Joe Vaz fights the inequities of this world with a brilliant mind and a gladiator's ferocity, which takes no prisoners. He hates those born with gifts that claim those gifts as rights of being. Rather than seeing the body as a carriage for the delivery of life's gifts to others. This man is far from beaten. He is just a most unlikely looking warrior. And while it is true, Dr. Joseph Vaz lives with only one foot in this world. He is ready to die for his beliefs at any time.

And it is more than the defense of a middle-aged, lonely man. Age has only taught Joe not to snarl at anyone who does not understand his words. He has never fully breached the wall of love, now believing himself far too odd to find a mate. In its stead, he nourishes and adores his fantasies. Which he sees as a substitute for being loved. Joe Vaz is also a genius--and an idiot about loving. He is the man responsible for saving a hundred million lives. Dr. Joseph Vaz feeds the Dirties.

The railing ends at a metal door. His hand runs up the cold metal until he finds the lock. Opening it, he enters a noisy underground cavern. Below, large garbage trucks light other trucks by their headlights. They are being loaded with food. Joe Vaz, along with being an idealist, is the most dangerous man alive for the Patrician Order. He not only feeds the Dirties. He gives them hope.

Watching the trucks load, satisfied that all is well, he walks along the perimeter catwalk, by the battered parts bins used for repairs. Then he crosses through another door and up a flight of fifty stairs into the dusk. Beginning the trek to his home, around him is a red-lit evening. The sag of girders in burnt-out buildings, some hidden gardens, a few machines running, and the unending tents mark the sides of his path. Scrub grass grows through cracks in the asphalt and concrete. He detests the ruins that sag overhead, the Bay Area Rapid Transit System. The white concrete "T's" supporting sections of track look so tired to him. He knows that sooner or later the tracks will collapse. Even though they only support wooden platforms, tents, and dirty people. Rope ladders sway in the gusts of sea-smelling winds mixing with the smells of sweat and pain. The shambles of civilization appear this evening to have always been here. Unlike the technology Joe loves and trusts.

Ahead of him, children play hide and seek. Their squeals and yelling hooks his mind, luring it into their games. "It's the Food Man," a young girl calls out. Like mice, twenty children wiggle out from beneath a rusted school bus. They stream from its doors or drop down from the empty engine compartment rushing towards him. "Play with us until the trucks come back. You said you would," pleads a small blond girl with soot on her nose.

Though Joe can't remember saying anything of the sort, he nods as they crowd around him. "A quick game of tag. The trucks for the Wall are almost full of Kandy," he replies.

"Okay," a tall, dark-skinned boy says. He looks around at the others. "But...You're it." They run in different directions. Everyone loves teasing Joe. It is their defense. A man who once thought that ability and skill would attract friends and lovers, he scoops up love whenever he can find it, like a street bum seeking a stogie. He fears his loneliness, and endures it.

The children love him, but like their parents, they keep their distance. Too late in life, Dr. Vaz learned ability and skill have no quarter in love.

"The bus is safe," somebody yells. After a few minutes, a skinny girl with a shaved head--it keeps the lice away--runs right near him. Joe intercepts her. She let him catch her. Everyone knows the spindly man cannot run well. She darts out after a boy in shorts. Joe hurries to the bus and rests against it. Over and over they get him. Soon he is sweating. Leaning back against the bus, his hip barking sharp pains. When they see him tire, the children ignore him. Their smiles are there for him so he feels happy. The game continues with Joe being the one everyone wants to tag.

The eighty garbage trucks from the food factory appear. They rumble by on their daily trip to the Wall. Three children jump on the back of a truck and wave to their friends. They are off to fight. Joe waves good bye as well. He is tired and pleased; the children like him.

A second distant rumble and he looks up seeing a jet fighter streak across the sky. He admires its sleekness and no longer fears it. The jet tells him that the military knows approximately when he ships his food out, and how he uses garbage trucks at this main factory. But the jets no longer attack. Joe Vaz wonders if they are conserving their remaining weapons' stores for defense. The tide of battle has turned in favor of the Dirties up at the Wall.

He watches the jet turn in a wide circle and streak back to the carrier thirty miles out to sea. Despite the worldwide packs of carrier groups, with their bombers and missiles, every day the people outside of the Wall get stronger.

Joe wonders why these people still attack the Wall and sacrifice so many. They already know the tunnels have weakened it and it is just a matter of time before large sections collapse down into the earth. Joe has spent hours with Phillip Stein working the numbers and making suggestions for positioning the tunnels and munitions. Joe has a head for systems and logistics.

Still, he cannot see the logic of it all. So far as he can tell. Other than a few material comforts that taunt those outside the Wall. Those inside the Wall have no future. When asked, he has argued that siege--rather than attack--is the solution to the Wall. He is ignored. So he asks the others, "Why bother?" In his opinion, the Wall is a prison for the remains of a junta that commandeered a nation and were beaten back by the citizens of that nation.

Joe Vaz also claims he cannot understand what drives the unending suicide. Other than as an expression of anger from those who had trusted in a system that took them for fools. Phillip, Joe believes, is the quintessence of this anger. A brilliant researcher and strategist who had overestimated his worth to the Patricians, that overestimation had cost him his wife and children. Now Phillip lives only for revenge. Paradoxically, Joe is envious that Phillip Stein ever even had a real family. Though he pities him for the loss.

At the top of the hill, a bell tower stands at the intersection of the Glade Lane and Mission Boulevard. Crossing under it, he strolls down a narrow lane. At the end of the alley, the remains of an old office building wraps around a set of cabins in a U shape. With twisted steel girders and windowless frames, the luxury office building is now occupied by guards using the four-story structure to observe the surrounding area. A female guard in the burnt-out building stares down at Dr. Vaz as he approaches. She is narrow and blond, once an occasional lover. He has no real interest in her. Joe believes she pities him and that is the source of her attention. Joe Vaz grew up without love.

His mother had been raped continually as a child. An older brother with a sense of entitlement and a lack of boundaries had been the culprit. Tanya Vaz met and married a violent man at the age of sixteen whom she believed would protect her. A gang-banger, the assaults stopped after his first visit. Joe's father never knew of the sexual assaults against his wife. Joe's mother had wanted to protect the life of her older brother. Unfortunately, her hatred and pain from so many years of abuse left her angry and empty. In effect, Joe Vaz grew up an emotional orphan. Or in other words, he is a walking miracle.

He pushes aside the dirty blue curtain to enter his bungalow. His small cabin has no door. Of course, the cabin doesn't need a door. No one would steal from him. Doctor Vaz has given the children life.

Tan book-shelf-walls, a stained ceiling, and the shiny plywood floor of the small room sparkle with cleanliness. The small chair of dark wood to his right sits tight against the tiny white plastic desk. Fresh dandelions rest in a clear glass vase. Wood waits, stacked in front of the small stove in the center of the room. His bed against the side wall has been straightened. The stained blanket tucked in around the edges. The books he had been studying last night are no longer on the desk. They sit edged alphabetically around the base of the desk. Hundreds of other books sit jammed into the wall-shelves. Bright yellow ribbons hang over their backs for easy return to where he had stopped reading. It is not that Joe is naturally neat. Two years ago he had tried to find out who came in and built his shelves. Then they began cleaning his room and mending his clothes. All anyone would tell him was they wanted him to be comfortable--so he could make more food. That response left him bewildered. Joe Vaz does not know if he is being used, or cared about. He believes he is being used.

Then he broke his favorite cup. A replacement appeared--almost an exact copy--within the week. Yet no adult, he notes, speaks to him on a social basis. Other than the blond woman he saw today or an old man who lives next door. So, he considers the homage of neatness payment rather than affection. Joe Vaz is sure that for some reason, in this life, that certain gifts are denied to him. He has no knowledge of what it means to be ignorant, desperate, and uneducated. As a result, conversations with him make others uneasy, or insulted. They walk away. He ponders what he did wrong.

With former lovers, as a young man at the University, he had noted they all said they could not find him. Along with his brilliance, Joe Vaz is astoundingly creative--and therefore a difficult lover to understand. He does not know that he is a puzzle, and that because of his fears, he hides the key. So as an adult he considers loneliness just a part of being hyper-intelligent.

Joe shakes the dust from his cloak and hangs it on a nail over the desk. Turning, he spies a scrawny white mouse on a wooden shelf above his bed. Sitting in front of a rusted blue ice cream scoop on the shelf, the mouse, watches him. As it does every evening now, twitching its snout.

"Shoo. Get away," Joe says, raising his hand. The rodent leaps onto his bed wiggling its hindquarters, scurrying across the woolen blanket, then jumps down to the dark floor. It hurries out the opening to the gutted kitchen area, disappearing into a drainpipe until tomorrow. This daily ritual has gone on for three weeks now. Joe has named the mouse Mousey. Sometimes, he leaves it food in the ice cream scoop. The need to do this makes him feel stupid.

Joe kneels beside the stove and lights the fire. It is always full. Ready to be lit by a small candle that sits in front of it. He blows out the candle and watches the fire. A knock on the cabin wall disturbs his stare. Joe doesn't hurry to answer it. No one will be there.

Eventually he gets up.

There on the threshold, a yellow-painted metal sign that says Yield. Holding a cup and a pewter pitcher filled with fresh water, between them sits a small orange carrot no bigger than his pinky. A tear wells in his eye as he carries the wonderful treat into his home. He has no idea why today is special. Around here, some might consider a carrot more valuable than life. He mistakenly assumes the thin blond woman is courting his favor. Brilliant as he is, Joe misses the obvious about his fellow humans because of his rabid idealism. He cannot comprehend love existing in what he calls evil--unmitigated desire.

Sitting by the small cheery fire, he pulls a small cake from his jacket pocket and puts it on his tray next to the carrot. Dr. Vaz again ponders the strange people and their anonymous benefactions. He just cannot understand why people would be so kind, but never speak to him. It never occurs to him they are merely following their needs.

Joe takes a tiny bite of the sweet carrot. After savoring its almost magical freshness and placing it back on the tray. He bites through one of his food cake's exterior of crunchy protein--into the curry flavored hot pepper filling. These white cakes are his favorite ones. Joe prefers the very spicy filling to the sweet blue cakes that taste like vanilla, or the chewy red cakes that taste like pizza. He is content with any of the cakes. The people in training to take over his factory have experimented with other flavors. So far they have developed only brown cakes that smell like, and taste like, an old shoe. Joe has told them it is because of the birth control chemical they are adding. They will not listen. Priestess Etu has ordered an experiment in birthrate reduction as a way to make peace with the far side of the Wall.

Joe admires Elena's idealism and needs her beauty. He cannot escape the ugliness and brutality of the world around him in any other way. A woman's beauty is an elixir for him. He drinks it in as if he were an alcoholic on a binge. While he analyzes in awe the way another's beauty nourishes his spirit and soul.

Occasionally, he thinks of a Brazilian woman whom he had adored. She had refused to follow him north saying that he would stay with her--if he really cared for her. She was an idealist as well. Joe left her because of his duty. Without any sense of nobility. Joe Vaz knew there had to be a food factory in North America, like the one he had built in Brazil. It is the key to ending the savagery that roams the planet as well as the key to destroying the last remains of an order that says it has no responsibility to the rest of humanity. So he is pleased and driven to perform a task that damages Hell on Earth.

Despite the bombings that destroy progress around this main food factory, Joe sees his stealth has given the factory longevity. The factory in Brazil was destroyed soon after he left to come north. Other tiny factories cover California. Many of them build either food or weapons. Some are so well disguised that they cannot even be seen even by walking up to them and staring at them. Heat signatures, smoke, waste, transport, power--all of the tracks of civilization remain disguised. As a result, the small factories flourish.

Joe finishes the carrot and steps out back to the long ditch and washes his glass under the faucet. It drains rain water from the roof cistern. Just then he hears the ritualistic tapping of rocks that occurs every evening about this time. The sound of a few hundred-thousand people tapping rocks together penetrates everything, like a great idea. The people call it the Earth's Voice. To Joe, the rumble seems like the coursing of blood, or chi, though a living organism. He loves the sound and quickly reenters his hovel so he can join in the ceremony. Picking up the pair of small, smooth hand-sized river rocks from a shelf, he exits his front doorway.

Tap
Tap-Tap
Tap-Tap-Tap
Tap-Tap-Tap-Tap
Tap-Tap-Tap-Tap-Tap.

It is a repeating beat:

Tap
Tap-Tap
Tap-Tap-Tap
Tap-Tap-Tap-Tap
Tap-Tap-Tap-Tap-Tap.

The dusty drive fills with others clacking rocks together. A fierce intensity unites them. Joe smiles at those around him. Unaware he hardly ever smiles at others outside the dark cavern of his factory floor. The men, women, and children dressed in sacking, return his kind smile--proud to know him. They are glad the Food Man no longer scowls at them all the time or drifts passed them like the breeze. His efforts have saved innumerable lives. Everyone considers him a saint. Night after night, when they are out of Joe's hearing, people old and young, tell and retell stories of how Joe found a way to manufacture food from the past's waste.

Tap
Tap-Tap
Tap-Tap-Tap
Tap-Tap-Tap-Tap
Tap-Tap-Tap-Tap-Tap.

His neighbor, the old man, looks over and nods hello. With a rutted face and a horrible scar that arches from his left eye to his right ear, the man seems lost in the sounds. The wounds to his head during the fall of San Francisco have scattered the old man's thoughts. He looks muddled most of the time. Until his mind fills with equations. He had used them in his previous occupation as a teaching physician at a hospital down south.

The equations cloud out the confusing details of a painful life. For brief moments the man's world is clear. His mind caresses the symbols cascading through his head, treasuring the feelings he receives from the interplay of numbers--and their beauty. The old man waves to Joe with tapping rocks and examines the health of the man who has saved so many. He senses no change and goes back to the rhythm of the beat. To Joe, this old man is simply a friendly trash merchant.

Other neighbors stand in front of their homes and watch the two men glance at each other. The old man speaks as the rock tapping dies. Joe turns away. The old man looks at the dust below his feet and sighs.

Long before the horrors of mass starvation had turned the disenfranchised into the mob they call the Dirties, Joe learned not to hear. When it calls he listens only to it. He had turned away from the old man because he had an idea for a new way to move more food onto the trucks. The loss of genius scares him more than death. He has told himself more than once that if he loses his genius. He will kill himself. Ironically, if he tried to end his life, his neighbors would restrain him. They need him.

Back in his room, Joe reads for a while, studying the old encyclopedias on Africa. Egypt has asked about constructing a factory that makes food from petroleum waste. Joe believes the facility for Africa, would be triple the output of the San Francisco factory. He has been considering how to efficiently stage the resources. Joe is an incessant planner.

After reassuring himself that he can handle the distribution problem, Joe maps a path through the radiation belts of Africa. Then he rechecks his list on what he will need to acquire for the new factory near Seattle. He expects to leave within the month for the Wall. He checks his list of tools as well.

Joe Vaz isn't merely a wanderer or a saint. He knows that the Patricians on the other side of the Wall will come looking for him as soon as the Wall is down and so he will have to start moving to stay alive. He believes getting into Portland is the only way to keep himself safe and so he plans to offer his services to the Priestess once the Wall fails and his factory is safe. Still, Joe has a concern about going to Portland. He believes the Priestess will ask him to help her wage war against the Patricians. He thinks he will not do that.

He knows that saboteurs and assassins will remain in Portland after the Wall collapses and they will target him. It is the way of the PO. He also knows the opening of the Wall will invite ground-based saboteurs to focus on his factory. That is what happened in Brazil after the battle of San Luis. Had he not abandoned the factory when he did, he is sure he would have died with the factory.

Night falls. He listens to people speaking as they walk back and forth. Often they speak in a foreign language. Just as often he hears his name in conversation. It seems to him that millions of people shuttle through San Francisco on their way to the Wall. There are often comments about how civilized this city is, compared to many of the other large cities left on the planet.

Lying in his cot this evening, he considers the Priestess Elena Etu and how much she has achieved these last few years. *She tries so hard to help these people. Her desire to control the growth of population, as a method of negotiation seems an impossible notion.* Joe cannot understand why she will not recognize that those on the other side of the Wall see a unified population as a threat to their power--regardless of their numbers. *It was never about overpopulation. It was about a society outside the Patricians' control.*

The Priestess' plans for peace through population control make him feel stupid about his ideals of feeding more people. That concerns him also. Worst of all, her heroics are encased in beauty. He is jealous of her physical gifts. Unable to recognize that, he tells himself that he admires her beyond words.

Elena is like that young woman who saved my life. Both of them know exactly how to negotiate this world. I wish I did. I wonder what that soldier is doing now? He gazes at the moon's light as it bathes the floor trying to remember the woman's name. *She's probably up at the Wall. But I'll bet she hates what she does. She probably flies one of those air ambulances.* The thought warms him.

Occasionally, someone will stop nearby with a friend and tell a story of the old days or fabricate some heroic pursuit that always ends in happiness. Joe listens to the stories with intense pleasure; his saw-like snoring putting an end to the tales outside his window. No matter where the tellers are in their story. A story on skiing begins outside his window. He lies awake hearing the end of the first story. He then hears about how to drive a car.

Joe feels the scar on his hip wondering if he will ever see that pilot again. He drifts off to sleep; a man in love with his fantasies.

CHAPTER TEN

You will die in my arms. The memory cuts through Ewalt's unconsciousness. Seeing the earliest light of dawn outside his window, he closes his eyes. *Still here. Fuck me.* His throbbing leg nudges him awake again, the burning on his ankles forcing his eyes to open. *A bandage around my chest. That crazy bitch zapped me with a taser.*

A woman, her back towards Ewalt, reclines in the next bed. "Then, so once I heard they were about to breach the Wall, I decided what the heck. So I lit the stove." He hears how the washed-out Wally in the bed lost both legs from a stove exploding at a rest area. She had been just trying for a less debilitating wound to get her away from the Wall and miscalculated the boom from gasoline.

Ewalt stares up at a ceiling fan listening to the woman babble on about her intrigue. It takes Ewalt more than a minute to realize the fan doesn't move. He looks to his right. A boy, both arms splinted tight against his chest, sits on the chair taking in this woman's every word. A patch covers his right eye. "I'm going back to the Wall tomorrow. What do I do?"

A small beep. The morphine drip kicks in. In a stupor, Ewalt fades back into memories; his mind wandering to the evacuation of

Coeur d' Alene. It fixes on Xandra. The woman who had said he could die in her arms. A woman whose long hair fell like cool black water over his face. A woman whose deeply set blue eyes still stare at him. He hears her laughter. It is a chirping bird outside his window that has just met the spring of its life. Of all the women he has known, only Xandra haunts him. If Amanda Feiss hadn't killed Xandra, he believes the prediction he would die in her arms might well have come true.

His mind falls through time.

The Dirties had begun raiding Idaho in an effort to find a way through the irradiation zone that had begun at the Arctic Circle and was making its way south into Idaho. Everyone knew that if the Dirties succeeded in controlling any corridor through Idaho, the entire strategy for the Wall in Redding would fail and the remaining states of Alaska, Washington, Oregon, and British Columbia would be overrun by the Dirties.

Even though no one wanted their state turned into a nuclear dead zone. The citizens of Idaho protested and wrote their senators. The militants took up arms and were slaughtered. The religious prayed and the mercenaries became rich. The Patricians believed they were being backed into a corner. Wholesale death in the name of safety was dealt out to citizens with unheard of wrath. Canadians joined the battle because no one cared what the locals wanted. The hostility of citizens became rage when rumors of death camps spread throughout the cities of Idaho.

Ugly and brutal, Idaho was the beginning of a long education for Ewalt Rader. That spring, a large number of insurgents descended west into Idaho. Another group charged from the south hoping to split the US forces overseeing the irradiation. Ewalt saw his chance. A gunnery instructor who occasionally escorted engineering teams to Wall construction sites, he was bucking for something new. Anything to make sure he would make it to the other side of the Redding Wall when it was complete.

Corporal Rader approached a Captain with one arm named Cavanaugh who ran the weapons support program for Idaho. Desperate for good gunners, the Captain began his interview with Ewalt this way: "We are looking for gunnery support because the Seventeenth is currently in the shit. The Constellation helicopters are the weak part of the Heavy Lift Command. While capable of carrying thirty-five tons of debris and scattering their cargo in precise patterns, they are just too damn slow. Our job is to protect them. But that means you'll go slow also. Too slow make it home, unless you are a hell of a gunner. You dumb enough for this assignment, Corporal Rader?"

"Well yes sir."

"Volunteers need to know that many of the Connies have been hit. As well as too many of my gunships, the new Tenark Rapier gunships are at least a year out. The Dirties clearly understand the importance of this last corridor into the Northwest. While we think they know the effort is useless. They continue to fight. We also think they are trying to use up our resources. They are fighting a desperate battle and inflicting serious loses and we can't afford to lose many more Connies. Our job is to kill as many of the little bastards as we can. To keep the Connies safe. Your job, as gunner, is to make that happen. And frankly we don't give a shit about you. As long as the Connies are safe. Can you deal with that?"

Ewalt was brought in as a belly gunner for one of the older model gunships, brought out of moth-balls to protect the Constellation helicopters. He quickly learned that his task was far from being irradiation support. His real job was to escort and protect engineers into places where they would secure material and precious metals for some corporate project.

Idaho was being raped in the name of civilization and its citizens left to die. Ewalt could plainly see that. The radiated door in Idaho would slam shut no matter what and the citizens were to be ignored.

The process would take almost three months. As he watched the destruction, he learned the meaning of evil and how to ignore it. This was lesson one of the Idaho campaign for Corporal Ewalt Rader.

Initially shocked by the wholesale killing, he saw that anyone who stood against the task of the engineers was considered an insurgent and immediately killed. Doctors, clergy, lawyers, statesmen, other soldiers, he saw them all become casualties of avarice. Then he saw that truth was uncovered in the battlefield and hidden from the population. In what he decided was his search for truth, he made the military his career. The barbarity of humanity he concluded, came from protecting what one had. Rather than the desire to fix problems or make things better. It meant the skills of a soldier would always be in demand. That was lesson two. It changed Ewalt from a man wanting survival into a killer. He was twenty-nine years old, believing his only play in this life was to deal death.

Ewalt quickly began to view himself as a wiser man who had learned that society was evil. In response, he sought the solace of women. Corporal Rader had come to believe, their warmth came not from love, but from their need for security in a brutal society. Women were still toys for Ewalt Rader to this point.

At nights, and on his days off, Ewalt began studying battle tactics, or getting in fights, or copulating with any woman who would have him. On one of these binges he met Xandra. Ewalt assumed she was just a bar-girl. Even though she claimed she had been a doctor--as well as a mother of two. She told him a story about how the Dirties had captured her home by a lake. Her children and husband were burned in their home--while she escaped. Ewalt didn't believed her.

A briefing before the assignment, supposedly to keep the troopers safe from scams, said almost everyone would have fake hard-luck stories. The instructors had gone down a list of likely stories. Number two on the list was the death of loved ones. Psy/Ops had then came in and said the stories were thought up by the cunning minds of the insurgent leaders. To undermine the troopers who were the bulwark of civilization against the barbarians. Until Coeur d' Alene, Ewalt was a believer of that nonsense.

Ewalt soon told Xandra he didn't believe her story, saying there is no way they'd allow a beautiful woman like her to escape unharmed. She began to cry, excusing herself for the powder room. When she returned, her eyes were red. Ewalt bought her some bourbon, having figured out his blunder. He apologized, asking her to tell him more. She claimed she had stayed to help the defenders of Boise. Then after it became an irradiated hell, she had come to Coeur d' Alene to help as well. She thought she could do some good--she said--before escaping into Washington State. Also drunk by that point, Ewalt had laughed at her, knowing that escape was an absurdity for the indigenous population. The problem was over-population. He didn't say it--but he knew another bar-girl on her own would never gain entry to the United States.

A week later he was still with her. Ewalt found that he liked her smile and big words. Her long black hair felt nice on his chest when she swished it back and forth. Xandra made sure he didn't get cheated. That pleased him. She also didn't talk like a bar-girl--he decided. And her breath smelled like cloves. He kept her at a motel and started to take care of her, still believing she meant nothing; Ewalt Rader had many lovers.

Every morning Xandra would stand at the window watching the clouds mingle with smoke and ask him: "Are you going to leave me, Ewalt?" He would stare at her from the bed and say, "Those that want to get out, will get out." As he had been taught.

Ewalt cannot remember when he decided to try and save her.

One morning he surprised her with an invitation for breakfast at a field kitchen: eggs and bacon with pancakes. Ewalt knew the breakfast meant the end was near. He wanted to give her something special. Waiting on line that morning, Xandra spoke about how the population--which was supposed to number in the two million range--seemed to have deserted the city in the last day or so. Ewalt replied that there was only a tenth that number. The rest, he said, were already in Washington.

She scoffed at that saying there was a rumor alleging that most of the city's population had disappeared down in the shelters. Ewalt had seen the engineers working on large gas canisters used in the underground shelters. He had also seen the skull and crossbones on the trucks that carried the liquids used to filled the containers. His response was to ignore the question and mention how good the bacon smelled. He followed up with a conjecture that perhaps some of the population had gone east to join up with the Dirties. Xandra replied by saying she always enjoyed a big breakfast.

After they ate, Ewalt and Xandra headed back to the motel passing a couple making love beneath a statue of a man dressed in a nineteenth century waistcoat. The couple and the statue were oblivious to everything on the street. Ewalt had made a joke about blind love.

Passing soldiers moving items out onto rail cars and trucks, they both noticed the dismantling of cranes was under way. She whispered, "Thank you," into his ear and gave him a soft kiss that still lingers on his cheek. That night she cried, and come the morning she didn't ask him if he was going to leave her.

Over the next two days, they were together every spare moment. The closer the battle came to the city the more she clung to Ewalt. The last day she kept saying she needed electrolytes. He laughed and said there was no power for lights. So what did she need them for? She nodded and told he was an idiot. He went over to the medics. Found out what she was saying and returned with a case of Pedialyte before he went on duty. He then asked a friend about getting her safe passage. When he found out he needed connections to make it happen, he called his friend, Jack Porter. His secretary had said he would call him back. He was fitting his tuxedo for the upcoming wedding.

At seven that evening he was on the steps of an old hotel, by that statue of the man in the waistcoat. She was never late and it was usually she who was waiting on him. He planned to scold her then tell her that he had arranged for her transport into Washington through Jack's connections. He also began thinking about how he'd introduce her to his father. Ewalt's mother had died in childbirth.

Ewalt never saw the men who appeared from behind the statue. One of them plunged a blade into Ewalt's back, just above his left kidney. Another hit him on the head with a piece of pipe. The force threw him down the steps. He tumbled to rest in a bloody blur on the cobblestones.

The next thing he knew, a female was leaning over him, firing a pistol. His vision was blurred with pain, and his ears were ringing. This woman was defending him. Then someone fell across Ewalt's chest. He found he was powerless to remove the figure. It was Xandra, her eyes opening just briefly. She said, "Then I'll die in your arms." Then there was the report of a weapon and her head jerked over to the side. Only after the woman with the weapon pulled the body off Ewalt, putting her leather flying jacket over him, did he realize the woman protecting him wasn't also Xandra. He remembers three other events from that night: The feel of the knife in his body, the pilot's confident smile, and the feeling of Xandra's blood all over his face.

The next morning, he found the down-facing body of his lover at the makeshift morgue. A bullet had entered Xandra's skull from the side. Another had entered her back. Standing over her, he cried so violently, his wounds opened. By nightfall, he was rushed back to the same hospital that he had escaped from that morning.

Amanda Feiss came to visit Ewalt that next day. His wounds had abscessed and he had to stay in the hospital for a few more days. She sat by the side of his bed for hours, talking about the upcoming final evacuation of Coeur d' Alene. When he asked her how she was there and what happened. She replied that she was passing by and saw

"...Four of them jump him and stick a blade into him..."

The next day she returned with a TV. Amanda had hired a combat photographer to make a video of a battle. Back then free-lance combat photographers would make videos of any engagement--for a hefty price--and sell them. Soon after Coeur d' Alene, photographers were not allowed into battle.

Ewalt and Amanda watched the torching of suburban tracts while eating pastrami sandwiches and pickles. He had never had a pastrami sandwich before and liked it. He soon figured out this woman had money and power. He also had no idea why she was taking care of him. Still, she looked like a ticket to fun and that was all he needed to know. He decided she was taken by his rugged good looks. Ewalt made sure not to speak about himself. He was common. The son of a baker. She was clearly Patrician.

For her part, at the time, Amanda had no conception that any man might find her unattractive. No matter what she said or did; however, after seeing the anger in his eyes, she knew gaining this man's love would push her skills. Amanda decided the game was worth it. She wasn't yet sure if he was worth it.

When she visited him there was always some wildly expensive treat: shrimp, chocolate, and even something called caviar. He would ruminate on Amanda's conversations because they were so strange. It got to the point that he wanted to talk about anything other than Idaho. But, the beautiful auburn-haired pilot was taking days off solely for the purpose of getting closer to Ewalt. So they discussed whatever she wished to discuss.

To this day, Ewalt believes Amanda is attracted to men whom she believes are trash. It never occurred to him that her initial interest in him might be based on his gunnery skills--which it was--or that she genuinely came to care for him.

His third night in the hospital, he was transferred to a hospital in Victoria, BC. She showed up there as well. That night he heard a doctor and nurse discussing how everyone died in the Idaho hospital--supposedly from a suicide attack. Only Ewalt and a dozen senior officers had made it out.

As he healed, she described how the locals had fought alongside the Dirties. They had infiltrated into the city, and how heavy the casualties had been among the troops. Then for hours she would describe the fury of the population after they learned they were not going to be evacuated. She talked of the male and female hookers who mutilated soldiers. She dwelled on the looting of the city. The last day, the ground forces had "joined the party as well." At the end, she laughed at how the US had frozen the assets of the population and that her dad, Luke, stood to make a billion dollars off the evacuation. That was the day he connected her name to the name of the people that supplied all the weapons: Feiss Industries.

A poor-man's son who didn't understand the weaponry of commerce, he found her impressive. Though truth be told, he found her distance from suffering to be distasteful and ugly.

Then, on the day of his release from the hospital, Ewalt changed the game. He asked her why she killed Xandra. Amanda immediately left and didn't come back. Amanda Feiss became a loss to him--which was okay with him. Even though he owed her his life, he felt a debt to Xandra.

Over the next year, Ewalt drifted from assignment to assignment teaching new recruits to use the weapons of the Eisenhower 501 SWAT. After a nasty fight with a young lieutenant with extensive connections, he was relieved of duty and again assigned to supporting the Constellation helicopters. They were ferrying loads of nuclear material from Hanford to the reactors in the Skagit Valley. To that point he had not heard from, or seen the pilot who had saved his life, and killed his love.

Then one night, he watched large swarms of gunships appear through a misty rain. The new Rapiers were being delivered. The egg-shaped helicopters landed on the tarmac one after the other. Supposedly the helicopters were to stay the night then get delivered south to begin service. But Ewalt had heard rumors that the Rapier had weapons problems.

Lights flashed on and off the puddles as crews scurried back and forth. Civilians with instrumentation swarmed over the gunships. The flight crews from the helicopters were immediately driven to a debriefing. Ewalt could see confusion; there were definitely problems. He stood behind a chain link fence watching Amanda Feiss among a group of suited men. Pointing her finger at them, she railed at them for almost fifteen minutes. Before she threw her helmet to the ground and stormed by him. A few minutes later, listening to the engineers discuss their challenge, he decided he had a win.

Rader asked a bearded guard with a large Rottweiler dog about the suits. The man eyed him suspiciously; more than was his job. When the guard wouldn't respond, Ewalt talked about the weather. Then he pointed at the gunships. "Those came from Amanda's dad, you know," Ewalt had said. "The guns are shit. Luke Feiss asked me to solve that. Can you help me get to the right people?" The man then pointed to the Operations shed.

Ewalt bounded up the three wide stairs and opened the door, wiping his feet on the mat, and brushing the rain off his arms. An officer sat typing on a computer keyboard. Rader was surprised there were no guards or security inside the shack--as was the standard practice at all the other buildings.

Ewalt saluted and produced his ID. "My name's Corporal Ewalt Rader and I'm looking for a pilot named Amanda Feiss. I am a gunnery instructor, here to fix the gun systems on the Rapiers."

The man didn't look up. Or even bother to look at his ID. "Sure you are." Ewalt glanced at the phone on the side of the desk. "Captain Feiss just returned from a mission and she'll be out of debrief in..." He looked up at the clock on the wall. "...About ten minutes. Go out the door and make a right. You'll see her at the Officer's Mess. If she doesn't want to see you, there will be hell to pay. Just walk away."

"How can you be so sure?" Rader asked.

"That's my job. So think it over before you do anything stupid." The conversation ended. Ewalt saluted again and picked up his ID. He ran through the rain to wait outside the mess hall.

Amanda, of course, spotted Ewalt long before he spotted her. She had also seen him outside the fence an hour before. She walked straight over to him. Ewalt noted the pilot's expression was concerned rather than bored.

"Hi," Ewalt had said. "I didn't get a chance to thank you." He watched her examine his face.

For the last hour, she had been wondering if he might be useful. "We're going back up for another shakeout. It should be quick and easy. The weapons systems are screwed up on the Rapiers. I hear you know gunnery. I want your help. How's your gut?"

"Fine. I can solve your problem."

Her eyes had brightened. Their glow surprising him. "Tenark has a team of engineers here. They have been working on the issue for weeks."

"You mean months."

"They've come up with nothing. You say you have the brains, experience, and capability that they are lacking?"

"I'm a gunnery instructor. I can't explain why your engineers are idiots. But there's nothing I don't know about your Tenark weapon's systems. And I can't imagine a better first date for us."

"Forget that. I need to know why my weapons systems sputter to a stop every so often."

He was pleased. "I can solve it."

Amanda arched her back to stretch. She faced the falling rain. "My body doesn't know how tired it really is." She smiled weakly wondering if this was all just too easy. "Look, I'm glad you came by to see me. I need a problem solved more than a lover right now. Can you deal with that?"

"You fly. I'll scope the problem. I'm Tenark air-class three qualified and I scored a 3.97 three months ago in live fire. I can smack a gnat with a twenty from 4oo yards and I am a hell of a dancer. Besides, I owe you for killing the bastards who stuck a shiv in me. I can solve the problem. I will not disappoint you, Captain."

The last sentence pierced her armor. He remembers wondering at that moment if she was falling for him. "See the Major in charge." Ewalt nodded. "If he says you check out then okay you're on. If not. Forget it."

"Done," replied Ewalt.

"Are you sure you can shoot?" Amanda already knew he was death-plus on a gun. It was the initial reason she had been following him around Coeur d' Alene. "You sure your wounds have healed from Idaho?"

"How about I just let you tuck me in when we get back and you can check me out," he had said with a grin. "I hear you have lots of pull."

The flight was boring. Ewalt, as SGR, protected the ship per standard orders on the live fire range. He told her on the way back that the problem with gunnery system was the mechanism on the trigger system caused the computers to self-test too often. He said he'd seen it often on the Tenark gun systems. Then he asked why the manufacturer hadn't fixed it on the new gunships.

There was no response from above.

He followed with: "Now you know why daddy's gunships have a bad rep with the gunners. A little spray graphite along the top, and only the top will solve it. Impressed?"

Silence.

Annoyed, Ewalt figured his analysis should have won him a little more than silence. He remained perplexed by her lack of response on the flight back, while working to keep his anger in check.

Amanda was walking the flight line on her way to Operations when he caught up to her. Before he could say anything, she suggested they go out for dinner.

Then she stood him up.

He sought her out the next morning, asking Amanda what her game was with him. Her response had been simple: "Corporal, I don't date the help."

The game had begun for them. Amanda Feiss was seeking forgiveness from him. Even though she knew Ewalt Rader wanted revenge for the murder of his lover. Ewalt was seeking another lesson from life.

CHAPTER ELEVEN

The day, after Amanda Feiss stood him up, Ewalt was tossed from his cot by MPs and marched to a transport. He had been assigned to duty by the Wall--as a maintenance person for land mines. The last person he saw before he left the ground was the officer from the flight shack who had told him to be circumspect. His smile told Ewalt that he had been had.

Later that day, the company commander glared at him. Ewalt's hair was combed back, and the stubble was gone from his face, a fresh uniform and a bright smile said "Oops." He doubted it would matter. "You're a charmer, Corporal Rader. Do you know that? I would have never believed this kind of social climbing crap from a man like you. You're a grunt, get it? Just what were you trying to achieve by telling the daughter of Feiss industries that her dad's gunships are pieces of shit?" The gravel-throated man leans back resting both his arms on the squeaky chair. "I asked you a question," he roars.

Stunned, he doesn't know what to say. "Yes sir, a charmer sir," Ewalt replies. Ewalt had prepared a speech for why he had bent the rules to fly with Amanda Feiss, but this accusation about the Rapiers didn't make sense. He did them a favor. Ewalt thinks this is a joke and wonders if he is in any trouble at all. His analysis of the weapons defect was perfect. Ewalt had seen the maintenance memo outlining the fix last night--using spray graphite--so there is no way anyone could complain about that. He also had few doubts that Amanda Feiss would be anything less than enchanted by his actions. Plus, she could not have missed the fact that her ship was the only one that did not take any simulated damage, even with the glitch. Ewalt did wonder why the others took so much damage. The training exercise was easy for him.

The skinny, very angry CO, stares at him for a moment longer. "What makes you think you can use the military to further your love life?" He is not just angry with the young corporal's insolence. He has been having troubles with the well-healed Ms. Feiss and her family for months. Worse, the MPs had woken the company commander in the middle of the night so he could discuss Ewalt Rader with General Howell. For officers like this CO, the Feiss family is royalty and General Howell is their executioner.

Ewalt continues speaking: "Sir, I heard about the weapons problem and so I just stepped in. This doesn't have anything to do with the pilot. I was just doing my job--helping out the team."

"You're a moron. Shut the hell up." Then the phone rings and he grabs it. "Yeah?" His dark eyes dart up to Ewalt and the color in his face drains. Ewalt works not to smile. The company commander stares at him, listening to the voice on the other end. He begins to nod; jaw clenched. His eyes finally leave Ewalt and wander to the rain-covered window. "Yes, sir, I understand. No, sir... Yes, sir... Yes, sir... I know there are some who are more equal than others. Yes sir. Brilliant of us to send one of our instructors up. We learned a lot. I see. All of my requests were filled? All the supplies I asked for? That's great news. Of course, I understand. Yes sir. Sorry you were bothered with this, General Howell. Yes I will tell him. Thank you, sir." He cradles the phone staring passed Ewalt to the file cabinets behind him. "Corporal, I thought you were just some ass-hat with a hard-on--a boot like me. But I guess your social climbing skills are to be legendary. That was General Howell in Seattle. The General just received a phone call from the CEO of Feiss praising your pluck--and talent."

The CO stands up, circles his desk coming to within two inches of Ewalt's face glaring at him. He speaks quietly. "Rich, snot-nosed little bastards are ruining the military. Did you know that?"

"No sir."

"So I suppose you think that those pricks are going to get the last laugh after all?"

"No sir."

"She's poison. If you're smart. You'll stay away from her. At best you'll be a toy for her. At worst, she'll hunt you down and hurt you--just for laughs." He steps back and circles his desk taking his seat. "Corporal Rader, you've been reassigned. You will enter training as a tank commander for a 501. Consequently your rank will change to SWAT Commander. Now get your face out of my office. Or I swear by the almighty, I'll pull you out of here by the nape of the neck, strap you to the front bumper of my truck and run you into a building."

Ewalt looks at him. "Just try it...Sir." Among his other traits At the age of 30, Ewalt had too much pride at times like this.

The man smiles. "You think you won? Good luck, son. She's death. Now get the heck out of here and hang on because you are nothing more than new meat for those people."

"We all are, sir. I just don't want to roll over and make it easy. Like some." Hurrying down the stairs he opens the door to a rainy evening. Amanda Feiss stands in front of him under an umbrella. She wears a black knee-length skirt and a white blouse. Over her shoulders is a cashmere scarf--the size of a beach towel.

"Hi, big boy. How about a snack?"

"Oh," Ewalt stammers. "That was your help in there I guess. Stay out my business, lady. I don't need your help." He doesn't move.

Amanda's eyes sparkle for him. "Everything okay, stud? You didn't like my joke about mine maintenance?"

Ewalt scratches his head. *This woman is everything any man could every want. And she wants me, a dumb grunt. I'd be an idiot to let this all go by me. Nah, fuck it. I could be dead tomorrow. The COs right. She is poison. Still, I should settle the score. And that fucking tank, I want that ride.* "Someone put pressure on the big boys in Seattle to give me gifts. Friends of yours I'd imagine."

"I'd never interfere with your life," Amanda says, with a crooked grin. Her cheeks glow slightly red in the damp winds. Her clipped smile has bright white teeth, the way a model smiles.

"I am assigned to a 501." He pauses. "Can you drive me to the bus depot? I need to get to a facility in Eugene. There's a two month wait for tanks and I'd like to make sure it's no longer than that."

She threads her arm through his. "Quit being a clown. That's not what you want. They'll deliver that tank to your doorstep in a week or so. I thought we'd have a slow dinner in town. Or are you worried about someone giving you a bad time for being late?"

"So....Not to worry. You're on the job?" He sees she has the whole situation in her pocket. "I am not sure I like this."

"I had a beef with that bastard Howell and it was a pleasure to kick him in the nuts. You're incidental." She winks at him.

"I can tell." Ewalt, rather than trying to calculate the mess he is in, decides that sooner or later it is going to blow up with her. *This woman gets her way and she is nobody's dog. Only a fool would target her for revenge. But all my battles are deadly. Still, to step on this tiger's tail--that's real danger. I owe Xandra to make it right.* "Thanks. Dinner and dancing with the elite. Pretty darn good for a bum like me. I'll assume I am just a slum-lark for you tonight."

"Never." She smiles at his style. "There's a tofu palace called Pappa's. Have you ever heard of it?"

"No."

"You can take me there," Amanda replies. "You pay--because

you're such a liar. You try to act like I don't impress you and that you are not planning to get everything you can--before I toss you out on your ass."

"You're dead on. I am trash and your kind is a murder of crows."

"Or maybe you think you are going to win my heart by that sweet talk and then disappear in a blaze of glory. I hear you are quite a stud."

"I better disappear before you figure out what has happened here. That's for sure." He watches her with the assurance that some men have, sure of their power over a woman. "I have nothing. You have everything. Let's go for that ride, Cutie. I do not disappoint."

"I'm not stupid, Commander. That's the right term isn't it?" She feels her heart skip a beat and frowns. "You don't love me, yet. But you will. Then I'll win and I'll toss you overboard and laugh as you drown. That's who I am. As consolation you'll have your tank and a chance to make it through this mess. But we're never going anywhere. You're dirt under my fingernails. Fair?"

"And if I don't fall in love with you?"

"It'll be a first."

"Okay, then we have a bet. I bet you take the sucker punch on love and you bet that I do. Same old game, fair enough," Ewalt says confidently. "You can't buy me, lady." He sees her lean down and pick a daisy. She rubs a rain drop into the yellow center of the flower, then places the flower in a small side pocket of her skirt. Though he tries not to believe the false front, he does believe he sees a crack in her wall. "A keepsake?"

"Yup."

"Nonsense. You can do the broken heart dance on someone else." He points to the pocket with the flower in it. "Oh so heart-warming."

Her hand reaches up to touch his cheek. She feels his warm cheek then pulls back her hand. His view is calm and untouched by her action. "We're just grabbing a bite and a dance, okay? I've got a car."

"A car ride too? Something flashy I hope."

Amanda's eyes spark as she reads his interest in her car. Trucks rumble by and the occasional bright of lightning fills the sky. Neither seems to be able to move. The rain, the cold, the odd silvery light, each other, the world around them, the scrim of liquid on their skin; this is more than maybe and they both feel it. "We're going to celebrate your new tank tonight. No mischief."

"Oh of course," and they warm together.

"Come on, Commander."

As they walk around the corner to the parking lot, a set of pilots pass them eyeing the couple. The mumble of their awe is audible. "Feiss with a grunt?"

"Damn, did he win a prize or what." Then laughter.

Ewalt takes the warning and finds himself able to center. Amanda scowls.

Crammed full of brightly colored vehicles, the officers' parking lots have stunned Ewalt every time he has seen the bevy of cars, trucks, and motorcycles. This version is no different: fifty beautiful vehicles all in one place. "Nice lot? Yours?"

She stops in front of a dark green sports car that sits low to the ground, its shiny copper wheels glowing with the sunset. "Like it?"

"Nice ride. You flight-jockeys, anything fast, huh?" He admires the low slung convertible. "There is probably nothing on the ground that can keep up with this--except maybe that Kawasaki over there." He watches her. "Yours as well?" He would have been surprised to know this car is one of six vehicles she keeps in this lot, including the motorcycle.

They climb into the thick leather seats and Ewalt relaxes into the leather womb. Amanda pulls the steering wheel towards her and waits on the gauges to show green.

"If I'd known you were rich, I'd have never considered flying with you." Rader glances at her legs. Her black skirt has ridden up to mid-thigh. "Beautiful, sexy, rich, you might be good enough for me. But I doubt it."

She flashes him a smile "You don't like money, sex, or power?" She doesn't bother to adjust her skirt.

"It's not that. Every time I'm with someone who's rich, I keep thinking of ways to take advantage of them. My friend Jack says its virtue. I don't like it."

"Well, you really are a boy scout." The car rolls back slowly.

"I'm no boy scout. I'm just a poor kid working for the man--or the woman in this case." He looks around at the luxurious tan interior of the car. "So now I understand. I go out and kill people just like me. So you can have this ride. What a crazy world. What luck you have."

"Luck?" She backs the vehicle out of the parking lot, turning the nose of the car toward the main gate. Amanda catches him staring at her legs again. "I turn you on, Ewalt?" The rain flies off the windshield as blowers keep the windscreen dry.

"I was staring at the floor mats," he says jokingly. "Nice mats."

"I've never heard them called that." She taunts him by moving her legs. "I suppose there has to be one man who will not fall in love with me. Too bad for you it's not you." At the front gate, she slows, winking at the guard. The guard snaps a salute giving Ewalt the evil eye.

Moments later, they race down the Stark Street heading towards downtown Portland. "So what else do you want?" She asks.

"To keep my ass out of a sling. Where'd your money come from?"

She glances at him. Her cheek bones raised high. "My grandad made a ton of money during the rise of pharmaceuticals. My dad is a real go-getter. We jumped from genuflector to gentry in three generations. Drugs are our main business. We started importing those years ago. We now supply all the gas and drugs to keep you military guys and gals happy. We branched out into armaments, bought Tenark, and now we run the game." The brightness that had glinted from her eyes pales for a moment. "We're not that different, Ewalt."

"Yeah, I hear it happens that way all time." Ewalt sighs, embarrassed he doesn't know what a 'genuflector' is. The car cruises down the road passing the trees and buildings of Laurelhurst. In those days, Portland was a secure city.

"Are you worried about the promotion?"

"No," he admits. "The battle is going badly. And it is going to get worser. The Dirties know we have a problem. They're never going to stop. They'll constantly attack us. They fight and dig--fight and dig. The country needs me."

Amanda slows to sixty and turns sharply into a corner. The car handles it as if it were locked onto the road. The pillow-soft leather caresses Ewalt in response to the turn. She accelerates to eighty passing the Burnside Bridge on their right. The Rose City glows pink.

Amanda speaks: "Sooner or later I think we'll pull back from Redding--once the new Wall is done."

"What new Wall?"

"They are considering a new one on the other side of the Columbia. My guess is we fight them for a few more years if they build it. Then we pull back. Between the river and the radiation out east we have established a stalemate. Then we negotiate a peace. Once there is peace. We slowly screw the bastards and take back what we've lost. That's when the real work begins. This war stuff is just establishing everyone's negotiating position The real battle begins once we all put down the guns and we start goosing your kind all over again. It's all a cycle."

Ewalt has never heard this viewpoint before so he cannot tell if he is hearing insight or madness. He begins to understand his boyhood friend Jack Porter a little better. "Well, this part is going to be a hell of a long battle. The Dirties aren't going to stop and they keep piling into California by the millions. You guys can't keep bombing the entire planet to keep them down."

"Says you. We are in the armament business. Bombing is us." Amanda glances at him and smiles. "Sooner or later they'll give in."

"I doubt they will negotiate with you or anyone else. They got too much hate."

"History is full of people fighting wars, losing them, then winning the peace. Look at the corporations. They lost two World Wars but eventually they took over the whole planet."

"Until all this."

"A minor setback. Just an economic cycle bottoming out."

"I'm surprised the Dirties got so much firepower. You guys supply them as well?"

"Nope. They are the enemy. We don't consort with the enemy. We are patriots. Besides, the Dirties have nothing to do but try to force their way into the US," Amanda says. "They don't need to be efficient in their weapons. They just need to keep reproducing--the little bastards." She laughs as they drive along the east shore of the Willamette River.

"I suppose you are right." Ewalt did not know about a second Wall or an expected pull back. He also now realizes that any information he gets from her will be helpful in keeping his father and he alive. It is in this moment, so many years ago, that he begins planning his father's journey behind the Columbia Wall. "I just want to go out fighting."

"To defend truth, justice and the American way?" She says smiling at him.

"I just like to fight."

She grins. "Me too." Amanda Feiss has a bit of the black widow in her.

"I want to be a pilot at some point."

"Everyone does. You can't get into flight school without pull because those with the lever get to pick their fights. Besides you're too old to enter training. You're almost 31."

"So I hear," Ewalt says. "I guess I'll be happy with my tank. I'm a good boy."

She slows the car and pulls onto a bluff that overlooks the water. "Look, if we're going to be buds, your going to need to cut me some slack. Just because I see what they do--it doesn't mean I am like that. And just because I tell you what I know--that doesn't mean I am an idiot for telling you. I know you are looking to get anything you can from me. I told you that. I expect that. It is how it has been all my life. I am a target for anyone else's advancement. But that doesn't mean you are my boy."

"Nice speech. You still think I am going to fall in love with you?"

"I do." She touches his arm.

On their right sits a huge red shack. A red neon sign on the roof says Pappa's. The front sports a painted-on crescent moon--like an old outhouse. "You like tofu?" Amanda says, shutting down the car.

"Sometimes." Ewalt looks out to the water. The glow of the city pleases him. He has never seen the city from the northeast. This is a restricted neighborhood. "Nice view."

"I see. Let's go have some food." She gets out of the car, knowing that he is hiding something from her. "Where are you from, Ewalt?" The night wears the thick scent of sweet, wild roses. The smell annoys her tonight.

"Here. My dad has a bagel shop over on the west side."

She already knew all this. "Are you a Jew?"

"Aren't we all?" It's his standard response to the question even though he is Greek.

Amanda puts her arm though his. "That's too bad. I don't like Jews. They aren't in touch with their emotions because their ego is so big. Makes up for a lack of love from their parents." They stroll over to the building that has been designed to look like a rickety outhouse. She stops and breaks free from his arm. "You need to get over this class warfare thing you've got going. Should I just drive you back?"

"I'm not a Jew," he says.

"Now that you mention it. You do have kind of a big nose." She stops in front of the apparently precarious wooden staircase leading up to the front door. The rain has turned to mist. Beers labels randomly pasted all over the outside flap in the light winds. "Can a Jew drink?"

"You're nuts." They walk up the stairs. He notes the well-hidden steel supports.

"Not yet. Give me time. So do Jews drink?"

"What do you have against Jews?" Rader says, opening the door for her. The interior of the restaurant smells of garlic and old beer.

She steps into the large room with him following. A beautiful oak bar runs floor to ceiling--and wall to wall. Next to it, a clear space serves as a dance floor. The cherry wood floor has a bright shine. A man and a woman in matching white suits dance cheek to cheek. Three burly men, who Ewalt assumes keeps peace in the bar, stand by the tables that run along the back wall and up the right side of the room. The room is big enough to park a pair of tanks. "You'll like this place--lot's of fights," Amanda says.

"You really do like to fight, don't you?" Ewalt responds. He follows her across the room as she sits at a table by a far window.

She points out the window. A white platform that looks like a fight ring floats in the river by the promenade. A ten foot wide wood-planked walkway separates the ring from the metal grate of the promenade. Surrounding the platform are benches. There is a staircase from the restaurant down to the promenade.

"I'm surprised you like this place. It's more my taste."

"Finally." She gestures upward to the ceiling and the twist of clear plastic tubes that cover it. The tubes extend out in all directions. Inside the tubes, brightly colored cylinders that look like shell casing course around the ceiling. Some knock into others and bounce off in the opposite direction. He watches the three story kinetic sculpture with a child-like smile.

"Funny, you have a reputation that would make a mugger blush. Inside you're okay. Where did that killer thing come from?"

"You know a lot about me." He still gazes at the ceiling. "Even my religion. But I guess your kind does research on people before they meet them right? When did you start?" His eyes drift from the ceiling, to her.

"I don't help just anyone. I did my research. I first heard you were a hell of a gunner. It's not typical for a Jew. Then I heard that you told your trainees to turn off the gas and think. That's a no-no."

A thin, dark woman in a yellow sari brings two filled beer steins made of shell casings. These have brass handles brazed onto the sides. She nods to Amanda.

"They know you in here."

Amanda picks up her beer. "To our Jewish friends."

Ewalt hefts the large mug and tips the rim. "To the ignorance of the upper classes--may it never cease." Ewalt notices repressed laughter in her eyes and decides that he likes her grit.

Another young woman approaches; this one is dressed in blue jeans and a sheer see though top of yellow gauze. Long straight blue hair cascades over her shoulders. It almost covers her dark extended nipples. He decides this is a test and so he stares at the waitress. She offers them menus made of plywood, then withdraws. Ewalt watches her posterior as she leaves.

"The food is great," Amanda says, looking at her plywood menu to hide her pique. "I have eaten here a lot."

Ewalt looks at her, then out to the boxing ring. "Been out there?" He points with the menu.

"Don't worry," she says. "We'll be gone before it really gets rowdy. I don't want to scare you off. You'd never come back to me."

Printed on the menu are seven items of food ranging from a tofu salad to fried tofu enchiladas with blue cheese dressing. "I said, have you ever been in a fight out there?" He puts down the menu waiting for her response.

She looks up over her menu. "Yes, actually." Her cruel smile seems hollow to Ewalt. The waitress returns and they order their food.

"So where are you from?" He asks.

"Originally DC, now the Widby Island area."

Ewalt scans the slowly filling bar. "What does your dad do beside run big companies?"

"Not much. Other than walk around the house with a hard-on."

Ewalt narrows his eyes. "A tough guy, huh?"

"Luke is a tough guy. What I mean is he walks around with a twenty-four hour erection."

Ewalt almost chokes on his beer. Her laughter fills the room and he ignores it, or tries to ignore it. "Is that the way you folks spend your money? No wonder the Dirties hate your kind."

Pleased with herself, Amanda smiles. Ewalt is losing his demeanor. "About fifteen years ago, as my mom tells it. Dad developed a hydraulic problem in the southern regions. The doctors said they couldn't do anything about it. Well you don't tell my mom 'sorry, you can't have what you want.' She found a darling Indian doctor who did a little surgery. Voila, she put Dad in a constant state of ready."

"Must be kinda' hard to piss," Ewalt remarks as casually as he can. "Nothing's off limits to your family is it? So what do you do for fun?" He asks, baiting her.

"Now you're getting it," Amanda says laughing. "Mostly, I just like to masturbate in the shower."

"Of course."

The young woman in the sari returns pushing a brass cart. A silver tray with a dozen small compartments containing a dozen different colored pills sits on top. The woman pulls out two pristine white cloth napkins and places them on the table. Then she produces two pairs of dark wooden chopsticks from a small compartment on the side of the tray laying them on the napkins. She tips the small silver tray for inspection. "Oh, of course the family business has come to call."

He is about to say no when Amanda says, "Two hits of Roadies." The young woman nods. With a knowing grin, she picks up yellow pills with her chopsticks, putting one pill on each napkin. Removing the salt shaker, she bows, rolling the cart away.

Amanda swallows one of the Roadies quickly. "Are Jews against drugs? I forget."

"My shabby exterior is a gaffe for you." He stares down at the five-hundred-dollar-a-hit designer drug. He has always wanted to try these. They are supposed to be the best high that money can buy.

"You should talk. I hear your joy juice was off during our battle. You always fight straight?" Amanda says.

"Yes."

With evident envy, she exhales: "How do you deal with all that horror?"

"It just doesn't bother me."

"But wealth does. Are you sure you're not some Dirties' spy?"

"In your dreams. So why'd she take the salt shaker?"

"Family secret. I want your deepest secrets and salt defeats the drug."

"So what?"

Amanda finds she likes him a bit more. "If you ever sit down with Luke and Margrete over coffee, don't forget the salt."

"They spike the coffee they are so famous for? With Roadies?"

"Roadies slow people down and it get's people to talk. We all drink the same coffee and so nobody worries. We take a salt pill before the meeting so we win. You lose."

"Thanks for the tip." He chugs back the pill with the rest of his beer.

"Is that why your kind hates us? Because we are smart?"

"Don't you get it? Your kind can have fun anytime. We can't. For you, life is a smorgasbord and so that bothers us. Therefore we hate you." He grins. The waitress arrives again. She puts their food on the table and withdraws. Ewalt begins tearing at the enchilada with his chopsticks. Then he stops and looks up at her. "Look, Amanda, I don't hide. If I can help it."

"I can see that. That's what I like that about you." She picks up a piece of tofu and places it carefully in her mouth.

"So are all men just some kind of challenge to you?"

"I thought you understood women." She bats her eyes. "I may look like a hard case, but I think I'd go nuts if I had to remember everything I've done. Imagine fighting straight. There can't be ten of you lunatics in the entire country."

"Other than a few million Dirties." He shakes his head. "Battle is too damn confusing for me. I don't need any assistance to fog it."

"So you're just a dumb grunt doing his job. Is that what you're telling me?" Her mouth curls tightly shut. "Dad would call you a Ford. That means basic transportation in life." She places some rice in her mouth. "If this Dirties problem continues, they're thinking of putting Roadies in all the soldiers' food as well as the joy juice."

"At five-hundred a hit? I doubt it. Do you really have that much control over the government?" Ewalt replies, his brain fogging. "I hope this drug helps. You're boring me."

"First of all there is no government. We won. They lost. We run the show and they can't talk about it. That would be gauche. Second, the Feiss family makes a fortune off selling drugs to troopers. With drugs, a large volume of use means we can make the price a lot cheaper. And if you fight better. That's a win."

"And we're all the less capable after?"

She winks. "Exactly. After a decade on these Roadies your kind will have the collective IQ of a tree stump. What television has started, our drugs will finish."

His body feels light. A second or so later: "First a Jew and now I'm a Ford. I guess bigotry isn't against the rules for your kind." He wears a stupid grin from the drugs.

She stops eating and places her chopsticks on the plate. "You're no dumb grunt. You're a brilliant, ignorant peasant." She turns to one of the bouncers and raises her hand. The lights switch on, illuminating the arena. Two men who look like soldiers climb into the ring. Bouncers stand outside the ring.

"And now gladiators for our entertainment?"

"Look at those bouncers," she says ignoring the comment. "Their chests are so large their shirts could include the street address, the city, the country and the name of the planet where the bar is located. Are you blind, Ewalt? Are you a blind, Jewish, Ford?"

"So you spend your whole life trying to cure your boredom? That includes killing people, right?" The drugs are too much for Ewalt.

"We'll get back to that later. Here they go." Amanda watches the shorter of the two men charge the taller man. He is immediately pounded onto the ground by an elbow. The taller man's much longer reach controls the action for the next few minutes. The fight doesn't last much longer. Soon, the smaller man is flat on his back.

"Hey, Ford," Amanda says, "You ever duke it out with a woman?"

Ewalt looks at her, then down at his enchilada. He tears off another piece of tortilla. *I knew it.* "Sure, what do you think I am some kind of chauvinist? You don't want to fight me. I can find some coward for you to punch out. You're no match for me and I don't fight the weak. I'm not a member of your class, remember?"

Amanda leans over. Then with a quick, open right hand connects hard with his cheek. The force of the open-handed slap sends Ewalt's chopsticks across the room. Before he can figure out what has happened, a man, who appears to be another bouncer, stands beside him.

"This man bothering you ma'am?" The bouncer asks. His shirt

wears a yellow happy face.

"He says he wants to fuck me. I said no. He got fresh."

The man laughs at her. "No. He didn't."

Amanda drinks her beer. "I challenged him." She tilts her head toward the ring. "And the pussy says no."

The bouncer stares down at Ewalt and grins. "Now why'd you do that, sonny?"

Ewalt remains seated. The young waitress reappears with a new set of chopsticks. She puts them down on the table and hurries away.

"So Ford, let's go." She cocks her head again to the ring. The bouncers drag an unconscious man out of the ring.

"It's either me or her, sonny," says the bouncer.

Ewalt feels warm blood on his cheek. "Mind if I stand?" He asks the bouncer. "I'm going to wash."

"Long as I don't have to knock you down," comes the reply from the bouncer.

Ewalt places his napkin on the table. "You won't." He gets to his feet. "Okay lady--you got a fight. First I finish my enchilada. Then I promise I'll kick the piss out of you before we have desert. And you, Chunky. You're next."

Amanda stops sipping her beer. "Ford--I like this. A quiet meal discussing class warfare. While we each contemplate how best to kick the stuffing out of each other. You show uncommon élan." Looking down at his crotch, she says: "But none of that. Okay, we finish dinner on one condition. No questions about the fight. No 'why did I hit you and why the fight stuff. Period."

"I don't need to ask. You're one of those women who likes to fuck hard-pounding men. So long as they appear to be gutter trash. Then you blow them kisses, talk sweet love and get them all wound up in their emotions. Once you have that. You wait for the wrong moment. Then you kick the guy in the gut and leave." He spins and drops the bouncer with a roundhouse kick. When the man tries to stand Ewalt jumps him and pummels him into a unconscious. He braces looking for the other bouncers. They are keeping the crowd back.

"Nice," Amanda says with a grin. "You didn't want to go to the loo? You were fibbing to me to get some leverage? See? You could be a Patrician."

"The what? Oh the head. No. I didn't." Ewalt sits down to finish his meal. "So tell me, how long have you been a dragon woman, baby doll?" The bouncer remains unconscious on the floor. Ewalt decides he does not like this woman.

Amanda stops mid-bite. Her chopsticks pause an inch away from her mouth. Her eyes drift slowly up at him. He is far more interesting than she ever thought possible. "One way or the other, you're going to get passed this class thing and see me as an equal. Once that's done. If you still want out of loving me. No sweat. I think you'll see I am as tough as you. You have already discovered I am as nuts as you. Of course, once you see how tough I am, you're dead meat."

She notices his gaze is no longer knife-edged. The change pleases her. "Now we are getting somewhere, Ford."

"You suddenly have those dreamy warm eyes." He points at her face with his chopsticks. "The ones every woman has when she senses a kill."

She nods taking another small bite of food. "And you like your women predictable I see. Tough luck, Ford. I am going to kick your ass." The bouncer stirs.

Ewalt keeps an eye on him as he gets to his knees. "There's a big difference between predictability and bizarre behavior."

She laughs. To his surprise, so does he. "So I've got you, Commander Rader, haven't I? Like the food?"

"Yeah, it's good. Even though the company's a bore." *Or nuts.*

She winks. "Thanks for saving me the trouble of pointing it out. Tell me. How perfect are we?"

"Fair enough," he says stuffing a bit of broccoli into his mouth. He watches the bouncer stumble away. No one helps him.

"Keep that thought. We wouldn't want to lose you. That's the collective America--we. There aren't many of your kind left."

"My kind?"

"Oh, you know--old school: brave, courageous, and bold. Willing to do a crummy job and like it. Your family must be proud. Say when did they teach you that Jew dough?"

Rader puts his chopsticks down. "Funny girl."

"Touche." She grimaces at his homage. "You kicked that bouncer around like he was a punk."

"That's enough. You said no discussion. Let's go."

"Where?"

"I thought this might be a good time to bust you up."

"Done." Amanda folds her napkin and places it on the table. Ewalt follows her lead, wondering what he is going to do. He's unsteady due to the drugs but he already knows she is no match. Ewalt has been in lots of fights. He has fought women hand to hand on the battlefield. This event is something new. *How can she expect anything less than getting the hell kicked out of her? Why does she want me to hurt her? Because of Xandra?* He trips on the door threshold going outside.

"Careful, Ford, I don't want you tripping and breaking your neck. Or maybe we should wait until the drug wears off?" Her facetious offer is meant to enrage him. She cackles, then continues down the stairs.

The stairs flatten out to the long platform leading to the ring. Ewalt notices no one from the restaurant looking out the windows. It surprises him. He would have been glued to the window had he not been a combatant.

The damp air cools him. Amanda unzips her tight skirt. Underneath she wears skimpy tight green shorts. He realizes he has been set up. She climbs over the ropes and bounces over to the far side of the ring. Ewalt checks her position and quickly climbs in, turning rapidly in case she is coming at him. Her back is towards him and she appears to be staring up at the dark sky. She bends at the waist stretching her leg muscles. Had Ewalt hurried across the ring he could have pounded once or twice and left her unconscious on the mat. Instead he stares at her posterior, admiring it. *What is this?* Ewalt notices dried blood droplets everywhere on the cream-colored mat.

A bouncer steps on the edge of the platform and begins to speak: "No rules. When one of you can't stand up; or if either one leaves the ring. The fight is over. But, as long as you're in the ring, you're fair game for anything." He rings the bell. "Ain't love grand?"

"You sure you want to do this?" Rader yells over the sound of a motor patrol boat racing along the river.

"You bet your butt," Amanda says. She begins circling slowly to Rader's left. He advances into the center of the ring and readies himself, expecting a kick to the groin. Amanda continues circling. She spits at him, then charges.

Ewalt picks up her kick, steps back and blocks it with his knee. She steps back. He ducks allowing her roundhouse kick the stir the air. She quickly spins out with a low kick meant to trip him. He merely backs up. Amanda comes to rest, staring at him. She circles slowly left, then charges again. Ewalt steps aside. Grabbing her waistband, he sends her passed him through the ropes and onto the wooden floor. She immediately stands up and rubs the blood from her mouth. Amanda jumps back in the ring. Neither of the combatants note the patrol boat has circled and its armed sailors watch the bout.

"So, Ford, you're afraid of hitting a woman? Is that a Jew thing?" She says, slowly walking towards him. Then, putting her hands up to guard her face. "If I were a man. I'd hit me."

"You certainly deserve it." As soon as she is within his reach, Ewalt punches out straight from his waist hitting her square in the gut. Amanda collapses immediately, grabbing her abdomen and rolling over in pain. She is no match for him--and she knew it. "Your skills are poor to say the least." Rader backs away. In case it is a ploy. Watching her trying to catch her breath, he notes the bouncer appears to be waiting for something. Ewalt remains distant from her. As she slowly works her way into a crouch, he exits the ring watching her. "I need a cab." Ewalt speaks to the bouncer. The rain begins to fall again. He looks back at her. "And maybe you can help her?"

The man remains where he is. "Not my job." Ewalt nods. "If you're leaving, make sure you pay the bill for the ring. Loser always pays for ring time."

Rader stops and tilts his head. "I'm the loser in this?"

The bouncer shakes his head. "It seems to me she has gotten what she wanted tonight. I don't think you have gotten shit--except a case of the guilts. Plus you left the ring first. Therefore she has won."

"I'll pay," Amanda says. "Hey Rader, you still pissed at me for popping your girl in Coeur d' Alene? Is that what this is all about?"

His eyes blaze and a dark place in his gut seems to clamp tight around his being. "You did this on purpose." He walks back to the ring.

"I did not. It was a mistake. I thought you were a pussy."

Because of the drug, Ewalt cannot help but grin.

Climbing to her feet, seeing what she perceives as pity in Ewalt's eyes, Amanda angers. She stumbles over to the edge of the ring and holds onto the ropes. "But it is okay. Because she was really just your whore." She laughs.

Ewalt takes another step towards the ring. Then he stops. "How often has she done this?" Ewalt watches the fingers on the bouncer's beefy hand unwrap then retract.

"Never happened. She never fights. But trust me. The real fight hasn't even started yet, stud. Like any real war, the ring is just for show. She's planning to eat you alive. They call it love where she comes from."

"You know I keep hearing that?" He says stupidly.

"The real battle is in here." The bouncer points to his head and smiles like a man who had seen all Ewalt's cards in a game of poker. "Did she really kill your girl?"

"Yeah." Ewalt, unwilling to show any weakness, climbs back in the ring to help her.

She tries to kick him once in the groin. He easily avoids it. Amanda falls to the mat again, laughing. The rain washes her hair flat to her face. A moment later he sits down beside her unsure of what he wants to do. Then he sees she really cannot move anymore. The bouncer rings the bell. "Game over, ladies and gentlemen. As soon as Mr. and Mrs. America finish their date we'll get onto another love-fest going. Take your time you, lovebirds. The wall of love has no enemies."

Ewalt, to that point, had believed he understood the insanity of that evening. "You felt bad about killing her? You thought you were protecting me? So you thought I was pissed at you. This was so I could get that all out?"

"You're a fool." Amanda then leaned closer to him, kissing him on the lips. "I wanted you. So I killed her. Can you forgive that, tough guy?"

Ewalt stares at her. "So you're a murderer? You admit that?"

"Hit me if you believe that, Ford. Let's get it done with. And then I could use a massage."

Instead he extends his hand to help her to her feet.

That night had been a TKO--for both of them.

CHAPTER TWELVE

Two weeks after his fight with Amanda Feiss, Ewalt stands by the motor pool fence watching a Tenark flatbed truck pull into the motor pool. The truck driver, a man with green hair, ignores the sergeant in charge and approaches Ewalt. "Excuse me, Commander Rader, would you please sign for this?" Ewalt does, then ambles over to the huge machine, staring at the outline through the green tarp.

Lifting an edge of the tarp, Ewalt sees foil gift wrap: red, white, and blue. "The entire tank?"

"Yup," replies the driver.

The motor pool sergeant whistles. "Your tank has arrived, Commander Rader." The man salutes Ewalt then punches him in the shoulder. "You are a legend, my boy. Fuck you."

Watching them unload his Eisenhower 501 SWAT tank, Ewalt takes pictures for his dad. Then, after leaving the motor pool, he calls Jack Porter in Seattle.

He learns--among other things--that a SWAT Commander needs four years of college before being permitted to command a SWAT. Ewalt has never even been on a college campus--except to watch a basketball game. There is also the three month training course in

Marysville. Ewalt has already been told he can attend training, or skip it, because of his gunnery skills. "Oh, and by the way--there is a four month wait for a tank, not two." Jack Porter ends the conversation by calling him Walt--instead of Rader--the first time in five years. Pleased with events. Sure of the cause. Enamored with his new love: the half hot-rod, half battle-tank, Eisenhower 501, Ewalt decides he will take the training.

Once the SWAT is unwrapped, Commander Rader goes over the tank inch by inch. Tightening screws and tuning its systems every free moment of the day and night. Within a week of delivery, everyone in the huge fort knows him by sight. It is the first 501 delivered to Fort Shasta in almost two months. Everyone discusses how Ewalt could have made it to the top of the list. All they know is he is tied into Feiss Industries and that makes him worth their respect.

During the second week of SWAT training in Marysville, he receives a letter from the IRS saying there has been a mistake in his taxes from each of the last four years. The enclosed check quadruples his savings with a single refund--almost to the dollar. Ewalt immediately sends the check to his father so he can bank it for the move out of Portland. The refund is just enough to pay the landing fee for his dad and he in Washington. Processing will take two years.

Upon his return to Fort Shasta, when he isn't babying his tank, Ewalt spends time in the non-com office learning all he can on strategy, while waiting to be assigned a driver and a forward fire-base. One foul-up leads to another and he continues to remain unassigned. Somehow there is always fuel and ammo for his practice runs and shakeout trips through the hills. He becomes a skilled driver as well as deadly gunner. The other Commanders begin calling the shakeout missions the EVT: "Ewalt's Vacation Trip."

This is years before the Dirties and their tunnels begin to effectively breach the Wall. Then one afternoon, while sitting in the non-com office, with its pool table, smelly chairs, and a jukebox that had everything from rock and roll to klezmer music, the front door opens and a chopper jock with bright teeth and an easy smile enters. "Commander Rader?" Ewalt, reading a manual on the tank's engine systems, stands to attention guessing the next pull-of-the-string by Amanda Feiss has entered the room. He is wrong. She has not sent TJ to talk to him.

Returning the salute, Ewalt watches the pilot pull over an old metal folding chair with a stencil on the back that says St. Bonaventure--Modesto.

"Mind if I sit?"

"Suit yourself." Ewalt sits back down on the battered leather recliner waiting for the punch line. The man looks around the room. "I'm, TJ, Tom Lippman. I am Amanda's copilot."

"We met." Ewalt unconsciously looks down at his training manuals. He had already noticed they were published by Lippman and Company; so he wonders if they and his tank are about to disappear.

"This note is for you."

Dear Ewalt,
    Friends? All I want to do is fight with you.
    Amanda.

The note looks like it had been crumpled and thrown away before this man found it. Ewalt refolds the note and places it on the table. Noticing a white bandage sticking out from the copilot's collar. Rader points to it.

"One of the gliders delivered a metal message to us--at about two hundred miles an hour. I forgot to duck." Lipps pauses, waiting to see if Ewalt will ask about Amanda. In an uncomfortable silence, TJ folds the sunglasses in his hand and looks around. He gets up. Strolls to the jukebox then laughs when he sees a selection in the jukebox. "Klezmer music? She's a pistol isn't she?"

"Yup." Ewalt wonders what the guy is talking about. When he finds out he will also laugh. The clarity of her joke will be enough to force him to action.

Ewalt pulls out a chaw of chewing tobacco and offers the man a piece. TJ shakes his head no. "These are from your company?" He holds up a manual

"Yes." He walks away from the jukebox heading for the door.

"How do you like working with her?"

"She's a good pilot," TJ says, rubbing his nose with the clear plastic tip of one eyeglass arm. A truck rolls by shaking the shed. "I guess I'll be going. I didn't mean to disturb you, Commander."

"She's okay?" Ewalt asks.

Lipps looks at his glasses. "I'm not sure how to say this, so I guess I just better say it. The week before you two duked out, there was a party at that restaurant you went to. Some guy came onto Amanda. Her friend told him to get lost. One thing led to another and there was a fight in the ring. The guy connected real hard a few times. And her friend--a woman--was pretty badly hurt. She died during the next mission. Amanda believes it was her fault."

"So?" Rader stares at the small lump of cotton on the side of the man's throat.

The man looks away. "Anyway, this friend defended Amanda by putting herself on the line. That may not mean much to you, but Amanda comes from a place where no one takes a punch for someone else. Amanda believes she killed her friend. Of course she didn't. It was like that woman in Idaho. She has this responsibility thing all screwed up inside her. Amanda really thought she was doing the right thing."

"You believe that?"

Thomas Jefferson Lippman nods yes. Ewalt Rader is a weak poker player, but he has some knowledge of the bluff. He spots a hollow core in TJ's act. "Sad how she kills. Feels bad, then poor-missy walks away in misery. My heart's just breaking for her." Watching the pilot nod yes, Ewalt tries to figure his game.

"You may be right there. She grew up in a world where taking scalp is just part of the game. Amanda thinks you're pretty special. And don't tell me it's screwed up. I already know--better than you can imagine."

Ewalt tilts his head beginning to understand the visit. "You're saying she killed Xandra because she cares about me?"

"You knew that woman's name?" Tom Lippman places the glasses over his eyes and adjusts them. "Now I see." He shakes his head back and forth. "Commander, you're looking for saints in this world and they don't exist. She defended you against some people that stuck a blade in your back. I don't know if the woman was a part of it or not. I know you're the first one into Amanda' heart in a long time. That's grace from God for her. I've never known anyone more lonely. I don't know anything else." He watches Ewalt's response, sees that he is taken by the reference to a deity, and continues his campaign to remove Ewalt Rader from the equation of Amanda Feiss. "Let me tell you something. Do you know why we fly together?"

"No idea."

"We're supposed to fall in love and then combine the two families, Feiss and Lippman, into a corporate monarchy."

"And what, you're gay?" Ewalt grins.

"Amanda isn't my type. You are her type and I think she is your type. Regardless of the class issue you both suckle on like it was your mother's gland."

Ewalt doesn't believe him and thinks he has it figured. "I'm a target. A clay pigeon in an armored vehicle. I guess she got me the 501 because she wants to make it fair. Her view of fair. I am a game for her. Just like I am a game for you."

He nods. "You could be wrong. You could be right. Or she might be feeling bad about what happened, knows she can't fix it, but she is trying to make it right. See ya' hard case." Lipps crosses the dim space quickly and places his hand on the brass doorknob. He stops, knowing he has not yet accomplished his mission. "I've been flying with her for a while now. Amanda thinks if something goes wrong and she's around, she's the cause. She's got this thing about controlling everything. She has to make everything right if she is involved. On the other hand, she thinks everyone on the planet is her servant and they want to goose her. It's driving her nuts. Regardless of my other agendas, I'd like to help her through that mess."

What is this guy's game? He's no angel. "Me? So I am making it worse?"

"Well, loving you. Don't you see it's keeping her from fulfilling her responsibility? I think avoidance of responsibility is why she cares about you."

"That just proves your crazy too," Ewalt says. "Why do I want a crazy person near me? She and I have nothing in common. I'm a real world person and she is off in fantasy land. I have no interest in helping the poor rich girl. That means you're corporate monarchy is safe from me. Just let me be."

"See. I knew you were just like her. Commander, she's got pain, that's for sure." Lipps opens the door. "What pissed you off? Are you afraid of her?"

Ewalt starts to say no, then takes in a deep breathe. "Maybe a bit. I figure if I can last a few weeks out there with her flying cover I'll make it."

"Like hell. She is the best pilot on the line. Change the transponder signal to a different tank if that's your worry--one that's staying offline. She'll never find you."

"Like hell I will," he mumbles.

Lipps stretches his shoulder to relieve a knot of pain.

"Then I guess one way or the other you will soon find out the truth, Commander. You might also be interested to hear she moved heaven and earth to get you your tank."

"Is that supposed to mean something to me?" Ewalt remains seated in the old leather chair.

Lipps steps into the light washing his features away into a silhouette. "I hear you also have a promotion."

"Yeah."

"Funny thing, isn't it? You're the last guy I'd put in command of a weapons platform. Word is you're a psycho who fights straight and likes to kill people. How'd you get the promotion, pull?"

Ewalt laughs. "I don't owe anyone anything. The promotion is long overdue. I'll take it any way I can get it."

"I guess you must be the living proof we live in a meritocracy."

"I don't like people who take advantage of others or feed them bullshit, because they can."

"Fair enough--so here is your punch line: Her as well and that's the problem. Commander Rader, she is a target for everyone she meets. Mom, dad, friends, strangers, the media, you name it. It's driving her crazy. When she sees a chance for something real, she goes for it. That's not a crime in my book." The grin that passes over his face is lost in the shadows. "See ya' chump." Lipps leaves the room as a pair of mess cooks push by him for their afternoon pool game. The door shuts and Ewalt sits blind in the dull light.

For nearly three hours Ewalt listens to the two men as they talk about cooking turkey while they play straight pool. By the time they finish, he cannot tell if he is worried that he may lose the tank or he is angry at his own sanctimony. Then he asks one of the cooks about klezmer music.

Dusk the next day, Ewalt finds himself wandering among the olive-green buildings that have been erected in Medford for the new Rapier-class helicopters. The airfield reminds Ewalt of a supply depot. With palettes of materials stacked everywhere, many of the boxes say either, "Feiss Industries" or "Lippman & Co." It makes the walk all the more difficult. Ewalt does not need powerful enemies.

As Ewalt hikes passed row after row of freshly painted warehouses and new hangers, he watches the tractors and technicians working on the helicopters. He keeps asking himself how to say thank you. While erasing the target he now believes is glued to his back from both Amanda and her copilot. *Where do I get off playing on their field? I gotta' solve this.*

When he spies a group of pilots examining the new gunships: "Captain Feiss?"

"She's over there, Commander," says a cornstalk-thin southern boy. He points Ewalt towards a khaki green sheet metal structure where air crews are receiving new gear.

Inside, men and women sit at long tables. Officers are assigning crews their equipment, inoculating them, or just answering questions about new tactics that tie the SWAT and the gunships together. Some of the air crews gather in clusters, refusing to wait on the scraggly lines that extend from the tables like tentacles. Ewalt approaches one group, but they are speaking in French and Chinese. He can't make out the words. After waiting a moment, he moves on to the next crowd.

Outside of his gaze, Captain Amanda Feiss places herself behind a brawny mechanic named Stanislaus. Every one of the eight people around her note the action and spy for a threat. They recognize that their cornucopia of supplies are there for her protection--so they take their job of protecting Amanda very seriously. Seeing the brawny tanker, a few of the men gather, placing themselves between Amanda and Ewalt. Until Lipps sees Ewalt. He nods to the rest of them and they disperse--watching Amanda act like a school girl hiding from a beau. She keeps her eyes on Ewalt as he wanders from crew to crew. Her hand wanders to her hair, straightening it--looking at her reflection. Her throat feels itchy and tight. Her other hand checks the wrinkles in her uniform. She continually glances at her reflection, then back to Ewalt.

When Ewalt finally circles closer, Amanda adjusts her position so that he might see her. Ewalt waves and she scowls--before she looks away to engage again with her crew. Lipps, in the middle of a lawyer joke, watches them without moving his head or glancing into Amanda's darting eyes. As Ewalt approaches, her suspense increases. She cannot fathom why he is here and Amanda has no intention of talking with him if he appears angry.

This fidgeting of hers declares that roadblock-jumble of emotions Tom Lippman fears so much. He knows Amanda will never consider him as a partner, so long as she feels for Ewalt. That is the problem he was working on with his visit.

TJ has also concluded that Ewalt Rader is an angry man who will never forgive Amanda--so he has nothing to lose and everything to gain by playing ball. Watching Ewalt's hesitant approach, TJ mistakenly thinks perhaps Ewalt has tacitly agreed to TJ's wants, as away to keep his new toy. In any case, TJ figures pushing them close, before they are ready, is the best way to make Ewalt bolt.

Amanda notes her copilot's casual smile. It gives her a sense of security. Ewalt circles the small group to stand beside her. Neither of them can find words. The group of men and women slowly move off in other directions. Never letting their attention leave the couple. The two people stand next to each other--without looking at each other--for almost a minute. Then there is no one near them.

TJ Lippman believes Amanda Feiss is happier than he has ever seen her. To calm himself, he reconsiders what really happened in Idaho. *There is no way he can forgive her for killing that woman. It will be impossible for Ewalt to see murder as an act of loving him.* Thomas Jefferson Lippman tells himself again that Amanda and Ewalt's time will be short--and the linkup between Feiss and Lippman is secure. Nonetheless, he keeps an eye on the two lovers.

"What are you doing here?" Ewalt says foolishly. Amanda's eyes dart to Lipps as he winks and walks away.

She goes outside, standing under a single goose-neck light by the door. "Why are you bothering me?"

"Your copilot talked to me," Ewalt says, to her eyes.

Amanda puts her hands together, as if she is trying to catch something. Frustrated, she lets them drop. "You hate me and you think I'm psychotic." She watches him, trying to calm her breath. "What did he say to make you come see me?"

"Nothing much--except to congratulate me on my promotion. Have you heard I've been given a 501?"

She shakes her head no. "It doesn't surprise me. They promote idiots around here all the time. Of course sometimes we need people who can kill." She looks away. "They protect me."

He is about to ask her if she had planned to kill Xandra, and why. Then he decides instead to try and let it all fade into the myths of war. Ewalt Rader has decided that the truth no longer matters to anyone and it is all about now. It is this moment that dooms their love. The rest is icing. TJ Lippman's plan will be successful. He has wrecked their time by pushing them together too soon--though he will never reap its rewards.

Ewalt speaks quietly: "I've also been informed that there was an accounting mistake in my favor." He stares at the white paint of the corrugated walls. "My bank account has increased by four-fold. I used it to get my dad landed into Washington. Or I will--once the forms are approved."

"Christ--another Jew--there goes the neighborhood." She crosses her arms, propping her right foot back against the wall of the warehouse. Watching to see if he smiles--he tries--she speaks. "Go away."

Ewalt scrutinizes the flight crews going back and forth. He isn't surprised to see surreptitious glances come and go as well. "Those people care for you."

Amanda smiles in their direction. "My dad gets them the best supplies possible. They're my buddies. Other than that, like you, they think I am a crazy spoiled bitch."

"You are."

"I know. Go away."

"So you tried to buy me?"

She looks at him. "Are you my buddy now? Oh, I see. You think I am going to take your toy. You're looking for a way to keep it."

Ewalt shakes his head. "You're on the hunt to cure some kind of issue. But I don't understand what you are doing with me. You act like a kid in love. So I win? That's easy. That's it. Game over? You love me and I don't care? The common grunt wins because of love?"

Her gaze remains fixed on his face until she looks over at the boxes around them. When she glance back at him, Amanda wears the same beaten look as she had in the boxing ring. "You're a dope."

He has an uncontrollable urge to grin. In spite of himself, Ewalt asks: "Did you mean to kill that woman in Idaho?"

"I did. I didn't know what she meant to you. It looked to me like she set you up with the guys that stuck a blade in you and crowned you with a pipe. Are you ever going to get over that mistake of mine?"

"She was a doctor. She wouldn't have hurt me."

Amanda tries not to laugh at him. "Oh did I forget to check her CV? Damn."

"Her what?" When he sees her pitying him, he clenches his jaw. Then her eyes begin to glow more brightly than the moon above them. It touches him. He tries to shrug it off. Confused, he cannot. He also sees that her pain has been made lighter by his discomfort. Still--he resists the connection--reminding himself that he is here to cover his assets with this woman. Then, thinking he can finesse the situation; he tries a lever. "What makes you think I want you to interfere in my life?" He works at trying to appear stern and fails. Ewalt was always a terrible poker player.

Her eyes brighten further as she centers on the man in front of her. "You're not angry about her. You just want to make sure I am not angry at you. You think I'm a fool and you're pleased by that. Aren't you? That tank is something you wanted a hell of a lot more than me. It was supposed to piss you off, Ford. Instead it turned you into a slut, like the rest of them. I'm glad I could give that to you." A cruel smile forms on her lips. "You can go now, Commander. You said thank you and you have the answer to your riddle. I will not take anything more from you. Just try to stay alive out there. We need whores like you."

Ewalt cannot deny the truth of what she says. "You have a strange way of talking to me." He does not understand why he remains here talking to her. "You know the truth about me and you act like you care. And then you say something stupid, like calling me a whore."

"I don't love you, stud," Amanda says. "So give it up." For Amanda, gifts are the opposite of affection; understanding the wants of those around her means leverage. This instilled viewpoint is a slowly festering wound. "I can have your love anytime I want it. And that's the point of all this. Get it?" She smiles. Knowing he will miss the point.

"You don't want me?" Ewalt grasps his hands behind his back squeezing them trying to understand it all.

"No, I don't want you. I just wanted to say I am sorry. It's possible to give someone something and not really care about them. Look at all this junk around us." She finds herself sweating.

I never sweat, damn hill ape.

"Do you want to give me a chance to do this right?" He feels the words have come out of him without his permission.

"See ya', Ford." She turns.

"Okay, I give up. Why the hell would you give me something. Then say you're glad you did it. Because you did it so you could feel you don't care about me? Or even better you gave it to me so you could tell me I'm a whore. And behind it all: You want me to care about you? Tell me what you did in Idaho. Were you following me around or something? What the heck went on?"

"Again?" She looks at her watch as if she has someplace to go. "I needed a gunner. Your name was at the top of all the sheets. I made inquiries and you seemed more and more interesting. I was walking down the street, recognized you, and saw a mugging. I stepped in and helped you."

He believes she is lying. "Why would you kill her?"

She places her fingertips in the front of his mouth, as if he were an adolescent, then quickly removes them. "I am saying you have a right to walk away. No harm. No foul. But if you keep this up--you must understand that I answer to no one. It will not go well for you." She doesn't know she is lying to herself.

"What do you want from me? People like you always want something?" His eyes stay locked to hers. "This is crazy."

"Can we be friends?" She asks.

"I'd be taking advantage of you. I am here covering my ass. Remember?" He will say nothing about revenge or Tom Lippman. "I don't really give a damn about you. That's not right. I don't know. Fuck me. I don't know what I am saying. I just wanted to come by. Say thanks and make sure I didn't have my ass in a sling."

"So you really don't like me?" She says, now knowing he will collapse into her. "Let's just forget this."

"Let's put it this way--you're the last person I would want as a lover."

"Because I'm so ugly?" Her smiles broadens and she watches his eyes glaze over into stupidity.

"So I should go." He doesn't move; he stares at her.

"I'm flying cover for your group now," she says mischievously.

"I haven't been assigned. Oh, of course. When do I find out about this?"

She can practically see Ewalt's brain working on how to interpret what she wants. "You should hear in the next couple of days." Her hand brushes aside a lock of hair--sparking the diamond's light from her ear lobe. "Ewalt, you look at me like a queer. My beauty, my money, my connections, none of it is worth a damn to you. You want your tank and you want me to let you be. Is that real?"

"I want peace between us."

"So then I am more like a train wreck than a flight of Harpies aren't I? Ewalt, I don't want you to be afraid of anything."

"What are you talking about?"

Her hand moves to his chest and she touches him with her finger tips--for the briefest moment. "Is that what this is about? The second bell of our fight? I won the first one and you are going to show me how you can win all rest?"

"You didn't win the first round." He considers his words and feels out of his league. This visit, rather than making things better has made them worse. "I don't see why I am a challenge to you."

"You're not a challenge, Commander," she says with a smile. She sees that he misunderstands her. "Of course I don't impress me much, Ewalt. I'm spoiled and privileged. I am the madness. I am what we are all fighting about: an indolent, uncaring gentry. But you don't care about me. You fight because you like to fight. If I, and my caste, fall, so what? We're nothing to you." She laughs. "You're just like those crazy bastards on the other side of the Wall--except that you appear to be winning."

"You have a life of pure pleasure, Captain Feiss."

"I don't understand why you and they, envy us so much." Her hands sweeps the air in front of them.

He wonders what that was about. "They don't envy you. They hate you."

"You don't. Maybe that's it, Ewalt, you honestly don't hate me and that attracts me." Her weak smile has bright eyes above it. For the first time in years she wonders what she is doing with a man.

"So this is love in the 21st century?" He asks.

"Not for me," she says quickly. "I didn't expect to see you again. Why are you still here? Go away, soldier."

"Okay. I give up you win this round. That is one apiece." Before he turns away, he catches that odd smug smile from her. "I don't like crazy women."

"Of course you do. You're a warrior. Did you know that's what the name Walter means, warrior? If you can win this fight, you can have me. That would make me sane. Do you want to help me?"

"My love to save you? Not interested." He looks at the pistol on her hip. "Nothing can save you."

"Sure of that?" She asks, hiding her hurt.

"I am."

She kisses him and feels his ardor. "Liar." Amanda Feiss leans back against the shed supporting herself. She is lost.

CHAPTER THIRTEEN

Two days later Ewalt is assigned his first mission. In that first briefing, the tankers are informed that a squadron of brand new Rapiers will fly cover. As advertised, Amanda's squadron has been assigned to support SWAT.

As she flies support for Ewalt's SWAT, she sweeps the enemy with such precision, that Ewalt returns from the mission with a third of his weapons stores unused. This happens three more times over the next three days. He hasn't yet taken Lipps' suggestion to change the beacon on the 501, but he thinks he finally understands the comment. Her skills as a pilot are unequaled.

That Friday afternoon he shows up at her apartment with a box of dominoes in hand. Within thirty seconds, the dominoes lie scattered on the rug. The MPs are called twice because the cries from her apartment sound like a mugging. Feiss security keeps the MPs at bay assuring them everything is fine. Neither Amanda nor Ewalt are heard from for almost a week--and of course there are no repercussions.

When they are not in bed, Amanda teaches Ewalt to play Bridge and he teaches her to play Dominos. On free weekend nights, they go into Portland and dance. She leaves him in the city and goes home alone sometimes--then waits for him to show up at her door. One morning she goes to his dad's bagel shop and waits for him there. By the time he figures out where she is and finds her, Amanda is mopping the floor. She is covered in flour. Over the course of the next month, Amanda becomes less protective. Ewalt begins to take control of the ground battles.

Then one evening they go sailing on Lake Shasta; Amanda says someday it will be unsafe to do so. Ewalt finds that he loves to sail. To this day he remembers the long sail up and back upon the lake. Sadly, the memory takes him to a sailboat in the moonlight--not her.

The clear and cool night had bred short waves tapping the boat and pine trees creaking in the breeze. The sailboat heeled when the winds blew and Ewalt stretched out over the waves. When they finally approached the dock, the smell of the lake mixed with camp fires. She had leaned into his arms seeing genuine joy in this man's eyes. It was the same kind of snuggling he had come to adore from Xandra. The destruction of his caring for Amanda was now complete.

Onshore, he lifts her around a log; as if he were dancing a Fox Trot. His favorite dance step. She swoops out arching her spine, pauses, then slides back into his arms. One arm rides up his, as if she were doing a Tango. His free arm announces the end of the dance. Something is wrong. Her eyes blaze with the moon's light and the fire in her loins. Holding his face in her hand, she kisses him.

"You should have been a dancer," Ewalt says sitting back on the log. "You might have been...Happier."

"A boxer yes, a dancer no. Too big on top." She snuggles against his warmth. "I want to die so I don't have any children." She watches his eyes.

He is surprised to see a different kind of pleasure in her eyes. Rather than the eyes of a happy hunter stalking game Ewalt sees a teen-aged curiosity. "My dad is concerned about his seed. I think that is why he liked you so much. That really wasn't fair going to see him." Ewalt rubs his finger with a white linen handkerchief she had given him, putting it back in his pocket. "When I wasn't picked in the birth lottery for my year, he was crushed. He wants a grandchild. You're the answer to that for him."

Amanda blocks the jab. "Once you meet someone dumb enough to care about you. Let me know. I will make sure you can breed more Fords." A bored stare surprises her. "I'm never going to have kids so I don't see a problem. You might as well have children. You're much more decent than I. People like me and my family are animals. We claim to be the civilized ones, but we are the real Dirties. You said that." She notes her words no longer shock him. "I am having much more fun than I thought I would."

"And that's a fact," Ewalt says as he looks back at her. "The next time I seduce someone can I borrow your boat?"

"The boat is not mine to lend, sorry Commander." She grins. "It belongs to my lover."

He kisses her and she responds. When they look at each other, Ewalt shakes his head wondering why not her. Then he thinks he knows that sad state of men when they lose their clarity touching the needs of a woman. "I'd like to have kids," he says with a good natured smile. "But reversing my vasectomy would take an act of Congress."

Her heart leaps and she again finds herself angry at the stupidity in her breast. "That was low. Say that BS again and I will take away that tank you treasure so much."

"No way. Round three is mine. Sorry."

"Fair enough, jerk." Her back stiffens. "I worked with Congress for a while. I have friends there. I can get your vasectomy fixed--or increased." He misunderstands the growing anger and smiles benevolently.

"Did you really work in Washington?" Ewalt asks, still impressed by her connections. Ewalt had wanted to be a Senator until he found out he didn't have the guile--or connections--necessary for the job. Ewalt was a naive young man. "What did you do?"

Amanda puts her head on his shoulder. Her eyes drift off then she speaks, just a little sadder than a moment ago. "I was a page working for our Senator during my junior year in college. After pilot training I did work there again. I didn't like it. There was this one man who had this wonderful idea to feed everyone. So they killed him. I almost saved him. Can you believe that? Me, a hero?"

"I do. You seem like a traitor to your class. Why else would you be here with me? Maybe that's your problem. You can't deal with being a traitor to everything Mommy and Daddy hold dear."

She slaps him on the chest then rubs his chest where she hit him. Feeling her heart quicken she notes his does not. "Creep."

"So who tried to kill him? Why?"

"The people he threatened. They thought more food meant more people and that he was breeding more trouble-makers. I am done here. Time for us to go."

He helps her up. "And?" Ewalt asks.

"They shot him as he testified inside the Senate hearing room." She sticks out her hand forming a gun with her fist and forefinger. She points it at Ewalt. "He was a dreamer like you." She mimics the report of a pistol.

"What was this guy testifying about? Was he a criminal?" He takes her hand, disarming her, and they walk along the shore.

She stops to dig her toes into the gravel. "He was a nice man, a gentleman. He wanted to feed everyone because he said that if people were fed they wouldn't be so crazed. He had a way of making food very inexpensively. When he wouldn't be reasonable and let the poor and weak die off--they killed him."

"Why? Why would they do that?" His face turns brittle. She sees him glance around. That means trouble.

"They weren't bad people. I mean whoever did it, didn't get up one morning and say: 'I think I'll go kill a good man.' It wasn't like that, Ewalt." She pauses, measuring her words. "This population thing, all these people, it's a terrible problem. Our leadership had to make some awful choices." She turns to him and places her leg in between his legs, but just to the knee.

Her body in his arms, he gazes at the sailboat. "What was the government's awful choice?"

"I said leadership, not government, Ford." She pulls back and looks up at him. Surprisingly, she sees Ewalt feels as if he has the situation under control. It's odd how a man can be completely right and still miss the facts of his life.

"Okay so what did our corporate fathers, the Patricians, see as the solution to population control? Oh, I see: breed more trouble-makers means breed more people."

Amanda sees she has lost this man but she is unsure of when it happened. She speaks slowly. "If people keep doing things to save lives, then the population grows--and eventually you have everyone starving and the planet strangles on their wastes. You also get more power in the hands of the many. If you sit back and do nothing, the people who are suffering will say you're a murderer of innocent people. As if their suffering is the result of your prosperity. That leads to insurrection." She pauses, waiting to see if he finds her explanation plausible or if she is a demon.

He nods. "So you are saying that people are nothing more than a liability. Your dad decided to kill a good man because he wanted to help the weak?"

She has her answer. "People like my family made a decision not to interfere. The man in the witness stand wouldn't listen to the logic of how his plans were a threat to our power. He suggested there might be a very public review of our intransigence."

"But you tried to save him?" He says, taking her hand, unaware that he has done it. Until he feels her coldness and wraps his other hand around her. If only Ewalt had more time to think about this part of her life, and Amanda had the time to finally trust him; they could have saved their love. Poor Amanda feels only the warmth of his body at that moment.

"You're silly sometimes. I used to be silly. Things are not going to change. We both know that." She waits wondering how his hands can be so warm.

"Were you in love with him?" Ewalt asks. "I can tell you cared."

Her eyes widen as she sees jealousy. *He likes that I was stupid. How strange.* "I may have had a crush on him. I think now I just admired his idealism. On the other hand I don't love you. So you can forget the moon eyes and warm hands. You're making my palms sweaty." She pulls her hand away.

Ewalt picks up some gravel and throws it out into the water. He is done.

"I didn't sleep with him. Stop being childish."

He stares at her. "You are a Martian," Ewalt says righteously.

"I did save his life and I did help him to escape. Isn't that worse than sleeping with him? I risked my life for him. I wouldn't do that for you. Not now. Not ever." She laughs. "But he is dead. You don't have to be jealous. You would have liked him. He was brave and did what he thought was correct. Like you."

He scratches his head feeling as if he is being lied to. "Well you're consistent. Am I a game again or do you care about me?"

She slaps him playfully. "I am not going to deal with jealousy from you. I don't have that many friends and I certainly don't need another jealous jerk."

"I'm not jealous." He raises his voice sure he is just a game for her.

"You are lying." She walks away. The gently lapping waves of the lake caresses the shore, sliding up and back, jumbling the sliver rays of night, softly murmuring rise and fall. Warm winds roll around the couple. She stands on the shore wanting to doubt what she sees.

"All right. So I was jealous." Ewalt, needing to find the exit, steps toward her.

"You really are a slut." A mallard duck calls and Amanda cannot help but hate it. "You're playing with me because you want out. Why don't you just go away?"

"That's not what I am doing here. Remember I just mentioned kids?"

"Don't be like that, Ewalt." She backs up three steps, into the water. "Oh, now look what you've made me do."

"I guess I made you wet," Ewalt says quietly.

Her breath comes in angry bursts as she steps out of the water. Her eyes remains fixed on him. "I don't want to hurt you, Ewalt. Go away. We had a fling and nothing else. Our castes don't mingle. I give up. On the other hand, I am wildly attracted to your rejection."

"What are you talking about?' He closes his eyes for a moment. When he opens his eyes, her lips part briefly. The glow on their wet supple curve taunts him. "You are a problem for me You are beautiful. Everything a man could ever want. But you are a devil."

"So you see that part of me and you react like a boy?" Her eyes seek solace in his and finds nothing but purpose. "So maybe we can go sack it in the sack so you can see the rest?" She asks sheepishly.

"No. Then you will reel me in again so you can say: I'm moving on. At that point, if I am lucky, I will be happy to have gotten out of this with my hide and a ton of remorse."

Her eyes widen with anger. "You won two rounds out of three. You are not mine, Commander Ewalt Rader." When Ewalt steps back she looks up at him, disturbed at the sight of his fears. "You could love me except that you are afraid of me. Perhaps some of those good old Feiss battle drugs might help you fight...Soldier."

He grabs her behind the legs, tossing her over his shoulder. Amanda Feiss kicks him. With his strong arm around her knees, she can do little but squirm. He carries to the near woods. "Ewalt, what are you doing? Stop this caveman crap."

He places her to the ground. Her back on a bed of thick grass, a fawn's bed. Then he rips off her blouse. She grabs at him, pulling him into her embrace. They slam into each other tossing everything into the wood, grunting like animals and caressing like lovers. But for them, there is not enough grace in this world's treachery, or for their sins. They make love for the last time.

Caressing their wants and sipping desires throughout the blackness, they will both never forget this last night together. Come dawn, Ewalt will lean closer and kiss her along the neck. Then, sure it is over, both lovers will stand in silence. Ewalt Rader's parting glance at the sailboat will guarantee its destruction within the week.

Amanda and Ewalt see each other frequently over the years-- often from a distance. Neither one will engage the other in conversation or attempt to make contact, until the day of Amanda's death. On that day, Amanda will simply ask Ewalt if he likes her mother's coffee.

Years later, Ewalt Rader will open his eyes on the bus as it leaves the hospital in Chehalis. He will watch the fir trees on the side of the roadway. They are shadows against an almost dawn. Passing the shadows, seated on the bus, Ewalt considers that perhaps Amanda had never meant to hurt him on the battlefield. *Maybe she really wanted to protect me. So why did she cook my ass? Maybe the medic was right, she just doesn't know what to do.* The clarity makes him feel a little less important. He finally concludes that perhaps Amanda had figured he never could love her--after Xandra's murder--no matter how much she cared for him. Certainly Tom Lippman knew that.

In a tiny corner of his being, Ewalt hates Tom Lippman and his facility with deceit just a little bit more. He wonders again if they ever got together. Still, a notion of Amanda's tragedy never enters his thoughts. Amanda Feiss owns too much for him to consider the truth of her pain.

CHAPTER FOURTEEN

The metal cab of the truck is rusted and gouged. Paint doesn't exist in California and getting the local plant dyes to stick to a truck's metal is like trying to get a message across the Wall these days: impossible.

The Priestess Elena Etu's mind wanders to an apple grove near her family's home. Remembering the falling yellow leaves as they swirled down from the trees, she wishes she could go back. To put her feet in the cool stream and push her toes into the muddy bank. The last time she was able to do that it was just after the frogs had been reported as an extinct species. Nine years before South America fell. She was just a teen then. Living north of New York City to escape the emerging squalor, her family had bought a farm near Monticello so she could ride. Elena had wanted to be an Olympic equestrian when she was young.

Her bedroom window faced the stables and the rows of apple trees. The stream wandered between orchard and the corral. Inside, Elena had posters on the musty walls of the farmhouse bedroom. One was of a soldier smiling, a surf board in hand. He had thumbs up and a bad-boy wink. It was Baylor's first modeling job---a recruiting poster for the Navy. He had still been in the military.

Six people were scalped last night in San Francisco. Her beautiful man has degenerated into a wild beast and she finds no place for him this morning. Elena wishes her memories of loving him would disappear. The pain of his madness bounces in and out of her as the old dump truck mugs each rut of the decrepit interstate.

How long has it been since I have seen a horse?

The dust swirls around. There are no windows to the cab. The smelly scarf over her mouth feels like it is strangling her. The driver, about as old as the ancient truck, has no sense of the dust. She merely works to get the vehicle to the Wall looming ahead of them.

To distract herself again, Elena wonders about the young boy with the deadlocks who so skillfully made it back before she left this morning. She was surprised to see he had red hair. He made sure to clean himself up before the trip and now rides in back with her guards. He wants to be left at the Wall when she leaves. So that he might see Disney. Instead, Elena plans to have him tied up, if necessary, and brought back to San Francisco. The city and her people need smart men and women. That plan will not happen.

Sitting in between Elena and the truck driver rests Phillip. Eyes closed apparently from sleep; his head hanging forward as if he were dead. The unbraided white beard covers his chest. Phillip Stein was the first person to step forward on the beach when the fish washed onshore. Phillip has been Elena's friend for years--since the riots and the madness. His first words to her were: "Just don't ask me to believe your fish thing is a miracle. You represent order so I will help you." Since then Elena and Phillip have protected each other and prospered.

There were even times when she told herself that Phillip had forgotten about his dead wife and children. That he held his pain with a clear heart. Then she heard that he had gone to visit them again. The trip netted six new recruits and some valuable information about the defenses of Portland. As well as the location of an arms factory. She wonders if it was worth it for him and why the fury in his gut never fades.

The old man churns hopes that today's event will not ruin their friendship.

He hinted, before they climbed in the truck this morning, there was news about Patrician defenses. She could see he was upset. So she had asked how the visit with his family had been. He nodded with a smile, saying his family was still there. Then he closed his eyes. Elena has concluded there is a problem at the Wall. She is waiting for him though; if he has no report on the trip back she will insist he share the data with her by this evening. She has called for a meeting with Joe Vaz for getting food into Portland once the Wall is down.

Elena considers Phillip may never get Joe Vaz to look into the birth control project. Phillip and Joe Vaz have never really gotten along. They are cordial--respectful of each other's skills--but they remain distant from each other. On the surface of it, they should be friends. Yet neither man will talk to the other--except to compliment a perceived skill set or to help solve a problem. The whole dynamic frustrates her. Even though she relishes the male rutting because it takes her mind off the horror that surrounds her.

She worries that Joe cares too much about feeding people and keeping them alive. It is his strength--but that myopia borders on madness in her opinion. She doubts Joe will help her with the birth control project. He just doesn't want to. So Elena searches for a lever.

In reality, Elena is fascinated by him; Doctor Vaz is a decent man because he has no other choice. It is just who he is. She finds his fear of losing that decency amusing and sweet. Phillip on the other hand thinks Doctor Vaz a technocrat. Again, a confusing situation since Phillip is a pragmatist and Doctor Vaz is a former humanities professor. *Perhaps that is the issue. Joseph Vaz sees an ethical gap in Phillip and Phillip reacts to the insult: Men are annoying some times.*

"Almost there." The driver speaks, seemingly mesmerized by the Wall and its outlooks sticking up into the bright blue sky. After spitting out mud out through the door frame, she rubs her misshapen nose again and curses the Wall. "Sometimes I think all I ever want in life is to come up over that hill and not see that horrible thing."

"The undermining is working, Louise. It'll breach soon," Phillip says, without opening his eyes. Elena wonders if he ever really sleeps.

"You used to live here?" The Priestess asks the driver.

"I'm from Marisol, down south. My sister used to live here. Until she was murdered by some crooked attorney who said he owned her land. The Wall goes right through their farm. That stinking heap of Demon-waste is on her grave." The driver sighs. "It didn't used to be a desert either. There were lots more trees, olive and fruit trees. A lot of eucalyptus too."

"We need more fruit trees," Phillip says, distractedly. "Louise, please take us directly to the Wall. The ceremony will be starting soon." His eyes open and he grimaces at the hordes of people lining the sides of the old interstate. Their numbers fill to the horizon this close to the Wall. He wonders how civilized beings could have done this to their children.

When Phillip was young, he had always wanted to be in a parade with people staring at him. Now he hates going to the Wall because people always stare at him. Those he sees are the best off. They can walk. They appear like manikins to him.

Staring at the clouds of dust that have settled on their faces, Elena ponders the ease with which humanity has shed its former cloak of hygiene. "You know that man who wants to open the fake shopping mall with the big showers in Red Bluff should be supported. At least they'd have fun when they wash. And they could practice their gunnery with the water cannons. It's not right for us to subject these people to Victorian notions about morality, if the result is better hygiene. Who cares if it is both men and women in the same shower?" She is speaking to Phillip, passing the time.

"We need the resources for other things," he replies, looking out the window. "Showers can wait. Keeping the tunnels dry are more important."

"Food can take us just so far. We have extra pumps. They will be happier if they are clean."

He smiles. "In time, a few months after the Wall is breached, I will have extra pumps."

Unlike Elena, whom he knows longs for civilization, Phillip imbibes the drug of revenge. Like the alcoholic who thinks only of alcohol, he seeks only one release from his pain. The obsession with revenge is slowly poisoning the old man. He does not care. The architect of the undermining process, he wishes to watch the world of the Patricians fully breached. The acid-bottle of hatred thrown in their faces. The broken glass stuffed down their throats. Today is worse than most for Phillip because he fears failure. A patrol from the other side has confirmed there is a second Wall.

Worse, one of the officers from the tour yesterday claimed the new Wall was impenetrable. He had said limitless tunneling had been taken into account in its design. Nothing could have seared the heart of this man more. A brilliant individual, he could not sleep last night or this morning, for fear of an impregnable Wall. It also makes today's events even more import. He has to learn more about this new barrier. "Priestess Etu," Phillip says. He would never call her Elena except in their private conversations. "The flowers' colors are so brilliant and their smell is so divine this year. The people look so healthy and happy. I am filled with hope."

"It is the Food Man's work. It makes everything possible." She speaks the words quietly, staring up the Wall. Stunned that this epitaph to avarice seems even a little uglier than the last time she saw it.

"The flowers and you, Priestess Etu. They are beauty," Phillip says with a note of bitterness. The truck driver remembers the jingle and warms listening to them converse.

Up ahead the blacktop of US 5 changes to gravel ahead of the immense Wall. The driver pictures herself running the truck into and through the Wall. Even though she knows this action has been tried and proved utterly useless over and over again. She begins to downshift and pulls up by a wide row of azaleas in pink bloom. The vehicle rolls up a small hillock, finally coming to a stop near a set of food tents. The truck has no brakes.

Workers quickly unload food as the Priestess Elena Etu exits the cab onto the running board, waving with her plant-died wrap of purple and pink canvas. The crowd cheers. She bows to them. Then her hands are in prayer in front of her chest. The crowd, with a ripple of respect rolling back, returns her bow. The Priestess covers her shoulders with the filthy shawl stepping off the running board onto the dusty ground.

Phillip follows her slowly. Glad his bones feel so healthy, he wishes for an old-fashioned town car instead of the monstrous trucks. Baylor, who had been riding on the roof, arrives beside the Priestess holding a wooden staff. He struts about. The deranged man sees himself as master of this universe. The guards flank the three of them as the crowd forms up around them. Everyone knows Baylor has Wall-madness, a death wish. They know, but do not understand, why he is so special to the Priestess. They also know that no one can approach her hastily. It means death. So in reality--the guards are trying to protect the crowd. When Baylor finishes circling her, he places himself between her and the line of sight from the Wall. As if he could stop a missile.

Elena's hand reaches behind her to touch the truck's hood. Hot, like a frying pan, she steadies herself as she surveys the rapidly growing crowd. Translators fan out into the crowd. She looks up at the young boy from San Francisco sitting on the truck. His mouth is open and his eyes seem stunned. His right hand pulls on long dreadlocks twirling them back and forth in his hand. She points to him. A guard gets the boy down and lifts him onto his shoulders. The boy's grin spreads under sunken eyes. He feels a bit safer now.

The Priestess Elena Etu speaks to her people: "See how our children grow? Not in height, or happiness, but in spirit--they know how close we are to winning. Those on the other side of that wicked Wall also know this." She points at the monolith that extends out on either side of the crowd. "They are the past. We are the future." Her words live like waves, rolling out to those in the far reaches of the crowd. The translators explain her words to people clustered in language knots all around them: Spanish, Chinese, German, and so forth.

"Many have been killed by the Demons," she pauses. The crowd echoes her words. "But we are stronger. They are weaker. Soon it will not be this Wall that stops us from killing them. It will be our humanity as we take back the freedom and liberty entrusted to us by our forefathers." The Priestess speaks as loudly as she can. "Teach the children it is not the weapons aimed on us, or those who would kill us with their weapons, that are our enemy. Our enemy is our own horrible blindness. Our desire for convenience. Our refusal to stand for our country. These are the actions we undertook as we were hypnotized by comfort. When we allowed the vampire of consumerism to suck out our humanity. That has ended. This monstrosity will soon end as well."

The Priestess Elena Etu takes two small river rocks, both of them flecked with pink spots, and holds them over head. The crowd cheers. Phillip immediately produces another pair and holds them over his head. The Priestess waits. Everyone in the crowd has similar stones. Parents send children to tents while old people are helped retrieving their stones.

Soon some four-hundred-thousand people stand waiting. Their hands extend above their heads. "This is the Earth's Voice. It speaks for us It cannot be silenced. It will spread over the Earth, piercing the evil of the towers with its sound, showering the Demons with our strength, and proclaiming our mercy as a civilized people."

She slaps the rocks against each other once, then twice, then three times, all the way up to five. During the pause, a count of five, she scans the crowd. Their numbers astound the Priestess as she looks about her. Elena can see no end to them.

Tap
Tap-Tap
Tap-Tap-Tap
Tap-Tap-Tap-Tap
Tap-Tap-Tap-Tap-Tap.

At first, the sound is like a swarm of crickets. Then the repeated cracking becomes a synced malevolent thunder. It spreads out into the dry plains calling more people into the ceremony.

The tsunami of unified purpose echoes back, rising up to the Wall then over it. A rattle of hate floods the valleys behind the Wall. The blinking blue lights of the barricade turn red, indicating an alarm. Baylor points at the Wall with his spear. The Priestess watches her influence spread as the lights of the towers begin to change color as far as the eye can see in both directions. The closest towers begin to strobe. Baylor dances in a joyous madness.

Tap
Tap-Tap
Tap-Tap-Tap
Tap-Tap-Tap-Tap
Tap-Tap-Tap-Tap-Tap.

She stops. Then the Priestess speaks again, turning toward the Wall. Their surveillance recorders will be on her now. "I am the Priestess Etu. Hear me. Know of our weapons. Know your crimes will soon be tried by us. We are healthy and we are getting healthier. Our number grows at incredible rates. There is no escape for you. We have factories and we have new weapons. We are not content to wait and win. Our land is stable. Yours is not. That means we will attack your Wall and win. Of this I am certain."

The crowd cheers.

"Tell all your friends and relatives of my truth. You will soon feel the sound of a billion souls--and the Earth's Voice--screaming for justice. Our roar will not stop. We will crumble your Wall." The tapping begins again and continues for ten more refrains.

Tap
Tap-Tap
Tap-Tap-Tap
Tap-Tap-Tap-Tap
Tap-Tap-Tap-Tap-Tap.

The ceremony ends in cheers. She raises her hands and the crowd is silent. Their silence is her control and the people's acceptance of her power. For the Wall guards her ability to control the mob is scarier than the clamor of rocks.

Phillip looks at the crowd and smiles. *Why don't the people out there wonder why the guards haven't fired a missile at her?*

She speaks again: "I will lead you again, later. Our roar will wake the old lion who pulls the Sun to sleep." She turns from the crowd and looks at Phillip. "Did they hear me?"

"Everyone did, Priestess," Phillip replies. "I'm sure of it."

"There must be a better way to get them to negotiate with us." She watches his response knowing he will never betray her truth.

"If there were less of us, then they would kill us off. They wish to control us--nothing else. It appears to me you have taken some good steps to ending that." His old eyes seem threadbare with lies and so she inadvertently steps back. "They have to know they can't win by now."

"What do you know, Phillip?" She sees he is well-bothered by something and so she will not wait to hear of it. "They've known for a long time they cannot win. You have heard we have a problem. What is it?"

Tired from the trip he attempts a smile. It comes across worn and empty. "Perhaps they just want to be slaughtered. I need more time to research a rumor. Please give me to the end of the day. It will make sense, soon."

She stares at him. Ashamed she does not feel his hatred of those on the other side of the Wall. "When do we meet with the local leaders?"

Phillip looks down at the sundial beside the truck wondering if those are the last civil words she will ever say to him. "Let's walk over to the other side of the truck," he replies.

Elena follows Phillip putting the truck between her and the Wall. The thought crosses her mind that some kind of danger lurks. That he had arranged for her safety in that quiet way she has grown to appreciate and admire. *Phillip can always be counted on to get the job done.* A set of men and women, the local leadership, approaches them. They begin to speak about the need for more water and food.

From an outlook on the Wall, Lucien Feiss stares out through field glasses watching Elena on the far side of the truck. He listens to the recording of her speech, then scans the infrared camera as she seems to speak to the old man and a small group of men and women. Luke Feiss' elbows rest on the black vinyl cushion that runs under the window of the guard outlook. When the recording is done, he marvels at her control, and his foresight.

A General named Howell speaks: "She certainly has their attention." He is a brawny man with jet black hair and sharp chin. His eyes are dark stones.

"How many of these ceremonies do they have a day, General?"

Lucien asks.

"Four times a day. She is here every few months or so." The officer dressed in whites has an authoritarian poise, and no emotions to speak of. He is a killer in every sense of the word. General Howell began his career as a Wall guard. "During the ceremony, the High Priestess of Jelly Beans is always just where she stands now. We were going to set the guns on her. As you can see we continue to stand down--as ordered--Mr. Feiss."

"High Priestess of Jelly Beans?" Inquires Lucien Feiss.

"A local term," General Howell replies. "Her rocks, and those of her captains, have small flecks of brightly colored minerals. The last few weeks the guards have come to label her derisively."

"Put a lid on that." He stares at the General. "Also, make sure I get a recording of that girl and her tribal ritual," Feiss says. Two dark-skinned soldiers glance at each other then quickly return to their work

"Yes, Mr. Feiss," the General replies, "I'll get it to you. The gist of it is always the same. She says this noise should scare us--and that they wouldn't need to attack the Wall with anything else but their sound and their shovels." He laughs, even though he knows the undermining is far more effective than the guards in the outlook know.

The General wonders who will get caught behind the new Wall. He is a gambling man and some senior officers have bets on how many guards actually make it to safety. He doesn't doubt his own escape. Sadly, General Howell will not even make it through the day.

Lucien Feiss puts the field glasses down on the dark mahogany ledge between the bullet-proof glass and the cushion. There is a long scratch in the wood. He looks at the General with a raised white eyebrow. "This looks bad, General." Lucien Feiss examines a scratch in the wood as if it were a mark on his living room furniture. "Have this fixed," he says. The rest of the polished wood glows in the sun.

"Yes sir," the General replies, pulling out his black note pad and jotting down the instructions. He knows Lucien Feiss will have it checked to see if he has carried out his task. Seeing a look of inquisition, the General looks around at his officers. The smell of their fear fills the room. He decides to tell Lucian Feiss about Jack Porter--deciding it will do him no good to keep it from him.

Lucien Feiss watches the General think. "Your idea about setting guns or rockets on them, isn't such a bad idea. But others tried it up the line. She would be protected by their bodies and the resulting anger isn't worth the cost of the munitions. Four or five hours later they are back hitting those rocks together. There's too many of them just to gun 'em down. Killing her will not make any difference. Besides, we understand she is pushing for birth control. She is our best friend out there." These are words for the soldiers not the General. He already knows the facts.

Lucien slowly brings the binoculars back to his eyes to watch the crowd. "It really is a cult. Isn't it?" Feiss then hands the field glasses over to General Howell. "Okay, I've seen enough."

The General escorts Lucien Feiss from the guard outlook down a short staircase lined in red wallpaper and wainscoting. The steel elevator doors open. The interior is hardwoods and soft lighting, making the elevator interior look like an exclusive club. They exit, passing through a mahogany door into a small room that looks out over a hillside and small lakes. In contrast to the dry wilderness on the other side of the Wall. This looks like Eden.

"Sir, may I speak frankly?" Asks the General.

"You better," Lucien Feiss replies.

"It's not Elena Etu that's the problem. It's that lunatic who's supplying them with food. He and his factories are clearly the lynch pin to defeat the Dirties."

"We can pull that pin anytime we want," Feiss says sitting in an wooden chair by a small table. "We need control systems if we are going to defuse this problem long term. Ms. Etu and the food are our controls." A Hispanic woman in a short skirt delivers a pot of coffee and some cups. The delivery of coffee into meetings is a Feiss trademark. Coffee is impossible to get for most people. The woman retreats like a shadow. "Have there been rumors among the guards about the food yet?" The gold trimmed cups glow.

"No. We've kept the lid damn tight on this. Some of the senior Wall security people know--but no one else. And they won't say anything. For them it's just another piece of information to be kept in the family."

Feiss watches the tree tops sway in the breeze. "Keep up the good work." His head tilts back to release a tight muscle in his neck. "Has my daughter been contacted about dinner yet?" He is speaking to a pair of administrative vice-presidents who sit nearby.

"She's on a mission. She should be returning around six," says Packard, a man with a lean face and beady eyes.

Lucien nods, relieved he doesn't have to see her. "That will be too late. Have someone contact her when she gets back. Tell her how sorry I am that we couldn't get together this time. Her mom will be by later in the week."

The two men in business suits nod in unison. The other man hands General Howell an ebony colored suit case. "This is your payment for this year. You've done a good job."

"Thank you, sir."

Lucien Feiss speaks to General Howell: "And don't forget to tell my daughter I'm sorry that I missed her this trip. Anything else I should know about?"

Howell takes his opening. "One of the Seattle businessmen you wanted me to keep an eye out for, a man named Jack Porter, has been snooping about. He's looking for friends, including a certain SWAT Commander....Ewalt Rader."

"Him again. I swear that guy is a bad penny. Where is the Commander now?"

"Security says Commander Rader was wounded by a launch

plume from a Hercules missile recently. He was in the hospital at Chehalis. We can have him detained if you want."

"Where is he off to next?"

"He is on his way to Portland. Then he leaves for Everett. Where we think he will be meeting with Mr. Porter."

Feiss nods. "Rader's unimportant, but do I have to keep an eye on Mr. Porter. What's your take on it?"

"I think Porter wants to enlist Commander Rader. He's looking for someone to act as liaison and cut a deal for him with the Dirties. He appears like a man betting we will lose this war. He also seems to be looking for someone who can get behind the Wall and then get back. Someone he can trust. They're old friends. Who better to buy off?"

"Mandy would laugh at his corpse." Lucien sees a quick sideways glance from Howell to his vice-presidents. It says he has it wrong. Lucien concludes that the rumors are correct. She saved Commander Rader's life the other day instead of taking it.

Children!

"Keep an eye on them. If Porter gets to Rader and he says he will help Porter let me know. Don't stand in the way of it. Assign our people to assist. Also make sure our people handle the logistics. But don't let him across the Wall unless you get a Feiss okay." Lucien Feiss's eyes glow with the game. He turns to his vice-presidents to leave: "Gentlemen, shall we proceed?"

One of his vice-presidents grabs the door. A low bump moves the room and the door jams. As the man struggles with the jammed door Lucien Feiss shakes his head.

"Here let me," says Howell. "It's a wonder anything works."

These words are the last sounds Lucien Feiss will ever hear.

CHAPTER FIFTEEN

Through her dirty silver slippers, Elena feels a low rumble rise from the earth. Sand coughs from every hole in the ground. The earth heaves. It thrusts up. Then down, shaking the truck and tossing Elena back against it. An earthquake-like nausea rolls through her body. She grabs the truck feeling it bounce on its wheels. Thinking this is an earthquake, she has the time to consider the irony of a quake bringing down the Wall. The crowd panics as the rumbling becomes louder and more violent. She watches a blast of rocks out to the west blow skyward. Phillip pulls her down, another blast. The explosions spread out between the flowers and the Wall base. Her unfocused gaze sharpens. Then she is looking at Phillip's wry smile. But he is not seeing her. His inquisitive stare tunnels under the wheels of the truck to the Wall. Another huge explosion tosses the truck up on the two side wheels. A moment of silence. Then the rumblings begin again. Geysers of rock fan out both east and west. The tremors become more intense. Elena stumbles around the truck uncaring about the danger, she is sure she knows what is happening.

Puffs of what appears to be white smoke come from the gardens in front of her. Then a dozen geysers of dirt and rock fly skyward with deafening roar. Thrown to the ground, Baylor is immediately at her side. Weapons drawn, his eyes alert to the panicking crowd. Explosions march closer and closer to the Wall in a curtain of exploding rocks. Phillip appears beside her and tries to pull Elena down beneath the truck. She will not budge. Rocks and debris shower the area.

Then it happens. A low rumble, a moan from the depths of Hades, and the Wall heaves backward. Then it tilts forward like a piece of flimsy paper waving in the wind. The topmost vertical section cracks open. The guard outlook directly in front of them topples forward sliding down the front of the Wall, crashing to the ground. Exposed hallways and armaments lie bare to the day. People lose their fear and they rush in to attack it. Another explosion rips upwards from inside the Wall, sending the bared sections in every direction, scattering people back and sending new pieces of the Wall structure up and out like an opening gate. The next two flanking guard outlooks curl down in slow motion towards the breach. They fall inward in a cascade of bodies, concrete, and steel.

Most amazingly, there is a moment of quiet. The crowd stands. Then after what appears to be a wide cough of smoke from the other side of the Wall, a one-hundred-yard section of the Wall just slides forward and drops down into the ground.

For the first time in a decade, those south of the Wall see the verdant green hills, the meadows, and the farms. The collapsed mound heaves up a fourth time, bringing down more of the Wall--including those next two flanking guard posts. People rush the guards.

Elena looks to the left watching new explosions appear. They multiply a few hundred yards away in each direction. She turns back to the wide gap in the Wall. To her amazement the two shattered ends of the Wall suddenly seem to rip away from the rest of it and fly skyward. Huge pieces of concrete flying backward into the meadows and trees. The explosions stop and the breach settles. Then off to the west, another section of the Wall collapses. Its mass dragging huge segments of the structure into the depths turning the top of the Wall into a mass of rubble that quite neatly fills each hole into which it fell. The precision astounds her. Within ten minutes, sets of 500 yard runs of the Wall have disappeared into a maelstrom of dust and smoke.

Arcs of fire shoot skyway. Secondary explosions come from inside of the now deflated Wall sections. From the intact islands of the Wall, machine guns open fire, but the computer systems are down. Only the size of the attacking crowd makes the guns effective. From the south there is the rumble of engines and Elena turns back to see a fleet of a hundred or so trucks streaming towards the breach. For a moment she wonders why. Though the Wall is down its shattered bulk still remains a blockade of rubble--and the helicopters will be here soon. Then the trucks disappear into caverns. One after the other, until all of them are gone. She then understands why some sections of the Wall, and their tunnels beneath, remain in tact. The trucks will use those tunnels to egress on the other side of the Wall dispersing troops within a few minutes. The battle for Oregon has begun.

More trucks appear, streaming up old US 5 as thousands of people run at the remains of the Wall without any plan or purpose to engage the helicopters and SWATs which are sure to come. It will take three hours for an effective call out of reserves.

At this point three tanks from Fort 54 and their helicopter escort are approaching the problem area. They do not know that the Wall was built with a surety that said it could never be breached. With the segmented destruction of the Wall, the non-redundant communications system deep inside the Wall have failed. Teams on either side of the breaches know something has happened, but due to the dust clouds have no idea the extent of damage. The masses of people will overrun the tanks and kill everyone they find.

A killing field will be set up north of Weed so the SWATS and Rapiers can begin guarding the retreat to the Columbia Wall. The islands of Wall will remain secure and they will be abandoned anyway. The guards in the Wall will hold out for a week. By then, the anger will have quelled and many will get out alive. Today though there will be no mercy from the crowd. Elena leans over to Phillip seeking to maintain her composure. She is certain Lucien Feiss had been inside one of the towers that collapsed. "Phillip, we should have talked first--"

He looks around. Seeing they are alone, he speaks before she says anything further. "Priestess, they never fired on you. I know you work for Feiss. So I really couldn't risk saying anything. I'm sorry. If you like I will resign and never do anything further. I wasn't going to go to my maker without seeing that abomination destroyed and my children avenged." The old man stares at her. His fogged-over eyes and deeply rutted face appear placid for the first time since she has known him.

"So why would you remove our support on the other side of the Wall?"

"We never had any support from anyone," Phillip says.

"You're a fool, an angry, presumptuous fool." Elena is unable to speak further. She watches people charge the Wall despite the remaining weapons' systems coming back on line. The carnage mounts as they get closer. Behind them others begin to smooth the rubble that had once been the Wall. She is amazed at how organized it is. How plans they had discussed for a distant future were underway before her eyes. Thousands of single-minded people dig, pick at rocks, and smooth the destruction to facilitate a new roadway. With no concern for their safety. "You sent sapper teams in those trucks?" She asks.

"Those first trucks you saw have three missions. Destroy the gas systems in the cities, confirm or deny the existence of a second Wall being built along the Columbia--then we are going to try and secure access to the armaments factory."

"A second Wall?" She stares at him. "When did you learn of this?"

"I was told of the possibility a week ago and had it confirmed by a prisoner yesterday. I still couldn't be sure. We also couldn't wait any longer. We have to get to Portland to find out--before they complete it. I am sorry. I just gave the go ahead."

"If there is a second Wall, what do you think have you done? The bridges will stop a small force. Now that they have three-hundred miles to prepare for them. Especially if the Wall has the Columbia River in front of it. We will never do any damage to the new Wall. By the time we have a sizeable force to assault it their new Wall they will be ready."

"If it is there, they are going to try and destroy it. At minimum, they will confirm its existence and start feeding me data so I can draw up a strategy. Then our people will disable the gas systems in Portland. I am not going to allow those bastards to gas another few million people."

She sighs.

"We are unstoppable, Elena."

"We always were." She turns and notes the young boy with the dreadlocks scampering across the fields heading for the breach. The Priestess looks for her guards. They are too busy keeping a perimeter around her. Elena watches the boy disappear into the dust. "Was it nuclear?" She looks back at Phillip.

"Nope. Just a hell of a lot of people digging. And some unused ordinance I happened to know about from the Monterey area. Clean as a whistle and effective as all get out. There will be six more breaches all along the Wall. You saw the first six. The rest will begin in sets of two. They are set to begin thirty minutes from our detonation here."

A reconnaissance helicopter from Portland appears. It is immediately blown out of the sky by six missiles. Elena speaks: "They are on their way to kill more of us."

"It'll be hours before they mount an effective assault and they will do nothing but guard their retreat. We'll be in Portland before the end of the month."

"And if there is another Wall?" She asks.

"That's why we are going after the munitions factory. I've run out of explosives." Phillip will not look at her. "We have those helicopters."

She angers. "Paperclips with tin foil and spitballs. They'll blow them out of the sky as they see them."

"I will not condemn the civilian population of Portland to the same kind of death as my wife and children. And if we can secure that munitions factory, we have a big lever."

She glares at him. "Tell then to find medical supplies." She watches the surging crowds scale the exposed flanks of the Walls. Gunfire from guards defending their islands of concrete leads to slaughter of the assailants. "This is to keep attention from your sappers as they move north?"

Phillip nods at her comment knowing her anger. "Right. The Border Patrol will be lethal once they recover from the shock," Phillip says. "Priestess, so far as they know this is all your plan. You are now a genuine force in this conflict. Those are your soldiers assaulting the bastards that now call themselves the United States."

She sighs. "You are a smart man, Phillip. But you never understood. We are the United States. Those are pirates and murderers holding our citizens hostage in a hijacked a corner of our country-- nothing more."

He nods surprised at her patriotism. "I know you were wanting to broker a peace with them and I know they were just using you-- like they used me." Phillip and Elena both stare at the storm of colors attacking the Wall. Those climbing the Wall soon slip on the rivers of blood. The flame throwers are brought back on line and they start burning people alive. The defense swings into full gear. A retreat begins. Phillip looks away unable to bear the slaughter. "We need to get out of here. Baylor find the driver and get this truck started."

The mute protector of Elena waits for her confirmation. She nods and he trots off to find a driver.

"Phillip, everybody knew they were at the end. We could have made peace."

"You're naive," he says. "Once you make peace all they will do is seek a new way to kill more. They are animals."

"And you're so full of loss from the death of your family that you're blind."

"You misunderstand." An explosion followed by smoke fills the horizon from the north.

"Here comes the counter-attack," she says sadly. "Or perhaps those are your sapper teams being picked off. It just doesn't matter to you that people will die. Just so long as the bastards that killed your family pay in blood." Her body shivers in the dusty heat. Elena Etu is now less a Priestess and more an angry woman.

Phillip points to Baylor as he runs around looking for a driver. "He means that little to you?"

She ignores his words. So much of her work this last year lies buried in the debris of the Redding Wall.

By nightfall the population on the north side of the Wall will be informed of Lucien Feiss' death. Tomorrow will be declared a national day of mourning.

CHAPTER SIXTEEN

That evening, Joe Vaz fidgets, trying to insert a large skeleton key into the lock of a mausoleum. The news of the Wall's breach has reached San Francisco. He is so excited, he cannot work the keyway. Finally he turns the lock. Pushing the tomb's well-used door, taking in the familiar smell of machine oil, Joe looks around the headstones and edifices of death. Before closing the door, like a boy fearful of ghosts, he slams the door.

Inside, the touch of heat from the ovens below and the music of a tuned factory reaches out, caressing him. He hopes his assistants have completed the process of lighting the fires and playing the recordings that will distract ordinance. Joe wants to hurry the work of distracting bombers and others. Doctor Vaz has seen more over-flights this evening and he assumes tonight or tomorrow the attacks will begin. With the Wall down, the destruction of his food system will be a key to the Patrician's defense.

Avoiding the many booby traps, Joe steps through a second door. The smell of curry fills the area today. Down a flights of stairs that lead deep into the ground, he stops on a metal catwalk suspended over the production floor. Below spreads an immense cavern, he crosses to a new catwalk and begins strolling above the apparent cacophony of equipment, moving red lights, and blinking green lights. Pipes and cauldrons fill the room below. Robots steam here and there as large metal crates fly along the ceiling, suspended by chains.

In the dark, above the production floor, listening to the mechanisms resonating from the stone walls, he calms as if he were in a sunny park. Below, bumping, chugging, clangs and clicks, whirls and whines, tapping and ticks. A symphony of purpose: Feed the hungry. The great machine that nourishes him also nourishes hundreds of millions of people. Intimately tied to its environment, harming nothing, it generates food from waste.

Below, automated carts zip down the aisles, their red and green lights flashing in syncopation. Joe pauses and watches the ballet. Both hands on the railing, his mind picturing the processing for which his eyes take credit; his ears supply the rest.

And like a God looking down on the red and green stars he has created, Joe feels a sense of home among the great mechanisms in the once empty black cavern. He places his right hand on the railing and taps it with his old college ring. The sound travels out along the fifty catwalks: Father is home.

He stares at a large steel cylinder that Phillip has had brought in. A set of tubes runs around it from a set of smaller containers. It is not connected to his machine. This test system creates the hormonal imbalance that precludes unwanted birth. Joe ignores it as he walks above it. He tells himself it will be a cold day in hell before he allows anything that isn't pure nutrition--let alone chemicals to alter the reproductive system of the species--into his food manufacturing system.

Joe Vaz recognizes the problems of too many people. He just hasn't gotten the time to solve it. Ironically enough, he can do it. Some people are like that: demigods some would say. Problem solvers, others might say. Idealism is the curse of people like this. Capability is their grace. Loneliness is their companion and fear their secret.

Inside this geometry, Joe Vaz prioritizes his actions to develop the most effective schedule for solving the problems of the other members of his species. It is an irony that the species he believes ostracizes him, demands his love. And while he knows that his plans may not be perfect; he also knows his plans are doable. Joe Vaz sees himself as a freak: A human with the ability to deliver success, day after day, year after year--regardless of the challenge.

Many years ago, when asked if he thought he was a great man and that was why the Senate should listen to him, he responded that he couldn't help being great. "Everyone has a curse. Something they cannot change about themselves. Mine is greatness. It is no better or worse then the megalomaniac or the artist. Greatness just is. And yes for that reason you should listen to me. How many of you could be considered great?" Then they shot him and a young Amanda Feiss began the process of her destruction.

On the floor of this dark place, where humanity is served by its machines, most humans would certainly die in seconds. The machines have no sensors and their tasks are hard-wired in. It's not that the environment, or the climate below is dangerous by nature. It performs a function and any humans that decides to enter the realm must take care to respect the forces at work here in Doctor Vaz's world. This factory, Joe has often told visitors, is a model of the Earth's processes. Except that the factory has much less tolerance for human meddling or interference. It functions for the good of humanity and in return demands respect for its processes. There is no mercy for those that are served--just purpose. Before the anarchy, Doctor Vaz taught environmental philosophy at a university.

A few weeks after the factory opened, some teens broke in and entered the factory floor. Nine of the ten died. The last one lives in a bed. Joe fretted that Priestess Etu might shut the facility down because it was so dangerous. "Priestess," Joe had argued, "We need to see that the system is here to feed us. We are its only reason for existence, making us part of its results--not its processes. That also makes it dangerous, not evil. A functioning system provides little for those that ignore process. And we have disrespected processes for too long. That is our sin. It has always been our sin--as a species. We continually sacrifice results for ego satisfaction. The result is we now cannot rescue certain members of our species."

The Priestess responded by saying he sounded like a Patrician. Unruffled, Dr. Vaz then said. "They and I see the balance of life and responsibility. But I do not use it to stroke myself. I serve." The Priestess ruled against the complaints of the parents.

Not surprisingly, Dr. Joseph Vaz can wander with impunity on the factory floor. Having created the world below, it lives both inside him and outside him. Ironically, the factory is more like a family to him than the crush and madness of the people he helps feed. Others rarely understand what that means for Joe. Mostly they just conclude he is a Renaissance man. That this is his home so it protects him. Elena recognizes the creator and the created are one because each lives inside the other. Their distinct nature only arises at the edges of their existence, otherwise known as the perception of others. The factory excretes food like Joe's being develops solutions to problems. Neither functions if it is disrespected. Dr. Joseph Vaz is not a Renaissance man--the term is archaic. He is a man fully connected to his ecosystem. He is simply man.

He laughs when others say his work is a take off on the old corporate farms that raised pigs and other livestock in hellish conditions. Slaughtered animal delivery of protein is no more on this side of the Wall. Murdered for food a decade ago, the farm animal is a memory: too energy intensive, too resource intensive and too time intensive to fit the human needs of this time. Joe argues that process must evolve just like a species evolves. But with the constriction of economics as humanity's core, as he sees it, certain processes just did not evolve, like food production.

Joe Vaz sees humans as processes inside other processes. A collection of cooperating systems, some of which are housed in a body. Their output is a convoluted awareness called life. He has figured out how to harness the interconnections of his ecosystem more efficiently than anyone else. As a professor, too late he had tried to teach the technique to his students. His success rate approached zero as society collapsed.

Had he lived a hundred years ago, in a blinder world, Joe believes he might have been an entrepreneur--wealthy and angry-- erecting a partition of power and influence between he and the people who mock him. Joe considers how he would have controlled a great empire. Perhaps buying his way out of loneliness. In that belief, Joe Vaz is a fool.

He occasionally ponders if there might still have been no bond between him and those around him--even with wealth. Joe chides himself at night with the notion that in another world, those on the other side of the Wall would be his progeny. The convoluted scenarios of what might have been, keeps him safe in a mad, rabid world. Joe, like the rest of humanity, has been driven partially insane by sadness and horror. So at this time in his life, only the complex functioning of machine are his friend.

Continuing along the catwalk, listening to the factory below, he watches fluorescing robots picking parts and supplies from a wall of bins. Moving like bright purple honey bees on a barrier of square flowers, the robots dart left and right. Their single arms pull parts from the bins, putting them into bags that hang on either side like holsters. The contents of the bags are later put on conveyors, or emptied into pipes, so the materials can be distributed to where they are needed in the factory.

Huge pipes snake along the underside of the catwalk like intestines, taking different density parts to subsystems for processing. The mixers below him, like giant organs, take compounds from other pipes and break them down into a chemical and yeast soup. It forms new organic compounds used by the machine. The results are mixed, baked, and then flavored.

Unaware he steps in time to the pumps' beat that sends bits of plastic and starch through the ten foot diameter pipes, he begins to smile. Joe is at peace. Leaving this corner of the production floor, Joe approaches the shipping area. He sighs knowing humans wait beyond the next set of doors. *The Priestess' people will be there with their guns and beady eyes.* Guarding the stairway to the surface, they wait to take him to his cabin.

Exiting, he sees hundreds of soldiers. Once, many had been his students. Now they watch him. This main factory was turned over to Elena's people today, as were the satellite food factories all around the state. The battle has started. He wonders if the new custodians will be jealous of his wanderings. The Brazilians became possessive before he left. Never considering his remorse in turning his factory over to his students. This facility is far more efficient. The best he has ever built. He worries he may not be able to improve on it. It is the continuation of this demigod's factories that now weighs on him, not the battle up north or the expected attack.

For the first time today, he thinks of the young woman who had saved his life, wondering if she is alive on the other side of the Wall. He ponders the traitorous actions of the female soldier who saved his life. Curious about the price she has paid for saving him, Joe Vaz has never forgotten that a beautiful young woman once saved him. She remains the one person in his life he wishes to spend more time with. He fantasizes of a fireplace and old chairs, tea, conversation about his machines, and games of the intellect. She had said she played bridge--as she carried him through a dark hallway. He always assumed she meant that. Despite the blood that flowed from him.

Now with the breach of the Wall, he believes he may one day find her. Occasionally, he considers trading his knowledge of food production for finding her again. He does not think beyond that. Joe Vaz has no reliable experience with love. Though he does believe that the search for a lover invariably disappoints the searcher. So he tells himself his romanticism is only a speck in a larger cosmic joke. In the final tally he is a fool. Doctor Vaz has no notion this longing for love is part of a system far more complex than his factory--and just as debilitating for the dilettante. Ironically, he has also never considered it the salvation of his species--just dangerous.

He pushes open the door to the night and sees the cautious faces of guards waiting for him. "They'll come through the loading platform. It's the obvious entry. Keep an eye out for anyone you don't know. There will be a series of attacks. When they approach, listen for their weapons. Do they jam like ours?" Dr. Joseph Vaz is back on task.

CHAPTER SEVENTEEN

Media reports declare that as a result of the Wall's breach, the legs of power have been cut out from beneath the Dirties--but no one says how that can be possible. The battles in southern Oregon are called skirmishes. Even as engineers and technicians dismantle equipment, load heavy lift transports, and drive trucks that rumble through Portland. The vehicles will be parked across the Columbia River and their drivers ferried back for more. On their last trip, the drivers will help destroy the city's infrastructure.

The news on the Dirties reflects despair, degradation, and inaction. The results of a failed attempt to breach the Wall. A minor collapse will be mentioned as an engineering failure--and the withdrawal associated with it--a brilliant strategic plan to draw the last of the starving Dirties into the open and then slam the door shut behind them. Other reports say "...Some of the starving cretins are inside the Wall perimeter, wandering about like a herd of crazed buffalo who occasionally rush the containment perimeter. Concerned soldiers stand ready to alleviate their suffering..."

Or: "...Relief supplies are being rushed to the Dirties."

Op-Ed commentary states: "The poor, sad humans will be

contained by the brave fighting men and women of the Wall for their own good, while keeping the safety net to protect civilization." In cafes and bake shops from Oregon to Alaska, the debate on how best to feed to Dirties is in full swing. A relief fund has been set up through Google. Other commentators declare: "... The demise of the Dirties is the inevitable result of disease, unclean water, and poor hygiene. California is just a few years away from being liberated, once the great die-off of the Dirties takes place." Court battles on who owns what part of California are now broadcast every evening.

Captain Amanda Feiss watches a Hercules swoop in low and release munitions killing troops and their machines to her right. She banks the chopper to survey the burning truck hulks and the thousands of bodies that lay scattered around them. The infrared scanner beeps a fifth time saying another set of Dirties has appeared on a hillside behind them. A set of three SWAT tanks approaches until WeatherEye reports the force to be well over ten thousand. She watches the tanks reverse. Then two of them explodes in flames.

"What the hell was that? We're losing tanks by the gross today," says her gunner.

"Not a single tanker has made it back to refuel. They've got saboteurs in the field and fire control in the hills," Lipps says.

A figure waves from the ground. A bright yellow triangle identifies the figure as a SWAT soldier. Amanda checks the signal to see if it is Ewalt's ID. It is not. Amanda swoops low so Ernst can kill any of the approaching Dirties and clear an escape path for the soldier. In the distance, the broke-back ruins of the Redding Wall still smolders up into the sky. It is 05:30 in the afternoon and her team has been in the battle since the breach at noon yesterday.

She speaks into her radio. "This is Warbird One. We have another set of bugs with broken wings. The transponder signal is weak and I doubt the satellites will pick it up. The location is thirty by thirty-one, my sector. I also confirm another two bugs squashed and thirty-eight-thousand dead. Hercules is in process. This latest force numbers somewhere over fifty-thousand and they are advancing quickly." She stops staring at the number, unsure it is correct. "That's incredible. Proceeding north after this fight to refuel."

"Roger that, Warbird. WeatherEye has confirmed your location. More hawks on the way. We will handle the chick."

Amanda blinks her chopper's lights to let the woman SWAT driver know that she has been seen. Then lowering the ship's nose, she sets the attack computer to kill humans on the hillside. "Lipps, check the far hillside for rockets; Ernst you handle the near side. We do this by the numbers. Fire first, then we'll talk." The death of her father has burned the last bit of humanity from her soul. Amanda Feiss has become a killing machine.

She banks the Rapier and begins flying fast and low, killing everything in the ravines so an inbound Hercules can stop this latest force from advancing through Weed. No one is bothering to seal the tunnels. There are a dozen roadways over the remains of the Wall. All day there have been dead tanks and crewmen. The tanks were never designed to fight on the flat plains. So the Dirties use ravines to wait for the tanks, springing up and killing them with multiple missiles. That tactic had been unheard of a year ago. She is impressed with the tactic of concentrating on the tanks and ignoring the helicopters. The losses are staggering for both sides. Though the loss of life doesn't seem to matter to the Dirties, so far as she can see. Amanda assumes Weed will be lost to the insurgents by the morning.

The gunship begins to rattle with the release of munitions as she banks the helicopter to allow for more effective fire. "We need to burn these bastards where they live," Lipps says. Amanda glances at him. Amazed he has lost his celebrated composure, she begins to fear the future.

Telemetry confirms another force has entered the valley. Amanda examines the readout. This group appears to be poorly armed so the gunships fire their weapons with amazing accuracy waiting for the Hercules to come up and destroy the main force. Surprisingly, the infrared says the numbers are staying at close to a thousand even as they methodically sweep death upon those in the valley. As she directs fire at a possible underground missile emplacements, she looks down noting the dark rutted ground. Erosion from the rain last night seems darker and deeper than it should be. At that moment, the computer blips and slows the chopper. The front window of the chopper displays four sets of two-foot wide tire tracks in the soft mud. "WeatherEye, this is Warbird One. I'm showing four--please confirm my number-- four ore trucks with entry paths in the valley. Location: Whisky X-ray- five at three. Paths converge from east and south. Do we show a kill on any new class eight trucks, my sector?"

"Negative on that Warbird One. Be advised a second Hercules will ETA in two-point-five minutes. We do have a report of Dirties burying trucks. That is unconfirmed. I repeat unconfirmed. Note that we've lost two Hercules this morning."

"Thanks, WeatherEye. Warbird One ascending." Amanda begins a quick scan from the valley. "Here we go." Amanda hates this new strategy of sticking their head up so they can ping the ground a few times to find the buried assets of the Dirties. The Rapier rises out of the valley in an easily predictable loop.

"Three-hundred feet, all clear. Four-hundred feet, all clear. Okay we're pinging."

Amanda waits, puzzled. *Could the Dirties have entered the valley, buried the trucks, then just retreated back? Waiting for what?*

The gunship loops but there is no attack. The wide flat fields lie blackened by battle. The majesty of Mount Shasta's cinder-cone profile dominates on the far side. Smoke from destroyed vehicles swirls with the winds. "I hate this place," she says to her copilot.

"Bad place," Lipps responds. "Too flat." They continue to

ascend. "Got 'em." The gunner loads the magnesium rounds. "Contact, three, four trucks, confirming launchers--plume! One, two, three, four, six. I got 'em, go. Captain, go left," Ernst calls out. The tracking computer displays the information.

"Flares out," Lipps calls. "Suppression on."

"Banking left. Returning fire. Missiles away."

Amanda watches the missiles from the Dirties to make sure their heat seeking ability has not improved. Two missiles fly off and crash onto the far hillside. "WeatherEye, this is Warbird One: tell the Hercules to hold. HUD telemetry coming to you now. Six Plumes, four trucks--all buried. They were waiting for the Hercules to get here. Now on the move. We could use some SWAT. Confirming these as the dug-in trucks with launchers. Trucks are now heading north at grid thirty by twenty. Should be clear for assault by the bugs in three-zero. They are running north for the cities."

A missile streaks past them and blows up in the middle of the three flares. Her gunner calls out: "Hill missile sites, two. No I don't know how we missed them. Plumes: Two, bank left. Returning fire." Two missiles sail past them. One missile just stops running and falls back to earth. The last loops over and comes back at them. Ernst fires as they drop more flares. The missile explodes fifty feet away, sending a chatter of metal against the skin of the gunship. "That was uncomfortable." The Rapier tosses. The engine quits.

"We have a fuel line breech and a hydraulic coupling that's just bled dry. Switching to auxiliary drive system. Negative," says Lipps. "WeatherEye, we have a problem. Warbird Two take CnC. No secondary power. Transponders on. Mayday. Mayday, Warbird One. Mayday."

Amanda puts the ship into position to auto-rotate to the ground. The blades pick up speed and slow their descent. Lipps and the gunner begin firing weapons. *They'll be useless as soon as they expend their stores. The point now is to get to the ground in one piece.* She feels the ship launch four air-to-ground missiles and kill two trucks. Miraculously, the secondary power system comes on line and the blades increase their speed. "What did you do?" She asks Lipps.

"Who cares? Who knows? Clean living? We're flying again." The chopper comes to a hover two hundred feet off the deck. They will be dead if another salvo of missiles comes up at them. "Ernst, will you please remove those hill launchers and those last trucks?"

"Yes, and...I've just...Right--taken out the last hillside launcher. Two trucks still heading north. I'm counting fifty or so scattering from the wreckage."

"WeatherEye this is Warbird One, Warbird Two will retain CnC. We've taken some damage and are running home on back up. We've tracking two of the trucks. Enemy hill launchers destroyed, repeat, but two enemy transport systems functional. Fifty plus in the weeds--send in the Hercules. Warbird Two, your turn, boys."

"Thanks for that, Warbird One. Warbird Two, on point. Out."

Amanda looks over to Lipps. "This is crazy. Where'd they get all these resources if they are staving to death? Let's find those bastards in the trucks and then go home."

"Yup, you're sane," Lipps says with a good-natured smile. A moment later they are flying over the interstate heading north. "There they are--on the freeway--at close to sixty."

Amanda sees the twin clouds of dust ahead. A pair of trucks motor up the roadway. "Smart bastards. How'd they know WeatherEye would ignore them because of the speed?"

"Captain we have Dirties. I am counting thirty," say Lipps. "Those bastards just popped out of the hillside."

"There are more now. They're distracting us from the trucks." Amanda calls out.

"I've ranged the trucks." Small arms fire pings off the sides of the chopper.

Lipps fires the rest of their air-to-ground missiles taking out the trucks in two bright yellow explosions. Ernst kills the soldiers.

"What the hell were they carrying? Sulphur?"

"Tom, shut down the speed-blades. We'll claim the secondary overheated on us."

Lipps shuts down the small blades that add so much speed. The helicopter jumps to the left. Then it starts to fall. "Tell WeatherEye we're having some problems," says Amanda.

"What are you doing?"

Amanda nods taking the gunship down in an erratic pattern that might suggest an engine malfunction--to any monitoring platform.

The chopper lands near the pile of smoldering bodies and the burning trucks. The smell of excrement, rotten eggs, and vomit fills the air. "Wait here," she says, unbuckling herself. Running over to three dead men who look like they crawled out of a sewer, she scans for survivors. There are none. The dead all wear similar multicolored rag pants and paper shirts.

A red object on the ground beside one man is exactly what she had been expecting to find. She picks it up, astounded at the truth. Flat, like a small pillow, it is Doctor Vaz's food. She breaks it in half. The red crust is harder than the interior which had a soft consistency like stew.

She takes a sniff. The food smells like a pepperoni pizza. *Dad said Dr. Vaz was dead. So that's it. It was so obvious. I wouldn't see it. Damn it. Why did you lie to me?* Hurt and astonished, she rifles through their pants. She finds four more of the little cakes. *White, red, and blue, just what he said he'd do.* She puts the cakes in her pocket and leaves the burning trucks. The smell of sulphur fills the air around it. *Now what the hell were they going to use that for--to try to blow up the Columbia Wall? Too dumb.*

"Lift off," she says climbing into the helicopter.

"What did you find?" Lipps asks.

"It was sulphur in the trucks."

"What the hell are those?"

"I said lift off."

Her copilot takes the helicopter up. Amanda stares straight ahead. "WeatherEye, Warbird One is on the way home. We are four by four. Warbird Two you remain CnC."

"And this is?" Lipps asks pointing to the Kandy.

"An unlimited food source."

"How do you know?" Lipps asks.

"I know."

"So the rumors are true," her copilot says. "They'll never starve." A cold chill rolls through his gut. "Amanda, my dear, I would conjecture our trust funds are in doubt. I'd say our posteriors are not so secure either."

CHAPTER EIGHTEEN

The night-rain has stopped in Portland. It is almost dawn. As the bus parks at the downtown bus terminal, a burst of moon breaks though the running clouds painting the ground a light blue. He marvels at the shiny new buses parked nose-in to the building. The outside of the building also glistens. Ewalt looks at the clock. *Five in the morning. Must be something big going on if they are making a show of the buses and cleaning the terminal.* He peers inside the station. Brightly lit from halogen lights taken from a local soccer park, a work crew paints the walls white.

Still tired from the drugs. The memories of Amanda Feiss and the numbness in his body, he doubts the reality of the bus terminal around him. Or that he is here in Portland. Then he leans over and feels a burst of pain from the wounds on his back, Ewalt settles into the now.

Two sets of side doors open with a hiss. Ewalt exits the front set and begins walking north toward his father's store--half hoping to not find him there. Following Broadway towards Burnside, sensing the streets are too quiet, he keeps to the shadows. The dark alleys and dirty gray buildings in this part of town provide perfect nests for an ambush or snipers. *Cities are the worst. Once they get inside, it's all over.* The fact that he has walked these same streets for years and knows every inch of them offers little consolation. Ewalt has been in battle for too long. He measures every situation in terms of its lethality. Seeing impotent street lamps, most of their mantels broken from rocks or bullets, he senses desperation in the city. Two months ago, the last time he was here. The lamps were functioning.

This morning, the squalid buildings of the old downtown huddle silent, the streets littered with packaging debris. As he walks, his eye catches the free-form neon designs from tall buildings reflected off shop windows. *The rich parts of town always glow.* In this neighborhood, wet newspapers choke the gutter where the building walls meet the roadway. When Ewalt was young, he used to like the way wet papers rounded the base of the buildings. Then one day he pulled them aside and found a dozen pink baby rats living in rotting pulp and excrement. That was the last time Ewalt remembers being disgusted.

At 18th Street, Ewalt stops. This is the same corner where he'd committed his first and only mugging. The victim was a man about forty, six inches taller than Ewalt and a good forty pounds heavier. Ewalt had chosen him because he thought it was fairer to mug a man who might be able to protect himself. The man froze at the sight of Ewalt's knife and gave him everything he had. Then he'd cried like a baby. Jack Porter had stood by and laughed. An arrest three days later led to enlistment.

Thinking about it, Ewalt realizes Jack was always in the shadows and again wonders why Jack has asked him to come up to visit him in Washington. Ewalt never spoke of Jack's involvement in the mugging.

Four more blocks and the carnage of broken street lamps miraculously ceases. The boarded-up windows are gone. Small shops, cafes, and clothing stores line Burnside Street--their precious contents guarded by steel framed mesh. Occasionally, a shuttered tofu bar or tea parlor breaks the monotony of insane cuteness.

Ewalt stops at a boutique window. The gowns and lace blouses all seem so soft to him. He cannot imagine a woman dressed in such finery. Seeing women in battle has irrevocably changed his opinion of the "weaker" sex. He doubts a long cherished belief that women exist for love; he now believes they exist for a man's lack of love.

Turning the corner he sees the church that Ewalt's father once said would save him. The twin spires still leans to the south. His dad always calls them the leaning towers of Portland. Ewalt hadn't understood the allusion until saw an old news report about a hungry mob tearing down the Leaning Tower of Pisa. Ewalt Rader was nineteen at the time and had been in battle for three months.

Walking by the church, Ewalt intentionally spits through bars at the stained glass windows. Ewalt believes churches teach passivity. A sin so far as he sees it. Footsteps come from down the street. A figure darts across the intersection in front of him. Yelling. It comes from where the runner had emerged. Rader ducks into the shadow of the church. A group of pursuers rush by carrying chrome telescoping batons. These self-defense batons had been handed out to the city last year so the citizens might protect themselves. Then when the authorities tried to retrieve the batons a month ago none came back. Ewalt still laughs at the absurdity of it all. The people running across the intersection disappear around a flat building with a chain link fence around it.

The mists begin again.

Running his hand along the metal fabric, he looks through the school yard to a circular glow of light over the wet street beyond. Ewalt heads toward the huge yellow bagel sign, slowly entering the brightness. Soaking in the rain, he stands at the window staring at a big man. Lester Rader wears a white tee shirt covering ape-hairy arms. An apron covers his wide chest. Tossing a tray of bagels into a rack, the man rubs his hands on the white pants. A jaunty chef's hat covers his brow. A set of small, shiny brass stars circle the brim making the big man look like a sultan of some sort. Embroidered in black across the hat is the moniker: "Moose."

Ewalt raps on the window.

Busy turning bagels by hand, Lester waves without looking up--indicating he isn't open yet--and goes back to turning bagels. Ewalt raps again. The man looks up angrily--then sees Ewalt. A huge grin breaks out beneath an absurd, pencil-thin black mustache. Lester grabs a towel, wipes his hands, and hurries to the front door. Ewalt notices his father has a long scar on his arm. It's a knife wound. A switch has been turned. Ewalt is now dangerous.

A set of six ancient locks turns and the door swings open. His father immediately embraces him, pinning Ewalt's arms to his sides. And although he could have easily pushed out of the bear hug, Ewalt does not. The one time he had, as a teen, his father had barely spoken to him for the rest of that day. Ewalt adores his father.

"Why didn't you tell me you were coming by? I would have met you at the bus station. You look okay. Your wounds have healed? Imagine it, getting burned by a missile. Man, how do you do it?" Laughing, his father steps back tilting his head slightly. "If I put another star on this hat my neck will break." He erupts into another short laugh, pulling Ewalt into the store and locking the door.

"How are you, dad?" Ewalt asks.

"My garlic bagels!" Lester hurries back behind the counter. "I'm fine, son."

Ewalt examines the store: Everything is bleach clean. The white counters still run along both side walls, then across the store. They still separate the customers from the baking area. They were supposed to have been removed for the trip to Washington. Ewalt also sees the tables remain bolted to the floor. His father was supposed to remove them as well so he could bring the tables north.

The glass front of the counter shows the bins are not yet full of bagels. Ewalt takes off his tie and leaves it on the metal chairs. He rolls up his sleeves and folds his blue blazer; there is work to be done. The scarred black and white tile floor is as clean as ever. Ewalt had mopped that floor for more than a decade. He hates it with a passion. The smell of eggs and onions washes over Ewalt and he closes his eyes, glad to be home. "You didn't remove anything yet," he says, looking up at the quiet fans.

"Nope, I got new everything. The store in Washington should be done this week."

Surprised, Ewalt watches his dad turn a row of egg bagels on the yard-square metal rack and put them into the proofing oven. The rolling metal rack of baskets is half-full of cooked bagels and bialies.

"There that's done," Lester says.

Ewalt watches his father wiping his arms. It seems to Ewalt his father has been using the same frayed towel--it once again hangs from the silver handle of the oven--forever.

"Aren't you tired?" His father asks. He reaches in the basket of bagels and tosses Ewalt a plain bagel.

Ewalt catches it coming around the counter. He lifts himself up; his legs dangling, just like when he was a kid. As Ewalt takes a bite of the bagel, Lester watches his son's expression. Ewalt nods as he chews, then holds up the bagel. "Still the best."

"I know," Lester says, turning to open one of the lower ovens to inspect some garlic bagels.

"So how come you're doing this alone? When are you moving? It was supposed to be yesterday. Where's Robert?" Ewalt says between bites.

The old man looks at him. "He got a draft notice. Can you believe that?"

"Robert?" Ewalt says with genuine amazement. "He was almost as deaf as you."

"Worse." Dad pulls out the rack of garlic bagels and places the tray in a cooling rack. "He ignored the draft notice. They came for him last week. His trial was supposed to be next week. But I guess with what's happening at the Wall...He's not coming back."

"What have you heard?"

Lester leans closer. "They said there was a breakthrough."

"There's always a breakthrough. Remember that's what I do?"

"I know." Ewalt's father places the pan in the oven then crosses over to the industrial mixer sitting on the floor. He pulls back the wet towel and stares in the huge dented mixing bowl. "The Wall, it's down in some places. They say it isn't, but my customers know. They say it's down and we are retreating across the river."

Ewalt considers what he has seen this morning and it now makes sense: another rumor. "You need to scoot out of here now."

"This is my last day, son. Your old man ain't no fool. But I can't find anyone who I trust who'll get up at four-thirty in the morning and make bagels while I am in up north. And those damn Californicators are paying janitors twice what I pay for a baker."

"Forget the store in Portland. You need to get out of here."

His dad looks up from the batch of dough. "Will you stay today and visit? I won't ask you to mop the floor."

"I can stay until this evening. Then Jack Porter has me on a flight to Everett. We're getting together at some hot-shit restaurant."

"What's he want?" Lester asks with a sneer.

"I think he wants to hire me for a job."

"Son, why don't you just move up to your mom's old farm? You can work with Jack. It's right near Everett. Then you can forget this mess here."

"You worry too much, dad. I thought you sold that place."

"Your mom's ghost would kill me. She wanted you to have it. In fact I hired a new man to manage it. A bright kid with crazy hair. You'd be a great farmer."

"You need a girl to do your thinking for you," Ewalt says with a smile.

"I do, a live-in girlfriend." His father winks. "She's packing up the house now." He points to the front of the store. Ewalt looks for a picture or some tell tale trinket "Did I tell you about the window?"

Ewalt wonders why the girlfriend situation has been so quickly passed over. "Screw the window. Tell me about your girl."

"Later. You can meet her after the quitting bell."

"You are a stubborn man." Ewalt looks at the plate glass windows. "So, what happened to the window?"

His father points to the one on the right. "Some kids busted it out and wrote 'Dirty Jew' on the other one."

Rader begins to laugh. "I keep telling you to hang that sign I made. The one that says: "I'm Greek, you dumb bastards.'"

The older man points to Ewalt, laughing. "I did. That's the point. I had it hanging in the window. They stole that too." The two of them laugh as his father begins scooping dough from the huge metal mixing bowl.

Ewalt hops off the counter. "You got some whites for me?" Ewalt grabs his coat and tie.

His father begins adding more flour to the mixer. "Stupid question. In your locker."

Ewalt walks through to the back and opens the locker. He hangs his clothes and puts on his whites, surprised to see a new steel door leading into the storeroom. After closing the locker door, he pulls on the new door. The overhead lights come on and he finds himself staring down a long narrow room. It is empty, painted white, and clean as a whistle. There is a new round door at the end. He walks back to his dad, tying his apron. "What's happened to the storeroom?"

"Civil Defense came by almost two months ago and paid me a ton of money so they could put that door in and take over the old storeroom."

"What's with the weird door at the end? Did they put a submarine down there?"

"The other end of that room leads down into one of the new shelters. They're putting some kind of air pumping system in. It should be done by Saturday, they say. Paid me enough so that I could get the window fixed, buy the new counters, tables, and get a baking system for the store up north."

"Keep an eye on them. They don't give you money for nothing," Ewalt says.

"I am not going to be here, remember, Einstein? Besides, I take what I can get from them."

"Oh that's where I learned that." The men begin to work.

By six-thirty, opening time, Ewalt's white apron and baggy white pants are covered in flour. He opens the front door and switches on the small rotating light over the doorway. The bell over the door tinkles within a minute and a young athletic-looking woman in a gray business suit enters the store.

"Hi, Moose, new man?" She says staring at the baskets of bagels and apparently ignoring Ewalt.

"Just for today. This is my son, Ewalt. This is Ms. Klein."

She smiles at him and quickly looks away. "An onion bagel with butter and a black dandelion tea, vente, with no whip--please." She places a white ceramic mug with a hinged lid on the counter for Lester to fill. The mug says: "Kiss the CPA."

Ewalt grabs a bagel, cuts it and butters it. His father fills the cup, snapping the lid down. Ewalt puts it all in a canvas bag that she has placed on the counter. She hands him the money and leaves without conversation. Rader watches her close the door before speaking. "What was that about? She walked in the door like an old time neighbor. Then it was all silence." Ewalt puts the coins into the drawer beneath counter.

"Suits, they are immigrants from Weed and Yreka. They're all over the place now. Or maybe she has the hots for you. Nah, never. You're too ugly." He grins. "You seen the old shopping mall?" His father wheels two carts of bagels over and dumps them into the last two empty hoppers under the counter.

"No, I came from the bus station." He hears the door open again.

"You should see it. It's a financial center. They're redoing the bowling alley that shut down also. Can I help you folks?"

A tall man and woman in matching sweats and silver baseball caps that says Feiss Corporation look at the bagels. "Two lemon bagels and two chamomile teas--ah--please."

Ewalt leans down looking for lemon bagels. When he cannot find them, he turns to his father and mouths, "lemon bagel?" His father points to a small bin behind the garlic bagels.

"I saw new neon lights from the new Pearl buildings on my way over here. Not the same old Portland. I guess nothing is the same," Ewalt says putting the bagels up on the counter. The couple snatch the bagels and tea ignoring him. "Put it on the corporate account, Moose."

They leave.

Ewalt hears the woman say: "You should have paid him." The door shuts.

Ewalt watches his father write out a bill to Feiss Corporation. "Do you really charge them sixteen dollars for two bagels and tea?"

"You bet your butt. They demand the lemon bagels. So I give it to them. They have more money than they know what to do with. Did you see their hats?"

"Yeah, I know Feiss. They make weapons I hear."

"Girlfriends too." He glances at his son briefly. "Feiss took over the old Red Mill site last month. They buy eight-dozen bagels a day, six days a week," his father says, slapping Ewalt on the back. "In fact their driver will be here in about fifteen minutes for pick-up. Go get some cold milk containers, son. We're running low."

Ewalt smiles at his dad, who seems happier than he has been in years. Curious about his dad's new girlfriend, he walks to the back door. Bags of flour and green-colored milk containers sit piled alongside the door. His father's security baton leans against the wall, in exactly the same place it had been two months ago.

The front door opens and a group of kids come in. Before they are gone, two more couples enter. Both couples are dressed in business suits. Ewalt begins to fill the milk containers settling into the tasks. *Now this is life*, he says to himself.

The sun touches the skyscrapers to the west. Ewalt locks the front door. Dad hands him a wire bin of leftover bagels. "Take these out back. They are waiting."

After unlocking the steel door in back, Ewalt places the excess bagels on the small plywood table beside the door Ten ragged men and women who had been leaning against the brick walls come forward. The alley smells like the Redding Wall: urine and vomit. The people each take one bagel. One eye on their selection--the other on Ewalt.

Ewalt locks the door, though not for fear of the men and women in the alley. They are grateful, not dangerous. Returning, he sees a man in a black duster inside the store. Ewalt knows he locked the front door. Looking around the back room for the baton, a cold chill rises in his gut. It's gone. From beside the oven, two men in black coats appear. "Surprise, no baton, hero." A fat man waves a large hunting knife. The other man giggles--jazzed on some drug. They push Ewalt into the front. "Now, open the drawer, pops." The man in the duster grins at Ewalt.

Lester sighs glancing at his son. He has no fear for his life. He just wants the mayhem to end as quickly as possible. "Don't make a mess, Ewalt." He opens the till as Ewalt measures the men. Eyes drifting over their faces, he notes their scraggly beards, the color of their eyes, scars, and the type of shoes they wear. These aren't Dirties. Ewalt will do nothing yet. This is just a robbery. There is too much chance his father might get hurt. The two men finish shoveling the money into a bag.

These men are going to try and buy their way to safety across the river.

The man in the duster takes the money and pushes Ewalt's dad, banging him against the mixer. A puff of air escapes his father's chest; but he quickly puts up his hand to keep Ewalt still. There is no need though, Ewalt already has a plan.

"Thanks Kike. Now you, chump, unlock the back door." After he does, the three leave the store without further incident.

"Son," Lester calls. Ewalt has already found the chrome baton. "Ewalt, it's not worth it," his father says. "I have insurance..."

Ewalt throws open the back door. The men and women who were still eating bagels freeze at the angry figure and drop their half-eaten bagels. "Where did they go?" They all point to their left.

Ewalt runs up the alley. As he runs, he twists the metal tube, telescoping it out to almost five feet and checking the charge. Locking it in place and releasing the charge safety, he sees the three criminals heading towards the grammar school. They are laughing.

"Hey, assholes," Rader yells. He lopes across the street. The three men turn to him.

"Oh please." They laugh derisively and spread out, producing their knives. "The baker boy is going to hurt us." Rader stops in front of them, the baton horizontal. "Hey look. He thinks he's a tough guy. Go away, Jew-boy, and live." The speaker is the man who had been standing in front during the robbery. Ewalt smiles. They begin slowly circling, spreading out around him.

"You garbage-eaters are about to have a bad day," Ewalt says.

The man in the middle, lets his coat fall to the ground. He wears a vest of body armor and he holds a sawed-off shotgun.

"Really?" Ewalt says.

Before the man can level the weapon, Ewalt lunges forward, hitting the man on the wrist with the tip of the baton. Even in the daylight, the arc of electricity is blinding. The man screams and drops the shotgun. Ewalt measures the other two assailants. They lunge from either side, surprised the baton is more than just a hunk of metal. Ewalt blocks the guy on the left by bringing his baton up into his neck, missing the fat man with it as he turns. Much faster than Ewalt expected, the fat man's knife slices into the underside of Ewalt's arm cutting his shirt and skin.

Ewalt responds with blind, brutal anger. He spins and kicks out, landing his boot toe in the crotch of the fat man. The blade that had come out from the boot cuts deeply into the fat man's crotch. Rader pirouettes, dragging the blade across the man's genitals and into his leg artery. Blood pours onto the roadway. The man howls in pain as he falls.

Ewalt drops low as the blade of the second man slices through the air. He slaps the man on either side of his head with the baton. Both hard shots strike the skull. The man collapses to the street, already dead. The man who had the shotgun tries to run away. But Ewalt tosses the baton. Sending the man face first to the concrete sidewalk, Ewalt jumps on him, grabbing the man's nose with his finger tips. Pulling back quickly, he rips the soft skin, raking the man's eyes with his fingernails. Now blind, the man screams. Ewalt turns him over. With one short jab into the man's throat, Ewalt collapses the brigand's windpipe. The man gags, then dies.

Ewalt stands. Walking over to the last man with the gored gonads, he grabs the man's neck pulling his head back at the same time. Everyone on the street hears the man's neck break. Reaching inside the robber's coat on the ground, he retrieves his father's money: nine-hundred-and-fifty-eight dollars. He grabs the baton and heads back to the store.

A crowd forms. The three brigands lying dead in the street are a diversion; however, the maniac who has killed them speaks death.

Ewalt notes his father's empty expression as he takes off Ewalt's apron and wraps it around the wound. "You're hurt. We'll call the police and get you fixed up. If they ask. You tell them we chased them from the store together."

Ewalt looks at his dad and laughs. Walking back into the store, they ignore the small crowd forming outside the bakery. No longer lost in the horror of what he's seen, Lester conducts Ewalt to the back room and concentrates on dressing his son's wound.

"Dad, we don't even bandage wounds like this," Ewalt says. Then like a drunk, his eyes glaze. His body shakes. He begins to sweat. A few seconds later, his eyes refocus on his father. He tries to speak, but cannot. Lester works on the wound, whistling a tune Ewalt has heard all his life. He does not know the name of the song and forgets to ask again about the tune. Ewalt believes the music is famous.

The police arrive. They stay for less then fifteen minutes taking information on the robbery and the resulting battle. Their final comment is that if Ewalt wants to do more good there is plenty of scum down by the river for him to kill. There will be no further investigation or questions. Ewalt asks if those three men are Dirties. Saying that he has heard something about a breach in the Wall. The men walk away without comment or acknowledging Ewalt's words.

"Ever since the Californians took over the police. It has been like that. Their view is if someone isn't a producer, they're crooks--and open to any form of vigilante activity. I've heard it said the only time someone gets into a court now is if both parties have a lawyer." Lester Rader examines the bandages once more.

"Why?"

"If only one has a lawyer it's a fait accompli they will win."

A few minutes later they lock the bakery and walk across the street. Ignoring swarms of flies snacking on the puddles of blood in the street, Ewalt's father wears that concerned expression Ewalt fears so much. There will be no more talk about the robbery or Ewalt's violence. Discussions like that lead these two men into an argument.

One of those arguments had been the reason Ewalt stayed in the service after his first tour of duty. Ironically, his father now blesses his son's violence. It keeps his son alive. Lester Rader has also given up trying to understand or eliminate his son's insane anger. He just wishes his son had more peace.

As they pass by the high school, he looks at the children playing baseball. *If they'd just leave him alone. It wouldn't matter. But somehow, they can sense what's in him. He is their executioner for crimes they really had no part in.*

"Dad, you have got to leave this city."

"I know, son. I know. We can talk more when we get home."

CHAPTER NINETEEN

As they walk in silence, Ewalt notices the stores are hauling merchandise from the shelves by the truckload. This morning when he walked by, it seemed normal. "What is everyone doing?" Ewalt says, finally breaking the quiet.

"I told you there is a breakthrough at the Wall. It's no rumor."

Ewalt looks down at his cell phone again for messages. There are none. *Why aren't they calling me up? Miller's death shouldn't matter. There's always drivers.* He finally wonders if this is Jack Porter's work. He knows it isn't Amanda Feiss' work. Ewalt considers phoning the base. He decides he will first get his Dad to the other side of the Columbia Wall. After that he'll meet with Jack and find out what he wants. Then he'll consider calling in--maybe. By the look of the box-mayhem lining a street, the expensive boutiques will be empty by tonight. He figures the city hasn't much time. Memories of Coeur d' Alene rise fresh in his thoughts.

"Dad, I am going to get you across the river today."

"I know, son. We've got the truck parked at the house now."

"You left the shop like you were coming back tomorrow."
Ewalt notices the big bookstore has workers scurrying around packing

books into boxes.

"I guess I just couldn't do anything else after forty years." Lester Rader smiles at his son. "I just don't know if I am going or not. I need to get her safe."

"She must be special." Ewalt nods, chewing on his lower lip as he had when was a child. When he realizes it, he immediately stops, and looks down the street. "If you stay here you'll be caught on this side of the Wall. You'll die."

"Everyone volunteers for extra work to help the guys and gals at the front. Did you see that new movie Cannibal Express? Bagels might make a difference. Are they really still eating each other in California?"

Ewalt shakes his head. "I don't know. I don't think so." He does not know what to say about the city's future and its people.

Along the side streets, trucks are being filled at an insane pace. Items dropped on the pavement are left for the scavengers. Old appliances, plastic toys and tiny boxes made of old printed circuit boards fill the gutters. The dark green circuit board boxes were the newest rage two months ago--among the young and wealthy--cages for crickets.

Lester speaks: "Most people get very little news about the battle. I know a pilot who says his duty is the most boring assignment there is. They fly out. Find some people building something, kill them. Then they fly back to their carrier. What about the new Wall?" His dad asks. "I hear they are still working on sections by Richland. Will it hold?"

"The old one didn't." Ewalt kicks a small pile of newspapers with his foot.

"The Columbia Wall will keep them out."

Ewalt shakes his head yes.

"So we're in trouble whether I stay here or not."

"You've got no problems once you get to the other side of the Wall." Whatever Jack Porter wants he will get. So long as he looks after Ewalt's dad. "I know what to do to keep you safe." His dad quiets. Ewalt waves his hand out of embarrassment. "Dad, we can't just roll over and die."

"They need food, son."

"Fine. Grow it on my mom's farm. Ship it south. Catapult it over the Columbia Wall. When they first get into a city they go crazy. You'd have to make it through the first six months--and you won't."

"I can go into the shelters. Or, look." His father points to a new set of buildings on the eastern hillside. "That's one of Feiss's new facilities. They employ five-hundred people there. And over there," he points to quiet smokestacks. "That will be a new industrial park for Lippman Industries. We're becoming quite a city. There is no way they will leave us to die."

"Sure, and our great economy will trickle down to the poor and hungry." Ewalt remembers saying that and meaning it, not to long ago.

They turn to enter a residential neighborhood along 21st Street. A street Ewalt has known all his life, it has never looked so clean. The long rows of attached apartments and freestanding homes are painted every color imaginable. Neatly tended vegetable gardens sit in front of every home. "See? I told you the old neighborhood would come back," his father says. They circle a small park, swings and a slide.

"You did indeed." Ewalt looks up at the gable-end roofs that line the street. After walking a bit more, they stop at the middle of the block by a deep blue house. "What are we doing here?"

"Do you ever hear from that pilot, Amanda?"

Ewalt smiles knowing his father still wants to be a grandfather. That isn't why Lester asked about Amanda Feiss. He knows she can keep his son safe.

"She was transferred. I haven't seen her in years."

"She was some catch, Walt. She was a real Feiss wasn't she?"

"That she was--a real Feiss. What are we doing on this topic in front of this house?"

"Because you are still lying to your old dad." Lester grins wearing one of his I-told-you-so grins. "Is there someone new?"

"There's always someone new."

Lester opens the gate looking at the wire-fenced front yard. Ewalt sees the unmistakable mark of his father's gardening: tall threads of aluminum foil, meant to protect the cherry trees. "Nice garden. Let me guess, you bought this house for cheap?"

"It was very cheap." His father laughs. "Okay so I am a lousy business guy. Look at the size of this garden. You know there's seed stock available all the time now. Every home around here has a garden. Last fall I went to the seed exchange in Lake Oswego. This year I'll get artichoke seed. It's good anywhere in the United States. I'm also number eight on the list for Asian Pears." Tomato plants line the walkway on either side. Lester leans over and picks a small bug off of a leaf. "Pretty nice, huh?"

Ewalt has been around destruction for so long that he finds himself uncomfortable with such a hopeful little garden. He finally blurts out, "I'm amazed. And it's so quiet. So where's the truck? We gotta' get the heck outta' Dodge. Now."

"Around back," his father says. He hurries up the slate walkway to the white door. The metal screen door has an "R" fixed in the scrollwork.

"Where in the name of Christmas did you get that?"

"I always wanted a screen door with my initial on it. Business is good. So I bought one at Macy's downtown last week. The door comes with us to Washington. You're in charge of that." They enter the living room. On one side is a long stairway. The hallway created by the stairs leads to a large country kitchen. A sliding glass door opens to a tiny side yard. His father's prize roses are in bright white bloom.

"You even brought over the roses."

"Want a beer?"

"A beer? How the heck can you afford beer? Are you spending my inheritance?" It is an old joke. Ewalt notices the inside of the home is bare. Only a few boxes remain by the kitchen door. He calms a bit. "Where'd you get the brew?"

"A man down the street makes it. We gave him some of my corn last year." He leans over melodramatically to his son. "We were planning on making some real hooch this year, vodka." He winks. "I'll get us a beer."

"We?" Ewalt follows his father down the hall into the kitchen. Light blue lace curtains hang over the window by the sink. Ewalt looks closer and sees unfamiliar pitchers and glasses in a wooden box. "Dad, we need to get going."

"Here you go," Lester says, handing his son a beer after screwing off the top. "And don't break the bottle, okay?" Ewalt takes the good-natured reference to his younger days in stride.

"Cheers, I'm happy things are so good." He drinks the cool bitter liquid scanning the area. The empty space where the refrigerator had been is sparkling clean.

"Dad," Ewalt says slowly, his curiosity getting the best of him. "Who's living here--with you?"

"Lester, who are you with?" A voice calls from upstairs. Ewalt watches his father blush.

"And you let her call you Lester, not Moose?" Ewalt teases, tilting his head to the side in mock reproach.

"Come down, Marcy. My son is here," Lester calls out. "He is here to help us move."

There is silence for a moment as his father sips his beer. Lester Rader looks up at the ceiling. As if he can see through it, he calls out again: "Did you hear me, I said come down. We need to get going." Then looking at Ewalt, he adds: "She's a little deaf." His father speaks softer. "Oh, and don't say anything about the robbery--or what happened--okay?"

Both men remember how a statement like that would have sent Ewalt storming from the house. "No problem." Ewalt drinks more beer. "Good stuff."

"Right?" Replies his dad.

The woman on the stairs calls to his father. Ewalt follows him, still holding the beer in his right hand. A heavy woman in a yellow and green dress over blue jeans appears at the bottom of the stairs. Her face is fleshy. Her eyes are a beautiful deep blue. Long blond hair hangs to her waist and there is something familiar about her, but Ewalt cannot place her.

"Ewalt," Lester says. "You remember Marcy Swift. She was your art teacher in grammar school."

He nods. "Mrs. Swift tried to have me expelled after she caught me selling glue to other students."

"So you and Mr. Porter burned my car in retaliation."

"No Ma'am." Then everyone laughs.

"Hello, Ewalt." She wears a soft grin on her face. "You're not still angry with me are you?"

Ewalt shakes his head. The woman he remembers had been thin and angry. Not the grandmotherly figure who stands so close to his father. "No. Of course not. But I was wondering if I might borrow your car?"

Gently putting her hand in Lester's hand, she looks down and spies a spot of blood on his shoes. "Well..." She pauses a moment. "I guess we need to be moving along?"

"Join us in a beer first," Lester says.

She shakes her hand back and forth. "No thanks. I'd like a hug." She is speaking directly to Ewalt.

He hands the bottle to his father and embraces her. Marcy glances at the freshly bandaged wound. It seems to her that one just like it had been there the last time she saw Ewalt, years ago. "How did you convince Lester to leave with me today? Your timing is great."

Ewalt nods. "I am not sure that I have convinced him."

The older man shakes his head back and forth. "If the driver from Feiss Industries is right the breakthrough just happened. There is no way they will get to Portland any time soon. I could stay and see what happens."

"Dad, if the Wall is down, they will send in saboteurs. They are probably already in the city. Plus the retreating forces will burn or destroy anything the Dirties can use. A bagel shop is a food facility. That makes it a target."

"But son, listen. That room they added in back is for some kind of gas system. To make sure the air is clean in the shelters. I hear the population of the city will be safe down there. They're going to gas the Dirties. If they get close."

"Dad, I have seen three cities give way to the insurgents. I don't know anything that keeps the population safe during the insanity that follows. I do know that unless you get your keester out of here some Dirty is going to throw you on the BBQ and have you for Sunday supper."

"Ewalt." Says the older woman.

"Sorry."

"Lester, if you stay. I stay." Her tone is firm. Ewalt believes she has now played the trump card and that she will win.

"Baloney, Marcy. You packed the truck. You packed it because you are going." Lester crosses his arms.

"I packed the truck," she says softly. "Because you are going. Now go get your stuff. If Ewalt thinks we're in danger we get going. Now." She turns without waiting for an answer. "My coat is upstairs. Your stuff is in the truck."

Ewalt watches his dad bite his lower lip. When he sees his son catch him, Lester breaks into a smile. "Damn."

Twenty minutes later, after Ewalt removes the new screen door, the three of them are climbing into the pickup that functions as the delivery truck for the bagel store. It's jammed with furniture and other items. Including a couch and chairs strapped to the roof. "How the hell did you get the couch up there?" Lester asks, starting the engine of the truck.

"Jessup and his son helped. I sold them the equipment in the bagel shop for his help--for his beer making." She watches Ewalt turn away and fears for friends who will stay in the city.

Lester is peeved. "So there was no choice for me?"

Marcy is silent.

The truck rolls along 21st until it enters the freeway bridge crossing the Willamette River. The lack of traffic confuses Ewalt and he fears the retreat is premature until they roll down the ramp onto US 5. Two SWATs sit on the road, fully armed. A nest of soldiers works the area adjusting wires for the explosives laid into the bridge. Ewalt checks for his ID.

The traffic remains light until they get to Hayden Island and the bridge into Washington. It is five o'clock in the evening and the lamps set up along the road force the drivers to squint and slow down even further. Red taillights begin their dance and the truck crawls forward to the checkpoint. "Dad, do you have the pass and the papers for transit?' Ewalt asks.

"In the safe."

Ewalt opens the ash tray and pulls out the pan. From a small compartment he grabs a wire. A panel drops near his legs. He reaches up and pulls out the paperwork. "Make sure you tell them that she is your assistant, not your lover," Ewalt says.

"I know." Lester guides the truck around the maze of concrete barriers. Ewalt lowers the window examining the soldiers and their emplacements. They are temporary; the soldiers haven't even bothered to tape the wires into place. "I hear they are going to destroy the 205 bridge and keep one of these spans open."

"How come you have such good intelligence?" Ewalt is impressed. The truck stops. They are two vehicles way from crossing the river.

"Those people from Feiss know everything that's going on. I make sure they get the bagels they want and they have no problem sharing their world with the poor baker. Who I now gather they pitied because I was about to be left to die. Imagine that SOB saying I should put the bill for the lemon bagels on the Feiss tab. Asshole." The older man tightens his jaw and Marcy touches his arm.

A soldier waves them forward. Ewalt's dad lowers the window and hands a soldier the papers. A second soldier comes around to Ewalt's side and asks for his papers. The moment he sees Ewalt's papers he levels his weapon at Ewalt. "Step out of the truck, Commander."

Surprised, Ewalt exits. A team of soldiers begins a thorough examination of the papers, the truck, its contents, and its passengers. "What's wrong, Corporal?" Ewalt asks.

"Commander, you're from the 54th?"

Ewalt nods.

"So far as I can tell you are the only tanker left alive from that unit."

Ewalt's eyes widen. "Check me out on the CPU. I was in the hospital at Chehalis. I am due back at the base tomorrow at 6 PM. And I have a transport leaving for Paine Field in an hour."

A Captain arrives with a canine escort. "Your base is no more, Commander. Luckily you have survived." He begins to examine the papers. Then he picks up a small portable computer and runs Ewalt's name through the system. A moment later he looks up shutting the laptop. "That's your dad, Commander? You're making sure he gets across?"

Ewalt nods. The soldiers have opened the back of the truck and are checking for other soldiers. "There's been a deserter problem? Is that what this is all about?"

The Captain ignores him and speaks into a cell communicator. He is getting confirmation on Ewalt's flight to Everett. A few seconds later he nods and hands the papers back to Ewalt. "You won't make your flight if you cross. There's another checkpoint on the other side of the river and processing takes a good two hours."

Ewalt glances at his dad, then the Captain and his dog.

"I'll be alright, son."

Ewalt looks back at the Captain. "Okay. I'll stay. I want to see them get across the river."

The Captain is already onto other items. "Let 'em go. And put this hot shot on the next jeep to the airport. He has a plane to catch."

Ewalt hugs his dad and Marcy, then watches them drive off across the old bridge. When they are out of sight he turns back to see the Captain waiting for him. "You've got pull, Commander. Normally, I am supposed to drag your ass back to the front as soon as your family leaves.   But...It seems your pass is irrevocable. How are you tied to Porter Industries?"

"Jack Porter is an old school friend."

The man looks around nervously. "This pass probably saved your life because the tanks aren't getting back. You just remember I paid attention to all this. I didn't have to. This whole retreat is a disaster." The Captain hands him a business card with his contact information. "I'll get you to the airport, Commander. Don't forget my help."

Ewalt nods, seeing a new world opening before him. *So that's what it is all about. When it gets real, the money doesn't matter. Pull does.*

CHAPTER TWENTY

In the bunk, her feet up against the cell wall, she feels like she is on a vacation. A parallelogram of sunlight from the window paints a grid on her stomach. The concrete floor smells of urine. The blue steel cot, the window, the door, and her excrement--there is nothing else. Amanda has no idea why she is here. Her Rapier hadn't been on the ground five minutes before she was escorted to the prison by four MPs, put in the cell, and left. Per standard procedure she was gassed the moment the cell door closed. She waits, placidly. Overall she finds the curious surroundings interesting--like a ride on a carnival.

She shivers again and wraps her arms around her chest, wondering why the people who run the prison will not give her a blanket. Another whiff of her urine invades her thoughts. Originally, Amanda hadn't minded the smell of the room. Then she realized why it stank. When she realized they had supplied her with a bucket for her excrement, she had just grinned. She knows the last laugh will be hers. *Mother will have a fit when he hears about this.*

Her stomach growls and the dryness in her mouth has cracked her lips. Amanda stares again at the bucket by the door, then to the loaf of bread next to it. A set of roaches scampers around it. The sounds of whimpering rolls down the hallway. A trio of captured insurgents, who have been tortured all day long, are returning to their cells. No one seems to know who engineered the collapse of the Wall. Everyone knows Portland will be lost soon. In the hours that Amanda has been in the stockade, the area outside has turned from a bike trail beside 205 into a roadway. Trucks and cars beep horns. The drivers curse each other. She has heard some gunshots. *Seems no one cares about Portland anymore. It's not going to be like San Francisco.*

California was a prize to be owned at the end of the war. When California is retaken--as everyone assumes it will be--there will be wealth for all. It is a place where no one wants more damage than absolutely necessary: to its main cities or infrastructure, while destroying the human population is paramount. There is money to be made and the less bombing and destruction, the less investment costs later. The sooner the Golden State is back under control, the sooner it will pay dividends. This had been one of the key arguments for falling behind the Redding Wall and regrouping. No one wanted to turn California into a wasteland of battle. Not so for Portland--it is a gateway and no more.

Interestingly, as of this evening, various fiefdoms inside the private sectors are arguing about how to destroy Portland, while a few of the participants suggest it is a bargaining chip with the Dirties to get back some of California. With the destruction of the Redding Wall, many argue for reconciliation with the government of Elena Etu, until they can get rid of her.

This is the main reason Amanda waits in the stockade; her mother attends these meetings and feels keeping Amanda in the dark about negotiations is best for all. Margrete Feiss doubts the powers behind the Wall will be able to control the California prize without Elena Etu's cooperation and so she is at this moment listening to discussions. Keeping silent about the connection between Feiss Industries and Elena Etu-- she worries the act of sabotage was also a statement of independence. Margrete Feiss watches the players arrange themselves as she tries to assess her daughter's anger at Elena Etu. Elena is, after all, a Feiss asset and needs to be protected, at all costs.

Her hold on California has kept Elena Etu alive so far, since the common wisdom holds that whomever controls California--will eventually control the rest of the planet. So Elena Etu could be a huge asset. Regardless, she secretly thanks Elena Etu for her betrayal. Margrete believes it is her time to run the show.

Even after losing an entire planet, the PO still do not recognize that corporate subjugation based solely on profits is a poison pill for the corporate state. Instilling greed kills every family structure--even for the families of the Patrician Order. So unfortunately for the Feiss dynasty, Amanda Feiss also believes she should run the show. As her mind drifts in the gassed cell, she plots her ascension as her mother plots her neutering.

Amanda wonders where Elena Etu is at this moment and if she

knows she is the walking dead. Her dad had said Elena was the key to finding peace. The key because Joe Vaz was supposedly murdered, having died in the defense of his Brazilian factory.

Amanda's strategy for ascension centers on the Corporate Council believing Joe Vaz is alive. Everyone knows he treasures her for saving his life. Finding him and killing Elena Etu means she gets control of the situation, not her mother. Amanda Feiss tells herself that her mother is not up to the task of running Feiss Industries. That makes getting down to San Francisco to find Dr. Vaz her path to success. To achieve her goal, she plans to lever her mother's ignorance, believing her mother will support actions to find and secure Elena Etu.

All I need is proof he is alive. From then on Vaz doesn't matter.

Amanda grins as she works up a plan to get down south and control the food of the Dirties. She remembers eleven years ago, sitting in on hearings regarding the options for national defense. As an expert witness on helicopter tactics--she was really there to explain how wonderfully the Rapier helicopter will perform. She had supported a negotiated peace against her father's wishes. Amanda believed even then that food was the key to peace. Others did as well. They therefore feared anyone who controlled the food of the Dirties.

Regardless, the factions of power had decided to pull back behind the Wall. So arguing peace was encouraged. It would allow the populace to focus on their jobs--while the elite prepared for the life to come. The hearings were also a sham because everyone started their testimony with the statement that the Wall would be impenetrable. Amanda Feiss had laughed at the absurdity of it all with her father over coffee. She loved sharing mastery of the puppets with him or watching the other power factions battle over the wrong information.

The best example of that was the Corporate Council's plan for the US military to be exclusively defense oriented for corporate interests. It was hidden under a ridiculous debate for rebuilding California. At that point, the Dirties were considered just bad neighbors. When the correct military alignment was finally agreed upon, the different corporate factions believed they had a way to divide up California-- upon the collapse of the Dirties. In the mean time, Feiss Industries continued to develop Elena Etu into an effective asset.

Amanda remains amazed at what the population believes from their sources. She should not have been. Their illusions are no more absurd than her own illusions. For example, she believes her father had needed her help but was too proud to ask. She also thinks he had become non-communicative because of his age. Amanda has little understanding of her father. He never communicated very much to her, except his wants.

Amanda's education, her friends, her vacations, they had all been manipulated. Learning experiences about the cold, greedy world, Amanda's work in the Senate and as a page in her college years- -ostensibly to train her up--had been intended to show her what happens when institutions became weak. "They sold themselves to the highest bidder, like a whore." Lucien Feiss's agenda had always been to demonstrate to Amanda how she needed to be tough. As well as how the corporate structure is the answer to the chaos of the Dirties-- not their cause. His desire to see Feiss Industries run the planet was sprinkled in every dinner conversation--and that Amanda was to be his heir--was unquestioned. Except by Margrete Feiss. And though her mother never spoke on the subject to Amanda, Margrete's wishes were ignored behind closed doors. Mr. and Mrs. Feiss had never been a team.

Even so, they taught Amanda everything they knew about the weakness of society, and the weakness of its citizens. In their opinion, power is gospel. Its use is everything a privileged, pretty, intelligent girl should know about the world. Luke Feiss was grooming Amanda to take over the world. Margrete agreed in principle but kept truth to herself. Although in the end, both parents believed it would be Amanda's turn--once they were finished with the planet.

When Amanda ran off to fight in the border war, Lucien hadn't been concerned. Amanda always appeared a bit too soft. And since he appreciated high spirits, and had already recognized Amanda's need to rebel. He didn't block her exit. Lucien Feiss had felt Amanda needed to see the seamier side of life to become mature. For Lucien and Margrete Feiss, sophistication equals ruthless.

With that maturity, Mr. and Mrs. Feiss felt Amanda might someday return prosperity to the planet. An activity the Feiss' family considers on par with sainthood. So when Amanda had recently told them of her intentions to stay in the military for the rest of her life, they made plans to have her pulled from her job once the Wall was breached.

That all changed when Lucien Feiss died. Margrete Feiss took over the reigns of the company and within hours countermanded any efforts to bring Amanda out of the battle. Margrete Feiss was tired of being number two and didn't need competition from her daughter.

Margrete Feiss is currently considering whether or not to have Amanda find Elena Etu and Joe Vaz. Her military advisors have described the plan as suicide. When the doors close behind her at the meetings, the military officers speak with longing for Lucien Feiss's megalomania. Margrete Feiss is a brutal, unreasonable person.

As Amanda listens to the traffic outside, she believes that her mother is too overwhelmed by events to retrieve her from the stockade. In fact, Margrete Feiss is on her way over having completed the first round of negotiations with the Corporate Council. Her mother has no idea Amanda is becoming rabid. She believes Amanda is in mourning for her father. Even so, Margrete Feiss knows she has an ambitious child and that she needs to be handled. As Margrete gets into her limousine, she has an assistant phone ahead to have the gas turned off in the cell.

A few minutes later, lying there on the cot, Amanda has begun to think about her dad and his death. The collapse of the Wall angers her; suddenly, she only cares about revenge. Amanda begins to question how her crew is doing, and if Cavanaugh has bought the story about her forcing Lipps into the landing. She curses the Colonel and knows her counter-charge of sexual harassment might slow Cavanaugh down until the family lawyers swing into action. *I should have been out of here by now. Mom just doesn't have Luke's savvy.*

Amanda wonders is something might have happened to her mother. A smile blooms. Then a concern about her mother's intentions creep into her consciousness. As if on cue, from down the long hallway, a lock clangs. The whimpering from tortured bodies stops as footsteps approach. Amanda immediately recognizes the clack of her mother's high heels. Her footsteps make the same sound on stone as they had on the marble hallway outside her room when she was young. The tapping of her cane confirms her presence. Partially out of embarrassment, and partially because she longs to feel the moment of release, Amanda ignores her cell door.

A buzzer sounds. The cell door opens. Colonel Cavanaugh eyes the bucket on the floor. Cavanaugh was against this imprisonment from the beginning. They need good pilots. He glances back at the tall stately woman dressed in a long camel hair coat and brightly colored scarf. Margrete Feiss's pretty, dark eyes take in the scene of her daughter lying on a metal bed--as well as the smell of urine. She brushes aside her white hair. "Please step aside," Margrete Feiss says politely. "I'd like to help my daughter out of your prison cell."

Amanda's mother steps through the door. Cavanaugh glances at the two men who stand behind her. Both are dressed in gray suits and both carry weapons. They appear only vaguely aware of Cavanaugh. "Come along, Scout," she says, approaching her with her right hand out. "You've had enough rest for now. We have work to do."

Amanda rolls to face her. "You took your time."

Mother speaks: "You should be more concerned about a fool arresting you for having the pluck to see what is going out there on the battlefield."

She brings her legs down to the floor and notices her mother staring at her hair. Amanda self-consciously brushes it flat, then takes her mother's soft, cold hand and rises from the cot.

"Why didn't you shoot the lout?"

Amanda stands, confused at the response. It doesn't make any sense to her. There were four MPs. Her mother glances at her excrement. A moment of embarrassment passes over Amanda Feiss and she forgets her mother's odd comment. Mother leans close to her daughter. "You're not well, Scout," she whispers. "Come along. We're leaving this place." Margrete Feiss helps her daughter exit the cell; her eyes appear to be those of a concerned parent. She speaks to Colonel Cavanaugh. "There was a crew on her ship. Are they in the same condition?" Chairperson Feiss walks her daughter down the narrow hallway.

Colonel Cavanaugh would have never allowed this aristocrat to be here--without strict orders to do so. The play is in full gear.

Cavanaugh follows. Knowing his part, he answers. "Yes, Ma'am, but I think--"

"I don't expect you to think, so don't. I want the needs of her crew seen too--immediately."

"Ah, yes, ma'am, but, their discovery was considered classified."

Chairperson Feiss stops and turns like a hawk protecting her chick. "Are you saying no to me?" Cavanaugh glares at her, clenching his one hand, and then just stares away. The two men in the suits shake their heads at what they see is the bravado of an old man.

"But."

"But what?" Only with this question did tones of real anger appear in her voice.

"They must attend a debriefing," Cavanaugh says boldly. "The food is considered classified." He grits his teeth telling himself to stay calm.

"I run things here, Colonel. You take care of her crew. Food, water, exercise, anything they want. And make sure they have toilets. Buckets are disgusting." Margrete Feiss turns to Amanda. "That okay?" Margrete's eyes narrow as she looks at her two assistants. The men are the picture of concern--but little else. They know this is all an act for Amanda Feiss's benefit. Margrete Feiss could care less about the crew. She just wants to make sure Cavanaugh knows the crew is to remain sequestered in the prison. Nonetheless, Margrete cannot resist another taunt. "You are even a poor warden." Margrete smiles. "Incompetents like you have made the military what it is today."

"Yes, Ma'am. The corporate influence is well known." He looks away, having recently been told the Corporate Council has decided there will be no need for military prisons--on the other side of the Columbia Wall.

Margrete Feiss scowls leading her daughter down the hallway. Amanda wraps her arms around herself to keep herself warm. One of Margrete Feiss's assistants strips off his jacket and puts it around her shoulders.

"Thank you, Hewlett." Mother arranges the jacket on her daughter's shoulders and continues walking. "Colonel, my daughter and I are going to have dinner and a little chat. If you have a problem with this then you may shoot at my car." She turns to the man who had given Amanda his coat. "Hewlett, stay here until I come back from dinner. Make sure the Colonel follows my orders. If he does anything else skin him alive."

Amanda shivers at the comment.

"Are you all right, dear? It is so damp down here," says her mother. "I know you should rest. But I need your advice. Is that okay?"

CHAPTER TWENTY ONE

After a dinner peppered with questions and pandering, Amanda exits the bistro on Hawthorne Street eyes narrow with anger. Fury builds with every breath as she walks along the street passing hooch-parlors, whack-doctors, and speed-merchants. At 39th, she stops, gazing at the light oil rainbows in puddles. *Just who does she think she is?* The absurdity of her question bypasses Amanda. Still stunned at being patronized, she continues walking, passing the old food market. At the chain link fence surrounding the Feiss parking lot, she salutes a soldier. He opens the six-foot wide gate for her and steps back.

Alongside the rest of the family vehicles in this lot, is her ancient Harley Hog. She pushes it forward from the rest of the motorcycles. Amanda hops on, jumping down on the manual starter at the same time. The engine rumbles to life. Putting on her helmet waiting for the bike to warm, Amanda tries to calm herself. *Regardless of the insults,* she tells herself, *I have gained my mother's support for a plan to infiltrate Elena Etu's world. Bitch.*

In the beginning, her mother had suggested Amanda forget battle and work inside the corporation. Amanda argued that she needed to get behind the Wall to find Elena Etu--to open a negotiation. By the salad course, she began to suspect her mother wanted to make sure that Amanda was no factor in the running of Feiss Industries. Then, after hearing that Elena Etu should meet an untimely accident once negotiations are complete, Amanda pushed harder for the infiltration. Sadly, Amanda, like many children, are blind to the Machiavellian ways of a parent.

Margrete Feiss has no plans to allow her daughter leverage by infiltrating and contacting Elena Etu or Dr. Vaz. Margrete Feiss wants someone else on that job--someone she can control. Still, she is glad that her daughter has taken the bait and has decided to go behind the Wall. To keep Amanda's anger on high, Margrete made sure to end the discussion with a jab at her relationship with Ewalt Rader. That was a tactical error. Amanda knows her mother had found Ewalt Rader an attractive man.

Amanda guns the Harley forward, displays her pass to the guard, then bolts off, tossing small pebbles in his face. The ancient machine roars down Hawthorne toward the Willamette River. Slowing by the restaurant, she sees her mother's car is gone. Amanda speeds downhill. Cold air sweeps under her helmet. It does little to cool the heat of her cheeks. So far as Amanda is concerned, tonight's dinner had been short and to the point: It was time to forget the myth of a loving family and attend to life. Scout is expendable.

Cursing her way down the roadway, Amanda also tells herself she has tested her power and fumbled it. Her mother didn't seem to care that much about Doctor Vaz's food. She didn't seem to care that much about the breach of the Wall or the Dirties overrunning what was left of their lands. She cared about the foie gras. Amanda missed the parry. Then there was: "Amanda, don't you realize we have nothing to worry about? Leadership isn't measured by service. It is measured by example. The better we take care of ourselves the better they will. We are an ideal. We are not their parents. Live well and take care of your own. That's all we can teach them. That's all our Lord says we are required to teach them. So we live a good life and hope that someday all humanity will live a good life. They just have to follow our example. Of course don't expect that to work with your Dr. Vaz. He is a fool." Margrete's knowing smile ratcheted Amanda's anger up a little more.

Amanda did try her best to deflect the comment, but her anger at having her plans obvious to her mother had been too much for her. "We need your strong leadership."

Margrete Feiss didn't keep smiling. There was something amiss in her daughter's response. She stared in silence at her daughter for a moment before she took a sip of tea. "Do take some extra crab with you, Scout. I am sure your crew will appreciate it. Perhaps one of them can go behind the Wall for us?"

"So you do want me to deal with Dr. Vaz and his food machine?" Amanda retorted displaying her wit while finishing her creme brulle. Her favorite food.

For just a moment a look of pity swept across her mother's face.

Then it was forever gone. "We need to be smart and decisive, Scout."

Amanda slows when she sees a hospital. She pulls into the parking lot. Hopping off the bike and entering the main door, Amanda approaches the admitting nurses.

Captain Feiss asks for the location of Commander Ewalt Rader, flashing her Feiss Industries security clearance. The nurse scans the computers and informs her that he has been released from Chehalis Hospital. He is now on a flight to Paine Field. Glancing at the clock, the nurse ends with a comment that he will be landing soon. Full of efficiency, the nurse also asks if Commander Rader should be detained.

Confused, but not stupid, Amanda replies in the negative and leaves. There is no sense in alerting Porter and his group that something is afoot. Especially since she believes Jack Porter has some plan up his sleeve involving Elena Etu. Hopping back on her bike, she wonders what Jack Porter might want for his support. The thought calms her and as she drives passed the dreary bars, and the brightly colored love parlors with their noisy barkers. She doesn't like Jack Porter but she considers how an alliance with Jack Porter and Ewalt might help her.

At the Hawthorne Bridge, she slows to show her ID to another guard. The guard waves Amanda through after a quick glance at the driver. Everyone knows her bright pink Harley. The bike motors across the bridge and heads south. Following the signs for the Sellwood Bridge, passing through the decrepit part of town, the stink from a paper factory turns her stomach sour. She glides by cardboard huts and plywood hovels. A tent city has spread out under the freeway ramp ahead of her. Amanda wonders how many of these people are refugees and how many are Dirties planning their assault on Portland. The bike roars under the OHSU tram.

Bright red lights flash from a sign over the roadway. It announces a checkpoint for a roadway entrance into Contractor's Alley. A heavily fortified two mile strip along 43. Much of the munitions and repair work for the Northwest had been handled here. Once considered the safest place on the west coast because of the air and ground forces protecting it. The facilities are mostly gutted, having been moved north of the Columbia Wall. Amanda wonders how long it will be before the Dirties assault the area. A steady stream of heavy trucks emerge from of the checkpoint, heading north.

A single marine stands at attention. Amanda rolls up to the twin bullet-shaped bunkers on the south lane of the split road. *The Marines are here and Border Patrol is out. That's not good.* A horizontal white pole connects the two bunkers, blocking the roadway. Amanda produces her ID and the Feiss Industries badge. The white-helmeted guard recognizes the name; and his peach fuzz cheek twitches uncontrollably. Amanda glances in the slit of the bunker behind him. A small green dot is lit in the center. She looks back at the guard, his hand shaking. Neither of them say anything. Amanda understands. A red dot is normal. A yellow dot means caution. A green dot says an attack is expected. "See ya'," she says.

The white pole lifts. She drives under it, pondering just how many eyes are on her. With all this danger, Amanda questions why her mother stayed on this side of the river to have dinner. Amanda believes courage is not her mother's strong suit--not knowing her mother attends a late night meeting with the Corporate Council. This one is to discuss the destruction of Portland. Amanda's mother has no idea just how dangerous Portland is this evening.

Soldiers and contractors guard the trucks up and down the road. Passing the low factories lining up one after the other on both sides of the road, Amanda speeds the bike forward as quickly as she dares. Ahead, dark brown and squat, the buildings are more like bunkers. The lights are on, so the second shift has not left yet. Battle scars mar the area. A few truck hulks and some recent blast craters pock the ground. Amanda wonders how they keep the remaining civilians working with this going on. The pay is good--but the end is clear. This is a dangerous time to get left behind. She considers the workers as brave for just a moment. Then she realizes they probably have no place to go--or they believe the myths they are fed about a guaranteed exit. *This compound is a myth and a prison.*

"Sheep. You're all sheep waiting to die," she screams out over her engine's roar. She has no idea she has done this.

Ahead, dark green and made to look like a log cabin, the Totem Mall waits. It once offered everything, including shops, schools, recreation, and a large helicopter pad for vacations to the coast or quick evacuations. The six huge totem poles outside the mall, actually sniper towers, are fully manned. The locals call it Fort Apache; because in effect, it is the last refuge for the staff and their families. The Totem Mall is supposed to be unassailable. That is also myth. Built by the Feiss subsidiary, Tenark, after the retreat from California, the mall currently houses almost five hundred women and their children. The central shopping mall's lights are all extinguished as those inside wait for the next evacuation bus.

A pink and white striped bus pulls up at the mall exit. The armor-plated vehicle sports a yellow happy face where its license is supposed to be. No one exits or gets on the bus. It pulls away, empty.

Because of its protection and because of their desire to be lied to they wait to die. I guess a mall is the perfect place to hide from the truth. It'll make gassing them easier too. Who needs soldiers when the meek are so easily led to their demise in a shopping mall? Why don't they know the important people have already left the building?

Ahead of her, a large supply area by the river appears shuttered. Most of the supplies, including six of the twelve tunneling machines that had been used to make the large munitions complex under the amusement park and river are gone. Slowing to look at the remaining tunneling machines, she notices that on these machines, their flat drill-chuck fronts are gone. The tanks stationed on the ends of the row take an interest in her. Weapons slowly rotating towards her, the men and women in the SWATs have one job: Guard the machines and if necessary, destroy them if anyone attempts to move them without triple confirmed authorization. The mistakes in California that had given the Dirties sixteen mining machines will not be repeated here. As she scoots through the exit gate, the guns of the tanks follow her off the reservation.

Ahead, thick forests of fir and alder line the right side of the roadway. Across the river on her left, the displays of Oaks Park grace the river. She smirks seeing the park so well lit. *It's all a show.* The amusement park's lights blaze skyward. Painting the brown wash of the river in reds and yellow, the park hides the Lippman munitions facility beneath it. She downshifts making the left turn across the Sellwood Bridge. A tightness in her chest begins to grow. "Never complain," over and over, the words rattle in her head. She hasn't felt that tightness for years. A psychoanalyst had once said it was resentment of her mother. Amanda smiles wryly. *And the shrink didn't know the bitch wants me dead.*

Midway across the span, Amanda cranks the throttle once, sending a roar across the river and up the forested hillsides. Amanda, at one time, had genuinely loved the woods and would pontificate for hours against the incessant cutting of timbered lands. Today, the forests seem to be nothing more than pieces in a chess game. Her family holds the claim to all the timber tracts in the Sierra. That lobbying effort had cost billions.

The pain in her chest intensifies. Amanda decides it is fear. Fear that her mother wants her dead. Fear that she is losing control. At that moment, her mother's power seems unassailable. Amanda feels herself sinking back into her mother's words: "There is nothing anyone can do to you--except kill you. Your father's worries are over. He is free. Stop endangering your life on the little battles of morality and ideals. They are chew toys for lower class. Fight the big battles. You can either be a pawn or a queen in this world, Scout. Work with me. Don't fight me." Amanda also remembers her mother's cold hand on her cheek. "We've shown them the way. They messed it all up. Not us."

They messed up? How foolish. Did she arrange to have dad killed? With that thought, her tasks take on a perverse sweetness. Like a honeysuckle has released its odor to the winds. *The world is filled with evil.* Amanda knows the life she wants.

After crossing the bridge, she turns right down a grade. It is access to an entrance of the armaments factory. All the portals for the facility are disguised as docks, rest rooms, or cheap storefronts. And while the Lippman company is careful about its security arrangements, they are unaware that foreign observers have been watching the facility for hours, cataloging each entrance. New at the task--the observers discount a single motorcycle approaching an entrance. Their attack is on schedule.

CHAPTER TWENTY TWO

Amanda steers the motorcycle across the intersection of a rail line and the roadway. Large lights blink green. There is no train nearby--mostly because there are no functioning locomotives on this side of the Columbia River. Amanda slows further, scanning the area around her. The road dips before swinging to the right into Shoreline Park. She approaches the docks that extend into the water and sees another green dot on the top of a rest room building. This means snipers are on the hillsides and they have orders to shoot at anyone not obeying the signs. She does not know the snipers are dead.

Circling around an abandoned office building, recently scarred from a skirmish, smoke lingering in the scars, she slows further. *That's new.* The smell of blood fills the air. From the look of the blasted trees near the park there was a battle here not too long ago. She notes that the blast pattern suggests another random attack and that calms her a bit.

Amanda scans the huge four-lane bridge that dominates the view to her left. The red lights of its communications towers are dark and she wonders why the explosives engineers are working in the reflected light. To her right the amusement park is filled with people enjoying the night giving them plenty of illumination. She watches the huge Ferris wheel spin and the large roller coaster toss happy people about in their seats.

On the hillside, across the river, the darkened woods surprise her. Usually there are campers out there on warm summer nights like this. She decides things couldn't be more dangerous. Amanda needs to get equipment for the drop behind the Wall and then skedaddle out of here.

Ahead, two guards stand by a guard shed. Once disguised as a gift shop building, the piles of sandbags in front of it have been the source of many questions today. Behind the shed, six docks run perpendicular to the pier. Midway along each of the six docks are blue bathroom buildings. Four of these are egress to the factory located beneath the Willamette and the amusement park.

The soldiers are dressed in full battle gear. Amanda stops just in front, shuts off the bike, and gets off it. To her right she can see the lights of Portland.

A guard walks up to her looking about. Her small mouth seems barely able to contain her large white teeth; her name is Sally. Amanda had gotten her this cushy job. In return, she always makes sure that Amanda has access to the factory whenever she needs something. "You missed it, Captain Feiss. We're too close to the end of second shift. You'll have to wait until the crews come out."

"Okay."

The Willamette Marina tethered to the park seems quiescent. Its quays are filled with sailboats and a few of the new Sun Racers that use high tech water boiling systems for propulsion. The boats all bob in the water with a deceptive tranquility. Amanda checks her watch. Mobs of people suddenly emerge from the four exits disguised as bathrooms. Passing her, they filter into the park, which has just started its nightly fireworks display. Within seconds, the hundred or so remaining workers that had come up the elevators are in the park. The third shift has been cancelled. "I'll just park this." She begins to move her bike, steadying it on the kickstand.

Because of the fireworks, Amanda doesn't hear the first barrage of rockets. When she looks up, geysers of water shoot into the air. Buildings, boats, and dock sections explode in a curtain of yellow sparks. *That's what the sulfur was for.* The guard's shack beside her shatters, sending shards of corrugated metal everywhere. One piece hits Amanda's helmet knocking her backward. The Harley falls over on its side like a wounded beast. Amanda lands on the metal grid of the dock, her hand slapping hard against the armless torso of the guard. She turns, seeing the lifeless body and screams.

Hoarse-sounding horns begins bellowing as a second and a third fusillade of explosions rock the floating platforms. Rockets begin landing in the amusement park pushing the crowd away from the factory entrances amid screams of panic. New blasts are so close they bounce Amanda around, showering her with bits of concrete and hot metal. She slowly regains her wits in the glow of explosions and the chorus of screams. Crawling over to a tussle of sandbags for shelter, the second guard pops up and drags Amanda over the top and into the revetment of bags. "Where's Sally? Did you see her?"

"She's dead," Amanda replies.

A set of blasts rock the four lane bridge and Amanda tries to burrow under the sand bags.

"We need to--"

A second set of explosions run down the Sellwood Bridge like a parade. Amanda looks up as two lanes drop into the river, swamping them in a huge wave and drenching them in smelly brown water. They can't sink us," the soldier speaks again. "You stay here and use this if you need to. The guard hands Amanda a machine gun and tries to stand, but flops back down. Surprised that her foot is almost severed, she blanches white.

"You're torn up," Amanda says, her head clearing.

Another set of explosions rock the bridge. The top of a support tower tumbles into the water beside them. More wash and waves toss them back and forth. Amanda peeks over the sandbags and sees three of the elevator buildings and two of the wooden docks burn. "The Dirties are targeting the elevators too." Amanda sees the Ferris Wheel collapse into a crowd of people. Families scurry away diving into the water. "It always comes down to us flyers covering your ass, Bordo. How do we seal the factory?" Amanda asks, sinking back below the sandbags. "And where the hell is perimeter defense and the snipers?"

"If they get passed us and get inside the facility we lose the factory. Word is, the factory can hold out for six days, if it is locked down. By then the Dirties could be here," the soldier says, her teeth covered with pink froth. "Why are there so many damn screw-ups?"

The crackling of gunfire makes Amanda turn round. Her bike is hit by a round. The tires burn ferociously sending up thick black clouds of smoke. "The burning tires will give me cover," Amanda says. "What do I need to do?" Then, trying to get a better view of what is happening by peering over the sand bags, she receives a bullet along the top of her shoulder that rips open her shirt and skin. "Damn this," she screams ducking behind the sand bags. "When did those bastards get so good?"

"Captain, I think they took out our snipers and put their own in. You gotta' get to the poles out there. The old telephone boxes that are on the main pier." She points behind them.

"Those phone boxes that hang off the poles?"

"Yup. Just tear any of them from the pole. They were armed this morning. It will isolate the factory below until the cavalry gets here."

Amanda scans the area as bullets zip through the air.

"They don't know how many of us are left. But they're not going to wait that long to find out," says the guard.

"There's two phone poles. Which one?"

"Either one. Rip the phone off the pole. It'll also destroy a small section of pier between us and the land. That will keep the Dirties from getting to us. Here take my Mac, too." She hands Amanda her machine pistol. "I'll try and give you cover. Where the fuck are those damned choppers?" She glances at Amanda a moment.

"God-damned right," Amanda says with a smile. Small arms fire comes everywhere now. Machine gun fire rakes the sandbags in front of them. Mortar fire concentrates on the roadway and the Sellwood Bridge to keep ground reinforcements away. Across the river, a SWAT goes up in flames. Another set of Dirties are firing into the park. Others are in the residential area on the hillsides causing panic. "They're up in the hills around us," the guard moans. "Wait until the wind blows the smoke back over us. It's your best shot."

Amanda surveys the two hundred-yard pier and the docks. It is a perfect killing zone except for the guard rails and metal light poles. "Here they come." Dirties begin descending from the hills while others repel down from the bridge. "Well that explains why they didn't destroy the rest of the bridge. They have weakened it enough to keep tanks off of it; but not enough to collapse it. How'd they get so damn smart?"

"Look," the guard says.

Amanda turns toward the water. A small craft is speeding towards the marina crowded with ragged men and women. A solid stream of bullets rake the guard shack.

A single small helicopter dives out of the sky towards the boat. It had been on reconnaissance; but it begins attacking the boat with its single pair of machine guns anyway. The attack connects and the boat explodes. A moment later a missile streaks up from the bridge. The blast destroys the helicopter, killing its pilot, Mr. Tubbs. In concert, explosions begin to boom from the surrounding hills.

"Those are our Rapiers," Amanda says looking for the tank support. She jumps to her feet running down the ramp to the docks. Bullets whine around her as the roadway boils up small eruptions from bullets. She dives for cover. Rapiers begin obliterating life on the hillsides.

The men repelling down the bridge see her. A man lands giving his comrades cover from the very pole Amanda has to get to. Amanda remains still until the other men are just upon her. Then, rolling to her right, she sprays the men with a hail of bullets, almost cutting the first two in half. The guy at the pole gets off a few wild rounds as Amanda continues firing. She catches him in the shoulder with a round. It spins him off the bridge and into the water.

Another twenty yards to the pole. More Dirties repel from the bridge firing at her. Amanda tucks herself into the corner between the roadway and the low guard rail. She waits a moment. Reloads. Gathers her strength. Then fires a burst. She misses. A man landing on the dock returns fire. She fires again, rolling to the center of the road. The man jumps for cover, firing at where she had been. Amanda gets him with another burst, hitting the man in the face. It sends his head back and his feet forward. His weapon clatters to the ground. She kills the others with a short burst from her other weapon. A set of insurgents repel from the bridge as another set of soldiers provide cover fire from the bridge.

When she sees a team of Dirties rolling down the hill in a pair of armored delivery trucks, Amanda runs toward the pole. A SWAT that has rolled in from the park, fires missiles at them, but misses. Amanda dives for cover then pushes on the small hard spot beneath her ear. Her satellite transponder will hopefully identify her and hopefully keep the tankers and others from killing her.

Whoomp! The SWAT goes up in flames. Amanda looks around for the launch location. A spindly helicopter scoots up over the hill, running south. *They've got flight too?*

Gunships continue arriving, tearing up the hillsides. In spite of their withering fire, hundreds of Dirties advance down the hillsides. Without the SWAT, the Rapier is half of a weapons system.

If they get in the facility there will be no stopping them at the river. The first armored delivery truck rolls into and over the wounded guard, crashing into the guard shed. Men and women tumble from the truck heading directly towards Amanda. *They're heading to the telephone pole to keep me away from it. They trying defend it. They know what it does.* Amanda gets to her feet and runs to the pole in a footrace with approaching insurgents. With a lunge, she yanks the phone from the single cable that holds it. A second later, a set of explosions begins to march toward her from the shore in rapid succession. The Dirties turn in horror as the bridge explodes, enveloping them in the hell of burning metal. The other armored truck races ahead of the explosions, rolling towards her. Behind it, the remaining Dirties follow firing all their weapons.

Bullets begin to ping and whiz by her from all angles. Amanda fires back. Useless against the armored truck, her weapon quickly coughs empty. The trucks slows and ten of the Dirties rush round it coming towards her. Amanda dives forward and grabs a weapon. It fires once, missing all the targets, then jams. Amanda curses, then looks up expecting a bullet in the face. The armored car explodes. The men stop, staring at her as if they had been dipped in ice.

Now what the hell is this?

Then she hears the whop, whop of helicopter blades and glances behind her. Three gunships hover twenty feet above the river. Tom flies her chopper. Anger owns him.

The Dirties scream and begins to charge. Amanda drops to the grate as a typhoon of munitions burst forth from the three helicopters. Seconds later only blood, torn flesh, and bits of bone can be seen. The other two Rapiers rise to begin sweeping back up the hill killing anyone they see. Lipps lands the ship a few feet behind her.

Ernst unbuckles and jumps from the chopper. "Wow you are a maniac. You're hit."

"Just a couple of fat wounds on my thigh and shoulder."

Ernst begins to laugh. "Then I suppose that chunk of metal

sticking out of your helmet is decoration."

Amanda pulls off her motorcycle helmet. A bright silver piece of the guard shed about six inches square, sticks out of the side like a single deformed wing. *That explains why they kept pausing when they saw me.* She looks inside her helmet. Just the tip had penetrated, but it hadn't even scratched the scalp. She holds the helmet up and waves it back and forth. Lipps shakes his head.

"You're one lucky fucker...Captain. Come on," Ernst says, putting his arm around her.

"No. I need to wait here," she says stubbornly.

"We need to get you somewhere safe," he says.

"What the hell are you doing here anyway? You were in a prison cell the last time I saw you."

"We were called up in an alert," Ernst says pointing across the river. "Seems someone thought this was a diversion and the hospital on the hill was the real target."

Amanda tries to focus on the hospital battle. "Seems like two coordinated attacks."

"And do you think that shocked the powers that be? Command is in chaos. So Cavanaugh got us out. I think your mom pissed him off."

"She pisses me off also--and so do you. Come on, Crackers, let's go clean up those hills. I can't get into the hospital if it is under attack."

"Yes, Ma'am," he replies giving a thumbs up to Lipps. Amanda looks around at the remains of the amusement park. Her eyes glaze over. "It's going to take me ten lifetimes to pay for those dock sections I destroyed," Amanda says going into shock.

"They're cheap--should only take a rich fucker like you one lifetime," Ernst grabs her as she begins to tumble. "But don't worry, they're not getting the billing right these days. Captain, please sit down."

"Stop it. I've got work to do," Amanda says. She collapses.

Ernst rolls her over his shoulder and carries her to the gunship.

Thomas Jefferson Lippman opens the door pulling her into her seat. "Damn hero," he mumbles.

CHAPTER TWENTY THREE

The remains of Oaks Park smolder in wisps of windy smoke curling up, then disappearing into the dark sky. Amanda sits on the dock watching the firefighters retrieve a hose from the river. Navy boats crisscross the lake guarding the two remaining entrances to the munitions plant. Explosives teams continue their task of wiring the facility for destruction. A dozen barges have lined up; the munitions factory is almost empty of anything worthwhile to the enemy. Her leg and shoulder are sutured. Her head is bandaged. Groggy, an island of drugged tranquility in the bustle of activity, she watches explosions continually erupt near the hospital on the hillside. The bridge remains standing though two of the four lanes are in the river.

Amanda wonders why a guard stands near her. His weapon at the ready, occasionally glancing at her, but saying nothing. He wears a Border Patrol uniform. From the small jagged "W" on his collar she knows he is from Security. There will be no point in asking him anything. Her head hurts from watching the choppers move around like angry hornets firing their cannons or launching rockets. The number of insurgents involved in the attack on the hospital is close to a thousand. Of that number, almost half are the angry residents of Portland. The alarms for herding the population into the Portland shelters are scheduled for tomorrow night

A figure in a dark blue suit emerges from one of the two functioning elevators. She searches the area then stops one of the soldiers pointing to the motorcycle slung across the back of a wrecker. Margrete's white hair blows across her eyes. The guard shakes his head. Speaking into a walkie-talkie, he quickly points to Amanda. Margrete Feiss waves at her daughter. Through the smoke Amanda sees her mother's shoulders fall in relief. Mom strides towards her. Amanda is confused by her apparent caring. Mother's attention is riveted on her wounds.

Amanda speaks to her as she approaches. Slurring her words: "I'm fine, just fat-wounds."

"Can I do anything?" Her mother looks deep into her daughter's eyes. "How did you know this was going to happen? I should have never let you leave the restaurant so angry. What were you doing here?"

Amanda grimaces. "I came by to get supplies for the incursion to the other side of the Wall." She shakes her head. "Getting tired of rescuing me?"

"No. Why are you out here in the night? Guard." She turns to the soldier. "Why is this wounded soldier out in the weather?" The man shrugs his shoulders, ignoring her. He obviously doesn't know Margrete Feiss.

Amanda giggles at how much trouble this trooper has just gotten himself into. Mother turns back to Amanda, her eyes blazing with anger. "How did you get hurt? How did they get all the way up here without us detecting them? They're still attacking the hospital." A set of explosions startle her. "My goodness. This is becoming a mess." Trees burn across the river. Staring at them, Margrete Feiss says, "I wasn't quite sure I could agree with this plan of yours before."

"They're closing tunnels on this side of the Wall before we find them. They are filling them with supplies. Then they bring saboteurs though during a fire fight. God knows how long they have been doing this," Amanda says.

"Looks like you need some rest." Her mother looks around the docks at the damage. "Scout, I swear we had no idea they were so well organized."

"They attacked from the hills. A second group came in on boats. A third group came down from the bridge--from both sides." She leans in. "I saw a helicopter. It wasn't one of ours."

Her mother sighs. "That's bad."

"The Dirties had exquisite fire control."

"They were trying to take over the factory, I understand that. But why the hospital? How could they hope to hold it?"

"They need medical supplies," Amanda says.

Her mother nods. "They will never get them." She starts moving Amanda towards the shore, ignoring the guard. The guard begins talking into his communicator. "We've set up a battle line at

Salem. There is a problem with the Rapiers and the tanks--some kind of hose issue. I swear I just don't understand why the lower classes are so unreliable. Regardless, we will hold them at Salem using the hospital tower or some other tall building for fire control. The Columbia Wall is secure. But there is a lot of equipment to move. I just came from the Wall. It'll be a patchwork. We will have full fire control by the morning," her mother says distractedly--watching a helicopter fire a missile into the far hillside. "Did you know there have been two attacks on the Wall so far. Some crazy lunatic spray-painted the words, 'The Dirties', on it. They are just animals, defacing everything. I don't see how we can help them."

An officer approaches them and salutes. He sees Margrete Feiss, casts an angry glance at the guard, then speaks to Amanda "Ah, Captain Feiss, your presence is required over there. Ms. Feiss you are of course welcome to join her." He points to a tent set up by the dance pavilion. "Debriefing."

"Who is in charge over there, Lieutenant?" Margrete asks.

"Ma'am, I don't know." He glances at Amanda, then back to her mother.

"I asked who is in there?"

"There's a General from Wall Security, Ms. Feiss."

"Thank you. We will attend in a moment." The man stands still.

"I said: Thank you." Margrete says firmly. He takes his leave and walks over to the guard. The point of the officer's finger means death for the young guard. He will be a corpse by the end of the week.

"They've got enough food. Your Doctor Vaz is as big a problem as your Dad said he might be. We need to control him and Ms. Etu." She slips an arm around Amanda's waist helping her stand. "We plan to do something about Doctor Vaz right away. You know I never agreed with your father's plans for him. I liked the man. Now though, after this--we need to forget the pleasantries. If they have helicopters they will eventually breach the Columbia Wall. We can't let that happen."

"Of course you are right, mother." Amanda thinks to herself: *What a mess. Luke would have never let it get this far.*

"So you are still game to cross the Wall?"

Amanda nods, thinking she has won. "I'll need a couple of days to assemble a team and then we will handle those on the other side of the Wall." Seeing her mother smile Amanda realizes this was her plan all along. Then, despite the drugs, her neck feels prickly. That sixth sense Amanda has developed in battle says it is a trap. She stares at her mother, sure of her sense of danger.

"Is something hurting you, Scout? Come on. We are going home for a rest."

CHAPTER TWENTY FOUR

From takeoff on, the plane has bounced Ewalt around like a toy. So wedging himself between the blue-black coffins (SWAT), and the pewter-colored coffins (Wall Security), he grabs the webbing and holds on. There are more dead than alive on the plane and he doesn't want to add to the number as a victim of some pilot error.

Soon, the only two not sleeping--on, or in coffins--are a skinny Captain and Ewalt. The Captain is a Feiss operative keeping an eye on Ewalt. The plane's large cargo bay is jammed with others in recline--both animate and not.

Approaching Seattle, the flight steadies, and Ewalt begins to peel the wood away from an alder branch with his pocket knife.

By the time the plane lands at Paine Field crescent bits of wood litter the floor. "What are you making, Commander? Is it a sailboat?" Asks the skinny Captain who sits across the wide center aisle. His arm is in a sling and he wears a purple heart on his chest. He looks like he is going home. The inquiries about Ewalt's carving are the first words the man has spoken during the flight. The two have been sitting across from each other for almost an hour.

"Just cuttin' wood," Ewalt replies.

"On your way home--or to see some friends?"

"No, sir, just some free time." Ewalt drops the piece of wood to the floor and folds the knife. Pushing himself forward off the casket, he walks to the rear door. Ewalt is no fool. He isn't in uniform.

He waits there as the plane taxies to a stop. The pilot lowers the ramp into the puddles pelted by a hard rain. The bright lights from Paine Field dart this way and that, sparking from the brass handles of the officers' caskets. He walks down the ramp watching the bounce of raindrops off puddles and personnel.

The whine of rotors and the smell of fuel oil fills his nose. Engines and beeping vehicles drown out the sound of rain pounding the puddles. Following an iridescent orange stripe to the processing shed, he quickly becomes part of the doorway crowd. Chilled by the rain despite the warm night breeze, the processing of personnel goes slowly as security teams check everyone's pass. He will be late for dinner.

Thirty minutes later, Ewalt sits in a van. Waiting for it to fill. He notices that new building frames are being added to the industrial park at the south end of the terminal. "More additions, huh?" He asks the flabby driver who rests his head on the steering wheel.

"Damn Oregonians. All they do around here is build things. I just don't understand. Why do all those rich mother-fuckers want to build right by the airport of all places? The traffic is terrible. Why the hell don't they just go north into Canada and hide like the rest of them?"

"Maybe they like being near the airports," Rader replies. "For a quick escape."

"Or they know the Dirties are about to fuck their dogs and eat them," comes the response. The man looks back at Ewalt from beneath droopy eyelids. "You back on leave?"

"Yeah," he replies.

"You from around here?" The man asks.

"Just north of Everett, but I live in Portland--or used to."

"Nice to be home, Commander?"

"Yeah, sure." Ewalt tells himself that he is being paranoid. There is no way, he tells himself, that the Captain and the driver are both spying on him.

The van fills and the driver closes the door.

Slowing at the triple wire fence that makes up the perimeter of the field, the driver hurls a friendly insult at the guards as the van makes the turn towards the yellow glow of the city. Watching the searchlights sweep the security zone, just beyond the fence that circles the airfield, Ewalt keeps himself busy by finding infiltration points in the fence. The road that separates the airport from the low buildings on the outskirts of town also has large mounds of equipment all along the road--all covered in blue tarps. *Loot from Oregon*, he guesses. He decides they are not too worried about incursions. Ewalt has seen two places he could drive a bus through and never be seen.

A quick left and they are in a shanty town of pimps, fast-buck artists, and gamblers. The van stops in front of a pink building lit by torches; most of the troopers pile out. The town vipers cluster around the troopers, calling out their prices and their services. The vehicle pulls away, Ewalt is surprised to see that no one gets on the van.

A car pulls up. "Commander Rader?"

The SansChic restaurant rests on the dock and pilings that had once supported an old sawmill. Located on the north side of town on the slough that divides the very-well-to-do north from the well-to-do south--one doorway looks north. And one doorway looks south. An open kitchen in the middle with dining at the poles, framed in heavy wood beamed walls, a barrel vault roof, and steel floor, the restaurant has just opened this month. Sound deadening glass separates the dining areas. An egalitarian veranda faces bobbing sailboats.

Fed by the gleaming apartments that disgorge their renters into the restaurant almost every night, the SansChic has become The Nightspot in town. It boasts an authentic Japanese sushi bar--which only the most well-connected people might access--from the north side. On the south side is a world-class charcuterie full of smoked and barbecued meats. All of the tables sport golden utensils. A joke on the part of management. Both entrances are framed with pristine arches of solid copper.

A reminder of the past, SansChic receives the kind of adoration once reserved for a church. This class of restaurant, open and opulent, had only been seen in the mega-cities of the first world until a few years ago. SansChic is one of a dozen world-class restaurants here in Everett run by the finest chefs alive. Consequently, for many of its patrons, food consumption has been elevated to noblesse oblige. Spending money on good food--it is said--delivers a good economy, good health, and therefore a healthy society.

Leaving the car, Ewalt calls his dad to make sure he is through the border crossing and inside Washington State. "You're sleeping in the bagel shop?" He asks.

"Got to. We're open tomorrow. Come by and I'll give you a lemon bagel and a latte."

"Funny. I'll see you in a couple of weeks."

"Jack Porter is a small fish, Ewalt. Remember that. Take care, son."

He forces himself to calm down, telling himself there must be some way to escape this madness. Ewalt has decided to go see the old farm before his flight tomorrow, thinking he might build a sanctuary there.

He surveys the small park and marina facing the SansChic. Turning his attention to the sloops and ketches with their bobbing masts, the sight fills him with envy. After his last date with Amanda, Ewalt considered the sailboat as a method of escape. Until he learned about the pirates who loot boats. And the perimeter defense tactic to kill anything afloat.

Ewalt walks towards the restaurant noting the guards that patrol the grounds are well-mannered. He sees many are ex-soldiers. Their task, he assumes, is to keep order and make sure those who do not belong, do not stay. For most people, to enter SansChic from the north side is more than a privilege. It is a free pass to Valhala. This is where the big deals are made these days. But being a practical man, Ewalt wonders what Jack Porter has in store for him.

Passing three large boulders decorated with plants on a verdant grassy knoll, Ewalt strolls around low benches to a small reflecting pool full of Koi. Crossing the arched bridge, he admires the Asian style and the gentle roll of the knolls. *Perfect defense positions, perfectly disguised for the patrons.* Ewalt then sees strobe lights bouncing upon the underside of the trees smacking the leaves in garish hues. The colored lights come from a dance area ahead that is disguised as another pond. Stopping to look below him, he sees clone-beautiful couples, apparently programmed to the colored lighting, dancing. Ewalt feels like he is looking into Hell. Then looking up, he sees the huge copper arches over the north portico.

A patrol of two men appears beside him: "Hey you, Soldier." Ewalt, not being in uniform, figures the voice is talking to someone else and continues walking. He takes note when a car door opens and slams shut behind him. "Hey, you."

Ewalt stops, keeping his hands loose by his side.

A beefy man with ham-hock arms stretching the material of his shirt sleeves steps in front of Ewalt. "Where you going, Wally?" The man is a head taller than Ewalt, but not as limber. The man who called out to Ewalt stands by the car holding a small charged baton in his grip.

"I'm going to dinner--there." Ewalt points to the restaurant. "If it's any of your damn business."

"Wrong side. No grunts allowed."

The guy in back taps his hand with the silver baton.

"Fuck you." As Ewalt walks passed, the man grabs him by the shoulder and spins Ewalt around.

Commander Rader stares at the beefy rent-a-cop. "Really?" He rams his shoulder into the man's gut and a swift second later is driving the man into the other guard. Ewalt makes sure the big man takes his partner's electric charge. As the man falls over, Ewalt rushes forward, kicks the second man twice in the head and waits. The man falls over. Ewalt grabs him by the collar and spins the wheezing man onto the glass top disco--face first. The beefy man remains immobile on the wet lawn. Ewalt looks down, sees no one is interested, beyond the amusement of it all. Straightening his blue sport coat, Commander Ewalt Rader struts up the railroad-tie-stairs into the restaurant.

Spun silver netting and pictures of old sailing ships cover the interior salt-gray wood of the restaurant. More beautiful men and women fill the bar. A huge aquarium holds various fish and sea mammals. The kitchen waits ahead of him; tables line the walls. A maitre d' stands by a glass doorway just right of the bar. An oval white sign above the door says: Fresh Fish. It strikes Ewalt that the concentration of people in the bar area is about the same as Dirties on the other side of the Wall. A tall blond man dressed in a tuxedo, waves to Ewalt.

Walking over, suddenly aware of his old blue sport jacket and khaki pants, Ewalt clenches his jaw wondering what he is doing here. "Ewalt, did you get in another tiff?" Jack asks as soon as Ewalt is close. With a slight of hand, he takes a chip of wood off Ewalt's shoulder.

"Jack, you look like the President," Ewalt says shaking his hand.

"Nah, he works for us." His old friend has that lean country-club look: Well tanned, slim, perfectly styled hair, and the school boy smile under a perfect mustache that hides a rattle snake tongue. "In fact, I look much better than the President. You look like a bull." The glint in Jack's eyes has Ewalt on his guard. "Ewalt Rader, this is Tom Grogan; he owns the SansChic Restaurant." Ewalt turns and shakes hands with the man, instantly disliking him. The handshake is wet and clammy.

"Jack, just take the table--and whatever else you want. I'll have that bottle of sake I owe you brought over." Grogan says. The man acknowledges Ewalt again, glances at his clothes, and grins. "Not bad." He looks at Jack. "And you've got that support you wanted for your project."

Jack winks at him and conducts Ewalt by the bar area. "You still have that way of letting people know exactly what you think of them," Jack says, with a grin. "Let's go sit down." They pass the maitre d' as if he were not there. Then Jack waits. The man opens the glass door with a flourish and they enter the sushi dining room. Thick leather chairs, white table cloths, and precisely dressed older men with attractive young women decorate this room. At the far end of the room, just past the sushi bar, a single table sits empty in the corner. A fire in the fireplace marks this table as the center of tonight. Jack points to it. "This okay with you?" He asks.

"It'll do," Ewalt responds. "Do I get kissed before I get screwed tonight?"

"It'll take a few days for you get screwed, Walt. But it will be your decision." Jack sits with his back to the crowd, facing the fireplace. Ewalt sits, facing a crowd that scans him then looks away. "I feel like a zoo animal."

"They think you are." A bottle of sake arrives. Jack Porter spreads his tan napkin on his lap, glances at the bottle, then speaks to the Sommelier with a smile. "You tell that skinflint our bet was for the best sake he has, not the second best. Take this swill back to the kitchen."

The man bows taking the deficient bottle of rice wine with him. After a brief silence, Ewalt speaks: "So you seem to be doing okay, Jack. You own this town? There isn't a face in the place that doesn't want to kiss your butt."

"Well yes, I guess you could say I have my own little fiefdom here. You know I haven't heard a person say a straight word to me in years. God, it's good to see you, Walt." Jack sticks his hand in the air and the waiter immediately appears. "A bottle of bourbon, two glasses." This waiter also bows before he leaves. "Have you heard that your almost father-in-law is a corpse?"

"Like you give a shit."

The second bottle of sake arrives and Jack motions for the Sommelier to open it. As he does, the bottle of bourbon arrives also. A moment later the sake sits in small ceramic dish of warm water. The bourbon rests on the table and the four glasses are filled with their respective liquids. "Cheers, buddy," Jack says, picking up a sake cup. Ewalt takes the squat bourbon glass and they toast. Jack slugs his sake back like he is drinking Scotch. "I hate this stuff, but it impresses the crowd."

Jack waves to someone and keeps talking to Ewalt. "I invested money in this town when the Californians started arriving. They paid a fortune for property that I bought for spit. I invested in some other junk as well and it also turned a huge profit. Everyone thinks I'm a damn genius and so they keep telling me their ideas for making money--or screwing over the Feiss family. I help either side when I find a sweet deal. Now I am the number three arms guy behind Feiss and Lippman. With Luke Feiss gone and his wife running things it is just a matter of time before I own the whole deal. You know the Dirties are only a couple of hundred miles south of Portland."

Ewalt sips the bourbon. "That means you will soon own nothing. You're a temporary lease holder. One with a big ugly target painted on his keester for when they break through the Columbia Wall. Then all these sycophants here will find you. Turn you over to the cannibals and supply the beer." Ewalt shakes his head at the absurdity of it.

"No way. They'd have to get through you to get to your dad and I'll put you up against anyone, anytime on that one."

Ewalt glances at the bottle of sake. He recalls Xandra introduced him to sake. He finishes his bourbon. "So they all make money for you. Then they pay you for the privilege?" Ewalt says.

"You now understand the secret of success."

"Stupidity?" Ewalt picks up the cup of sake. "Here's to Darwin and survival of the fittest." This old toast dates back to time when they had both belonged to the same street gang. Ewalt had been trying to make his way; Jack was trying not to be bored. Ewalt sips the sake finding he cannot taste anything. "If money bores you so much, Jack, why are you doing this?"

"I'm not as brave as you, Ewalt. But my smarts may save both of our asses." He leans close. "I think they'll get through the Columbia Wall also." He rests back against his seat.

Ewalt looks passed him then sighs. He sees those two guards who he had laid out talking to the owner. Two more guards are walking swiftly towards them. "They're here for you," Jack says seeing the commotion reflected in the glass.

"They tried to lean on me."

Jack shakes his head back and forth signaling the guards to back off. Everyone walks away. Ewalt pours another two fingers of bourbon. "Phew, too bad no one listens to you," he says. "Of course, you put those gorillas up to it. Pure Jack Porter--what a wonder." Ewalt holds up a hand. A waiter arrives immediately. "Take this sake back," Ewalt says without explanation. The confused waiter stares at Mr. Porter--who slowly nods his agreement. As soon as he is gone: "Fuck you, Jack."

The Sommelier arrives trying to understand the problem. "Tell the waiter, two of Renoir's ducks. Rare," Jack Porter says. The man leaves.

"You going to tell me about the bet with your friend, Grogan?"

Jack looks up at the ceiling. "I made him a bet you would bust up his best guy without ripping your clothes." Jack lifts his bourbon glass. "Are you becoming sensitive on me, Walt?"

"Too bad you didn't join up with me. Instead of spending your life playing power games with the lame and mentally deficient. You could have been a different kind of swine."

"Walt, what is it like?" Jack says suddenly.

"The Wall?"

"Everyday is life and death for you."

"You mean you haven't been there? I've seen hundreds of you guys touring the Wall and the forts in the last few weeks." Rader sips his bourbon.

"I've been there. I've been out to the Nevada desert, I've been on carriers off of all the coasts. But the military always keep us so far away from it all. It is hard to tell what is going on out there. I looked for you, but you are always blowing the shit out of the bad guys."

"I do that every now and again. Whenever I can get away from the club," Rader replies. "What do you want, Jacko? And what's in it for me?"

Jack pauses. He swallows his bourbon then speaks. "We each have our place in this world. Mine is to build a fiefdom and yours is to kick butt." Jack's face loses its cock-sure luster for a moment. "We're in trouble. Do you agree?" Jack never asks a question he doesn't already know the answer to--in triplicate. "I hear they have food and they are getting better weapons," he says quietly.

"Where did you hear that?" Ewalt replies as blandly as he can. A supply of food makes sense to Ewalt. On the other hand, it is standard operating procedure to never tell civilians anything about a battle.

Annoyed, Jack folds his arms in front of his chest. "I've heard they have heat-seeking missiles and a leader. They're already attacking our installations in Portland and they are developing air power. Word is some SOB already painted graffiti on the Columbia Wall. Walt, don't bullshit me. This is important."

Ewalt finishes his second bourbon. "You're pretty well-informed, Jack. What do you want? How come you're so well-connected to Ops?" *And how come you're so stupid as to ask me questions without checking if I know about it?* The plates of roasted duck arrive. Ewalt ignores them while he contemplates Jack Porter.

"I have a plan to end it." He looks at the duck and nods his approval. "Eat. Enjoy."

Ewalt looks down at the red-glazed duck, smiles, then looks back up at Jack. "My suggestion is you find a deep hole. If they get through the Wall they'll burn everything down and kill everyone who even smiles like you. No one is going to listen to anything you say." Ewalt picks up his fork and knife. He cuts into the duck. Thin red blood oozes from the pink meat.

"Walt, they've got a leader, the model Elena Etu. Do you remember her?"

"Jack, my subscription to Vogue ran out. Who is she?" Ewalt knows exactly who she is. There are posters of her all around the base--including one over his bunk. He thinks he now understands why. No one may forget her face. "Is she your monkey?" He takes a bite of the delicious duck. "This is good."

"She's not my monkey. She's Feiss' monkey. Or she was, but she was too smart for him. When she took out the Wall, she took out Luke Feiss as well."

"Smart woman." He places another slice of meat in his mouth. "And about as trustworthy as the rest of them."

"She's got food and more importantly the loyalty of the Dirties."

"So what's the problem? Go buy her a duck."

"Walt, I have two problems. One, she's is Feiss's lackey not mine. And two, she is smart enough to know she has the winning hand now." Jack cuts a small piece of breast and places it in his mouth; his eyes fix on Ewalt, measuring him anew.

"You don't want her dead. That's too dangerous. What do you want me for?"

"Information and contact, I have members of the military and a few members of the Corporate Council in agreement on a plan: I want you to tell me what's going on down there and what I can expect. I also need to speak with her. Most importantly I need a lever I can use on her." He has stopped eating.

"And I get?" Ewalt picks up a leg, glances at Jack who waves him ahead; then he bites into it.

"I'll give you whatever you want, Walt. You know that. You're not a good enough liar to compete with me. So I don't fear you. Except if I piss you off and then we both know I am deader than the ducks on the plate. So I am not going to do that. Second, with the information you get, we should be able to save me, you, and your dad. You get money, power, and the inside scoop. Then you get to retire to that farm your dad refused to sell to me. But I need the face time--to get Ms. Etu on my team." He takes the glass of bourbon and finishes it.

"That's it."

"Why me?"

"We were once friends. We may still be friends. You're also the toughest, meanest bastard I ever met. I can trust you to get this done--or die trying. It's as simple as that. That's the deal." He waits, hands folded in front of him.

Ewalt thinks, chewing a pommes frite. "You can get me to the other side in one piece?"

"I've already bribed two Senators and the Vice President. You have convinced the really important people tonight by your decisive pummeling of Security. It'll be you and a couple of spooks to guard you."

Ewalt puts his fork down. "Did my dad make it across this evening?" He watches his friend laugh.

"Moose was through that checkpoint in ten minutes. You didn't think I would fuck that up, did you?" He spears more duck breast, a bit worried about his plan. Jack had monitored Ewalt's earlier phone call to his dad.

"You'll make sure my dad is okay no matter what happens?"

"And after--if you say yes to this plan. Whether you succeed or not. I'll have a security detail on it tomorrow. When you get back, you'll find your dad has hired a master baker from the Marines. Who is about seven feet tall and tough as jerky. I promise to see to your father's needs, whether you make it or not. Health, financial, you name it. I'll also put enough gold in a vault to keep you happy for the rest of your days. In addition, you just let me know when you want out of the military. I'll make sure that happens. Then you and I can be the toast of the toasted." Jack Porter is not above the use of childhood allusions to close his sale.

"Very funny." Ewalt tears the other leg off the bird. "I ought to cap you right now."

"That's another reason I want you for this: your even temper and cool dispassionate logic. It remains is a bastion of sanity." Both men continue to eat.

"Jack, I'm not going to kill anyone without cause."

"Oh heaven forbid." They both toast each other. "This Etu woman is important, Walt. She has to be kept alive. If we have no one to negotiate for the Dirties, we're screwed. She can keep the peace. She has proven that. More importantly, she's your type."

Ewalt angers. He doesn't like being pandered to. "Right. We'll invite you to the wedding."

"Ewalt, if we are negotiating with my stooge, you and I are kings. If we are negotiating with Feiss' stooge, anything she says is useless to us."

Ewalt dabs his chin with his napkin. "That was good grub."

"As a backup plan, get me something on their food supplies. I can use that as well. I'll starve those bastards if I have to."

"Jack, they've been trying that for years. I'll keep the food information as my lever, you backstabbing son of a bitch." Ewalt stands to leave. "Thanks for diner, Jacko. Give Renoir my best. I'm in."

"Like I said, Walt, I trust you." This meeting has gone exactly as Jack had hoped it would.

CHAPTER TWENTY FIVE

Early morning mists swirl over the water. Carried by breezes and the sweet scent of damp wood, the fog begins to lift. Sitting on the deck outside the family cabin on Widbey Island, her left leg tightly bandaged, Amanda lifts her leg placing it on a stump that functions as a table. Despite the pain, she still believes she will be flight ready tomorrow but that trapped feeling has not left her, giving her pause.

She wonders about a phone call last night from the Joint Chiefs. The Dirties will be in Portland within the month--probably sooner. It was one of those grunt phone calls; she has heard them all her life. Though it used to be her dad who did all the grunting. Amanda hates those phone calls. They make her feel like her family is shutting her out. But even with the that, the concern on her mother's face was clear at the end of the phone call.

Amanda cannot find a trace of Ewalt Rader this morning. After his dinner last night with Jack Porter he seems to have disappeared. She needs to find him. Amanda wants Ewalt to put Joe Vaz someplace safe and then guard him. Until she is ready for him. *Mother will try to kill Dr. Vaz. It's time to deflect him and manage the asset of Elena Etu. The Corporate Council needs her help to evaluate the situation.*

Watching the fog roll out between a notch of the islands, Amanda can discern her mother's orange blur approaching from the distance, along with the four boats providing security. On mornings like this, Puget Sound is a ghost's bed.

She listens to the waves against the rocks and wooden pilings. The fir covering hillsides freshen with a breeze, then quiets. Amanda rubs her fingertip against the wooden deck feeling the cold wetness and then brings her hand to her face. Closing her eyes and touching the cold droplets to her eyelids, she calms with this memory of her youth. A crow calls. Pulling the black bearskin coat tight around her body, Amanda Feiss mourns her father by donning his favorite bit of wear. The fur carries a musty odor.

The sound of oars then the orange kayak shells define themselves through the mist. Margrete paddles toward the dock. *She paddles so slowly, now.* Amanda waves as Margrete maneuvers the boat alongside the dock and pulls herself out of the shell. Zipping open the front of her sweaty orange suit, she steps out of it and dives into the cold water. Mother pops up again about ten feet from the dock.

Two of the other boats dock. Security people emerge from the guard house and take up defense positions even though there have been no reported incursions north of the Columbia Wall.

"Don't you ever get cold?" Amanda calls, watching her mother tread water. In fact she thinks about her heart. Her mother didn't look that well this morning.

"What do you mean, Scout?" She says. "The water is as warm as bath water."

"How's your rash, still itch?" Amanda asks, watching her swim around the dock.

"It's just fine. Whew, you have the devil in you this morning, don't you?" Margrete pulls herself from the water. Amanda looks away watching peacocks waddle towards the house. "I was thinking about your plan while I was in the shell. We need to talk."

A few minutes later Margrete appears in the kitchen wearing a pink terry cloth bathrobe, a phone to her ear "...At least three to four thousand yesterday. So all of the Portland shelters were compromised? I see. Make sure that hospital is a corpse when we abandon it. They need medical supplies. I see...All right." She glances at the wall clock. "Have a helicopter pick us up at 12:30. Yes, six teams will be enough." She puts the phone down and looks over at Amanda. "We're forming teams to get current information from San Francisco. They will be in addition to your effort. We are going to talk with the Dirties about peace. I'll need you to help me with Elena Etu. Go make friends with her, Scout, and keep her safe."

Amanda nods at the comment. "You're going destabilize the reign of Ms. Etu and then negotiate with whom?" Amanda says as she sips coffee staring out at Puget Sound.

"You're too smart for me. We're going to see what's going on with Ms. Etu. Then we will decide. Can you leverage your past actions with Dr. Vaz? He is a possibility now."

"I see." Amanda leans back against the refrigerator. "I think so," she says. "Would we nuke California?"

"With what, spit?" Margrete scowls. "If we could have, we would have, last year." She sits down at the kitchen table and carefully fills a chrome tea ball with Oolong tea. Really good tea is now more valuable than copper. "We'll probably go after their leadership except for Ms. Etu and Dr. Vaz if they cooperate. Once we have them isolated we'll know the next step. If that doesn't work then we go after the food." She looks at her daughter's leg. "I am concerned about you and your leg."

"I figured as much," Amanda says with a smile. "I will be good to go tomorrow. What are you going to do if they break through the Columbia Wall before we are ready? With helicopters it is just a matter of time."

"How much time?" Mother fills a tea pot with water and places it on the stove.

"Once we give up Portland I'd say no less than a month and no more than a year."

Her mother looks down at the old stove and shakes her head. "We are expecting to have the hose problem solved within a couple of weeks. You will have a week to get back to me on what we can expect from Ms. Etu and Dr. Vaz. Pick a team. Make sure your transponder is functioning on Feiss channels. Use a supply drop to get over the Wall and abandon the helicopter. There will be a half-dozen other cells going in on foot as I said. Once you get down to San Francisco, meet up at the Museum of Fine Arts--three days after the start of the mission, at 6 AM."

"It would make more sense at this point to let me fly along the coast down to San Francisco and ditch the helicopter in the waves."

"We don't want to alert them."

Amanda's gut cramps. "Did you find Commander Rader? He's unstoppable."

Her mother faces her, considering her motives and the best course of action. "Word among the officers was you kept trying to kill him. Word among the pilots is you kept failing at it on purpose. What happened?"

Amanda crosses her arms bringing the bearskin closer. "Back in Coeur d' Alene, where we met, I made a mistake and killed a woman whom I thought was trying to help three muggers kill the guy."

"He couldn't take care of himself?"

"He had a knife in him and two inch pipe across the skull."

"And the woman was his woman. You didn't know that?"

Amanda stares at her. Margrete takes the kettle and pours water into her cup on the table. She returns the tea kettle to the stove and sits back down. "Your dad was a jealous man. Even after I married him. Had you been dating Mr. Rader already?"

"I was looking for a new gunner and his name kept coming up.

He also had a reputation for being fun. I was bored in Idaho so I made him a project. Then some doxy showed up and ruined my plans."

"And when you saw her attending the mugging--you took your shot--so to speak?"

"Not funny." Amanda Feiss stands up. "So where is Commander Rader now?"

"Too late, Scout. Jack Porter has him on one of his teams. They were boyhood friends. Is he critical to your mission's success?"

"He is the only one I know who will make it through--and I trust his word."

"So you were keeping him off balance, trying to control the asset? I see." Margrete sips her tea. "So he knows you killed her?"

"He is foggy about it but yes. I think he harbors a grudge. On the other hand, he is happy with the toys I gave him. You know the type."

"A angry man like that never forgets his rage. Believe me I know."Margrete's face tilts; Mother has a plan. "But you still think this is the way to go?"

"Yes."

"Then you'll fly the supply ship for his team. How you get him in tow is your problem. That way he will take care of you. Will he take care of you?" She points to the leg.

"I am sure of it. He is all duty, a pure soldier."

"Purity always did it for you." Mother leans over and kisses her daughter on the forehead. "Come on. Let's get moving. We have a flight soon."

At that same moment, Ewalt Rader walks along the dirt road just outside the old barn of his mother's farm. Up the hill he sees a set of swings that his mother had installed so many years ago. Before he was born. She never saw him use those swings; she died in childbirth. The old house next to the swings has been reduced to framing. The man hired to rebuild it sits on a scaffold watching Ewalt--unsure of what he wants. Ewalt doesn't worry about him. Ewalt slept in the wood shed last night to see what the new handyman is about. The man was asleep by midnight--after reading for a few hours.

Neither man bothers to wave as Ewalt approaches. "I'm Ewalt Rader. My dad was the guy who hired you." The man nods hello pulling the white bandana from his head revealing a bushy head of hair. "You're the handyman?"

"I'm Bob Wolf." The skinny man nods. "Have a good sleep? He points to the wood shed. "What do you want, Ewalt? Your dad mentioned you might come by."

"Just here checking out the barn. I might want to park a vehicle inside it for a few months."

"Right. Sure you do."

Ewalt grins, walking into the barn. The old cow barn has been straightened up and a small room added off to the side. Ewalt glances inside the new room and sees a tangle of wires as well as three computers.

Ewalt closes the door. Going in the far end of the barn, he looks back, to see if the handyman is paying attention. The skinny man nails siding to the studs. Ewalt studies the floor below him and stamps on the timbers. They remain solid. Then he walks to the tack room glancing at the roof. It's well tended and without leaks.

Inside the tack room he notes the stairway downstairs remains unused, the opening still obliterated with rusting farm tools. Ewalt believes the huge cellar below the barn will do nicely as a sanctuary if need be--*and the carpenter doesn't seem interested in much except his task and the computers*--so Ewalt considers the location safe. He exits the barn and waves to the handyman. Ewalt has a flight to catch.

CHAPTER TWENTY SIX

Ewalt hates not being up top, able to see what was going on. Of course, as he has recently learned, knowing "what was going on" is a relative term. Bouncing along a valley floor en route to the Redding Wall, he hears the ping of bullets through the armor. Sitting in the troop carrier, he is thankful he cannot see the battle around him. *Better to die in shock than see it coming when you're just baggage.*

Ewalt calms by breathing in and holding the gas. He'll do no fighting if they are hit. He'll be dead. And troops in a personnel carrier have no choice but to breathe the gas anyway. An explosion rocks the transport, throwing one of the soldiers onto the floor.

"That's what the harness is for," Rader mumbles. The man lifts himself back onto the seat and grabs the brown webbing that had hung beside him, pulling it across his chest. His code name is Rousseau.

The other member of the team is a woman with the code name of Locke. Her dark eyes remain glued to the amber light above the steel ramp that also serves as a back doorway. She has had nothing to say since they entered the troop carrier and appears like the strong silent type who only talk about the job at hand. Rader likes that.

Ewalt's code name is Voltaire. "So I don't suppose you'd like tell me who is paying you?" He asks Rousseau.

"You read the contract? We're here to fight and get information for Porter Industries. For that, we get paid a year's salary. We're a recon team, looking for targets," he replies.

"And you're just a gal who's here to check on their barbecue recipes?" Ewalt says to Locke.

She grins. "Actually, I'm more than that. I'm the boss. I am here to make sure you and Rousseau do as you are told. For that I will keep you safe. Now shut the fuck up."

An explosion rocks the vehicle tossing them from side to side. The dull amber light flickers off.

"Christ, you'd think after all these wars they'd have figured out how to keep the lights on," Rousseau says, rubbing his arm. The scratchy clothes are filled with lice--even though supply pronounced them clean. The smell of sweat and dirt fills the compartment. Locke scratches her armpit, then wipes the sweat on her brow. "Smell right. Then they will think you are one of them. That's number one." The amber light flickers back on.

Ewalt looks at the useless chronometer above Rousseau's head. There is no telling how long they've been rolling through the valleys. Asking himself again how he could have been so stupid as to take this mission without checking if Amanda Feiss has some part in it, he closes his eyes. *I was fat, dumb, and happy in that restaurant. I was a golden dope. Fresh meat ready to be fed into the grinder.* The explosions intensify. Shrapnel clatters against the armor, pulling Ewalt from his thoughts.

The speaker crackles to life: "Locke, we're in ravine delta-three-dot-two. A few thousand Dirties have been permitted to pour through a convenient tunnel to cover your injection. The valleys are filled with insurgents and the firefights are everywhere. We're okay, but they're taking hell up in the next ravine. That's where you are going. Also, we've gotten a signal from WeatherEye. When you exit the tunnel and get on the other side of the Wall, you'll be three kicks from the old interstate. Make sure you check in. There will be tents. Once you check-in, go up the ravine a few hundred yards. You'll run into an encampment. Stay there for a few hours. Then make your way to the interstate. I am turning the gas off now."

"We just follow the Dirties as they run away--no killing," says Locke. "We're them."

"Ironically enough," Ewalt says, shaking his head. He checks his weapon, looking up at the blinking amber light. Rousseau and Locke place small white battle pills under their tongues. *Who the fuck are these people?* All signs of stress disappear from their faces. They look at each other with firm, sure smiles. Ewalt snorts out a laugh. "No drugs for me?"

"We know about you, Voltaire." A red light begins to flash. The rolling cavern darkens. They are seconds away from entering the battlefield. A green light begins to blink. The door cracks open at the top and the smoky light of mid-afternoon races around the edges and into the compartment. Outside, dust from mortars and smoke bombs have eliminated visibility in the valley.

"Remove harness," Locke orders. "We go around to the port side, then advance south into the next ravine."

The back hatch falls to the ground and the team jumps from the back of the transport. The dusty battlefield smells of diesel, burning flesh, and cordite. The smoke chokes him. As soon as they are around the side, the vehicle begins to rapidly back up, firing dummy ammo for the first hundred rounds. She yells, "To the right. On me." The sounds of exploding shells and machine gun fire surround them. "Remember, we're supposed to be in retreat. Look scared."

"Duh," Rader scans the ground for fallen weapons. He sees none among the scattered bloody bodies. The team follows Locke forward, ducking as they run. A set of white phosphorus rockets explodes to their right, lighting a dead tree up like a match. Not every gunship has switched to dummy munitions. They run quickly over the dry stream bed and around the bend to a flat-bed truck. The ravine in front of them is battle-hell. Two bodies hang out the front windshield, draped forward like dummies. The tree stumps burn. Twisted metal litters the ground among the destroyed vehicles and dead bodies smolder. Six SWATs lie shattered in front of them. A Hercules helicopters smokes, buried in the hillside. They take shelter behind the remains of a truck. Scattered around the truck are jagged pieces of metal and body parts. Some gunner has scored a direct hit.

No weapons here either.

An explosion rocks the truck. A pair of trees collapse. Rader spots a weapon off to his left. He leaves the shelter, running the thirty feet to weapon, grabs the semi-automatic rifle, and takes cover between two boulders. Checking the weapon, he finds it is well-oiled. Also a bit primitive--but there it a full clip of thirty rounds. He throws his weapon in the mud as a big man dives into the protection of a blackened stump nearby. He is followed by a woman and two men.

"What's happening up there?" The squad leader asks Rader.

"Fucking tanks, five or six tracked vehicles, there's nowhere to go." A set of four shells lands in an almost direct line toward them.

"Shit, they see us," the man says. "Are you coming back or going north?"

"Coming back." Rader loads a bullet into the breach and fires. The bullet buries itself in a tree stump beside him.

"What the fuck did you do that for?" The man screams, staring at Rader as if he were some kind of idiot. "You think we got munitions to waste? Give me that." He reaches for the weapon.

Ewalt pulls it back.

"Don't try that again." But he doesn't try to take the rifle. The whiz of bullets boil through the air. "Let's get the hell outta' here." The man waves to his companions spinning his index finger in a small circle. They jump up and start to run toward the north. Then he faces Ewalt and his team. "You three--your mission has changed. Follow me.

Come on," he yells. Rader spins and puts a single round in the man's head. He falls back on a bed of small stones.

Rousseau's eyes turn midnight. "One more like that. I'll kill you."

"Please try," Ewalt responds. "We split up here and meet on the other side of the Wall. Got it?" Ewalt sprints toward the tunnel mouth.

Three SWATs make the corner so Ewalt circles behind a large boulder. The tanks begin to mop everyone back to the hole. Using boulders--from an earlier attempt to close this hole--for cover, he runs up the ravine darting from rock to rock. Bodies are everywhere. From their blued faces and bloated tongues, Rader guesses the Dirties have been recently gassed. Up ahead, groups of men and women are disappearing down a sloping hole in the ground.

A stream of bullet puffs the ground. A frightened boy with long dreadlocks runs passed Ewalt. Taking the direct path to the hole, leaving the shelter of the boulders, the boy is immediately raked across the back by gun fire. Screaming in pain, he falls to the ground--dead. Then the puffs of dust arc. The rounds curve towards Ewalt. He stops behind another boulder. Bullets pound the area around him, whittling the edges of the boulder. He waits for the last tracer, counts to three, and runs. The other two members of the team are now following him.

Up ahead, he sees a huge angled hole in the ground circled by a berm. Ewalt dives in. With a quick roll in the rocky dirt, he is back to his feet. Running down the steep slope and following the parade of people, he enters a large tunnel. Ahead of Ewalt, a woman falls from wounds and exhaustion. He stops and lifts her by the arm to carry her. She smells perfect to him, like blood and sweat. Her stink will hide his lack of smell. As he helps her along, he looks to see what has happened to Rousseau and Locke. Rousseau's left arm is a wash of red.

A hand grabs the back of Ewalt's shirt. The tunnel ahead is black. Ewalt reaches out with his free hand and grabs the shirt in front of him. Like a caterpillar, the mass of people scurry along the tunnel. The smell of diesel fills the air. Ahead, the yellowish light from torches form an eerie circle of light. The tunnel reverberates with people puffing and laughing. Then splashing--he is ankle-deep in water and mud.

"Crap. What pissed them off? I thought they gave up on closing the tunnels," someone says.

"They're closing this one," comes the alarm from behind. Everyone begins to run again. The woman Ewalt holds in his arms gasps for air. He thinks she might be at death's doorway.

A moment later a wall of air pushes through the cave like a piston, throwing some people to the ground. Ewalt's head feels like a hammer has hit it. "Hah," someone yells. "They screwed up--no gas." People hoot. Then a second explosion with a smaller push of wet air. "It's okay. We're sealed in." The comment is repeated in a dozen different languages. People stop running and lean against the tunnel walls to rest.

"Will they follow us?" A young girl asks.

"We own these tunnels," comes the response. Ewalt wonders if that is bravado, or if there is a security measure waiting at the end of the tunnel. A few others speak in a language that Ewalt thinks is Greek. Moments later the crowd passes three machine gun emplacements dug into the walls of the tunnel. Then the mouth of the tunnel seems to constrict: It's the crumbled foundation for the Wall. It has been burrowed through. A few yards more and they are inside the remains of the Wall. It's an officers mess and some sleeping quarters, or what remains of them. A second gun emplacement waits at the far end. This one has rocket launchers.

Anyone trying to get passed them would see God soon enough, Rader says to himself. The woman on his shoulder moans; then she gurgles out a muffled scream that dies in her throat. He carries her anyway. It will make for a convincing story on the other side. Ewalt hopes nobody there will know her and decides to say her name is Amanda, if anyone asks. The thought tickles him.

The cool tunnel smells of wet dirt and mold. Ahead, a target of light signals the end of the tunnel. The hot breeze of the day bathes him as he emerges from the tunnel entrance. A set of lines form at the exit of the tunnel. Rader stands and tries to peer over the heads of those ahead of them. He sees a table where people leave their weapons.

"Shit," he says to himself. He rapidly unslings his rifle and tries to get a few cartridges out of the magazine.

"I wouldn't do that if I were you. They frown on that," says a man with a bald head beside him.

"You're right." Ewalt shoulders his weapon and follows the crowd. He gives up his weapon. Seeing people greeting friends and loved ones as they return, he cannot help but think of the old airline terminals--and the returning business-people of his youth.

His shoulder cramps from the woman's weight. "Hey you, with the body, over here." Rader looks in the direction of the voice. "Yeah you." An African man with short clipped hair points to the ground beside him. The butt of the man's hunting rifle sits on a split timber table

Slowly crossing through another line of people dropping their guns and ammunition into a small parked wagon, he approaches the man who appears to be some kind of police. "Leave the body on the ground, buddy. We'll take care of her." The man taps the shoulder rest of his rifle against the dirt.

Rader swings her body onto the ground, slapping her head against a rock. He curses to himself leaning over to kiss the stranger on the cheek--surprised he can force tears out.

"Sorry buddy, gotta' move along. You don't have any bullets do you?" The man asks.

"No." Rader says. He gets patted down by another man.

The man nods and looks down at the woman. "A friend of yours?"

"Yeah."

"I'm sorry," says the man at the table.

Looking behind for his comrades, he sees only the crumpled

Wall. *A nice mess they made of that in a decade.*

The crumbled behemoth looks like some kind of strange ground snake. The view from the hillside is one of an undulating serpent stuck partially below the ground. The guard towers lie slumped on the front of the Wall having fallen forward for the most part; dynamited, some of them are still smoking. Far in the distance a large rusty ore truck kicks up dust as it rolls along US 5. The stink of rotting garbage that forms the interior of the Wall mixes with the sweet smell of flowers. Ewalt stares at the rows of flowers. *Where the heck did that come from?*

"Lose something?" Asks a young man with green shorts; he carries a pistol.

"No sweat. I just lost a friend. She was a gardener. It's nothing." Ewalt follows the others towards the orderly rows of tents and wooden shelters, which will turn out to be latrines. He passes what appears to be a man-made aqueduct. Wooden walkways traverse the open sewer as it flows downhill. Behind the tents, people mill about by a chain link barrier. Ewalt notices the encampment appears quite orderly. He had expected a patchwork of madness. Turning, scanning for his comrades, he keeps walking. Until the smell of food catches his attention.

He crosses over the greenish brown sewer water. Ahead, people talk together in various languages. Eating blue cakes, some stand by a long line leading to a blue tent. Another line that has split into two, each line going towards either a red tent or a white tent, Ewalt figures it has something to do with the food. And by the casual attitude of the people around him, he doesn't think the choice of line matters. He gets on the line leading into the red tent.

A dark-haired man in front of him jabbers. Ewalt listens to the man bluster about his accomplishments. A couple of weary women wait alongside him in the line. "So I figured the rocks would do it. Then one grenade later, bango. One Wally tank buried under a ton of stone." This had been a favorite trick of the Dirties a few years ago. It hasn't worked since the helicopters started raking the hillsides with their guns. The conversation makes Commander Rader feel more secure; he figures anyone who mouths off as much as this guy, will give him ample warning about any potential problems.

The smell of pizza creeps through the stink and Ewalt begins to wonder if he is having delusions. A moment later, inside the tent, he sees huge half-barrels of red cakes. The smell of pizza comes from them.

Flavored food, I'll be damned. What about money? Then he sees people are just walking by the cakes and grabbing as many as they can take. Ewalt turns and looks up at the defunct towers. *They could have seen all this. Or they couldn't before? Bullshit.*

He pulls out four of the cakes then grabs a plastic cup from the table beside it. He dips it in the dirty water. Ewalt follows the braggart to a hillside swarming with people. Many of them are trading different colored food with each other. Rader then continues up slope so he can get a better view.

When he turns, the scene shocks him: No chaos, no anarchy, all around him spreads a well-ordered encampment of probably three-hundred-thousand people. In the distance, like multiple oasis in the desert, other encampments populate the flats in front of the Wall. Noting the orderliness of the encampment, he figures this has been here for some time.

Ewalt takes a bite out of his cake. The warm pastry exterior gives way to the taste of tomatoes. Cheese flavor flows in a thick chewy paste. On his second bite, a bit of textured protein has to be chewed. It tastes like a sweet sausage and has a crunch. A trail of sauce spills down the side of his chin and onto his clothes. He wipes his chin with his sleeve--astounded at how good the food tastes. *What the hell do they want with us? The Dirties look like they are doing okay. I don't get it. Heck, I'd eat my food, take nice long siestas, and build a house in the forest. Boy, these fuckers are pissed.*

Locke and Rousseau appear wading through the crowd looking for him. Rousseau's arm is bandaged. Ewalt stands up. They see him and stroll towards him.

"They got better food than us," Locke says, as she sits.

"And decent medics," Rousseau adds.

Ewalt trades Locke for one of the other cakes and takes a bite. It tastes like vanilla pudding. She takes a bite of the red cake, smiles then sighs. "I bet it gets old eating the same old crap--but gents--we definitely have a problem here."

"Bullshit," Ewalt replies. "There's no way the Wall doesn't know all about this. So cut the crap. Who the hell are you?"

"I work for the other guys, Feiss Industries. The deal with Porter's people was that one of us had to be here. Or, there was no supply drop."

"Am I the only dumb son of a bitch who works for the good old US of A?" Ewalt says sarcastically.

"Don't be a fool, Voltaire," Locke replies. "You're the killer who is gathering information on these bastards. The good old US of A is a myth. I saw a special on TV that said the United States was made up by the Hollywood movie people in the 1930's so people would have something to fight for in the second corporate war."

Ewalt laughs. "Yup. You're well informed, boss." *She probably doesn't know about Jack Porter and I either. But I bet I know who is making the supply drop. Three person team my ass. As soon as I get the goods I am a ghost. Smart move, Jack. You knew I'd stay ahead of them.* Ewalt spies a tent off to the side by the open sewer. Men and woman separate to enter different openings of the latrine. "Gotta' pee." Rader walks over to the latrine tent and enters.

What do I do now? Hmm, nothing more than a large hole with men pissing into it. On the other side of the hole, a series of seats are suspended over a lateral trench. *This place must recycle its waste. Maybe that's what the food is made from. Some damn job that is.*

Tap
Tap-Tap
Tap-Tap-Tap
Tap-Tap-Tap-Tap
Tap-Tap-Tap-Tap-Tap.

Rader takes his time, urinating, wondering what is going on. The clacking of the rocks gets louder and he notices that everyone not urinating or defecating pulls out a pair of rocks from their pockets and hurries to leave the latrine. Suddenly there is howling and yelling that competes with the clacking rocks. "What is that?" Ewalt asks an old man struggling with his ancient plumbing

"Oh, they got another Wall-spy," says the old man. Rader walks outside. To his horror, Locke and Rousseau are standing twenty yards away; their arms pulled wide by ropes. A dozen people appear to be having a tug of war with their limbs.

A woman with no hair or blouse is screaming: "Kill the Demons. Kill the spies. They can't speak to the Earth. They're spies, just like those others. Kill the Demons." Rader backs into the latrine before anyone realizes there were three.

While the rocks appear to be no more than a ritualistic tool for making noise, in fact they are a simple and very effective mechanism to make sure the Dirties are not infiltrated. Once it is time to make the Earth speak, anyone without the rocks is taken away and questioned. A quick inspection of his comrades has uncovered the little white pills, which immediately gave them away.

Inside the tent, the old man has finished trying to urinate and turns to leave. Two small rocks are in his right hand. Rader pushes the man back quickly, clamping a hand over his mouth. Then jabbing his outstretched fingers into the man's throat, he crushes it. The old man collapses to the floor. Rader grabs the stones and kicks the man over the edge into the latrine. He knows sooner or later the dead man will be discovered. By then he plans to be far away.

Outside the tent, Ewalt begins clicking the stones in unison with the others. He makes his way through the crowd seeing two men pull long-bladed knives from their sheathes. They begin to skin his comrades. Ewalt strolls away knowing they will give him up so they can die. Hurrying through the crowd to make sure he is outside the vision of his former comrades, Ewalt considers his options. He needs supplies--but considering who the supply-drop pilot might be--he considers looking around for local stores.

Finding them all well-guarded, Ewalt embraces the beauty of getting Amanda Feiss alone on this side of the Wall. He wonders if he could really kill her in cold blood. Then he laughs at himself. *Any idiot knows it would be suicide for her to fly the supply mission with me here--even dumber for her to land. This will work out okay--no way she is flying the supply drop.* He takes another bite of a vanilla cake. *Man, these are good.*

CHAPTER TWENTY SEVEN

Locke and Rousseau misdirect their captors towards the Wall.

So the torture continues with salt and hot knives thrust into their bodies. Ewalt's former comrades finally admit that he is headed towards San Francisco and why. They also say they do not know his plans to get there, dieing gratefully a few minutes later. Soon search teams go east along the interstate and west up the hillside. Then they begin a circular search pattern.

Ewalt watches as Locke and Rousseau's remains are carted up the hillside. He had stayed less than a hundred yards from his former comrades until they died. Knowing what his pursuers know about him had seemed a good strategy. Ewalt settles in among the crowd.

Darkness falls into coughing and wheezing, the yells and clatter, the screams of pain. Around midnight the horror takes a new turn: He sees the misery of parents watching their child die from a cold. Knowing that in the cities north of here, their child would have been saved by a pharmacist. He is sure this kind of event has sent both fathers and mothers through the Wall with one thought: Death.

He lies among the others. Overhead, the canopy of clouds reveal the moon's cradle. Blues and red tracers own the northern sky.

Any attempts at crossing back through the Wall means death at the hands of his comrades. Going forward with the mission means he will have to know how to get back. And of course, Jack Porter wants to control the Priestess Etu. He considers that absurd since he assumes she has been fighting that battle all her life. The Priestess, Ewalt has heard from a dozen conversation, is a few hundred miles south in San Francisco. Supposedly, she will be present at the fall of Portland.

When he finally sleeps, the images of thousands of sick bodies charge his dream. While an image of the Wall dedication ceremonies dances in his head. In his dream, sick people sit in the audience while the dignitaries speak. The dream ends when a sick child runs up on stage and shoots his father. "We're the lucky ones," says his dying father.

In the morning, cirrus clouds roll overhead, reflecting the pale red dawn on their fat bellies. Ewalt hears the sounds of people making love in the distance mix with the wheezing, the yelling, the coughing and the crying. It will continue on into the day and night. He finds himself sorry for the suffering around him and hateful for his partnership in their plight. All he's seen so far are people behaving, hating the Wall, readying to take back what they believe is theirs. And then there are unending waves of anger at the evil of those on the other side of the Wall--in the form of the Earth's Voice.

Lying quietly, waiting to see the routine, he tells himself tonight he'll sleep tied to a tree branch, rather than endure another night so close to the suffering of others. A cold wind stirs the wheezing women, sick old men, crying children, and screaming fights between lovers. The brutality of their plight feeds their anger. This is why the flow of insurgents through the Wall never stops. Ewalt has never been so certain of the eventual fall of those behind the Wall. Fearful there is not enough time to save his father, he decides to resign his commission. When he gets back, he plans begin work on a shelter beneath the old barn. *Sooner or later these fuckers are gonna' come knockin'. It will be best if they find nothing on the farm.*

Looking to the right, he watches a woman cough and an old man snore. Ewalt finds the smell of them fading. A woman behind Ewalt clears her throat before saying: "Let him suffer, the Demon pig." She smells like death and coughs so violently she rocks back and forth against him with every fit. Ewalt keeps his back to her, fearing he might catch tuberculosis.

He glances to the western mountains. Tonight, there is a weapons drop at two thousand feet and he needs to be there. He wonders how many Dirties sleep under the trees. He also wonders how anyone could possibly think a drop in these hills might be secure. No matter. His choices are limited without weapons and supplies. And a single night in this horror is quite enough for him.

The women behind him moans and her body twitches violently. A few minutes later, he turns to the dead woman and dares her to blink. Others sit upright and look as well. A moment passes. He reaches out and shuts her eyes. A few say a silent prayer. Then they stand to get away from the diseased women. He does as well.

A couple wave at him without a word as they walk away. He returns their wave, then begins to wave at each person he sees. It is a custom among these people. A woman nearby, lying neat to her children, her arm hugging her two daughters, waves to Ewalt and follows it with a wink. He turns away. Ewalt tells himself he has no need of a shield. So far he thinks he is safe.

Other people stand up and make their way to the stream that serves as a toilet. In contrast to another stream a hundred yards on the east side that provides drinking water. The guards, posted all night to keep people from spoiling the supply of clean water or drinking from the sewer, are mostly asleep. Ewalt watches the people slowly pick their way over those who continue asleep. Not a person trips and not a prone person seems to notice. Stepping gingerly over nested bodies, Ewalt looks back at the woman who had spent the night touching him, kicking him, and then dying next to him. He will think of her in the coming weeks. She never complained. *That's three women who have died touching me.* His passivity for their suffering has begun to rub.

He continues his way through the crowd of bodies, careful not to step on those closest to the stream. They are older or sicker than the rest. The suffering here seems interminable. *What is so special about owning things when comfort yields this pain for others? There should have been a Suffering Channel in addition to the Sports and Movie Channels. That would have helped the problem.* He watches the pain and the nobility of suffering as he walks.

At last, he breaks out from the bodies to the smelly soiled bank of the creek. He urinates in the stream next to another old man who sings an old folk song about a man and his mule, named Sal. All around the banks of the stream, other people void their bowels or urinate. Any of them could walk into the dozen or so tents set up; but few bother with propriety. The wash of shared misery purifies ego.

Ewalt ambles back up along the muddy bank to begin his trek to the higher elevation. He keeps his eyes to the ground, occasionally looking at someone who either approaches or walks near him. He waves. Then sticking his hand inside his torn jacket, he pulls off a piece of the food and eats it. Surprisingly, it is still soft.

More and more people come down the bank to relieve themselves. The crowding makes him feel a little safer as he walks uphill, especially since no one appears to be taking any notice of him.

Ewalt takes the rest of the morning to climb, passing a tent and stocking up on food, then following the dwindling stream uphill. Another stream joins from his left and he fords it. Four guards stand at the intersection eating. They look at him, wave, but otherwise ignore him.

Then he stands on a small peninsula with no people nearby. He continues walking, occasionally looking behind him. None of the guards pays attention. Ahead are a few encampments. The numbers have thinned to almost nothing. His sense of alarm heightens with the tingle of fear. He looks for signs of disease or threat but sees none. Ewalt walks slightly crouched, ready to dart in one direct or another.

The stench is gone. Commander Ewalt Rader continues uphill, climbing a steepening gully wall. Dead dry grass covers the ground rather than mud; there are no huge gatherings of people. Surprised to see a few small knots of people huddle together, he also notes they are widely scattered and seem unconcerned with him. He looks back to the plain and hillside he has come from. Then he sees it. There appears to be a line of guards down the hill. Their fires mark a perimeter that he crossed back when he forded the stream. Behind the guard line, the press of people rolls as far as his eye can see. He curses incessantly as he walks. He believes there is great danger here; he just does not know what it is. So he fears the small camps are for defense against something evil and unknown to him.

Ewalt stops around mid-afternoon. The walk is so uneventful he feels both amused and afraid. From up here, he can see that he had slept in a valley floor in the center of three creeks. The flashing lights at the top of the guard towers--those that are not overrun--seem to call him for help. Those sections of the Wall still in tact are islands surrounded by fast moving vehicles and a carpet of people. *The men and women inside those sections are dead. There will be no rescue.* Rather than pity, he thinks it strange that so much time and energy is used to keep needy people at bay. *Surely, the defense costs more than cooperation. Oh, they make money off the weapons. They can't make money off of helping people. Who started this madness? They should be hung.*

Up hill and to his right, a group of people begin to light a fire. Three men walk towards him carrying what look like spears. Rader again concerns himself with survival, with a certainty that his riddle of danger will be soon answered. The men all wear loincloths and leather necklaces of strung teeth. Slicked black hair is tied into ponytails. Their leader is several inches shorter than the other two. The group comes within five or six yards of Ewalt, then stops. The leader leans on his wood-tipped spear waiting for the other two to join him. He is so casual Ewalt doubts his sense of concern. That doubt will soon disappear.

The leader's eyes are dark, and set deep into his skull. The three men spread out in a wide arc. "So you've had enough, eh my friend?" The man in the center speaks. "I don't blame you. It's hell down there."

"It's easier to die with us. There is nothing worse than the hell of disease or the weapons of the Demons on the other side of the Wall," says another. "No need to fear us. We are in no rush. We're the firemen. You can trust us."

"I'm just walking up the hill. I don't want any trouble from you, firemen," Rader says seeking to discover who might attack first.

The men laugh. "Of course you are. Would you like to meet those you will feed and be reborn in--or--do you want to just die here?

Ether way it will be painless." The man on the right has responded first and Ewalt has his plan.

Ewalt also has his answer: cannibals. "I'm not going to die, fellas'. But you will. Unless you leave me alone. I am just walking through."

The man in the center looks at his comrades. "We get more and more of this now. It used to be people would come up here and practically beg us to kill them." He stares at Rader. "But now it seems you cowards seem to want to put up a fight. I don't understand the reason." The cannibal shakes his head. "But you look strong. You'll feed us for days."

Rader makes sure his feet are firmly planted in the dirt. "Your little clan is going to have quite a feast."

"Oh that's much better."

Ewalt launches one of the rocks he took from the man in the latrine at the man in the center. The rock strikes the man squarely in the face and he falls in a heap. Ewalt dives after the spear avoiding the hurled spear from the man on his right. Rolling, Ewalt comes to his feet, ready for battle. Surprised, the two remaining men do nothing further. One speaks to the other. "Look at his eyes. I will not kill one who will poison our clan with that Patrician madness in his brain. Go. We will celebrate Cris here instead. He is one of us. You're crazy. There is something wrong with you."

Ewalt has to grin. "You're kidding?"

The men move slowly toward their fallen comrade, making sure Ewalt sees they have no further use for him. Rader thinks it a trick, until the two men make a slight bow and begin to haul away their comrade. Ewalt searches the area noting that those still in the campsite: men, women, and children, make no move. The morning's shopping trip is over. Meat is available; but it will be one of their own. Who cares? Certainly not Cris.

Ewalt picks up the smooth rock he had thrown, then hurries up hill, still carrying the wooden spear for defense. As soon as he is out of their sight, he runs along the high edge of the embankment, constantly scanning the area. When he enters an area with green grass and healthy-looking oaks, he slows. Curious, why the people below didn't just push up the hillside, he knows that their numbers would easily swamp these small bands of cannibals. Ewalt postulates the cannibals perform a public service. A quick and easy death has some worth with all this suffering. He then decides that the remains of Locke and Rousseau were delivered to the cannibals after their death. *But why give the cannibals all this land?*

He finally stops for a rest. Catching his breath before puling off another piece of food, he wonders if the little cakes are unavailable up here. *Perhaps the people are clustered below to be near the food. So maybe food transportation is their weak link? Thanks, Jack.* A moment later, he sits down on a log and pulls off his left sandal. Peeling the sole apart, he reads a small map etched into the rubber. It shows the stream with two arms. It doesn't show a third arm. Rader--thinking he is lost--climbs a fir then compares the Wall's guard outlooks with the map. Climbing down, sure he is in the correct place. Then he stares at the map wondering why the third stream isn't there. Until he decides the Dirties added that third leg as a latrine for sanitation.

Voices of men and women mixes with clanking sounds of metal and the braying racket of mules. Hiding behind a tree trying to locate their direction, he soon sees the noisy caravan of people and mules on the far side of the stream. Ten or so people leading the mules are well-armed with automatic rifles. They talk loudly making crude jokes. Iron ore fills the huge leather packs carried by the mules.

After they pass, Ewalt climbs a tree again and plainly sees their trail. It is wide enough for a small car or cart. Commander Rader groans to himself: *Those pinheads in operations have probably planned the drop right in the middle of a mining operation. Are they trying to kill me? Ruin the mission? Bad planning? The drop is run by Feiss Logistics. They're known for their planning capabilities. Oh crap, it's a set up. But a set up of who and why?* A second set of mules comes through the woods. He hugs the tree, motionless as five more mules and their handlers, pass along the trail.

This smaller group is also well-fed and well-armed. They have no scouts out and barely consider the forest around them. Ewalt considers what it will be like up here when the news of his arrival spreads--and why it hasn't yet. Perhaps when these caravans return up the hill they will carry the news. He plans to be on his way to San Francisco before that happens. A crow screams and the group of men and women immediately freeze. Rader pulls himself closer to the trunk. Immediately the platoon spreads out and takes up defensive positions near the trees.

What the hell is this all about?

The rattle of weapons' fire fills the wood. Two people and two mules are immediately hit. Screams and moans mix with hoots and howls. Another mule falls hard to the ground. The soldiers began to effectively return fire. The hoots and howls cease in the din of the firefight. The iron ore is safe again. Ewalt waits for a raiding party to retreat by him. Instead, everything falls silent. A few moments later a second firefight erupts from down the trail. It is followed by a few short bursts of celebratory weapon fire.

So it is not as civil here--as on the flats. Those guards mark the perimeter of Elena Etu's control. Out here it's anyone's game. No wonder everyone wants to talk to her. She's the government.

As night falls, Ewalt approaches some jagged rock tailings from the mine nearby. Flowing out from a rock wall like runoff from a deep red glacier, the rust-colored water forms a small stream. Various chemicals cause it to glisten, making it easily seen from the sky. By the pool, a tumble down-shack and an empty corral. *For mules*, he assumes. The beasts are somewhere on the path with their loads of iron ore.

He circles wide to the right into the spruce and fir, scanning for a sturdy fir, one away from the drop zone. He wants to spot the approaching supply helicopter as early as possible. It will make no noise. After a fifteen minute climb, Ewalt makes himself comfortable on a branch thirty feet up. He snacks on what remains of his last cake waiting for the moon to rise behind the mountain fir.

Picking pieces of pitch from his hand, watching the moon ascend, Ewalt listens to the forest life. Soon a young buck appears nibbling on weeds. Conventional wisdom behind the Wall held that all wildlife has been killed for food in these parts. Indeed, on Rader's hike up here, he had seen no signs of deer or the wild pigs that once roamed the area. This deer munches young wild flowers without a care in the world. *Perhaps,* Ewalt wonders, *the cakes have done more than just feed the population. By providing food for humans, the animal population has been allowed to recover--or perhaps the extinctions had all been just more spin.*

He remembers a news report about how the "horde of human locusts" had eradicated species after species on this side of the Wall. *Which locusts was that? Who the fuck am I fighting anyway? And why the hell am I fighting for the bastards who created this hell? Fuck me. This is a one big cluster-fuck.*

A fawn appears, followed by a doe presumably the mother. Ewalt watches them, astonished that the ecosystem functions in quiet harmony. So far the route of his mission is nothing like the briefing had indicated. They had said that he should expect a large mud bog full of dirty people killing and eating each other. *And once again, nobody gives a damn.* Ewalt sees a black helicopter rise from the north, then drop down again. He leaves his perch as quietly as he can. The deer bolt away. A pop, then the whine of a missile's plume lights the area around him.

Not thirty feet in front of him, a team of six soldiers squat, apparently looking right at him. Rader drops to the ground and then realizes they had, in reality, turned away from the fiery tail of the missile aiming for his supply helicopter. He is now sure this drop is a set up of come sort. *There is no way this ground-based team could have been so on the mark without battle-management support.* He watches the missile sputter and fall dark to the ground. *Good pilot.* Ewalt remains motionless in the grass as two of the soldiers hurriedly tug on a second tube and attach its fins. The others crank a crude handle that lowers the metal tripod so they can load a second mssile. Ewalt quietly rolls away so he will not be blinded--or seen--during launch.

The second missile fires. Ewalt tracks the flare. The missile makes a sharp turn. It is a heat-seeker following a pilot trying to evade it. Ewalt counts to twenty, hoping the gunner isn't a rookie. After twenty seconds the heat seeker missile will run out of fuel. At twelve, the gunship's Gatling gun opens up. Rader runs away from the tree he'd perched on as the missile detonates almost directly over the tree.

The pilot begins to descend.

That dumb son of a bitch is still trying to complete the drop. No one is stupid enough to do that here. There's no place to maneuver and that rocket site is perfectly placed.

Another launch plume and the Gatling gun opens up on the third missile. This time there is no room to maneuver. Exploding in a mute light, then a roar, the badly damaged machine begins to wobble, then fall. The missile team on the ground cheers. Rader watches the burning gunship dip. Instead of going straight down, it tilts back coming straight toward the landing zone, guns blazing, chewing up the area around the launcher and killing three of the Dirties.

No fuckin' way. Not her. They'd have carpet bombed the area first. No way Daddy would expose little Mandy to danger like this. Wait. There is no Daddy. Whoa, so that's it. That bitch of a mother wants little Scout playing soldier so she can run the company. I am definitely on the wrong team here.

The impact of the missile has severed most of the controls. The helicopter lurches as the yaw line jams. Lipps struggles to keep the chopper under control as Ernst fires at the launch location. The crash sentinel begins to beep and a synthetic female voice calls out from the speakers: "Emergency landing. Fuel lines compromised. CPU down. Fire--fire suppression on. Target acquired. Instrument failure. Mayday. Prepare for crash. Warning." Lipps signals to Ernst to put the weapons on manual and brace for a crash. He reaches out to shut down the fuel lines.

The ship crashes through the upper branches and turns sideways. Lipps smashes his head against the side window, the helmet protecting his skull. The nightmare of falling through trees, turning over, cracks and bangs, the moan of torn metal, hides his own sounds of fear. Then silence.

Thomas Lippman finds himself swinging like a pendulum. The harness holds him. He grabs hold of the frame and braces his legs against the instrument panel. Then with one hand, he lifts the safety from a bright red switch overhead and pushes on the release button. The front canopy falls forward like a hinged eggshell; it balances a moment on torn hinges, then falls to the forest floor a few feet below. TJ sees Ernst's dead body on the ground. He drops to the forest floor and stands.

"Freeze."

Thomas Jefferson Lippman lets his shoulders drop. He can feel a wound in his gut bleed down his leg. A woman and two men approach him. He waits for a bullet. One of them speaks: "He's scrawny. Let's just cook him and eat him here," a man says, laughing.

"I took my poison pill, Scruffy. Enjoy." Lipps smiles.

"You can't get back to the other side, pilot. So you're one of us now. Some joke, huh, hero? We're not going to hurt you," the woman says. "We want information from you. Then we'll get you a medic."

The shorter of the men approaches him while the taller man levels his weapon at TJ. The woman takes out a flashlight and examines the crash. "Your SGR is dead. I am sorry. We know you're making a supply drop. That means your people are close." The other men keep scanning the area. "Keep your hands up, pilot," the woman says. "What's your name?"

"Mickey Mouse," TJ replies. The shorter man shakes his index finger back and forth.

"You don't get it. Once you're on this side of the Wall they forget about you. I am Lieutenant Elaine Walker. Air-Ops-Supression, Alameda." The tall muscular woman keeps her distance. "Check out the Rapier."

Strapping a weapon to his back, the shorter man spits on TJ and climbs up into the chopper. A second small light from a flashlight then appears. "More weapons in a drop pack--pretty beat from the explosion. Food, clothing, and meds, it is definitely a supply run." The man sticks his head out. "We've got a winner here. The telecom looks good too. I bet it's for that nut we heard about from the cannibals." He begins to climb down.

"You stay up there, Carlisle."

The short man nods. He nestles behind the pilot seat.

"I'll send relief later. Pilot, you are bleeding down your boot. Come on, you," the leader says to Lipps. She points down a trail with her weapon. TJ lingers, thinking how little he understands about what is going on. The missile launch site was perfectly placed. He never had a chance.

Then, through the woods a familiar voice calls out to them. "Hey you. Don't shoot. I want to give up." It is Ewalt Rader's voice. The insurgents move slowly forward. Ahead, a figure on the trail waits, arms up, not moving. Lipps can tell it is far too skinny to be the bullish Ewalt Rader.

"So get over here."

The figure remains still. "Now." Still no movement. "Kill this mother-fucker first," she hisses. One of the men turns and fires a single bullet into the skull of Thomas Jefferson Lippman. He collapses to the ground unsure of why he can no longer stand. The woman hisses: "Okay, we're ready now. Let's fight, Bordo."

Someone snorts out a laugh.

"Bordo, your friend is dead. Running short on brains are you?" The woman motions for one man to seek cover by a tree. Then she speaks again: "You. Come in slowly and keep your hands where I can see them."

The figure doesn't move.

"Waste 'em."

The men let loose with short bursts of gun fire. Miraculously the figure doesn't fall. "It's a dum--" That's all the woman says. She tries to scream; only a gurgling sound comes out. In the same instant her pistol is torn from her hand. A naked figure darts passed. His middle finger raised in her face. The woman falls dead to the ground.

Turning, the other soldier sees a sharp stick sticking out of the leader's neck. The man spins too late. Ewalt kicks his weapon aside. A second solid kick lands in the man's gut. Ewalt tries to fire the pistol. It jams. Ewalt jumps on the man and slams his head against a rock. The body goes limp. The man in the gunship begins to shoot at Ewalt. He grabs the dead man's rifle. Aims, then kills the man hiding in the helicopter with a short burst from the weapon.

Searching the dead woman for bullets and maps, Ewalt finds a cake and another three clips. He quickly reloads the rifle looking down at Lipps--who watches him. *God, he's alive.* "Hang on buddy."

A grunt comes from Thomas Lippman, then words: "Ewalt, her mother set her up to die. She needs you." Nothing in Ewalt's life has prepared him for that statement. A few seconds later, Ewalt doesn't know when, the pilot lies dead on the forest mat.

Ewalt stares, mouth agape, confused and dizzy at the brutality between parent and child. Ewalt has no lever against that kind of madness: a mother wanting to kill her own daughter. Hours pass without his knowledge. His eyes remain fixed on the dead body of Thomas Jefferson Lippman.

So what if she needs me. She's a murderer.

CHAPTER TWENTY EIGHT

Elena stands, watching the day fade, still stunned by the day's events. The attack on the Portland munitions factory was a complete failure. There will be no high-explosives to breach the Columbia Wall. With her back to the desk, she scans the crowds below as functionaries move in the wrecked buildings across the way. Vendors crowd the side streets. Troops are positioned at various places keep order down below as thousands stream through the square on their way to the Wall. Other troops just below her guard the trucks that will take her north--to the other side of the Wall. *What have we done?*

To the left, teams of people still work to repair the cable car line. It is said the cable car system was the first item destroyed by the retreating troops. Its repair has become a city-wide hobby.

Inside, on the soon to be empty sixth floor, the last symbols of her power remain: a fourteen-foot square bamboo rice box with a desk and chair on top--and the red and yellow striped tent beside it. The Priestess, though she finds the tent a bit gaudy, thinks it far cozier than her bed space in the old administration offices. She has found tent-living to her liking. The tent supplies an unexpected stature to her meetings, and more importantly a nice view of the day. Her coo-corral, as she calls it, also looks through the glass wall to Union Square. The only object in the tent now, besides her futon, is a chrome hat tree. From it hangs her silver necklaces. They are the same necklaces she had worn that first day in San Francisco so many years ago.

Outside the tent, the large desk is waiting to be moved off the huge wooden rice box. Looking like a medieval court, old floor lamps burning tallow, forming a hallway from the escalator, by the old escalators, in the dark reaches, stand her floor guards. The rest of her ersatz seat of government waits to be moved. Some of it on the floor above. Some of her people still hard at work on the floor below; and the rest, in trucks traveling north.

At the stilled escalator, Baylor appears with a young man. The boy appears to be no more than eighteen or nineteen. He wears leather pants and a blue tee shirt. His black hair is tied back; and the features of his face seem muddled in thought. Filthy, his dark eyes show the light of intelligence. *That can be bad or good since he is not a local.* The duo walks in between the line of torches. The Priestess smiles as Baylor approaches. His lord-of-the-manor stride declaring an important message. With the young man in tow, he stands in front of the Priestess Etu. His head bowed.

She examines Baylor. Chicken feathers are stuck to his head and streaks of red paint cover his chest. The scalps are new, again. He pushes the boy forward saying, "Speak." Baylor then stands quietly. His arms are crossed in front of his chest and his bottom lip pushing out.

"Priestess, I am from Portland. They have begun to move behind the river Wall."

"You are sure there is a second Wall?"

"I have been a laborer on the Wall since I was sixteen. So I have worked on it for more than three years." He looks back at Baylor who nods. The boy looks back at her. His eyes wide with concern about the madman standing behind him. "They do not plan to defend the back of the Wall. All of their remaining weapons face forward, toward the water. If you can get behind the Wall and attack the Wall from behind--it has no defense--except for the helicopters and tanks. And their helicopters will not fly for long."

She looks at Baylor. He winks. "Has this boy talked to Phillip?"

"He sent him to me," Baylor responds. "Explain why the flying death from hell will no longer scalp our lives."

The boy rolls his eyes at the Priestess, asking why she has this lunatic near.

"Go ahead and tell me."

"The rubber hoses they use for their fuel and hydraulic lines are made by my uncle. He is...Was a chemist. He told me to tell you that some hoses are made for fuel and some for the hydraulic fluids. The wrong fluid in a hose will degrade it because it is not made for the fluid flowing inside the hose. As an insurance policy for our safety--he has been selling them the wrong kinds of hoses for the last few months. He had figured if they made good on their promise to get us across the river he would resolve the problems as they came up. If not, well that was just their loss." He looks at the small bowl of Kandy on her desk.

"Go ahead. Take one." She looks up at Baylor. "Do they use his hoses on the tanks as well? Did he say anything about that?"

The boy is eating the cake and thoroughly enjoying it. "This Kandy is fresher than the stuff at the Wall."

"The tanks?" She asks again with a smile.

"Yeah, them too. I guess they only use his hoses for the turbine systems not the hydraulics. So they will run for a while then stop--but not crash. Can I have another?"

She nods. "Why don't you go down the stairs and ask the guards to take you to the canteen. What happened to your uncle?"

The boy looks up from the food. His eyes blaze hatred. "When they destroyed the factory they killed him. My parents too. You just let me know what you want me to do. I'll do it." The boy turns passed Baylor to walk slowly toward the stairs.

The madman watches the boy start down the escalator then leans closer. "It is the will of Disney that directs our victory." He then wears a solemn gaze. "Also, three spies tried to kill the Food Man after his meeting with you yesterday. They underestimated the mob protecting him. Their bodies are missing but we are sure they were sent from the other side of the Wall."

"They are getting ready to deal with us--looking for leverage." Her voice is calm as her eyes search the lion-faced man with his flowing golden hair. The chicken feathers, the red paint, the mad darting eyes, they all pierce her like arrows. The sight of his physical beauty, her treasured memories of his courage, and his goodness, cause her to shut her eyes. Her former lover knows only to protect her. The rest of him has taken refuge down some distant hole of consciousness. She opens her eyes and sees him stealing a glance at her. "Baylor, do you think the Food Man has an army?"

"I don't think so. I think they love him, Priestess Etu. But they are not his army. I think some of the mob thinks you sent the guards. The Food Man is on his way here to see you now." He stands at attention. A twitch appears over his left eye.

She sighs. "Dr. Vaz is a good man." She leans back on the edge of the rice box watching her ex-lover. He immediately diverts his eyes to the linoleum floor. They have not been intimate for years. "Follow me." She walks across the floor to a set of stairs by the old rest rooms. Upstairs, a second cavernous room dances in the light from torches. She turns in between two wall-sized white plastic plates that hang from silver chains. This floor contains treasures she will load only when she leaves.

Ahead, written across other plastic panels hanging from the ceiling are the words "Today's Women." A pair of guards stands beside the plastic panes. Just behind the plastic panels are a pile of swords and axes. Old blood stains the floor.

Baylor follows her through the opening between the two panels to a narrow hallway formed by a dozen more white plastic panels. Life -size, they are all of Elena dressed in exotic looking clothes. Baylor will later tell his sergeants that he has been to heaven. No women he knows have such radiant, smooth faces, smiling bright red lips, and chalk white teeth. No women are so impossible to touch. Baylor will say he believes he has never seen such beautiful women. Deep inside him, he will wonder if he ever really touched beauty.

"Baylor do you remember why all this is so important?"

"They are what we fight for. I remember that much. I know this space is always guarded." He glances at the piles of weapons, then looks over to the small shopping corners: Punk, Rag, Business, Ultra, and Top Drawer. Once, to the sounds of demographically correct music, Elena had strolled this same area as a customer. At the time she had been considering the offer from Feiss.

Overhead, a huge blue box kite hangs suspended from the ceiling. It says: "Elena Etu. Elena and You!" Baylor reads the words furtively as he passes under it. The words make no sense to him. They enter a dark forest of manikins in furs and jewels. "Bullets?" She says, stopping in the middle of the manikins.

The wild-man starts, wondering about the manikins. "I don't understand." He thinks the question has something to do with dead figures.

"They wasted bullets protecting Dr. Vaz?" She stares at the furs around them.

"Yes, Priestess--but they say every bullet hit its mark."

She watches his eyes wander over the beautifully dress manikins. Baylor has been accused of some particularly perverse behavior--two brutal deaths by decapitation. "Does he pay them to protect him?"

"No. I don't think so." The man glances at the long furs. "These would make wonderful bed toys." He blushes red. "Sorry."

"Baylor, please look at me."

He snaps all his attention to her. She sees the crazy-killer-eyes. No one wants to be the next victim of this madman. That had been her steel. But with the fall of the Wall, she must promote justice to keep her reign in tact--not brutality. And Baylor instills fear in her now as well. "The world revolves around the battles of those who seek power." She points her finger at him.

The man hangs his head. "And those who stare, are cows to be slaughtered."

"Oh, stop." She watches him look up at her as he shakes with fear. She gives up again. "In your opinion, would the soldiers have killed the Food Man. Or did they just want to steal him away?"

"It is odd, Priestess. They were certain these spies were going to kill him. The men drew their weapons the moment they saw the Food Man. It is said they were going to kill him in your name--they said. To keep him from running away."

"Why do you say that?" She asks, her arms on her hips. "When I returned from the Wall I praised him." Elena folds her arms behind her back. "What makes you think people believe I fear the Food Man?"

"They heard the spies say it as they approached. They said you think the Food Man's task is done."

That doesn't make sense. They need me to keep order until they can replace me with a leader. Which means...Dr. Vaz. But they were trying to kill him. I don't get it.

"Baylor, should I fear the Food Man?"

"Never. I think he is strange. He only wishes to serve more people by feeding them." The man's brow breaks into a sweat, hoping he has answered correctly. "Priestess, I am not a troublemaker. I do not want to be leader, either. I wish to serve you. You run things. I am madness. I am no challenge to you. Do not be angry with me."

The Priestess watches the man look at the lifeless manikins.

"Please let me return to the land of the living. This is a dangerous time and I need to protect you."

"You speak to me with fear because you think this is the entry to death? Baylor, I am not upset with you."

"You are wonderful. How could you not be upset with me? I have failed. Once I was a whole man. Now I am an animal. They are trying to assassinate the Food Man to stop the flow of food. You ask questions because you see that whatever they do--it is to hurt you. Let me return to fight the Demons for you. After your task is done then take me to death, please. Just not now."

She nods quietly. "Take any of these furs. They will keep you warm. It always rains in Portland." The man stands motionless. His head bowed.

"Is there something wrong?"

"I will do better. I will become more fierce. You'll see. We will succeed." He grabs for the nearest long fur coat leaving the figure nude. Baylor bows to the Priestess Elena Etu. "Count on me for anything."

"You may go." After he withdraws to the stairs, she walks further into the forest of manikins to sit at a small table. On it, a small brass chime hangs from a golden loop that stands on a square of black-painted bamboo. Overhead, on a hanging poster, two lovers recline on the main deck of a yacht. The man in the poster sips champagne from a long glass flute. The woman stares longingly at him. Under them is the slogan, "Elena Etu. Elena and You! Shop With Me!" Her fingers tap the chime. A guard appears a few seconds later.

She speaks: "How long until the Food Man arrives?"

"He has just entered the square, Priestess."

"And Baylor has left?"

"Yes ma'am."

"Thank you."

He bows at the waist and leaves her.

Elena stares at the chime. Baylor had given it to her on their first date. She can no longer cry for him. Elena will soon give up trying to get him to remember that he is more than a machine dedicated to defending her life. *It was those first terrible days after the mad hordes that did it.*

Baylor had been covered with blood most of the time keeping them safe. Elena had never expected to see a fury so insane, or a blood lust so consuming, from an entire city. Baylor killed day and night. Then one day he had to kill a group of children who set upon them with bats. At the end of the battle, he had killed the twenty teenagers, and suffered a broken arm. The next day, Baylor scalped those he found dead and returned with his now characteristic skirt of scalps. The man was gone and only devotion remained.

In time, the guards began to model his fanaticism. Their fear and respect made everything worse because that fanaticism saved her life dozens of times. Even so, she thanks God that Baylor has not been called on to fight more children--rabid or not. She finds herself wishing his madness was an act to hurt her for all she has put him through. That kind of hatred, she can cope with. His dog-like devotion cuts into her over and over.

She stands and stares again at the man and his champagne. That photo shoot, in Miami, was where they had first met in person. Baylor had just been released from the military and she had requested him for the photo shoot--unknown to him. She curses herself for what she had sought from him. *He was just too beautiful to resist.*

Elena walks passed the parade of white plastic panels hanging from the ceiling and then goes back downstairs to her desk. A bell chimes from the floor below "Yes," she says.

Phillip tops the escalator. The old man is unbraiding his beard. "Elena, Joe Vaz is below in the glass lobby. He has bodyguards. Men with weapons arrived with him. They are peaceful and they have stayed in the square. They seem concerned."

She looks below and sees the men immediately. They have clustered directly across the street. She scans to the right and left. Two gun emplacements are trained on them. She faces Phillip again. That is his work.

He speaks: "I believe Dr. Vaz is worried about what will happen to those who killed the men impersonating your guards." The old man looks at Elena admiring her beauty. "They had identified themselves as your guards and they were killed anyway. He thinks you may not trust him anymore." Phillip tells himself he loves beauty above all else. Sadly, it is not true. "Joe worries about his people. They do not know where the assassins came from. I think your calling for that meeting might appear to have been a trap--to some."

"I want him in Portland. It's too dangerous here. They destroyed the factory in Brazil looking for him. They'll do it again. We have proof of that now."

Phillip nods to her.

"We have no munitions to attack the second Wall, Phillip."

He circles the chair to make sure all the guards are well out of earshot. "If the hydraulics are compromised we might be able to take out the guard towers from the rear by helicopter. If we can destroy enough of them, they will be blind in that sector without helicopters. We can attack that hole." He smiles. "I'll need someone to help me with the preparations and timing."

"That means Joe Vaz."

"I don't know anyone else with the horsepower to manage the logistics. It will be a very tricky assault. I have been examining the Redding Wall. I think I understand their construction design principles."

"We were premature in our attack." She pauses for a moment. Phillip remains silent. "He has no place to go but with us." She looks closer at her advisor. "I also need to know if others might consider him the chosen replacement for me. Now that Mr. Feiss is no longer with us."

Phillip smiles. "You took your time asking me about that. No one will obey him. They just protect him."

"Your timing on the Wall was poor." She stares at Phillip, wondering if he might be a traitor, rather than pragmatic. Elena immediately dismisses the thought. His hatred runs far to deep to desert it. "You should have had the sense to trust me to approve the plan."

"I am your advisor. This time my advice was a little more straight-forward than usual."

"Why?"

"I learned with the death of my family to follow my instincts." Phillip will never apologize for his actions of keeping Elena in the dark about the tunnels. He knows she needs him and he believes his actions were correct.

"I am not a Patrician."

"You are their chosen janitor for this mess here."

Her eyes remain calm. Her chest thumps. "So you do not trust me? That's why you did not tell me? Maybe I should be more cautious with you."

He blinks, shocked at the accusation. "I am your strategist and your friend. I have seen you perform miracles for these people. I had concluded that you would be angry for my insubordination, but see it was the correct thing to do. The Patricians are almost done for. Please let me complete my work. If you like I will withdraw so that you need not worry about my loyalty. I will go to Portland and make sure we get through the Wall quickly. I need Joe's brains to manage logistics while I do that. It is a ten-person task. Please understand that I have no need to lead and that I have no desire to live the day after the Patricians are dust. Elena, I am your servant in that task."

This second declaration of servitude angers her. "My life is a series of unforeseen events and selfless wanting servants. Sometimes I just want to laugh." She watches him melt in her gaze. "I'll make sure Dr. Vaz goes with us." A moment later she stands up. "Have Dr. Vaz meet me in the glass room."

The glass room is a hexagonal mirrored space that once

functioned as a private clothes-modeling area for the store's wealthiest clients. Walking towards it she nods to workers sitting at work-desks: energy, defense, food, water, sanitation, and development. Men and women work at these desks twenty-four-hours-a-day without complaining. These are people with one task; to get things back on track and growing. The perqs of these high level tasks once allowed others like these knowledge-workers to enjoy shopping trips, big homes, and large cars. In truth their job was to consume. The result was that they sought nothing more than perquisites. In contrast, these people love their tasks.

She watches a man scribble calculations on sheets of paper. With a computer, his task of food distribution could have been done in a few seconds. As things stand, it takes him all day to complete his calculations. Even with that burden, he never makes a mistake. The food always gets where it needs to be. In fact, the circle of food distribution widens every month. Elena once tried to give this man furs for his children. The man had said his children were fine. In his eyes she had seen happiness. In all of these peoples' eyes she sees happiness. They believe in the work they do. There is no need to quell the pain of a job that seeks to tear happiness from others to increase sales.

Two guards snap to attention as she reaches the double glass doors. She nods back and enters a dingy yellow hallway. It is no longer scarred with obscenities. At the end of the hall, a gold-lettered sign over the black door says: "The Gallery." Passing through the ebony door, she enters an eight-paned arc of a misted glass that lightens and darkens with the clouds overhead. Baylor greets her with a slight bow. She had not wanted him here. He apparently thought her in some kind of danger.

Joe Vaz appears wearing gray shorts and a bright green paper shirt hanging over his long torso. His stick-like arms protrude from the sides. Unkempt wispy brown hair falls over a bony skull. In the middle of all this disarray--deep brown eyes that stare out from an old soul. All around him is his image on the many mirrors. He sees them, but does not acknowledge them. Joe Vaz does not like the way he looks.

Elena sits in a wing-backed wicker chair in the center without speaking. The damp coolness of the plants placed along the walls touch her skin. A young woman appears from behind a door and places a wooden stool, for Joe, in front of the Princess, then withdraws. He stares at Baylor, wondering if his friend Elena would have the crazy man kill him for some reason. The Priestess' face appears suddenly stern, and more angry than he would have expected. It confuses him. He sits, hands folded on his lap.

"Doctor Vaz, did you know I had an adopted brother?" The rhetorical question is left unanswered. "Carlos was an orphan that my father, Emile, adopted when I was very young. One day I asked him what it was like to leave a horrible home and come to a beautiful home. He said it was like walking on the beach all the time. Then one day Carlos disappeared. He left me a note that said thank you for the use of my parent. I never saw him again. I would like to think he was a selfless man went forth to help people. Why did you have those people killed?" She asks.

Joe is startled by the shift and the question. He interlaces his fingers, then pulls them apart, replacing his hands one on top of the other. He speaks carefully: "We were on our way back from the meeting you called. My neighbors heard the assassins say that they were sent to kill me--by you. They did not riot."

"Did you give an order to kill the people impersonating my guards?"

"I gave no order," Joe says more insistently. "Those people were just trying to help me," he says. "What do you really want to talk to me about, Elena?"

"Why did you have the bodies hidden from me?" Her eyes flash. This kind of assault from her startles him.

"I don't know what happened to the bodies."

"Perhaps we should lock your friends up for rioting?" The Priestess asks.

Joe stares hard at her. Then, realizing it is the wrong thing to do, his gaze fixes itself to the floor. "Okay, you caught me. I did it. I gave the order to kill your people. Then I told my soldiers to disappear into the hills. I confess. All I desire is dominion over this shit-hole." He sighs. "I am here to take control of your kingdom. Me and Herb Caen. Repent, sinner." He looks up and grins.

Astounded by the commentary, she signals for another young woman to bring two glasses of water. Elena notes Joe staring at the woman's figure. With a gesture, Elena instructs the young woman to remain. The attendant stands in parade rest, hands behind her back, chest out.

Joe tries to ignore her as the Priestess slowly sips her drink watching him. "Why didn't you go with those men? Why would you doubt they came from me?"

His eyes dart to the young woman then back at Elena. "They were dead the first time I saw them. I have spoken with my neighbors and they now understand the Patricians are trying to divide us."

"Okay then, what do you want? Why are you here?" Elena asks.

He looks at Baylor and notes his confusion as well. "Okay. One, I want your word that the people who protected me are safe."

"Done."

"Two, that you will guard the factory once I go north. You want me to go with you, right?"

A slight nod of her head.

"Three, I want to know what is bothering you."

"Why do I have to convince you to do the work we need of you?"

Joe blinks over and over. His brain and his mind perceive the event; his body seeks only peace since he reacts to confrontations badly. "I, ah, I didn't know. But I have work to do and you might not understand my procedures." He clasp and unclasps his hands.

Elena can see he is unable to maintain his balance and slowly sips more water. "Would you like some food?" She asks, giving herself more time to think.

He shakes his head. "No, no thank you. Listen, Elena, Priestess, there needs to be more food factories. Those little ones we have built around the state are useless without the main facility here. The battle for the Columbia Wall will take as long as the battle for the Redding Wall. Your helicopters are no match for the enemy. And while I do not doubt the eventual breach I also calculate you have another five years plus before you get through. I know you are going north. In the time it takes your forces to breach the new wall, I can build a factory out east then return."

"It isn't safe for you to stay here. Or travel alone, you stubborn man." Elena hands her glass back to the young woman. "And you just lied to me. You said you are going to go north." She scrutinizes Joe's face.

He glares at her. "I didn't want to run into trouble like I did in Brazil. I thought it best to accept the obvious. Still, I thought if I made my own schedule, I might be safer."

"So you don't trust me. I thought we were friends."

"What?" Joe calms and tries to examine her face looking for the point. There is one but it's not the one he expects. He cannot compute the circumstance. None of it makes sense to him. "We are friends. For what that's worth--so why the inquisition?"

Anger sparks her eyes. "So then you are ready to leave with us?" She knows the answer to this question.

"The factory remains under attack. Some minor damage was done already. I am repairing it. We are setting up new decoy signals. I expect more saboteurs and assaults for a while. Once it is under control I can leave." He begins tapping his knee with his fingertips.

The Priestess waits before speaking to gather her thoughts. "Without abeyance, there is no authority. Without authority, there is no order. Without order we are all dead."

"I don't question your authority," he says, again trying to get his brain to understand what is going on. "Those assassins were sent from the other side of the Wall to destabilize you, not me. It's best we are in different places. But I will join you in Portland whenever you wish."

"Without the food we are weakened. Even with the fall of the Redding Wall. You and your factory are the keys to our defense now. Insofar as you and I, they can't just remove one of us because the other is backstop. They are continuing to send out reconnaissance so they can locate you, not the main factory. Until they succeed, I am protected. You are not. You cannot stay here," she says. "They have sent six teams we know of. That means there are probably a dozen we do not know of. One team made it close to you. The next team may be successful if you stay there."

"They'll never get to me and they will never find me," he says defiantly. "I've done this escape thing before."

"Luke Feiss wanted you to escape from DC. He is dead now."

"Nonsense." Joe Vaz loses his confusion. *She is worried about me.* He smiles.

She guesses his brain has made some odd connection. He has stopped fidgeting. "I need to examine the bodies." She wants to make sure they are from the other side of the Wall and not locals conscripted to treason. "I want you to find them for me before I leave. Once I have seen the bodies I will know the next move of the others on the far side of the Wall." She waits.

He reluctantly nods. "Alright. What's the plan?"

She looks to the attendant. "You may leave us now." The attendant quickly leaves, but only after smiling at Joe. He smiles back at her with no plan to pursue her. Elena frowns. That part of her plan has failed.

"Why did you tell me the story of your brother?" Dr. Vaz asks. "You know I am dedicated to our success."

"He ran away. Don't you do that. Not now when we are almost complete. I need you to help me."

"We have years of fighting."

"And if we didn't?"

He groans. She closes the trap. "Dr. Vaz, we have a source who tells us the hydraulics on the helicopters and the tanks are compromised, and without easy repair. That means our antiquated helicopters are the only thing flying for a short period of time. Could your factory run without hydraulics?"

"You are very smart. I see your point."

"We need your help to exploit that short term problem." She looks at Baylor. "Please give us a moment." The man exits out the door. "Please return to your factory and do whatever you can to prepare for saboteurs and God-knows what other kinds of assault. We will follow you by the end of the day tomorrow. Have the bodies ready for us to examine. Phillip will work with you to try to develop more defenses for your factory while we are there. After that you have to leave the factory and come with us. We may have only a small window of opportunity. Phillip needs your help to launch an assault. He plans on leveraging the hydraulics problem to punch a hole in the Columbia Wall. Then a breach, does that make sense to you?"

"I need to think about that. I am not sure how it would work--but the concept is sound."

"Do you believe that you were allowed to escape, Washington DC, Doctor Vaz?"

"I don't know. I do know a female soldier saved my life. I doubt a random act of courage like that could be planned." He stares at her. Sure of his trump card.

Elena pauses. "That soldier was there to act as an expert witness on helicopter tactics, right?" His shell cracks as he nods yes. "Her name was Amanda Feiss. She is Luke Feiss' daughter."

"I see. And I suppose they herded me to San Francisco as well?"

"So far as I know."

Joe stands up suddenly. "There was no way for them to know I would come back to the Bay Area once it fell to the Dirties. I was in Brazil. Are you saying they herded me from Washington to Brazil. Then onto San Francisco by destroying my factory?"

"The factory in Brazil was destroyed as a strategic response to threat. Doctor, you were born at the Mission Bell Motel, not a hundred yards from where you now live. Your mother worked for the city of Belmont. Your father was a TV and audio repair man who worked at local audio visual store right at the top of that hill in Daly City. His name was Matthew something or other. Then your family started building windmills in Daly City, until your brother was killed in an accident just before you went off to college."

"Well you have it almost correct."

"The point is your return was a certainty once the factory in Brazil was destroyed and this city fell. Now that the Redding Wall is down, it is also a certainty that you are a walking target. We both are. I'd keep you here with me until we leave, but I know you need to complete your plans to make the main factory safe. I'll give you a day. Then we have work to do up at the Columbia Wall."

He stands, resigned to the facts. "I can't tell if you are a devil or a saint."

"Unlike you, Doctor Vaz, I am a little of both."

CHAPTER TWENTY NINE

Marching in front of them, Baylor leads the Priestess Elena Etu's entourage up Market Street towards Diamond Heights. Other men carrying weapons surround Priestess Elena Etu and her small party. Off to their left, the remains of city spreads out like a broken toy: crushed buildings, sunk cruise ships, the wreck that was a baseball stadium, the shattered downtown. She calms herself by studying the fishing boats out in the bay. *The new Wall is impregnable.*

Baylor, dressed in a navy captain's uniform awash with an array of peacock feathers, scans the streets and wrecked buildings. Walking two steps in front Elena and to the left--like a well-trained--but brutal guard dog. He hums Anchors Aweigh. No one makes fun of him or even grins at the maniac.

This is the first time Elena hasn't insisted he walk beside her. Phillip feels a sadness for the long-ago lovers as Elena continues to watch the city and Baylor. "There is nothing there for you, Priestess. Let him live the life he chooses."

Elena, horrified that Phillip speaks of Baylor as if he isn't there, quickly says: "Baylor, you're sure they still have the bodies of the men who tried to kidnap the Food Man?"

"Yes, Priestess Etu. I am quite sure." He greets her with a subservient nod.

She can tell something is not right with Baylor. Elena glances at Phillip who will not look at her; she looks back at Baylor.

Phillip tries another tack. "Baylor seems oblivious to everything but protecting you."

She ignores Phillip, forcing herself to gaze over the crowds edging the hillside. Most are engaged in repair or commerce. The old and very young enjoy the parade.

After a few minutes, Phillip tries again. He is campaigning for Baylor to stay behind in San Francisco. "The city looks better, don't you think?"

Elena looks at him, annoyed that he still tries to manipulate her. "You will treat him with respect."

"I understand, Priestess. But look. The bodies are gone. People no longer defecate in the streets and they no longer kill each other for food. Shops are opening and we have fourteen real bakeries. We are becoming civilized."

"The Sunnyvale orchards are a godsend." Baylor's slightly slurred words drop like stones on those around him. Elena believes his comment is in response to Phillip's stance that he is just too dangerous to go north.

"Of course there is room for improvement," Phillip says as if he could read her thoughts. "There's still no power. The water and sanitation system will take years to repair. And that's possible only if they stop bombing our projects. Still, look around. Even the roofs have been repaired. And that office buildings that used to house an oil company now houses ten-thousand people. That's certainly an improvement in occupancy," Phillip says pandering to Elena's dislike of the old oil cartel, looking for an avenue of discussion.

"You can stop the campaign," she says, walking a little bit faster to fall in line with Baylor. They both watch the roof dwellers move about on the down-slope building. A dim memory of making love so many years ago suddenly seems absurd.

The dirty brown blanket of roof dwellers have erected scaffolding across the roof tops. Forming a freeway for commerce and safe travel. During the worst of it, the roofs of buildings were far safer than the streets. Even now, years later, many refuse the streets, preferring the tangle of scaffolding. Some of the structures are so elaborate they span Market Street. The city-sized jungle gym is a giant toy for the children as they swing and jump about. As they pass under one bridge of scaffolding, a young girl smiles at the Priestess. She hangs upside down, knees securely wrapped around a horizontal support bar.

The Priestess waves to the child, sure she does not have the children's capacity to live with the horrors. It shames her and drives her to empathize with Baylor's madness. Elena glances at him and he returns a tight-lipped smile to her.

On the upside of the roadway, dull-eyed people stare out from an unwalled building marked with red crosses. The sickly people seem like little more than animals in holding pens. This huge building is a hospice, still called a hospital, despite the lack of medicine, walls, heat, power, and water. The dying are brought here by relatives so they can see the remains of the city as they die. There is little else this society can do for someone once they develop a serious disease. At one point people were literally spilling from the buildings to the ground below. Now, when they have had enough pain, they jump. The area below them is kept as lethal as possible to any jumper. Elena is glad she cannot see into the deep ditches where the sidewalks used to be. A murderous collection of sharp implements covers the ground; except where the body-baggers walk--to remove the dead for recycling. Elena notes there is space in some of the building and she wonders if that is improvement, or if more of the dying have just left for the Wall. The terminally ill often volunteer to be used as decoys on the other side of the Wall.

One of the reasons Elena arranged for the trucks to meet them at the factory was to gauge the numbers of sick and dying. Elena anticipates negotiations soon--if she can live long enough--and medicine is a high priority for her.

She looks over to Phillip. "Phillip, make sure the people on this road have fresh water. I don't like people sitting around here thirsty." Her impotence frustrates the Priestess Elena Etu.

"You know they now call San Francisco Bay, Ganges West?" Phillip says, surveying the distant water. "I don't know how they deal with all this suffering."

Baylor speaks: "The people I find most interesting are the ones who have found a way to live on the hard outer shell of buildings." He speaks to Elena, ignoring Phillip, but still he does not face her. "You know--the makeshift platforms of steel and wood are simply artful if you examine them. I saw one the other day that was surrounded by wind chimes. It was a symphony." A hawk flies low. A murderous howl boils up from inside him as his eyes narrow and his lips part, revealing bloody, recently sharpened teeth.

She stares horrified at the sight. He immediately stops growling. Looking shamed for a moment, he looks away.

"They are amazing, Baylor," Phillip says quickly. "I visited a group once and even stood out there on the windy platform where a family of six lived. They had taken the metal studs of the interior walls and bolted them together like a raft. Then, they suspended it from the exterior of the building using huge steel screws to tie the whole affair to the I-beam frame. Triangular sides supported the project. Their view included the entire bay from Berkeley to the Golden Gate. They even used partitions from the office cubicles to make small rooms. A view like that used to cost millions. Now you couldn't pay one of those bastards on the other side of the Wall to live in this wreck of a city."

Baylor nods. "These days anyone can have the view. The walk up and down the stairs must be a killer. There are probably less joggers as well." He smiles at his joke. This conversation kicks Elena's soul. Baylor's grisly mouth leaks a pink froth down his chin. She steels herself and turns to her former lover. "Do you remember when we camped on the roof of Embarcadero-One that autumn?" She asks, examining him.

"That family rigged traps for anyone foolish enough to try and get out to us," Baylor says looking at her. His teeth and gums bleed. "They were nice--but I don't think I will ever be able to look a pigeon square in the eye again. Food is a curse. You ever wonder, Eli, if original sin wasn't eating the apple, but just eating?" She sees the eyes of man she once loved over a crimson mouth and looks away. "It's all right, Eli. I need my madness. If they think I am crazier than them they will leave us alone. But I am not dangerous." He wipes pink froth from his mouth. "Perhaps you should base yourself outside of Portland--up in the hills. Until we breach the new Wall. I can work the city making it safe for you and you need not see me. Will that satisfy you, Phillip?"

"No. We stay together." Her eyes wander over to Phillip who wants to rescue her. He is torn between her pain and what he sees as a prudent decision to have Baylor left behind. Even so, he knows Elena's moments with her deranged lover are better than the agony he lives with every day.

Baylor arranges a set of peacock feathers on his right hip and then straightens his captain's cap. "I was just thinking that whomever tried to kill the Food Man is probably going to try to kill you also."

"We'll see, Bay." Her heart cries. She continues speaking to him. Elena cannot help herself. "Supposedly they captured more spies at the Legion of Honor," she says quickly.

"They tortured them." He lifts a hand to touch her then stops. "So apparently that is the meeting point. We have people waiting there. Still, I am worried about you."

"I keep telling you not to worry about me. I am fine now."

"You cannot believe they will keep the peace and honor agreements," he says firmly. "Their kind always tries the evil path first. After they exhaust every loathsome trick they will keep their word."

"It is why we are here, Bay."

His eye twitches. "What if they decide you represent strength instead of order? That your demise equals another chance for them to win?" Baylor asks. The lucidity startles Elena.

"You don't think the incursions are death squads do you?" Phillip says. Elena shoots him an angry stare. She sees Baylor's eye twitch and knows what is coming. She looks out to the fishing boats off the Berkeley shore.

"All I know is the teams we captured were teams of three," Baylor says. "The death squads when I was in the service were teams of three--while the recon teams were teams of four." He still watches the hawk as he speaks.

"At this point we don't know how many people have gotten through--or their mission," Phillip says. Of course, had Elena not commanded him to respect Baylor he would have already derailed this conversation. Phillip is a need-to-know person.

"Did they ever catch the man from the other day? The one that escaped through the latrine and used the rocks to escape detection?" Elena asks.

Phillip looks to the ground trying to hide his frustration at her willingness to include Baylor. "He's loose and we don't know what this orders are," Phillip says. "The only thing we do know is that he was a SWAT Commander on his way to find you. Their tank commanders are college educated, well healed, and intelligent."

"So what does that profile say about him?" Elena asks.

When the hawk disappears behind a building, Baylor begins to hum Anchors Away again. He scans the sky for new threats to the Priestess Elena Etu.

Elena walks a bit slower to speak quietly to Phillip. "You knew about his teeth?"

"I did."

She continues. "It happened last night. Where were you?"

"Asleep. Priestess...I didn't know how to tell you."

"And you were saying about my leaving him here?" She is daring him to comment. Phillip knows the discussion is at an end. Baylor will not be left behind.

He looks at the crumbling roadway for a second, then looks up at her. "If our intelligence is right, the soldier was sent here to kill you. But he is still going to take care of number one That's our leverage."

She stares at him.

Phillip keeps trying. "It may also mean he has a way back through the Wall." He watches her frozen gaze move from object to object. "I am sorry, Elena. I didn't know what to do. I was shocked also."

She walks in silence for another fifteen minutes. Finally, she speaks: "What if the soldier has no connections on this side--if we were too efficient and we have already killed his links?"

"If he commands one of their tanks then he is an intelligent cowboy. He knows they will kill him as soon as they have the data they need from him. So that doesn't mean he is a definite supporter, but he is a maybe. Plus he's still alive. That puts him into an elite group of one--that we know about."

"So where is he?" She asks. "Make sure your people at the Legion of Honor know I want prisoners." She desperately needs to open a secure line of communication with the other side of the Wall.

"Already done."My guess is he is on his way to kill you or Dr. Vaz." A huge explosion sends a fiery cloud skyward. Within the second, Baylor is less than a foot away from his mistress. His Bowie knife drawn, eyes scanning everything around him. No one dares take a step towards the Priestess Elena Etu. It is instant death.

She looks at Phillip, confused at the rare explosion inside the city.

"That could be his calling card," Phillip says.

"Come on. Doctor Vaz wants as much time as he can get from

us."

An hour later, Elena and her entourage stand near the Church Street Tunnel; it is a few hundred yards away from the crowd. Phillip's eyes measure the mayhem through field glasses. Flames roar from the Mission Delores flicking thick black curls into the air. A third explosion collapses the bell tower in a geyser of flame. Angry mobs churn in small whirlpools under the smoke. The mob appears to crawl over itself to taste the fire's warmth--then it pulls back at the heat--leaving space for others to crawl forward.

"What are they doing?" Baylor asks.

Phillip walks back to her. "Those dark spots against the walls are burning bodies. The rioters are putting monastics against the wall. I suggest we leave this alone and continue south. This isn't an outside problem."

"Can I look?" Asks Baylor.

Phillip knows from experience Baylor is gearing up for battle. "In a minute," Phillip says as he examines the mob. "There's a woman against the church wall. They're about to burn her. She's not moving. Why doesn't she run?" Phillip looks away, rubbing his eyes.

"A believer," Baylor says. "She is defying them by not running. She is a brave one. I think I'll kill her and release her back to her God."

"No," Elena says.

Phillip hands the field glasses to Baylor and speaks to the Priestess. "That thick smoke is from the chemicals they're throwing against the building."

"They're burning another man with chemicals and keeping them there with arrows. The crowd seems to be dancing," Baylor says quietly.

"Baylor, you stay here with the Priestess. I'm going down there."

"We'll all go," the Priestess says. The guards follow grudgingly. Baylor steps in front to lead the guards forward and they form a wedge around the Priestess and Phillip. In one hand he carries three Peacock feathers as if they were a flag or banner. In the other hand is his Bowie knife. Elena objected to his ridiculous actions until she realized his antics are a magnet for the trouble makers. They always focus on Baylor, see his blood lust, and often depart.

Leaving their perch, Phillip glances at the tunnel and speaks a quiet prayer. Only Elena hears him curse when he finishes. Almost three-hundred-thousand bodies remain inside this part of the Muni system.

Closing in on the mayhem, Elena notices a father hoisting a feral-looking child on his shoulders. So she can see the carnage better. It is a common belief that if the children get used to the horror they will be less likely to be stunned by it. Circumstances dictate that the Priestess and her people ignore much of the brutality. It is an outlet for the frustration of those who remember a saner world--and a perverse kind of hope to those who cannot imagine a better one.

As they approach the mob, the black soot and clamor from the crowd flows over Elena and her guards. The chants from brown-robed men and women holds the mob's attention. "Kill the religious ones." A jar strikes a target. The crowd curses those being immolated.

"They're just letting themselves be burned as they stand there," Phillip says. Two thrown vessels strike another woman. She makes the sign of the cross and silently collapses, arrows keeping her in place. The church's adobe wall holds the curtain of flame. "It's like old Rome," Phillip says. "We're the same on either side of that Wall."

"There, that's where we go." Elena points to a cluster of encircled believers waiting to be burned. Her group pushes its way through the loose knots of people, close enough to see two sets of heavily armed guards circling a group of robed men and women. Dirty tan hoodies cover the faces of the guards. Baylor surveys the crowd as Elena's group approach the believers. She sees a large drum on a metal stand. A spigot spurts brown liquid into small jars that are then handed out to a long line of people. Each waits to take their turn lobbing the oil cocktail upon a victim.

Baylor begins bulling his way towards it. "Wait." The Priestess produces two pink-flecked rocks. She begins to tap them together.

Tap
Tap-Tap
Tap-Tap-Tap
Tap-tap-Tap-Tap
Tap-Tap-Tap-Tap-Tap.

Phillip takes stones from his coat and joins in as do the rest of her people. Then, despite the hysteria, people begin to turn at the familiar noise. The tapping sound grows in an ever widening wave.

Within a minute, the crowd joins the Earth's Voice. The Priestess looks unblinkingly at those around her. Slowly, she walks to the doomed believers. Great gusts of heat belch at the Priestess. She notices the woman dispensing the brown liquid has not joined in the tapping, but instead continues to fill jars. The Priestess points the woman out. A guard hurries over to her. On his approach, the woman reluctantly shuts the flow and produces her pair of small rocks to join in the ceremony.

Tap
Tap-Tap
Tap-Tap-Tap
Tap-tap-Tap-Tap
Tap-Tap-Tap-Tap-Tap.

"Wait here," she says to Baylor, and strides through the jailers into the human pen. When she folds her arms, the tapping dies away. The crowd moves, shifting its weight, surprised at her presence. Finally, after a brief silence, the Priestess Elena Etu speaks: "Tell me of their crime. Tell me why we are behaving like the Demons. Tell me why we burn a building when we lack shelter to keep the rain and cold from our children. Tell me," she roars. A man steps forward. He pulls back the cowling covering his face. He sports a pistol tattoo on his forehead and bows before speaking.

"Priestess, they are telling us again of a false kingdom of heaven. That peace awaits us--if we bow to the greed of those on the other side of the Wall. These are the ones that tell us we should not mind our pain. They are the ones who tell us we must be docile so we can go to heaven. We know this to be wrong. We know that those who stand up for themselves live on the other side of the Wall in wealth and grace. Faith leads to degradation. These liars must die for spreading beliefs that murder our ability to think. They are Vandals. They are the TV. They are tools of the Patricians." He bows again and steps back.

Elena looks back over her shoulder at the frightened people behind her. Then she looks again at the old mission. "Their words are words of hope for the hopeless. We took their words in and made those words an excuse to be docile in the face of evil. That is not their fault. Their message was beauty. Their message was corrupted. Why do you torture and kill these people for their words of hope and piety?" There is no response this time. "Answer me."

The same man steps forward, Baylor inches up closer to Elena. Surprisingly, the woman who had been dispensing the liquid speaks instead. "It is their teachings that have caused our plight. We should have fought the greedy ones--instead of making peace with them. We would be better off. There is no peace with Demons." The woman glares at the first man who had spoken. They are mates. "If we had any guts we would not be strangling in our own waste."

The first man speaks again trying to recover his stature: "If their churches were not power hungry and greedy, they would not have lied to us. They told us God has only one teaching: Give up this life for the next."

Another voice: "They kept us blind to the many faces of God by telling us that the supreme being had only one face in this world. They said this to divide us. So we would die in misery. God has many faces, this is the greatness of God. Heaven does not require our suffering-- only greed does."

"Amen," Phillip says quietly.

The Priestess speaks: "What you say is true. But these poor souls are not the rich and powerful who have benefited by stealing your faith and trust. These people are here, suffering with us. They are seeking and speaking their truth. You already know God has many faces. So why do you anger at the face of God they seek? Killing them does nothing to harm those greedy ones who spawned the lies of a weak God that fears hell and its minions."

"How do we know they are not spies like the others we have heard about? Maybe these men and women are soldiers who have come to divide us," someone yells out.

Elena glances at Phillip then gathers herself. "Look around. You torture and kill these worshipers as if they were beasts because they practice what you once believed. Consider them mad. Pity them if you like. Do not hurt them."

The handsome man who had first spoken looks to his partner, and then he nods to the two men behind him. They all advance in one step. The die is cast and Elena sighs. The handsome man raises his hands to the smoky sky. Three more men emerge from the crowd to stand with him. Baylor begins to howl. The men look to him then to their leader.

The woman speaks. "You see. She has turned a man into a dog. I say Elena Etu is a witch who is trying to turn us all into animals." She looks to her man.

He points to the Priestess. "I say there are traitors among us and you are looking at one now. I say she has entered our circle to protect them because she is a spawn of the devils on the other side of the Wall. You will--" The man pitches forward and collapses. Two of his comrades start to move. A moment later they fall forward as well. Behind the bodies stands Baylor. Eyes empty of all light, two thin bloody knives in his hands, the huge Bowie knife remains clenched in his sharpened teeth.

Elena feels a series of chills run up her spine. *The pain of holding that knife in those teeth. What have I done to him?*

Baylor advances toward the woman by the oil. He smiles and winks at her as he grabs her sleeve and cleans the knife of her lover's blood. She stares at the messenger of death, her body shaking uncontrollably.

Baylor then looks at the men in hoodies who remain quite still. Not a shot has been fired "Come, let us die together," Baylor says. His chest heaves as if he were in ecstasy. He cackles with the voice of death The men do not move. They see an insane killer hoping to die in an orgy of blood.

"There will be no more of this. Go home," Elena says loudly. The men in hoodies remains still. She walks to the men. "I spit on you," she says loudly. Then she does, right in their leader's face. Baylor spins slicing open the neck of the woman by the spigot, before advancing quickly to his mistress' side.

The men look at each other and back away from the burning mission. Baylor dogs their heels, occasionally throwing stones at them as they retreat. One after the other, the men fall to ground, dead from either a well placed stone-throw or one of those thin throwing knives. Only one of those men will live through the night. It is Baylor's way.

"Priestess Etu," Phillip says to Elena's empty, almost drunken gaze. He points to the men and women gathering about them. "Priestess?"

"Thank you Priestess," says a voice behind her. "We are truly in the time of the devil. When the master returns, we will surely be rewarded." Elena sees another young person leaning on crutches made of two-by-fours. She notices there is something peculiar about the boy beside her. Then she realizes he wears a thin black bar of hair pasted his upper lip.

Phillip speaks: "Your people will continue to be blamed for the evil that overtook your religions. It would be wise to remain quiet for a time. Let this calm down."

"We cannot be quiet. And we will not let you quiet the voice of the Lord," says the boy.

"It's your neck, son," Elena says. "But those people remember a time when fake preachers spread fear and derision, not the gospel. It makes the old religions unpopular. As you've seen today."

"And is your religion better, Priestess?" A man snarls from behind the young boy. He is old. Almost as old as Phillip, with a heavily-lined leathery face, he adjusts his robes in a show of nonchalance.

The young boy barks out: "This blighted land will die. We believers know we will be taken to heaven while the rest of you will burn in hell."

Elena looks to the still-burning church behind them. "Your group can go about its business without interference from me, but be clear. This will happen again. I cannot protect you."

"Thank you," a man says, leading his people towards the church. They scrape dirt from the ground and throw it against the still burning liquid that clings to the ancient walls.

"Madness," she says quietly to Phillip.

CHAPTER THIRTY

Later that evening, the Priestess Elena Etu and her group arrives at a cliff overlooking the rolling brown cemetery that stretches out to the ocean. This is Joe Vaz's kingdom. Orderly lines of people wait below--between headstones. The lines remind Elena of stripes on a flag. Constant waves of movement start from under the tarps on the knoll and roll up to the line. In the forest to the left, clumps of children sit eating their Kandy. No encampments are allowed; this huge graveyard remains dedicated to food distribution and the graves of fallen soldiers.

She rests her knees against the rusted freeway guardrail and surveys the sides of the road. Wrecked vehicles sit piled on top of others, waiting for an escape that never came. A ferry had tried to make a run down the coast to rescue the once pricey vehicles; it was sunk on its maiden voyage after being spotted by a sailing yacht.

Phillip brings her water and speaks. "The trucks haven't arrived yet. There was another set of engine problems. I've sent runners to find Joe Vaz." He watches a lone figure approach them. It looks like Baylor.

Elena sips the water. "I want you to begin examining the defense of his factory as soon as possible. Make some recommendations and make sure the fake smokestacks are finished tonight. I want Dr. Vaz comfortable that everything has been done correctly for the defense of his factory."

"I have already handled that. I need to get inside the factory to finish."

"I'll take care of that. What's that smell?" She turns and sees Baylor, covered with feces. Elena holds the cup for a second then sips from it; her eyes taking in the fetid man. "What happened, Baylor?" Elena asks, voice dead as the graveyard behind her.

"Women, can we ever please them? First she doesn't like it when I have spots of blood. Now she doesn't like my smell."

"The Priestess doesn't approve of the smell," Phillip says sadly.

Baylor replies with pique. "Oh, I see, I have not kept my feathers of glory clean. That offends you, Priestess?"

"Wash it off, Baylor," Phillip says kindly.

Baylor draws a bloody knife. "Make me."

"Come on. We have to go down there." Elena begins walking, hoping the fatigue in her body will kill her. "Baylor, you walk fifty paces to the rear until the smell is gone."

"I found those assassins," Baylor says from behind them. The group stops.

Phillip speaks. "I'll check. I'll be okay." He walks back and Baylor points to a cart off to the side. Inside are the headless bodies of two dead men. "Thank you, Baylor." He walks back to her. "Not them. What now?"

"We go find Dr. Vaz."

Despite the hundreds of thousands of people who come here to eat, the graveyard remains the cleanest and best-tended spot in California. Everyone cleans the grounds with a care reserved for a holy shrine. Even during the extreme madness of the first few years, the graves remained sacrosanct. One young girl had told the Priestess that she loved this place because the soldiers buried here had defended the citizens of the country rather than attacked them. Another old man had said these soldiers fought against greed, not for it. Elena figures it is simply the glory due to those who fight for ideals.

A nation's core.

Joe Vaz appears from a large mausoleum, walking up the hillside followed by a self-appointed protection force of four men. Elena can see another twenty or so men and women walking alongside, through the crowd. This group would be the tip of hatred--if anyone were stupid enough to attack the Food Man. The surge of anger would lead to a tidal wave of horror.

Another reason for the respect of this place, beyond nostalgia for the thousands of buried soldiers, is Dr. Vaz's food factory. Located in the old military base deep below the cemetery, the area has so far escaped the attacks from the sky. Elena believes she knows why but says nothing about her views. She nods when Phillip says he admires the factory's stealth as they walk towards Doctor Vaz.

Six more men appear carrying stretchers. Elena assumes the stretchers are supporting dead assassins.

"There," says Baylor. "I told you so."

"Good evening Priestess Etu." The stretchers are laid on the ground and the canvas covers pulled back. "These stretchers hold the remains of the men who tried to kill me yesterday. There was a second assault--on my cabin. While I was meeting with you. Six people died protecting me this time," Joe says. "Those most recent assassins were pulled apart and thrown into the ocean."

Elena stares at the bodies. Her guards, along with Phillip and Baylor, survey the corpses. From their well-muscled bodies, the lack of sores, and most revealing, their full set of teeth, it is clear they are from the other side of the Wall.

"Do any of you know these men?" She asks. Everyone's response is negative except for Phillip. Bent over the corpses, he tries to turn one over. Baylor steps forward and turns the body for him. Phillip examines the ears, and then behind their knees.

He stands. "Nope. There is nothing here," he says scratching his head and crossing his arms. It is a pre-arranged signal to her that he knows more than that.

"You can tell your people these men weren't my guards, Dr. Vaz. It is easy to see they are from the other side of the Wall."

Joe looks at Phillip before he speaks: "They already know. They also know these men have flea bites of a kind known only in the north woods of British Columbia. They are easily seen behind the knees and ears. That means this is what's left of a death squad since that's where they train." Turning to Phillip, "Did you see that, or were your failing eyes too weak?"

"I must have missed it," Phillip replies.

Joe looks at Elena. "Perhaps you no longer see me as an ally? Will you and your guards take me as a prisoner?" Joe wants to know why Elena seems so mistrusting. "Or perhaps a tour of my factory will make everything okay?"

Phillips notes the anger. Dismisses it, but he as well has become curious about her protective stance regarding Joe Vaz.

"We need to talk," Elena says. A nagging concern about internal insurrection has become a mania. Elena believes the men at the church earlier today were organized by those on the other side of the Wall. She also believes the attacks on Dr. Vaz will continue and wonders how she could have been so stupid as to trust Lucien Feiss and his people. The irony of Luke Feiss' death is lost on her at this moment. "Dr. Vaz, let's walk. Baylor, guard my back. Phillip, please check with those who killed these men. We need more information. Then please join us at the nearest factory entrance."

"One of my assistants will guide you," Joe says.

The Food Man and the Priestess slowly descend the hillside passing sets of tables fed by overhead hoppers. People who had been sweeping the food into bags or old backpacks stop to watch them.

Heads turn and the guards move a bit closer to the Food Man and the Priestess Elena Etu. They do not unshoulder their weapons. A cheer erupts from the crowd. Any of the people in this crowd would gladly give up their life for either of these people.

As Elena walks, she is surprised to see that they bow to her, while seeming to ignore Joseph Vaz. She had worried that the Patricians might see Doctor Vaz as a leader. The truth of that is clear. He cannot lead. This means he is only a target. So the next step for her is ensuring that he leaves with her for Oregon as soon as possible.

They exit the crowd, passing by the rusted hulk of a tank covered with vines, and walk under a set of eucalyptus trees. Joe reaches into his pocket and pulls out a bright red radish. She stares at it as if it were made of gold, not bothering to hide her astonishment. "It's real?"

"Supplementary food sources are springing up all over the south. I have seen carrots, a turnip and radishes. I am in no danger. This war is won."

"Your intelligence is impressive," the Priestess says. "Your conclusions are naive."

"Anything that has to do with food gets to me. And, you also see I am no threat to you. Yet you maintain that I must leave here--to protect me? While you look at me like I am a Cassius. I do not understand, Elena."

She measures his words. "Those behind the Wall see you as the enemy, not me," she says. "It doesn't matter about other food. You are the target of an unreasoning beast."

"Funny, that now that there is enough food, more is starting to be grown," Joe says apparently ignoring her. In fact, he agrees. Still, he plans to keep working on further securing the factory. He feels he needs another week at least. "The desperation seems to be fading on this side of the Wall and growing on the other side."

"That's why it is so dangerous for you," she says.

Again he appears to ignore her. "We are going to win this, with or without me. Why do you care about me going with you now?"

She pauses, chagrined at the question. The two of them emerge from the wooded area into the parade of headstones spread out flat like a fan. "What are these for?" Elena asks.

"I saw one earlier this week. Maybe someone was just bored and made the design. Or more likely, it is a marker for my factory."

"Probably easily seen from the sky," she says. "Why didn't you move it?"

"I did. We are a thousand meters from the closest processing point. I wanted to give them something to kill and we need some new latrines down the way." He points to the western slope dotted with tents. "Those empty tents are also easily seen from the sky and they contain magnesium. Should be quite a show. You know we're going to be attacked. I will be needed for repair."

Elena looks at the hillside and then stares at the false marker admiring Joe's forethought. "So why didn't they attack already? Do you think they need this information? What could they be missing?" She waits. "How can people be so dull?"

He pauses, confused at her pique and the questions. "No. It is something else. And you know why--but we are not going to discuss that. I see." Joe shakes his head. "Priestess, they have lost. I know it. And if I know it they do. That means they are planning some kind of exit strategy. Once we figure out that plan--we'll know what they are going to do here. We will also know how to negotiate with them. But we need to figure out their exit strategy before we sit down with them."

She nods. "Seems, easy to figure, Dr. Vaz, and tougher to implement." Elena looks around wondering if it is time to tell him of her affiliations. "Do you still believe it will take years to breach the new barrier?"

He shakes his head. "If you are right about their supply issue, then I'd guess less than a year. With their helicopters down and their tanks crippled, the only issue is the path for the breach. They will not know that we know about the hose problems. I am guessing they will be concentrating on barges as our attack method."

"We have reached Salem, south of Portland. Their helicopters are failing and the number of tanks is almost zero. But they have established a brutal battle line in the Salem area. We are stalled. I want Phillip to look around inside your factory. If he says it is secure then we need to leave. We need your help. But I want this to be your decision also."

"So I am strongly invited to go with you. I see." They walk slowly towards a factory entrance--a large mausoleum. Joe, no longer unable to ignore the smell, looks back to Baylor. "He will have to wait outside." She nods her agreement. When they approach the mausoleum that functions as a doorway, Phillip is waiting for them.

"The people I spoke to were forthcoming. They were protecting him. Preparations are well underway for misdirecting fire from the sky. That leaves a ground assault. So that's what I am concerned about now. I assume you are expecting both?"

Joe nods yes. "At the same time."

"Can I join you inside?"

Joe Vaz agrees as the Priestess reaches into her bag and lays her two rocks on the ground next to the huge brass door. Baylor steps forward and crosses his arms standing over the rocks--to wait for her return. Phillip follows Joe and Elena through the open door onto a small metal landing. An old white plastic steering wheel hangs from the ceiling. "Don't touch that. It's a trap that would kill us." Joe points to a dozen small gas jets in the floor.

They soon descend a hidden staircase, then push aside a set of glass doors that reminds Elena of an old supermarket entry way. When the doors close behind them, the dark space lights revealing a white marble lobby scarred with graffiti and obscene pictures. Once a waiting room, it now contains only the large white-stone cube that had functioned as a reception desk for security. Behind it, a bank of old mailboxes sit open like a hundred tiny garage doors.

"I remember this place. My company had contracts for the IT here," Phillip says. "This is the first time I've entered the facility through that door. There used to be a long hallway to a garage. I see your marker is pointing at that garage. You gave them something hit?"

"With a very large boom," Joe replies. "They are supposed to think we built the factory down the hill by the creek."

"For the water? Very smart, I hope it works." Phillip looks around. "Down below us was the data processing system for the old satellite net. There used to be a cooling pond above the desk area." He pushes open a set of metal-clad doors by the mailboxes. A childlike delight comes to his eyes when he sees the sizeable dark green pond. The artificial water lilies and tall bunches of fake grass charm him. A wooden bench on end sticks out of the water. Overhead, a white glowing pane of plastic leads to a skylight at the top of a mausoleum. "I always wondered where that light came from. It's beautiful on the floor below with the light coming through the water." He gazes at the bench. "And you added to the water garden," Phillip says sarcastically.

Joe speaks: "I added the bench last night. I was a bit confused. I will set a torch to it after we leave. I am guessing a bunker buster then a rain of incendiaries right where we are standing."

"What were you confused about?" Elena asks.

"Actually I was drunk." His eyes squint as he says the word drunk.

"You?" Phillip asks.

"A personal problem--it was nothing."

Elena cannot fathom why the revelation that his congressional savior was a sham is so charged for Dr. Vaz. Then she gets it. She was his Beatrice.

"Elena, why did you leave those stones outside?" Joe asks wanting to change the subject.

They'd get no more from Joe on what had caused the bench to wind up in the pond. "I acquired the habit of leaving stones during the first few years after the city fell. I use them to tell my friends where I have gone."

"We've known each other for a long time. I never seen you do that before. Or perhaps you're so worried about an attack you want to make sure they know where your body is." A trace of hollow humor flattens his voice.

"Neither," she says boldly. "I want to make sure Baylor knows I am safe. He has become unstable."

"I am sorry for him. I think he was once a decent man." Joe leads them down to a narrow hallway. In front of them waits a long dark stairway. "We need to move quickly," he says. "The light will shut off in four minutes and any movement in the stairs afterwards will sound an alarm. Then we die."

They walk down a long flight of stairs and enter another hallway. Joe hurries them along. Anyone approaching from this avenue would need to exercise some caution. The area is covered with debris. Phillip sees they would never have the time to get to the end without a willing guide. They descend another staircase.

Elena speaks: "It seems much quieter here." The first time she visited the factory--just after it stared up--the noise was unbearable.

"It's far more quiet than it was when you were first here. In fact it is far quieter than it was a week ago. On the other hand there are three locations near those fake smokestacks on the hillside that make a hell of a racket."

At the bottom of the stairs, he opens a door. Gears mesh and she hears the beeping of automated carts. Other factory noises crowd their hearing: The whirl of machinery and the clump, clump of material moving about--the sounds pulsate like a heart--but not painfully so.

The sour look on Phillip's face says it is still too loud. "We need to make it quieter in here."

"I'm amazed you can discern anything in this racket, Dr. Vaz," she says, following the two men.

"To me, this is a melody, to others a cacophony. I'll turn down the production rates when we leave tonight. We have a good stockpile of food." He has been working on ways to defend this Eden since he built it. "We have done everything we can think of to protect it. My people are tired. But I can do more." A tinge of bitterness haunts his voice. The destruction of the factory in Brazil hurt him deeply. Joe loves this place; it is like a womb to him.

"Are you getting sentimental about this place?" She hopes not. It is a prime target for the Patricians.

"I love systems that work. That's as far as it goes." He leads them along a catwalk. Below them, sets of pipes snake around each other while small carts full of materials race down the aisles between huge machines. Other smaller carts occasionally stop at hoppers beside the pipes to dump their contents.

Within a few minutes, Elena has no idea where she is. Joe doesn't like people to know more about the factory than they need to. His Eden also demands ignorance; it keeps others from claiming dominion or doing effective damage. The echoes of humming machinery and the chug-chug of pumps suddenly clang, then they squeal loudly. Up ahead, a bright red lamp begins to blink. It appears to be on a different metal-framed catwalk. "I wanted to talk--" She stops when she realizes Joe no longer stands beside her. "Where did he go?" She asks to Phillip.

"He's over there."

A white light pops on about fifteen feet away illuminating a thin figure sliding down a railing, ignoring the steps. The red light pulses ahead of him. He strides along the floor, stepping aside just in time to miss carts of materials speeding by him. He drops to one knee. She watches him, thinking he might be praying. Joe contemplates a large steel mixing bowl. A rotating shaft travels round, near the rim. A high-pitched squeal comes from it every few seconds. He bends. A cart rolls by, its wide structure missing him by inches. The red light turns off as the squealing gets worse

"I hope it doesn't cause a failure in the factory that only you can fix," she says loudly.

Joe stands up. "It will take just a minute."

"Phillip, do you think he brings women down here?"

Phillip looks at her. "What?" The strategist ponders Elena's directing of Joe Vaz's actions. "You think something is going on?"

"Watch him."

He lifts a hinged section of the four tube metal railing that runs alongside the vat and descends a ladder to the base of the vat like a teen sliding on a jungle-gym.

"I see. You think he wants you to watch him." Confused, he examines her.

She notes Joe vault around the side. A small truck with vertical metal tubes races by him. Had it hit him, it would have surely killed him. For the next thirty seconds, he glides by machines and pivoting robot arms. It is ballet.

"So you question if this is just a repair?" Phillip smiles. "That revelation about Ms. Feiss has let the genie out of the bottle for him. Maybe Doc Vaz has a hankering for you."

She sees Joe ascend stairs to another huge metal bowl--ducking just in time to miss a traveling rail cart that rides along ceiling under the catwalk. "What are you saying?" She asks, unsure of her own observations.

"His heart has been shown to be a sham. And as always, the most unlikely of events surfaces. Maybe Joe has every intention of going north. He seems to be displaying his charms for you--but you already know that."

Elena notices Joseph Vaz practically dance around his home. "Maybe he is just happy here." Around the sides of the large kettle where Joe stands is a pair of rails. He climbs up on the side with amazing agility. His flashlight lit, she can now see a viscous liquid being stirred. Joe moves along the edge of the bowl with ease. *Joe Vaz never let on for an instant he had any interest in me.* "It's not me, Phillip. I have never seen him happy."

"Of course," Phillip replies facetiously. "How could I have missed it? Or maybe he wants me. That is one gay son of a bitch."

She ignores the silly comment and watches Joe reaching down and jiggling the rail. The squealing ends. He hurries over to a small panel--ducking just in time to miss a small cart flying by his head. Elena starts. She sees him look up at her and smile. "It's okay." Then he reaches out and turns a switch.

A bright yellow light begins to flash on the side of the metal bowl and the shaft inside comes to a halt. Then, his flashlight in his mouth, Dr. Vaz moves a small cap aside and begins filling it with lubricant from a large gas can under the panel. He switches the mixer back on. Ducking again--just in time--as a second cart passes him. He moves to the second vat and shuts it down for the same repairs.

"Poetry, dear Juliet. Poetry." As the blinking yellow light shuts off, Joe Vaz returns to her. "What's in the bowls?" Phillip asks.

Joe doesn't know why, but he doesn't like Phillip at that moment. "That's where the plastic is eaten by bugs. Those smaller tanks that circle the large vats--the ones with all the pipes--they are where we form the organic compounds that the body can use: proteins, fats, carbohydrates etc. One in each vat, the pipe overhead collects the methane waste. We use it for energy." He glows, watching Elena.

"What about those carts that speed by? It looks dangerous down there," she says.

"Not for me," he says with too much pride. Elena sees Phillip smile at the floor. "Priestess, you didn't come down here to learn the wonders of manufacturing. Phillip, you can see I have this under control. So what else do you want?" He looks at Elena, waiting for her to speak. "We can speak here it is safe."

She is silent, thinking. *Does he think I came here to see him? He has heard or seen that Baylor is too far gone? Is he testing me, feeling me out?*

"Doctor Vaz, we are concerned that you may not come north with us tomorrow," Phillip says.

"You are safe. You don't need me. I think we are safer in different locations. But I will join you nonetheless if you insist. You understand those people on the other side other side of the Wall. I do not."

"Sometimes you remind me of Baylor, Joe." Elena says, watching him.

Joe Vaz sees her surety and looks away, making believe he is checking a pipe. She will not look at Phillip. She is certain he wears a smug smile at this moment. "Joe." He looks at her. "We need to use your brains to negotiate a peace."

"And you are telling me this, why?' He says. "You're not worried about the peace. I can tell you have a plan already."

"She means we need your help with logistics for the battle." Phillip waits for his response.

Joe looks around. "You want me as your weapon of war? Is that what all this is about? That is a joke, I hope."

Elena moans quietly. "I've had enough of this. I am leaving and I am expecting your support. Phillip make sure everything is secure as it can be. We are departing as soon as possible." She is tired and angry.

"I will not use his emotions as a lever." Elena watches the first of the sun coming over the east bay hills.

Phillips sits beside her, drinking his dandelion tea. "To be honest, I think he'd have helped us anyway. He told me after he showed you out that he believed you when you said we would breach the Columbia Wall in a few months. He knows sooner is better. He wants to act cool around you."

"Cool?" She works not to laugh. "So that's why he acted like he has to be convinced?" She watches the encampments. The scent of wood fires wafts by in the breeze. "We can win this." She looks back at Phillip.

He takes in a deep breathe. "So you know what to do."

"I do not. I know we are stronger." She watches a man and woman walking among gravestones.

He follows her gaze. "Elena, you have to prove to them that you can defend your people and your advances. Once you are able to do that. They will negotiate. At that point the battle takes on a new flavor: bargaining table brutality. War never ends for them, Elena. You know that. You were here as Feiss Industries' ace in the hole. Now you have taken over that game. They respect that. They will hate you for it and they will respect it. Any power you have acquired in this vacuum you will need to secure if you are to stay alive--and if the rest of these people are to have any chance at a decent future. You've got to keep Dr. Vaz working with us. I agree that if he figures you are using his emotions--he will leave out of spite. I am not suggesting you use him. I am wondering if you care for him?" He pauses. In his opinion, Baylor's madness has turned Elena Etu into stone.

Her eyes dart to his eyes. "Meaning what?"

"You saw it. He's head over heals for you. He will not admit it to you--and probably not to himself either. On the other hand, you saw it before I did. So I am wondering if the same is true of you." Phillip wants Elena to be happy. She is his family.

"Baylor and I are in love, Phillip. I don't love Joe Vaz. I admire him. Or if I did--I'd never put another man I love into the same circumstance as Baylor. I'd tell him to get away from me as quickly as possible."

He stares out to the Pacific. "So if you care for someone, you will never admit it because of what has happened to Baylor?"

"Did you watch too many soap operas when you were a kid?"

"But if you thought a friend was going to be hunted down and killed. You would try to defend him," Phillip says artfully. He is a practiced negotiator and an astute observer. "We can use his help,. On the other hand, it could be argued that the right action is to keep the two of you as far apart as possible. So if there is a problem we have some redundancy. Yet, you refuse that notion because you want him near, to protect him. I question your logic, Priestess."

"You think I care for him?"

"I think you wouldn't know if you cared for him. Of that I am sure. I also know you care a lot about what he does."

"Then the point is moot," she replies. "I will not use him, nor will I allow him in. I will protect him."

Phillip considers how similar this is to Baylor protecting her. He will not speak of it. "Elena, you use him. You use all of us. If you were sure your way was the best for him, you would turn him into a snake-oil salesmen. Unless it meant he was to be emotionally tied to you. On the other hand, he could use a guide. The guy has the emotional maturity of a teenager."

"Like you can talk. How's that rage thing going?" Elena looks away embarrassed by her words. "I am sorry. I don't know what got into me."

Phillip smiles. "I think you tell yourself that you admire saints." He watches Elena carefully. "I question that stance, as well."

"You need an outlet for your need to gossip, don't you?"

He smiles at her. "You're surrounded by success, Priestess. On one side there are millions of people who need you. On the other side your pact with the devil, Mr. Feiss, has been cancelled and you hold all the cards. Completing the triangle is Dr. Vaz--a saint by all evaluations. You're a sucker for a good man. That doesn't mean you should forget what happened to poor Baylor. But we are not here to support the growth of robots who do a job then wither away."

"You're embarrassing yourself. There is the minor issue of the death squads coming my way."

He stares at her. "I guess nothing in life is perfect," he says wryly.

"You're trying to manipulate me," she says flatly.

Phillip shakes his head: "This place is my home. I will not be buried away from my family. The same is true for Dr. Vaz and his factory. Yet both he and I are going north. You trust me and you have been unreasonably concerned with Joe Vaz's loyalty and safety. I want you to note my observation of that as well."

"I say we take the fight to them. I say with you and Doctor Vaz in Portland the fight will go quicker and less people will die."

"Because he, like Baylor, will spit out a lung for you at this point. Look, I don't know if he really is, in fact, in love with you. I do know you care for him. I also know that he needs to know that you are a decent person. So he has someone to believe in and protect besides his machines and their mission. I will also admit that it might just admire for the guy's goodness so you want to protect that. By golly you two are alike."

She tosses a cake at him.

"By walling yourself off from him it makes it all the worse for him and he deserves better. He needs to know the people he saves are worth it. You are the proof of that. Baylor is the past. Joe Vaz is the genius of our generation with a heart the size of the ocean. With him engaging that brain because he wants to take care of you we will kick the Patrician forces out that much quicker. But that genius is just a man. And you are just a woman, my Priestess."

"I don't love him, Phillip. I admire him." She has never seen this romantic bent of his before.

He puts down his cup of dandelion tea, then notes a glint coming from the western sky. It multiplies quickly into a series of lights, spreading out in an attack formation. His heart sinks and he faces Elena who doesn't yet see the approaching jets. "Elena, we need to run. Now."

CHAPTER THIRTY ONE

A large bomb has been dropped into the skylight of the mausoleum. Landing directly into the pool below and detonating out, the entire area has collapsed in on itself. Joe Vaz limps out of the old mausoleum doorway into the smoke and flames. He moves as quickly as he can towards where Elena Etu's tent had been. The area is a burning hell. A large ore truck pulls up near him full of soldiers. It is immediately hit by missiles from the overhead fighters. The truck explodes into orange flames that roar up into the night sky. Another explosion throws Joe to the ground. The scream of the six jets is quickly followed by another pack that begins launching missiles at the fake smoke stacks. Some missiles go wild. The ground heaves and shakes madly; it throws Joe up and collapses down.

He looks around, desperately trying to find Elena. The smoke and debris, the panicked people, there is no way to see her. He rolls into a crater and starts to scan the area trying to determine the extent of damage to the factory. So far as he can tell, the jets have attacked all the decoys and missed the factory. He prays his preparations will be good enough for the ground attack. A flight of helicopters appears from off shore and lands quickly. People scream as armed men and women exit the helicopters. The ground forces are ready and the mercenaries are slaughtered. The helicopters retreat, lit by the flames, shooting wildly at the ground. Twenty missiles are fired at the six helicopters bringing down five of them. Phillip's defense against the helicopters is surprisingly effective. The other veers away. Joe gets up and runs toward a gully. Tents burn. People lie on the ground screaming for help. Another set of explosions light the sky throwing him to the ground. The next waves of helicopters begin strafing the area as the jets howl off to the west.

He looks for Baylor, but cannot find him either.

Bullets whizz all around. "Stop firing at the jets," Joe calls out. "Shoot at the helicopters!" Joe notes how few helicopters there are on the attack. The total number is less than twenty. A bullet shatters a wooden pole just to his right. Joe sees Phillip, his legs covered in blood. Joe rushes forward as the strafing is now concentrating near the fan of stones he had set up earlier. "What happened?" Joe screams.

"The attack?" He laughs. "I just heard that someone started a rumor that the factory had been shut down and the distribution center is going to close. They must have a ground assault under way."

"Are you okay?" He looks at the man's legs and the flow of blood. It doesn't appear that bad.

"I am okay. I was with Elena when the jets appeared and kicked hell out of everything."

"Where is she?"

"I don't know. I saw the jets coming in and alerted her. And I'll be a son of bitch. Just as I said it, Baylor shows up scoops her up like a sack of potatoes, throws her over his shoulder and scampers off with her. A few minutes later he came back, finds me in the debris, and he carries me here. Fucking amazing, he saved her life. He saved my life. I am sure of it. That is one crazy heroic son of a bitch. I've never seen anyone like that." Phillip looks around. "Joe, they went after the decoys we installed. I've never seen such terrible fire control. Whoever is running the show out there is our best friend."

"They are trying to destroy the factory," Joe says looking about. The area looks like Armageddon. It is supposed to--but Joe agrees--the factory may be intact. "You stay here. Sorry, dumb comment."

The helicopters begin strafing random targets. Joe runs toward a grove of eucalyptus and then darts from cover to cover watching the gunships and their positions. A hand grabs him, tosses him up and over a shoulder, and begins carrying him along. It's Baylor, the God of War himself, covered in blood. He runs, firing a weapon at an approaching helicopter.

Ahead, in a gully, Joe sees Elena. Baylor has built her a shelter out of headstones. Short of a direct hit from a missile, Elena is safe. Baylor tosses him down the hillside, then surveys the structure he built. His eyes mad, in one hand on a rifle, in the other his bowie knife. He turns his back to them and begins guarding them.

Joe faces Elena. She is unharmed. The helicopters turn west.

He begins to stand and she grabs his hand. "Where are you going?"

"To make sure the factory is safe--if there are saboteurs--I know where they'll try to enter now." He stands. Elena gets up and follows him knowing Baylor will as well. They all run to a sloped gravel road that leads down to the waste removal ramp. Two trucks are parked there. Four bodies lay on the gravel a few feet from the trucks. They hurry under the shelter, Joe looks around amazed that everything is in tact.

Bullets whiz by them. "Cease firing. That is Dr. Vaz," someone screams. No one even mentions Elena.

Four men come running out from behind the trucks. "Are you all right?" One of them asks Joe. Then they see Elena and the Baylor. They back up. One man grabs Joe's arms and they form a cordon around him--using their bodies to shield him from Baylor. The brave men look at Elena, confused.

"It's okay."

Baylor nods. The soldiers escort Joe, and therefore Baylor and the Priestess, behind the trucks. Baylor walks backwards guarding the rear, one eye on Elena Etu.

"Paulo, what happened?" Joe asks.

"You were right about saboteurs, Dr. Vaz. You knew exactly what they'd do and we were waiting for them. They tried to get in just like you said. A small group blew the supply hatch while another group started a riot about the food. When the second set of jets came, this third group told us they were here to set the charges to keep the factory out of the enemy hands. So we killed them." The man grins. "Dr. Vaz, how did you know?"

"There were lots of possibilities. I tried to cover all of them. This team just tried this one. I bet the others are just sitting around thinking what a dope I am." Joe smiles at the men and does not see the amazement on the part of Elena Etu.

The sound from the helicopters begins to fade.

"But how did you know the men approaching you were saboteurs?" Elena asks the man.

"Their weapons didn't misfire," he replies with a grin. "Dr. Vaz told us to listen for that."

Joe looks around taking in his surroundings. Baylor stands covered in blood. Three large gashes cross his chest and arms. Joe Vaz is stunned by the heroics of this wild man The Priestess cannot seem to look at him. Joe Vaz feels her pain. He sees Baylor's courage is no surprise to her; but the costs for Baylor are too much for her. The brave man froths at the mouth like a wild animal. Joe finally understands-- and he pities her.

"Baylor, would you take a doctor to Phillip and see he is tended to?" She knows for the next few days Baylor will be a wild animal. The man pauses. "I am okay." He hurries off to his task.

A soldier rushes up the walkway to Joe Vaz. "A complete zero. They missed the factory. The worst thing they did was to mess up the loading docks and destroy a day's worth of food. I can have the trucks loading again in six hours. How can they be so stupid?"

Joe, pleased with his preparations, looks at Elena Etu for her approval. She nods. "You have saved us again, Dr. Vaz. Thank you." She looks away a little too quickly. "We will have an Earth's Voice Ceremony soon. Please let everyone know."

Joe watches her walk away admiring her strength. *And she remains so calm.* He reminds himself of the last time her saw a woman so calm in the midst of mayhem--Amanda Feiss. His eyes narrow and his brain engages, examining the similarities. *She really was calm about our victory.*

That night when Joe finally sleeps, it is in a maelstrom of pain. Ching-ching, the sound of sheet metal rolling along the ground outside his hovel. Ching-ching--the sound of metal skates on the frozen pond when he was a child. Ching-ching--the sound of his father and his brothers building wind generators. Ching-ching--the sound of the University's metal roof slapping in the winds as mothers cried for their babies. Ching-ching--the sound of spikes being driven into human bodies, so they wouldn't fall into the cooking fires. He cries out.

The sobs slice out into the night cutting into every home around him. His neighbors would have spanked any child who cries so much. Everyone knows he saved the factory today. Tomorrow they will spank any child that comments on Joe's scythe-like crying. An adult might be killed. Regardless, they all listen. No one will ever speak of it.

Many of the hovels are empty. Over the next few days, all his neighbors' will sob as well. Information flows slowly around here--but unlike life on the other side of the Wall--everyone eventually learns the facts: Those on the other side of the Wall will not let them be--ever. Peace is a myth. This is a fight to the death with the Patricians and now the will of the people must become steel.

Joe hears a knock on the door frame. The cloth covering moves aside and he sees the old man from next door enter. "Are you okay?" The man asks, entering the room. The smoky flame of the lamp makes the shadow of his nose dance along the lined face. "It's Brazil all over again. Time for you to leave."

"I'm fine." Joe is surprised at both the visit and lucidity of discourse. He didn't think the wounded man could speak so clearly. Joe sits up looking around. There is something odd about his room.

"There is a message for you on the door. I saw them deliver it. The Priestess Etu has sent for you. She is waiting by the factory."

"What now?" Joe asks angrily. "Why does she keep trying to keep an eye on me?"

"Their trucks arrived and they are in a hurry. She wants you to join them. It is important you go with her."

"How do you know?"

"I have read the message, genius."

"I have to prepare for the next attack."

"We are fighting Demons, Dr. Vaz. You do not understand the demonic. She does. You need to do as you are told."

"What for?" Joe asks. "You know my name?"

The old man ignores the stupid question. "Most of us are going north as well. We are going to fight the Demons. They have been trying to destroy us all along with their poisoned gifts and lies. We must liberate the last of this planet from their hell."

"There is no difference between them and us."

The old man steps forward. "You are young and stupid. Try and keep that hidden. These people trust you," the man says. "Fight for the beautiful woman and the ideals that guide her. By your own admission she is as good a reason as any to live." He turns to leave.

"So you work for her?" Joe asks thinking himself a fool. "I thought you were just the neighbor."

"Try not to be so dense either, Doctor. Her guards are down the street waiting for you to wake up." The old man laughs. "That was a joke." He leaves. A moment later Joe wakes up. He stands, then goes to the front just in time to see a pair of Elena's soldiers arrive. One of them starts to speak. Joe raises a hand to silence him. He looks at his door frame then down to their hands. There is no document. "The trucks have arrived and the Priestess wants to see me. She is getting ready to go north."

The men nod, surprised at his comment.

"Tell her I am on my way to see her. You can wait if you want. It will take me a few minutes to gather my stuff."

"There are people waiting to gather your possessions and bring them north. Nothing will be lost," says one of the men.

Swatting her thigh with a eucalyptus branch, Elena circles around the large brass fire pan in the center of a modified food tent. Crisp heat warms her. It gives her no pleasure. The efforts of reconstruction, the city's water lines and other factories have been destroyed. Repair will take months. Those behind the Wall are in no mood to negotiate. *Thanks for the message.*

"Dr. Vaz is almost here." Baylor appears like a ghost, his wounds tended, his eyes seem lost in some madness. Elena makes a wish, then blows out a candle--leaving Baylor in the dark. "Please make sure Dr. Vaz and I have privacy. I'd like a hundred yard perimeter please."

Baylor bows. "As you wish, Priestess."

Her guards escort Joe to the table outside her tent. Then they follow Baylor making sure no one is closer than two-hundred yards. Guards are posted every few yards in a circle. Elena points to two chairs and watches Joe sit. Expecting him to be impatient, he appears quiet and subdued. She smells smoke on him. He worked all day on repairs to the factory's stealth.

He speaks hoarsely: "They want to turn it all back into chaos. I understand that now."

"I'm surprised that concerns you." She sits as well.

The thin man sits quietly for a moment looking at her, glad she is not wounded. Then he cannot bear the silence. "Of course I care. I'm just not willing to give my life for your beliefs, or anyone else's." Joe notices the reflection of torches in Elena's eyes. Their glow causes him to blush. "Or, I don't think I am willing to do that."

As she rubs her hand over the dark wood table between them, and speaks softly. "You know, I've never met a man who didn't believe he was unknown treasure. Nonetheless, you are the closest I've seen to actually meeting the requirements."

Joe scratches his shoulder. "No need for that. I will go north and help you. They are finished and they know it. They have nothing to lose. I just want you to know I am not a follower of false beliefs. It will not get easier."

"If you do not help us you will be condemning thousands to death in the battle to the north. You are a game-changer, Doctor Vaz. That isn't a false belief."

Joe laughs derisively. "Hogwash. These people are sentenced to purgatory by generations of locust-like leaders instilling false beliefs and fear. While the capable ones claim they are too smart to stare into the face of the enemy that condemns them to hell. Of the lot, I curse those who join the bastards so they can all beat down the weak. But I will not be a part of any useless sanctimonious charge at the guns just to feed my indignation--or yours. I will help you sue for peace. I will make battle untenable for the enemy. I will not wage war for the sake of hatred. I am not like Phillip." His stare then holds the knowledge of her links to the other side of the Wall. She cannot figure out how he has made the connection.

"We cannot stop what is happening now. No more than I could have stopped it years ago. If we win a negotiated peace they will target me--and you--to take control again. The peace must be unequivocal. I don't know how to arrange that, Dr. Vaz. I will need your help on that--not just to make war."

"I can do that. I wonder why you do this." He steeples his hands on the table between them. "People are so uncaring. Yet they care for you. I care for you. I don't understand why. Is it just your beauty?"

She closes her eyes for a moment to reclaim what little of her composure remains. "So you think its okay to win this?"

"Elena, you've been boating up a waterfall since I met you. If you can begin a peace, I will build upon it. If you fail then we will die together."

She looks away. "What if I said I could stop what's happening--that I just need to get to the other side of the Wall?"

"I'd say you believe your own dream of an Elena Utopia. I would pity you."

"I represent the government of the United States of America," she says firmly.

"You represent Feiss Industries." Joe's eyes narrow. "Please do not lie to me now."

"I am here to ruin them," she says. "You have too much ego about your stealth capabilities, Doctor Vaz."

He pauses, nods, "So I figured it right. They missed my factory completely and I would be a fool thinking our success today was my work." He believes her. It makes too much sense.

"And speaking for the government, if you will help me--I, and the government--will make sure we are a free people again. We can win this war."

Joe stares. "The other side of the Wall is controlled by the remaining corporatist legions of myopic CEOs and insane stock holders. The US government has no power anymore. It was gutted by deficits and eviscerated by a corrupt elite, decades ago. You may represent a government in exile, but in truth you represent a ghost, a corpse, or worse, a false hope."

"And you are a fool for trying to feed a billion hungry people." She stares at him. "I'd say my credentials are better then yours."

"I succeed."

"And I am succeeding as well. You just admitted it." She looks around. "The use of power takes delicacy in times of war. Until the Patricians got to the point of vulnerability, the government was hobbled by insane laws crafted over a hundred years by the Patrician interests. I want your help and I need to be sure of it."

"If what you say has any teeth, they will try to kill us in the hope that the ensuing chaos will buy them more time."

She taps the table top. "I admire your precision, Dr. Vaz. They don't know about me."

"You believe." He considers this new information. "So Feiss hired you but you were already an agent of the federal government?"

"You'd have to have met my dad, Emile, to understand how all that happened. Still, that is exactly what has taken place."

He wonders if she is crazy or if she is just lying to keep him with her. He decides neither makes sense. He has already agreed to help her. "Do you have any other proof?" He says trying to give himself time to think.

She nods. "The fish that fed so many."

"The dead fish? I already knew that wasn't a miracle. I figured it was Feiss."

She cuts him off. "That was the first time in fifty years Mr. Feiss and his friends had the use of government assets and it acted as more than a prostitute."

"And the second time was the fall of the Wall they engineered?"

"That is not an example of it."

Joe tugs at his mustache thinking she could have said yes and he would have been none the wiser. "What about Baylor?"

"Baylor was my lover. Now he is my curse, Dr. Vaz. You and I are targets. So is everything we've built. We represent a society based on mutually supported goals and ideals--not herd-based consumption.

I believe the corporatists do not understand my support and the government's tenacity. We can help guide this country to freedom. The rational choice is a negotiated settlement. Instead, the Patricians will choose to destroy it all. It is their way. I hoped it would be different but that air strike last night is clarification that there will be no peace--until we win. Regardless, the PO are at their end. That end can lead to either chaos or peace."

"Did the Air Force have the armaments and intelligence to destroy my factory?" He asks quietly.

"So far as I know, they do." She follows quickly with, "but I do not know if that information is current. The Patricians have been known to do unbelievably stupid things. On the other hand, I do believe the military missed the factory because they wanted to miss it."

"Do they know about me?"

"Everyone knows about you. You are another Feiss ace."

"You lie just like them."

She shakes her head trying not to anger. "To be powerful does not always make one a beast."

"We disagree. You have been more protective of me recently."

"In a way." His eyes light and she sees the heart of this man. She cannot help but admire him. 'We need you."

Joe looks over to Baylor who stands by a torch in the distance and points to him. "We are just like him. We will fight to the death in defense of a madness--only we call that madness; an ideal."

"You may be correct, Doctor. Peculiar isn't it? Philosophy aside, Doctor Vaz, we must prove to the masses behind the Wall that the Dirties can be no threat to them. We can't do that from this side of the Wall."

"Even if you get through the Wall you'll have to fight the corporate media blockade." His eyes dart around the night. "Oh, Elena Etu, Elena and You. The famous model, returning from the land of the Dirties saying it is going to be okay. Who could resist the story? I'll be a dumb bunny. And the US military will support you? Are you sure?"

"Nice factory. Still run does it? Boy those guys in the jets are dumb."

Joe Vaz looks around. "Okay, you win that one. How do I trust this isn't some insane attempt at Utopia by a deranged woman with delusions of glory?"

She finds herself admiring the light in his eyes.

"Elena?"

She recovers. "So you are still not sure if I am a beast?"

His heads moves back and forth repeatedly. "You may be a beast, but you have guts. I admire that. I just do not want to be the fool of a lunatic."

"And that is why you are alone, Doctor."

He stands to hide the pleasure of her company--from himself. Elena remains seated quietly sure this man's attraction for her cannot be counted on in any way. *He is a boy.*

"What about Phillip. Is he also the government?"

"He doesn't know about me and there is more proof. Check on it. Don't wreck my cover, please."

Joe looks down at her, his eyes glowing. "I really admire you." He looks at ground. "I will work for your cause. Seeing that it is your cause, and for no other reason. I am not sure that I believe you. That said, there is no way I will believe anything Phillip tells me about you. You are his hero."

His words sadden her. "Thank you. Phillip knows as much as he wants to know. That is the story of him. When he is ready to know more his brain will kick in and he will inform me. I have learned to wait for him."

Joe's lips almost curl into a smile. He stops it. "Beautiful women drive me crazy. Just let me know when you are ready to leave. I am ready. Please don't make my life a joke." He leaves without waiting for an answer.

Elena Etu watches him walk away. "I've never met a saint before," she mumbles to herself. "I thought they'd know more." Elena notes to herself that whenever she speaks to Joe, she winds up marveling at his goodness. She remembers how she once felt the same way about Baylor. The door to her heart slams shut.

CHAPTER THIRTY TWO

Shivering in the damp morning, Ewalt zips up the jacket he took last night from the soldier. It smells of oil and blood. Owls flutter, seeking prey. The odor of cooking meat wafts up from below. It's a greasy, unpleasing smell. He looks at the wrapped body of Amanda's copilot, then stares back at the sky, realizing he had been staring at the valley below most of the night. *Everything once told me I wanted to be like this poor dead SOB; to own things and make a lot of money, that the money would set me free. You high-steppers said you had the right idea. Fuck me. Now he's in a bag and I am freezing. What the hell have I been doing all my life? I am a robot, a wind up toy. You silly dirt-bags out there don't want to own anything. You just want to be left alone. To live your life--but that angers people like this guy and Amanda. Why would they hate your freedom? They want to turn you all into tools instead of people. They got me fighting myself because I want to protect my dad. I don't get it. God, are those people on the other side of the Wall really Demons? Are corporations the godless soulless beings we were taught to fear in Sunday school? Wouldn't that be a hoot-fucking-fact? No, they're not Demons. They're just dirty rotten bastards like the rest of us.*

Grabbing the webbing that surrounds the body, he continues

down the trail. Within a few minutes, he sees a pair of guards appear. He nods at the fat cannibal and his woman. A fire crackles nearby, a haunch of meat hangs skewered on the branch overhead. "That ain't hamburgers," Ewalt says dropping the webbing. "I brought you some more victuals."

"Huh?" The woman asks.

"Food," says the male. He leans over the corpse and cuts open the parachute covering the man. "Looks tasty. Can you smell the rich texture of this meat?" He laughs at Ewalt. "This is Patrician."

"I'll say." Ewalt scratches his gray-streaked beard. "You grade them too?"

"We worked in a packing house for swine."

"Didn't we all."

"Join us?" The woman asks cordially.

"No thanks, as soon as I see a food tent I'll go get some of the other stuff." He looks at the body of the dead man, wondering why he dragged him all this way just to be eaten by the cannibals. "Can I ask you a question? Why do you eat other people?"

The man ignores the question, grabs the webbing, and pulls breakfast towards the fire. The woman looks at him a moment. "We were trained to. Don't look so shocked. You were trained to be a killer. Why are you any better? We're just the recycling side of what you do." She points to the weapon then walks away.

"So something turned me into a killer, them into cannibals, and brought hell to the rest of us. What the fuck is going on? Why didn't we believe in anything besides money? And now I am talking to myself. Fuck me," he says to no one.

He makes his way down the hill until he comes to a guarded area. Ewalt stops behind a rusted tractor body outside the view of the perimeter guards. Worried they will think him a cannibal, he takes the time to strap his weapon under the loosely-fitting jacket.

In the distance, the sound of something like a million rattling snakes rises. People, who moments ago had been dreaming, or loving, or arguing, or eating, make one small motion together. Their collective effort sounds like a storm.

Tap
Tap-Tap
Tap-Tap-Tap
Tap-Tap-Tap-Tap
Tap-Tap-Tap-Tap-Tap.

The guards start slapping rocks together as well. The sounds of the ceremony gets louder. The motions of the crowd seems so small to Ewalt, but he cannot deny the affect. Ewalt joins in, calling out his presence as he ambles toward them. The guards see him, and ignore him. Only an older man with a small-bore hunting rifle strung over his back watches Ewalt. He has been waiting for him. Ewalt sees the man as soon as he crosses the guards' line but ignores him.

Tap
Tap-Tap
Tap-Tap-Tap
Tap-Tap-Tap-Tap
Tap-Tap-Tap-Tap-Tap.

That is the sound of Armageddon. A unified populations sure of their enemy--and filled with purpose. That's why the Wall didn't work for the bastards. It wasn't really a Wall. It was a lens. Dummies.

When the rhythm stops, the old man with the rifle summons Ewalt closer with his wagging finger. His garlic smell overpowers the stench of human filth that now fills Ewalt's nostrils. "Breathe on me, chief." The man leans his face close to him. Ewalt puffs a breathe at him. He scowls. "This is no time to joke, genius."

Ewalt smiles and takes in another deeper breath and exhales directly into the man's face. "That's better." The old man stares at Ewalt from clouded blue eyes. "Next time, son, don't do your fucking in Cannibal-land. We don't want you winding up as sushi. Keep it safe, son. Best to know when to fuck and when to fight. Go ahead." He waves Ewalt by. A strange feeling crawls up Ewalt's back as he walks. He will not turn to check on the man.

Commander Rader eventually stops on a small promontory, looking over the plain below. When he glances behind, he does not see the man. He feels him. Ewalt then focuses on the road extending north and south; it is a torrent of bodies moving north. He wonders why the road seems to disappear beneath the collapsed Wall, rather than going over the ruins.

Looking away from the Wall, he sees that every half mile or so two-wheeled dirt paths arc off the old US 5 and disappear into the ground--paths for the food trucks and soldiers. In the median of the old freeway, small camps of heavily armed men and women lounge waiting to cross under the Wall. The two closest guard towers lie in the dirt at the base of the Wall. Their snouts buried, they are dark, scarred by explosions, and empty.

He picks his way along the crowd. After two hours he passes the large troughs of water and the tents of food sheltering mounds of Kandy. Hordes of flies circle above or light on the food. Children with long wooden branches keep the bugs away. A plume of black smoke and a roar: the exhaust from the smokestacks of a dozen trucks. Other trucks appear in procession. *One thing is for certain. There's no way to commandeer one of those trucks. Christ, there are so many of them.*

Just then his stomach begins to float in his gut and he vomits. The spray and partially digested food foul three children playing with small quartz rocks. Ewalt looks down sheepishly, their legs are covered with his spittle.

The taller of the two boys stares at Ewalt as if he were Ewalt's father. "Say you're sorry and clean it up," the boy demands.

"What's the matter? Were you born in an office?" The second younger boy chimes in.

Ewalt pulls a rag from the pocket, leans over and cleans the area. Then he deposits his dirty cloth on the ground as he has seen others do. The boys now ignore him thinking him an idiot. They plan to steal the cloth as soon as he is out of sight. A guard runs by him. The man wears a green tunic. Ewalt watches him run to the other side of the roadway to a pair of soldiers who sit in chairs under camouflage netting. Lines of teenagers wait to see them. Next to the tables are a private trough of food and a large metal drum that holds spring water. The messenger leaves, heading to a truck.

Ewalt sits and contemplates the man and woman as they talk to groups of teens. Occasionally they point at the Wall. Ewalt notes as one after the other, teens cross the roadway as if entering the gates of Paradise. They are met by another woman who leads them into a tent full of weapons and then out to a waiting truck.

That's a recruiting center if I ever saw one. Pretty damn efficient. Recruiting station, staging area, and local security all in one. I'd like to kill the SOB who thought that one up. He's dangerous. A moment later Ewalt thinks again. *Why the hell don't we have better intelligence on this? Why didn't we attack the staging areas? Would it have driven them underground and then we would lose intelligence? The military is just not that dumb. Or is it?* The most obvious answer eludes Ewalt. He remains a man lost in clarity.

Oberving more trucks roll north at thirty miles an hour, he considers that he will either hitch a ride south or cross north at night. Then he hears a conversation about the attacks on the cities south of Salem--and how the helicopters are falling from the sky. At that moment, he decides to abort his mission. Ewalt knows the Columbia Wall is useless without helicopters to sweep the river.

He laughs drawing attention to himself--laughter is rare here and everyone wants a piece of it. The old man with the hunting rifle appears again as a group of soldiers reveal themselves tracking Ewalt's movements. Others now wonder why this fit man isn't fighting. Suspicions grow rapidly as people watch the soldiers watch him. Escape is not an option. He counts at least two well-armed squads tracking him and Ewalt sees the will of battle in their movements.

Death does not achieve the goal of helping his father.

Ewalt crosses to the recruiting tent and walks passed the teens. He takes no notice of the dozen soldiers that move in closer to him, their weapons trained on him. He speaks to the two people sitting in the chairs. "I am here to see Elena Etu. I am an emissary from the other side of the Wall. We wish to make peace."

CHAPTER THIRTY THREE

The majority of Elena's advisors believe the emissary is a fake. Nonetheless, she has agreed to meet with him, siding with the small minority who believe the story. Because they want to believe it. That small group includes Joe Vaz who has taken over some of the battle logistics work. Phillip's wounds have laid the old man on a stretcher and he is unable to direct both battle and the supply lines.

Approaching the meeting outside her tent, Joe Vaz feels tired and edgy. A rudimentary communications system Phillip has set up has proven to be an effective method of giving out false information. That has led to numerous ambushes and a rapidly increasing cache of weapons. Dr. Vaz has begun deploying these weapons. With an efficiency that amazes the other advisors, his stature has grown quickly. Even though everyone thinks he is not a man made for battle.

Elena knows better.

Having sat in on the discussions between Dr. Vaz and Phillip Stein, Elena is astounded at how Joe Vaz sees the function of battle and measures the human cost of any event by the overall benefit of the effort. It isn't that he is ruthless--he is just so practical she wonders how to keep him safe while employing his apparently unending talents.

She is concerned about what Joe will do when the soldier who claims to be an emissary is brought here. All the reports indicate the so-called emissary is the tank commander who had gotten away a few days ago. Elena knows Joe is intent on getting through the Wall as quickly as possible and she worries he may be cruel or reckless in his actions--though she admits to herself--so far he has been a godsend. In truth, she fears that Joe Vaz may prove to be too practical and a display of brutality is more than she can stand. Elena looks again for Baylor.

He has not been around for almost a day. Baylor has been out killing snipers--while also having been enlisted to look for certain kinds of equipment. She is surprised that Baylor and Joe work so well together. Rather than the acrimony that she had seen from Joe these last few years, these last few days he has been respectful to Baylor. She has seen him joke with Baylor. While asking him to do what he loves. Joe Vaz sees Baylor as a mad hero. He pities him, and admires his courage. Elena's gut knots seeing them converse. Early this morning, Joe said he had Baylor out looking for one of their tanks. Elena considers what Joe might possibly want with a tank. She suspects that earlier speculation that the emissary had been a tank commander has something to do with it.

Phillip, on the other hand has no real interest in the so-called emissary, other than amusement at the man's strategy to stay alive. Phillip also believes this man to be the third saboteur they have been seeking. Elena's real reasoning for meeting with the man is more than blind hope. She believes he may present some new options as he is the only soldier from the hand-picked group of killers to surrender.

The Priestess detests cowards. Considering them weak and untrustworthy, she still wants to speak to this soldier to see why the Patricians choose him for this mission. It doesn't make sense to sign on a coward. Regardless, she has already decided to carefully measure the man's words just in case he is smarter, or someone different than he might appear; even as she plots to use his fears as a lever.

Elena therefore evaluates just how desperate they are on the other side of the Wall. She assumes they are very desperate. With the vassals seeking an exit strategy, pockets of those left behind in Oregon have shown an amazing willingness to do anything asked of them. Unfortunately these different groups have also shown themselves to be ignorant of any useful facts. The level of myth among the population astounds all of her commanders. The most useful group had been members of a corporate think tank outside of Eugene. They were discovered hiding under an old SUV that acted as a barrier to their basement laboratory. That group had known where the chocolate bars were hidden. Elena distributed most of the chocolate to the troops.

From the eastern hillside where she stands, she can see what had once been a city. The battle lines remain stalled in the city of Salem. While the flames from the dynamited buildings in the town center have died down, smoke continues to roil skyward from the ongoing battle for the city. Artillery from the retreating troops have defined a battle line that has proven surprisingly solid for another day.

The meeting continues to this topic. "Communications and control systems still function despite numerous successful assaults on their communications facilities. We do not know why."

"There are rumors of a functioning network in the remains of the local hospital but we are hard-pressed to believe it. Most of the buildings have been dynamited by the retreating soldiers or pummeled by our rockets."

"I can see no other reason," says Phillip from his stretcher. It's leaning up so he can see the small group of twenty advisors and tacticians sitting around old picnic tables. "There is no good reason why the remaining resistance around the capital complex could have such effective fire-control."

She looks out to the west. Her high capacity binoculars allow an almost flawless view of the battle. She watches the battle and wonders if the Patricians had figured out how much she values a hospital.

Another of her plans is to take the old hospital on the hills overlooking Portland. Joe and Phillip continually confer on that target, ignoring the other obvious targets of the city, and its bridges. Both men agree those targets are less costly, but a working hospital is far more valuable than land. Reports say sappers continually try and set up positions to assist the assault. Unfortunately, the area below the hospital is a place called Contractor's Alley where the munitions factories had been located. That area and the hills above it are heavily fortified. Elena doubts that battle will be anything other than dreadful.

A young man, a runner, appears wearing a green armband. Six of her guards escort the boy even though they all know him. "Priestess, there are problems at the city center and by the river. My commander has asked for your cannons to ignore other targets and concentrate their firepower on the remains of the hospital tower. He says he is sure it is the remaining hub of telecommunications in the city. He says he understands that you want to preserve anything you can of the hospital. The death toll is getting out of hand. He also says he is sorry."

Elena leans over to look at the remains of the hospital tower. It is the only tall building left in the city, though it is shot full of holes with large sections of the exterior walls on the fourth floor completely gone. Elena cannot imagine there could be any effective telecommunications, but she has watched the assault stop while enemy soldiers and the medical equipment make it to the river. Supplies continue to be removed north by speeding boats. Soon there will be no supplies left to commandeer from the hospital and that bodes badly. No one was expecting so effective of a defense now that the helicopters and tanks that have disappeared from battle.

Fearing the battle for Portland will be made worse, the longer they are stalled here, she faces the two women who command the field artillery. They arrived a few seconds after the boy. She understands the coincidence. Looking to Phillip, Elena sees he is just waiting for her to give the order. "Train the artillery on the hospital tower. Destroy it." She speaks to the artillery commanders. They rush off waving their hands. A moment later Elena sees the artillery begin to adjust their positions. She faces the runner. "And you tell your commander to fire a red flare as soon as he feels the area is secure."

The boy looks at her quizzically, but will not ask questions. He nods, briefly closing his eyes out of respect, then runs off down the hill to a waiting motorcycle. The cannons open fire a few minutes later. They continue their barrage. Sets of mortars that the field commander has had put in place fire as well. The barrage goes on for almost four hours before she sees the red flare. The hospital tower is a skeleton of steel and burning debris.

Within two hours, her forces are at the river. The battle for Salem is almost over.

That evening, as she sits in her tent, she hears only the cries of the wounded as she chews on her dinner--one of Joe's cakes--staring at a picture of she and Baylor when they were on their honeymoon. Midway through the cake, she throws the framed picture at the front flap of her tent. There is nothing that can be done for the wounded of either side. The hospital is a total loss.

"You almost hit me with that." Baylor stands in the half light. He wears only a loincloth and a skirt of fresh scalps. He picks up the picture and frowns as he approaches her. "That was us back then. You always wanted kids. Is that what is bothering you?"

"Where have you been? Bay, are you okay?"

"Getting the Food Man his tank--what a pain in the neck that was." He grins.

She hasn't heard any lucid words from him since the attack on the factory. He puts a hand out too quickly. She stiffens fearing his movement.

"That hurt. I thought by now you'd know you have nothing to fear from me." He sighs looking at her then steps back. He pulls something from the waistband of his loincloth. "I wanted to give you this. It's a gold watch on a golden chain. There was a cache of them at an old mall in Portland." He hands it to her slowly, then steps back again. His caring rips into her like a bullet.

Elena watches the second hand move. Baylor sees her eyes mist "I'm sorry. It's your birthday today and I wanted to give you something. I didn't mean to make you sad by seeing me crazy. I worked so hard to make sure I was sane when I came in. I guess the picture on the ground confused me. I wanted to make you happy with my gift and tell how much this battle has meant to me. We're going to win. I was in Portland today. They are giving up everything south of the city-- and they can't gas the people anymore so it's chaos there. We will own the city in a few weeks."

She stands and walks towards him. Her hand drifts up to touch him--but this time he steps back. "You're poison, Eli. Don't touch me. I owed you a gift for your birthday. And I always do my duty." He turns to leave, then stops. "Your never-ending game of making yourself feel good sickens me sometimes. Did you know they called me a stooge when we first met? Did you know that? You were so beautiful I missed why they said it. I am nothing to you. Was I ever anything more than a tool?" He laughs, but stops when he sees she does not laugh. "Have you ever wondered if maybe you are the result of the evil? A reaction to it, like my killing. Maybe you are nothing better than me. Or maybe I am just not sure you are a good person anymore. I think you do things to make yourself feel good. That isn't goodness. Goodness is doing things you don't want to do because they are right--regardless of cost." His right hands scoops under a set of three scalps and lifts them out, as if they were short wings. Why can't these dumb bastards kill me?"

A dull film seems to fall over her stunning dark eyes. Elena finds she can barely see anything in the room. A gong sounds; the young messenger from this afternoon appears covered in sweat and mud. His dark eyes fill with a mixture of fear and awe as he sees Baylor.

"Speak." Baylor says. Elena watches Baylor's eyes. They dart about like angry bees. He has returned to auto-pilot, a killing machine just waiting for the feed.

"The Demons are raining death from the sky all along the great roadway. They bomb us with the gas that opens sores in our skin and lungs. We can go no further because the gas must dissipate." The messenger gasps for air and waits for her response.

Elena says a silent prayer for the soldiers then speaks to Baylor. "Take him to the canteen. Feed him my chocolate and have him wait."

The boy, unsure if he has heard the words correctly, wonders if she is teasing him. He has heard of chocolate. He has never tasted it.

As soon as they leave she calls for a vehicle to take her into the city. "Priestess, Baylor said you are to stay inside until he returns."

She glares at the guard. "I will get your car."

When it arrives. Baylor is perched on top. A set of infrared goggles on his face and a machine gun across his lap. She gets in the car. "Take me to our soldiers."

Her driver turns to look back at the Priestess, then seeing her scowl, just nods. A few minutes down the roadway, a second vehicle full of guards wearing full battle dress, stops in her path. Her car's headlights show Joe Vaz sits in the front seat. He gets out of the car.

"You don't carry a weapon," he says, opening her car door.

"Neither do you."

"Where are we going?"

Elena realizes the men and women surrounding them are his guards as well as hers. They are very well armed--though she does not fear them. Dr. Vaz is now a military field commander.

"I am sick of sitting here like some coward. I want to thank our soldiers and talk to them. To let them know they matter to me. Why do you ask?"

Joe Vaz shakes his head back and forth as if were arguing with himself. "Priestess, these men and women fight for you. I have seen sacrifice that had I not seen it with my own eyes, I would never have believed it. There is blood, and horror. I suggest you let it go."

"I gave specific orders for you to stay away from the battle lines. Wait here for me."

He looks at her and grins. "You think I am so empty-headed?"

She scowls at his cavalier response.

"Elena, it is all so evil. They destroyed everything in the city that might help us. Not just weapons, but medicine, water, anything of value, I am sickened. Don't do this. There is nothing to see but suffering."

"Now you understand why I am going. They are the people who matter. The ones that choose unity over vanity. I am no better then them. They sacrifice their lives. I will go to them."

Joe Vaz looks at her. Turning away, he gets in his vehicle.

It is a quick fifteen minute drive into the soldiers' camps. When she arrives, she walks to the milling crowd. They face her like leaves seeking the sunshine. She ascends a fifteen foot scaffolding, waiting for everyone's attention. She is a perfect target and both Baylor and Joe Vaz climb the perch to put their bodies in the way of the most likely sniper points. As soon as they do, soldiers in the back of the crowd break off and begin move to the high points looking for trouble.

Elena holds up her hands then bows. "We are all in your debt." In an instant, her calm is reflected in eased faces and a shared sense of peace. Elena bathes in it. Her ability to calm a crowd's fears and help those in need remains her drug of choice.

She stares at the slapping of the multicolored wind-socks on old flag poles. "My friends," she waits as her words echo out in the crowd by her assistants. "Today we have seen new horrors from the Demons. They use a hospital for killing more people." She waits again. The crowd stamps their feet at the mention of the Demons. The ground tremors beneath them. "The Demons are like the rats. No smarter, no kinder, no less able to control their filthy habits or their evil thoughts. They are the rodent that kills its own brood. Their evil continues behind their new Wall. Just as the smell of rats remains in our memories."

Her voice continues to filter out passed the crowd into the surrounding area. Other stranded citizens of Salem begin to appear. There is a report of gunfire somewhere in the distance. Baylor stands closer to her. She smiles at his courage and turns back to the crowd. "We must not let our good be extinguished in their madness. Their evil must be like the passing storm. We must not be soaked through with their evil. We must remain as one people. We must ignore the rumors and we must work together to defeat the small band of terrorists that came into our country, stolen our land, our hope, and our national pride while trying to make us feel weak and afraid."

"Tell us, Priestess, what else have the evil ones done? I wish to know so that I may laugh at their horrors when I come to spit on their burning bodies," says one man's voice.

"Repeat that to all. It is a good question." She waits as the question repeats through the crowd in various languages. Laughter follows it. "I will tell you, my brother, of the Demons' latest high jinx. On this day, the Demons have begun blowing up all the cities north of here as they retreat while gassing the roads. It will be our task to try and save the large city north of here, called Portland. The Demons will kill their own people to stop freedom."

"The Demons behind the Wall never change do they?" Someone yells out.

"Repeat it," Etu says.

She sees Phillip. He is carried on a stretcher and commands a group of fifty soldiers that quickly spread out protecting the Priestess and the Food Man. She nods to him. He is incensed at both Elena and Joe Vaz. A bomb would have turned the tide of this war.

She watches him begin directing more soldiers. "The Demons never change because the Demons know only the desire of their want. They believe greed is more real than ideals--or you and I. We must recognize that the good which is inside us is not within them and we must never count on goodness to defeat them. They will always seek the most evil alternative. They do this because they know we are good and it is difficult for us to see their evil. They know it is hard for us to believe that anyone would employ evil with such joy. So you see they see our goodness as weakness. And that is their weakness. It is why we will win. Repeat this."

The murmuring turns into a roar of approval. Baylor kicks his foot against the metal supports in approval. Elena, outwardly calm looks over to him. In truth, the banging has scared her. She raises her hands and the crowd immediately quiets. "We are no longer at risk from the Demons. Their numbers and resources are too few. We are again becoming a free people. Only our countrymen and women to the north are at risk from them."

"We will never fear them."

"We are good and good is stronger."

"We are not afraid."

"We will keep the help flowing to our fellow citizens." The shouts of courage are repeated and the crowd amplifies its resolve, feeding off itself.

"Soon all humanity will be freed from the evil greed of the Demons."

"Grreeed." The crowd repeats the word in a rising crescendo. Then a new chant: "Freed from Grreeed!"

"Grreeed. Freeed from Greeed!"

A cheer rises up.

The Priestess glances up at the sky wondering where her show of force is. Then, she points up. "Do not be afraid. This one is ours. Look at what we have achieved." A small metal-framed helicopter suddenly swoops overhead and darts across the square. It crisscrosses three more times then rises up and hovers. "This aircraft was made in our factories, by our people. Soon we will have millions of them to breach their new Wall. The end is near for the evil ones that have tried to steal our freedom, our humanity, and our planet."

The crowd cheers wildly. The small helicopter does one more loop of the square then withdraws behind the remains of a shopping center. Princess Etu holds her arms aloft. She clasps two red-flecked stones and begins to hit them together.

Tap
Tap-Tap
Tap-Tap-Tap
Tap-Tap-Tap-Tap
Tap-Tap-Tap-Tap-Tap

The chatter of stones fills the square rising to a deafening roar. The sound saturates her with the growing strength of those in the crowd and warms her like a hot fire. After five minutes, she stops and bows once more to the crowd--which immediately returns her bow. She summons Baylor. "Go meet the truck that arrives from the south. There is an emissary, a man. I want the prisoner brought to me. Keep him alive, no matter what."

He trots off to intercept the truck. Phillip limps over to her. His weight on the shoulder of a brawny soldier. "We need to talk." She can see blood all over his pants and boots. The soldier helps Phillip get in her car, then stands aside as Joe Vaz appears on the run.

Joe gets inside the car. "I've got my tank." He slams the door shut then sees the old man. "Phillip, are you okay?"

Phillip looks over to Elena. "We have another prisoner. She was directing the fire control from the hospital tower. She stuck a nail file in my leg." He laughs. "Her name is Amanda Feiss. The daughter of Lucas Feiss of Feiss Industries."

Elena stares, eyes wide and unbelieving. "You're sure?"

"I have never met her, but I am sure it is her."

Elena speaks to Joe Vaz: "I am thinking you can tell us if it is her." Elena can identify Amanda as well; they had met on numerous occasions. Still she wants Joe's opinion. "If it is her--we now have a bargaining chip."

Joe is swamped by this news. He stares away from them. Thoughts of treason, race through his skull. "She saved my life. I can't let you hurt her," Joe stares at Phillip.

"This I am sure of. We will keep her safe. She is a key to getting us through the Wall." Phillip says.

Joe has a smile Elena has never seen before. She suddenly realizes why she did not believe his ardor the way Phillip did. *He thinks he is in love with Amanda Feiss.* "Phillip, please make sure to have Ms. Feiss brought to us in the morning. Joe, I want you there." She watches Joe watch Phillip--absolutely certain his people will find out where Amanda Feiss is and begin guarding her. She considers this turn of events for a moment then sighs. *Too many riches.* "Why was Amanda

Feiss left behind?"

Phillip looks at Joe as he speaks. Watching him, he has also begun to fear Joe Vaz's response to this prisoner. "I was told she was in the hospital for treatment. When the battle began she began directing fire control. She already had a team of telecommunications people and a set of computers in place. She apparently knew we would try to bypass the hospital or save it. So she must have a plan for us as well. This surrender was no coincidence. Amanda Feiss stayed behind to meet with us. She approached one of my officers and asked him to get her a car so she could meet with the man in charge. They brought her to me. Before I said a word she stuck the nail file into my leg. They subdued her and they now have her tied up. We need to be careful. She is dangerous."

"She saved my life," Doctor Joseph Vaz says again.

CHAPTER THIRTY FOUR

The Willamette Valley surrounds him as the truck rolls through the hills south of Salem. Smoke circles the horizon. Though it is only two weeks since Ewalt was in this part of Oregon, it looks like it could have been years. Structures along the roadway smolder. Power lines are destroyed and the freeway is a little wider than a bulldozer blade. Blacktop and concrete from the roadway litter the fields. A few burning tanks have dotted the roadway. He remembers that among his poker playing friends, only he remains alive. The rest have died guarding the retreat.

The state smells of napalm and the black stumps that had once been trees. The choking dust is awful. Corvallis was still burning as the truck traveled though it during the night. Passing through Eugene, gunfire continued into the early dawn. Weapons fire can now be heard from the west as well. He assumes the sounds to be armed citizens fighting Dirties in what they believe is a last stand for freedom and America. Ahead, a shopping mall burns and teams of insurgent soldiers stand about watching empty stores spit flames.

The trip north from the Wall has taken almost fifteen hours. The dump truck he rides in pulls over for any vehicle that wishes to pass it--going either north or south. There have been no fly-overs by either helicopters or jets the entire trip, and he has seen the Dirties move their troops north at will.

So far as Ewalt can tell, it appears to have been an orderly well-planned advance. He has heard the front lines are just north of the city of Salem. The damage by the sappers from both sides is extensive. He notes even the creeks have been diverted to flood the roadways--once the wet season arrives. Ewalt assumes they have been poisoned as well.

Bound and gagged along with a dozen other men and women, a black chain link mesh covers him. He feels like a netted animal. Looking around, Ewalt doesn't see anyone who looks remotely like a captured soldier. So he wonders why they are with him. They weren't treated like deserters and they appear too quiet to be criminals so their placement strikes him as suspicious. The truck pulls over again as another food convoy passes by. He wonders how far he is from Salem.

The three men who guard the prisoners act as though they are sympathetic to Ewalt. They all claim to be former soldiers left behind the lines when the Wall was completed. The tall leader claims to have been an explosives expert from San Francisco. Named Franks, the man balked when Ewalt tried to engage him in conversation about Elena Etu. The man now sits on the roof of the truck's cab, his back to Ewalt, rifle across his knees, a green-checked cloth around his head and across his mouth. He reminds Ewalt of the Arab traders he has seen in old movies. The other two men have positioned themselves along the back tailgate. They wear goggles and scarves over canvas dusters. The truck begins moving again.

Through the grated sides of the truck, between the other prisoners, Ewalt watches as a blur of people appear along roadway. This is new. There were no refugees on the earlier part of the trip. Many of them are well-dressed and look confused that their protectors had dynamited or burned their world while the enemy seems to ignore them or throw food at them. The sounds of battle gets louder. The truck enters the obliterated state capital. On the hillsides he can see the puff of smoke from primitive artillery.

A few minutes later, when the truck pulls over again. Ewalt stares out to the ruins of Salem. This center of liberalism had always been a thorn in his father's side. Three times his dad had tried to open a bagel shop here. He was told ethnicity was frowned upon in this area. He was even told that if he called his shop a bakery there would be no problem. When Ewalt smiles at the memory, it immediately draws the attention of the other prisoners. The guards ignore him.

The truck rolls forward to traverse a lesion in the macadam apparently caused by an explosion. Threading its way across the median, the truck speeds up until it comes to an off ramp leading to the remains of a shopping center. Taking the off ramp into the parking lot, the truck stops among other vehicles being serviced or filled with fuel and supplies. The guards stand to stretch their legs. The man in front climbs down to speak to the driver. Ewalt looks at the sign: Lancaster

Mall. It is the only item left in tact. The buildings and restaurants are rubble or burning. "Alright. Get on down." The back gate of the dump truck falls forming a makeshift ramp and the chain link fabric is removed. One by one, the people climb down. After Ewalt reaches the ground, two of guards pull him forward of the truck separating him from the others.

A smaller vehicle parked by the sign now comes toward him-- an old white ice cream truck. A muscular, lion-maned man stands in the passenger seat. The vehicle come to a stop and the man puts on an Indian war bonnet of peacock feathers. Getting out of the truck Ewalt sees the man wears a skirt of scalps and khaki pants. Twin bandoliers of bullets cross his bare chest, even though the man seems to only carry a pair of hunting knives. Ewalt smiles. *Now this is more what I had expected.*

On his shoulders, Baylor wears the epaulets of a Marine Major. Ewalt does not doubt the madness of this visitor and is not surprised to see fear in the eyes of his captors that translates to mute respect. *Whoever this guy is, he thinks he is the boss. Can't be. There is no way this kook planned their strategy.* So Ewalt wonders if he is about to die. He gauges the crazy battle-glazed eyes of the man who now stares at him. Ewalt thinks that this man would have benefitted handsomely from joy juice. *This guy is battle-worn.*

The odd smile that soon crosses the man's face is not one of madness, or cruelty, as Ewalt had expected. It appears to be relief. *He has been looking for me? They want peace? They believe the emissary story after all? Oh bullshit.*

"Coward, you will ride with us. I am not here to harm you. My orders are to keep you safe. Do you understand?" Baylor's words shock Ewalt to the point that he only nods. Baylor pulls out the Bowie knife. "I will kill you if I have to." Again, Ewalt nods, noting the sharpened teeth. *So he does the I am crazier than you thing, okay.* Measuring the man and making some assumptions on how he fights--just in case he has to fight him--Ewalt notes the way Baylor stands. The crazy man is well-schooled in battle.

A moment later, Ewalt is strapped on the hood of the truck like a dead deer, his head just above the wheel well on the passenger side, facing back. A man has joined them. He had been posing as a prisoner on the ride up. Ewalt notes the driver and the guard wear the same green scarves. Ewalt also notes the driver and the guard are relaxed seeing that the crazy man with the feathers has turned his full attention on Ewalt, like some kind of mad baby sitter.

Speeding through the remains of Salem and into the countryside to the northeast, Ewalt hears the clatter of weapons fire increasing and he knows he is approaching a battle line. Fifteen minutes later after climbing into the low hills, he sees supply lines, bivouacked troops, and shelters. The sounds of battle are close. He notes the soldiers are equipped with modern Border Patrol weapons.

The ice cream truck pulls off the roadway and enters an

encampment. The roadway ends at a bulldozer and a patchwork of tents. All the troops here wear green scarves. Ewalt concludes they are an elite force or palace guard. A set of glinting objects in the sky catches his eye. As they come closer, he cannot believe the sight of three spindly metal-framed helicopters flying west in formation. The helicopters break formation and dive for the hillside, each firing a small missile. Ewalt wishes he might see how accurate the missiles are. Quickly, the helicopters reform up after the run. One of the craft now trails smoke, but it is still flying.

At that moment, from the north, three parallel white vapor trails appear. The jets speed closer, circle a few times then head back north. There is neither engagement of the spindly helicopters nor the troops. Ewalt cannot imagine why trained fighter pilots would not engage the enemy in these easily seen encampments. Ewalt hears the driver say: "They're not ignoring us. They're out of ammunition." Ewalt knows that is not true and wonders if the civilians have taken control of military operations because the actions he has seen are so foul.

In front are a stunning mix of iridescent colors--and people. He wonders what it looks like from the air, with the arteries of empty black roads and the multicolored tents undulating in the bright sunshine. His mind--trained to examine the feel of battle--senses relief in these troops. Victory surrounds him.

Far to the north a parade of flashes roll across his field of vision from infrastructure detonations. He wonders why, then concludes these are explosions from the interstate.

"I'd like to see you gut-shot," says Baylor, as he releases Ewalt's bonds, and hauls Ewalt up to standing. Watching the man, Ewalt feels amused. He has never encountered an enemy in battle more insane than he. It's an edge he does not happily relinquish. So far as he can tell, this man called Baylor is the only real threat he has seen since his capture. The challenge pleases him. He notes his baby sitter has had a broken arm.

A soldier pushes him onto a low mound of tires. The man who had posed as another prisoner leans Ewalt against an old truck tire and chains him to it. "You see this, Demon?" His arm arches out across his body pointing to the remains of a small town. "You see this?"

Ewalt nods.

"I was born here. There used to be a hospital right where we are standing. I went to school over there, down the hill. I married here. I was a mechanical engineer designing parts for aircraft. I had a home down by Silver Creek. Then we moved to Los Angeles for a new job. Two weeks after I got to LA, my family was dead and I had to eat dog food to survive." The man wipes his nose with his sleeve. "Do you believe you are anything more than a pawn? You and your moronic story about being an emissary?" The man waits for a response, but none comes. "Oh, I see. You're worried I might hurt you. Don't you get it? You're the bad guys. Not us." He looks at Ewalt then turns to his subordinates.

"Cowards, I hate them. They just can't tolerate the truth."

Baylor returns with a spindly man who walks up to Ewalt and stares at him. "I would have to agree with you. He is no one. Just a man who wants to live, like the rest of us." The man's eyes examine Ewalt, as if he were looking for some hidden benefit.

"Then we have no place for him. He is only a coward," Baylor says to Joe Vaz. "Do not harm him. Feed him. We'll deal with him when we get back." With that, the two men walk away from Ewalt, get in the ice cream truck, and leave the compound. A few minutes later the guards beat Ewalt with their fists and leave him gasping for air.

Joe Vaz sits quietly in the ice cream truck as Baylor drives them to meet with Elena Etu. He believes Baylor's decision to leave the man behind is a mistake but he will say nothing. He is no emissary but something tells Joe the man is useful. In any case, Baylor is Elena's albatross and Joe is concentrating on saving the life of the woman who saved his life--not some poor soldier. As they ride though the morning, Joe is surprised to see that the retreating troops appear to have entirely left the area. Last night Salem was a battle zone. This morning it appears far quieter--only the occasional battle. He wonders how far forward Elena Etu has placed her encampment. Joe cannot help but be impressed by her courage, again.

Twenty-five minutes later they circle a wrecked overpass and enter the remains of a large shopping mall. Joe wonders why she continually sets up her base of operations in shopping areas. He guesses it is because the buildings are large and offer space for hiding. He is mostly correct. Elena Etu also retains some cultural baggage: She feels safe in a shopping area.

Ahead, the Priestess stands at the far edge of a huge parking lot. Behind her is a broken down child's play structure and a flattened tree house torn from its support. The faux tree and its coverings lie bent like blackened tinsel.

She watches Baylor's ice cream truck careen around the corner and roll towards her. *He was so pleased to have found it parked by the hospital. Am I that mad as well? I must be.*

The vehicle comes to a halt and she is surprised to see only Joe Vaz with Baylor. She sighs assuming the man who calls himself an emissary has been killed. Baylor adjusts his peacock feathers and straightens up his scalps as he approaches. She watches Joe Vaz slowly exit the truck and walk towards her. Elena makes sure he is not injured. Baylor hums to himself. "Baylor?"

He bows to her. His entire body awaits her command.

"You seem in good spirits."

"I am looking forward to dying soon. I hate the pain and the killing."

She pauses for a moment. "You wish to die?" And she watches an impatient Joe Vaz approach, his eyes darting about for Amanda Feiss.

"Don't you? Think about it. All we've done is give these people the shaft. But what the hell. We'll go down fighting, right, Priestess? Ah-hee," he calls out. "Ah-hee. Ah-hee." His wild cries echo up and down the open parking lot like a ghost racing to a graveyard.

"Baylor, stop that," she says. "You'll scare the others."

He stares at her. His mouth open. "We were never equals were we? I am sorry, my Priestess. I seek only to protect you."

Elena stops and places her hand against the cold concrete wall beside her. *His mouth has stopped bleeding.* "You remember this place?"

"We were trying to sell, now what was it? Gloves? It was gloves, really soft leather. You bought me a pair. I used them to choke people the second day we were in San Francisco. Then I stuffed one of them down a kid's throat to keep her quiet. My arm was broken, remember? Can we get another pair while we are here? I think I lost the other glove also." He scans the ruins. "What a mess, huh?" He blinks seeing her horror, apparently frightened by his comment. "I am your servant." Baylor then stands dumbly awaiting her words. Joe nods hello.

"What happened to the emissary?" She asks this question of Joe but Baylor answers.

"My conclusion was that he is just a soldier trying to stay alive. When Dr. Vaz here concurred--we decided his desire to kill you was just too much. We have him tied up at the supply depot in the hills."

Phillip approaches on crutches with four of his lieutenants. They break off and wait for him. "Phillip, would you please have one of your lieutenants retrieve the so-called emissary from the Silverton supply depot and keep him safe. I will want to see him." She says the words ignoring Baylor and looking at Joe--as if to say he had been bad.

It raises Joe's hackles and he turns away. Phillip tells two of his lieutenants to go and retrieve the man. The man and woman turn immediately and run towards a waiting jeep.

Baylor mumbles. "You messed that one up good, Food Man. Damn."

"Gentlemen, please follow me into the old sports store. We have some work to do with the prisoner inside."

At one time this had been a janitor's closet. Amanda Feiss hums in the candlelit shadows. She straddles a chair with her legs spread and her head resting forward on the chair back. Her hands are tied behind her back. She cannot detect the door when it opens, but the flood of light and sounds are unmistakable.

When she sees the madness that is Baylor begin to pull on the chair, bringing her into the larger room, Amanda stifles a cry, thinking her worst fears are about to appear before her eyes. In an odd way, she is absolutely correct. Of course, none of the people in the room plan to hurt her. She would be astounded to know at this point that if they had tried. One of the men in the room would have died first. She cannot yet see Dr. Joseph Vaz.

The large open room is lit by multiple holes in the ceiling. Smelling the man with the pointed teeth dragging her--she believes she can also smell a woman nearby. When Baylor steps back and spins the chair, Amanda sees a woman surprisingly well-groomed in a dirty blouse over khaki pants.

Elena Etu smiles at her. Amanda knows the face and smile but when she sees that look that decries Amanda as some kind of fish on monger's table, Amanda smiles coyly and turns away.

She sees Joe Vaz.

An uncontrollable shiver possesses her body as if she were in seizure. Her eyes stare wide, unbelieving, her breath short. In his eyes she sees concern, knowing he is the cause of her anxiety. Doctor Joseph Vaz appears to her, petrified with concern.

Elena cannot help but examine the unmasked beauty of Joe Vaz. She feels happy for the first time in days.

"Hello, Dr. Vaz. I am so happy you are well. I thought it was you who had been feeding them." Her smile comes from the heart of a snake and the Priestess circles to make sure that what she hears and what she sees are congruent. Elena Etu sees the truth and finds her dislike boils over into the room. Phillip politely nudges the Priestess on the arm.

"Whom am I addressing?" Phillip asks as Baylor lights candles in a sterling silver candelabra and sets them on the plywood floor around them. It is already light enough, but like a mother spoiling a child, Elena allows him to play and stay out of mischief.

"I am Captain Amanda Feiss. I am the person that stabbed you in the leg. I guess you forgot," Amanda responds. "And you are?" She asks Phillip.

"Phillip Stein. I am the guy that blew up your Wall."

"That was Feiss property."

"Isn't it all?" He replies.

She looks at Elena Etu. "I believe that you knew my father, Lucien Feiss. He mentioned that he had hired you to do some work for us on the far side of the Wall." Amanda watches the reactions of the men in the room and sees this is no revelation to them. She purses her lips waiting for a response.

The Priestess stares at Amanda, astounded at her audacity. Finally she speaks. "You have come looking for me. Why?"

Amanda recognizes her leverage. "So you are not just a fashion leader anymore, but a populist leader as well?"

"This is the Priestess Elena Etu. She is the government here-- now that yours has abdicated from the real world." Baylor roars.

Amanda appears bored. "It wasn't an insult. In fact it was a compliment. I don't usually remember the help." Amanda pauses as she formulates her reply. "Did you know my company has a standing reward for your safe return?"

"I cannot believe money would sway you from what you think is right," Elena responds watching Joe Vaz who appears to have heard none of the conversation; he continually scans the young woman to make sure she is well.

Amanda shrugs. "Actually, I'm here to talk with Dr. Vaz. After that you can negotiate a surrender with me if you like."

"Is that why your mother sent you?" Elena asks.

My mother? Amanda holds her composure. "I have taken some minor operational responsibility here--for this rabble of yours. Your desertion of your country has become mine to straighten out as well."

"Now that was funny," says Elena, certain Amanda is busy negotiating her own deal.

"Untie me," Amanda Feiss demands.

Elena Etu does not move. Phillip speaks. "What were you doing in Salem directing artillery?" He asks.

Amanda who had been ignoring the old man now sees a leader. Worse, there is something familiar about him. "I was handling fire control from the hospital tower. I had been a patient and rather than leave, I found useful work. I am quite reliable you know. And I am not a traitor like some." She smiles at Elena.

Baylor who had been quiet, immediately walks toward her to strike her. Elena sees Joe reach for something behind his back. "Baylor, please." She assumes Joe was reaching for a weapon of some sort. Baylor stops and bows to Elena backing up slowly, his eyes glued to Amanda Feiss.

Amanda stares at Baylor realizing this is the Baylor Grendel, Elena Etu's lover. For a brief moment she feels the other woman's pain. "And I thought I was tough on men."

Elena walks closer to Amanda and for a moment Amanda believes Elena Etu will hit her. "You were in the hospital and your mother left you there?" Elena watches Amanda's eyes.

Amanda ignores the comment to speak to Joe Vaz. "Doctor, will you come with me to the other side of the Wall and speak for this rabble? I am sure we can find a way to end this horror with your help."

The Priestess Elena Etu smiles at the impudence of the woman and waits to see what Joe will do. She sees the light in his eyes turn low. Amanda says: "I hoped you would remain loyal. You are a good man. Okay, Ms. Etu, you have the cards and I am your servant. How do we solve this mess?"

"The Patricians need to share power."

"Oh, my, dearie," Amanda says. "You are witty."

Elena nods hearing the words of Luke Feiss in her speech. "We are going to get through the new Wall. I believe you have seen our aircraft? Impressive aren't they?"

Amanda lifts her head and speaks, keeping her top lip absolutely still. "Dearie, you must like jokes."

"A deb will always fall back on that when they're in trouble." Elena pauses to look at Joe Vaz.

Joe still stares at Amanda, but he sees a conniving soul. He excuses it as her need to survive. Then he second guesses himself and figures that he misunderstands what she is doing now. After a few seconds he decides the woman is petrified with fear.

Elena scowls, then speaks: "Your mother wants the marbles--or what is left of them. You know that. That's why you presented yourself. You plan is to use Dr. Vaz and I as assets to grab power from her."

Amanda slowly blinks, thinking about her situation. She does not remember Elena Etu as being so smart. In fact her dad had said he picked her because she was pretty and a crowd-pleaser, but not too sure of herself. Amanda doubts his words now. *This woman's capabilities are too hard to miss and she seems to have no problem with displaying those capabilities.* "You may get though the Wall. Without me, you have no way to negotiate peace. It's a fight to the death for you without my escort into the halls of power. That's why you have me here."

"You will lose that surety, Ms. Feiss," Phillip says as a matter of fact.

"Do you know MAD?' Amanda replies as casually as she can. "Mutual Assured Destruction, do you think my family believes in the strategy?"

Phillip looks at Joe for some verification of MAD as a plausible strategy. Instead, he sees a man distracted and confused. "You have a bluff round. I will give you that for now--but I will call your bluff soon."

Amanda considers giving her own life away. Due to her upbringing Amanda immediately discards the thought. She watches Phillip smile. A man a bit surer of himself now, she curses herself. "I can arrange a meeting to negotiate a peace. The meeting will be in Seattle and I will personally guarantee your safety. It would include the three of you minus Rover over there." She sees Joe Vaz turn away and walk outside. He is too confused by what he has seen to stay.

Elena Etu feels for him--his Beatrice has again unmasked herself as a Siren. "We might need you to help negotiate a truce. We'll let you know how we want to do that. When we are ready. In the mean time is there anything I can get you?" The Priestess watches Amanda fake a thought.

"No. I am fine. A little water would be nice."

Elena turns away as she speaks. "I'll leave the lights on for you. Maybe we can all do lunch next time." Elena mentally kicks herself for the ruthless comment.

CHAPTER THIRTY FIVE

Ewalt has his blindfold lifted, just enough to see the wooden stairs, and not trip on the damaged risers. He assumes he is somewhere near Portland.

The other footsteps belong to the guards. Through holes in the stairwell wall he can see the rain pounding a host of mangled cars. *This is an office parking structure--or was.* Hands bound behind him, he counts two landings and notes that suddenly there are no breezes or smoke. He wonders why the building is in one piece. At the next landing, a voice tells him to halt. A door opens. Then it's the unmistakable scent of a boudoir even though the floor is concrete stained with oil and gasoline. Seeing a brightly colored tent with red and yellow stripes erected in the parking lot, he then realizes that boudoir smell is perfume. *There is a woman nearby.*

He hears the battle, a mix of weapons and explosions serenaded by the downpour. Truck engines and heavy transports chug as gears grind and equipment scrapes the concrete. He sniffs again, but the smell of perfume is gone. Scanning as best he can, he soon walks though an area converted into sleeping quarters. Ewalt counts upwards of thirty cots. The floor is a mess of cans.

Through a doorway where a breeze flows, there is the sound of battle again. He wonders where he is and why. Another door opens and he is back in a stairwell going up. After the next landing he is walking on carpet and then pushed into a chair. His blindfold removed, he adjusts his eyes to the room; the sight confuses him. On either side of him, long plastic panels hang from brass chains. In front of him, framed by the parade of plastic panes, a wide glass window opens to the evening. The battle of Portland rages like a scene on a large screen TV. The explosions and tracers, the smoke and flames, he feels a sense of omnipotence course through him and wonders if this is what it is like for the leaders.

Ewalt guesses he is somewhere up in the Portland hills, in one of the expensive offices, looking out over the Willamette River. He watches the fires and explosions as red tracer rounds move like angry darts across his field of view appearing then not. Off in the distance the huge Columbia Wall looks like a long ant hill. It appears to him that only this part of the city is in battle. He cannot detect another area where there appears to be a fire-fight in progress. *They are holding the line along Contractor's Alley.*

The Sellwood Bridge across the Willamette explodes thrusting itself upward then down into the dark waters. He wonders why he has the grandstand seat to the event. *Why would they allow me so much information?*

Titling his head slightly, he turns to the long white plastic panels. Models dressed in long coats and evening gowns grace the panes. Advertisements for a fur coat and perfume cover the two panels closest to him. Exotic women in evening dresses and sportswear cover the rest. Ewalt notices Elena Etu's likeness over and over on the panels. Some of the pictures he remembers from magazines and the Internet--others from the TV. His crust checks at the absurdity of it. He finds himself silently laughing--then that boudoir smell. "T'was beauty killed the beast," he mumbles.

"King Kong, I presume." Elena Etu, dressed in green camouflage appears in front of the window framed by battle. He notes she stares at him as if he were excrement. "Turn him around." He and the chair are repositioned away from the battle. Ewalt faces an old man lounging on leather chair, a well tended leg wound on his left thigh. Elena Etu circles to stand behind the chair. The crazy man stands next to her.

Mesmerized by her gold necklace, Ewalt studies the woman in the torch-light and cannot believe her physical beauty. He thought it was a myth created by computers and airbrushes. With pity Ewalt looks at Baylor beside her. *Now I see what has made him nuts. I bet they were lovers He gave it all for her. Who wouldn't? What a beauty. What a curse.* The flickering candles makes his eyes warm to her. The space now feels to him as if he were under water. He looks away to the old man.

The old man seethes hate from every pore of his body. The jolt helps Ewalt. "It wasn't me, pops. I'm just trying to stay alive."

Elena pours water into three cut glass tumblers. She places one tumbler in front of Ewalt and one in front of the old man. Ewalt's bonds are removed, but he will wait until she has taken a sip, to drink from the glass. "I am not here to trick you or kill you, Commander. I want information from you." Elena scrutinizes Commander Ewalt Rader recognizing that familiar look of astonishment at her beauty. "You say you are an envoy from the other side." At the end of her words a curt smile rises. Her eyes remain placid, but he can read their message. There is something about him that she does not like.

"I am Commander Ewalt Rader of the US Border Patrol." He tries to keep himself ready, looking for an edge, but her languid eyes defeat him. Baylor does a small dance. Ewalt stares. With a wave of her hand, Baylor steps back and calms.

"Nice scar," Ewalt says to her, pointing at her arm.

"Nice try," she replies with a pert smile. She sips her water.

He waits as the Priestess looks at the floor, staring his sandals. *They are tied exactly right. One large loop on the right sandal and another much smaller one on the left sandal. She wonders how those behind the Wall had learned about the new security measure on the sandals--without knowing about the rocks.* "You and the other soldiers are dressed to infiltrate us. Why?"

"Trick or treat?" He drinks the entire glass of water.

She shakes her head no.

"I'm not infiltrating anyone," Ewalt finally says. "I took on the emissary job because I needed to."

To his surprise she smiles at his words. "Why the show? You are not a brave man. You have skills that are used for killing. You do not have the skills of a negotiator. What skills are they then that bring you to me? And don't tell me negotiation. You have already failed that test."

"Nonetheless, here I am." Ewalt says. *The crazy blond guy has not taken his eyes off me.*

Phillip speaks. "Of the sixty people that have infiltrated as part of your operation, you are the only one left alive. You were very smart not to pursue the heroics of your comrades. Some might call that cowardice. I call that intelligent. Will you help us?"

"A man by the name of Jack Porter contacted me. We were childhood friends. He wants to talk turkey with you all." He sees surprise in Elena Etu's eyes and the old man is now fully engaged in the discussion.

"Porter Industries?" Phillip asks.

"That's Jack." Ewalt nods seeing he has gotten some respect. "We were boyhood friends. He trusts me. So he asked me to make contact. He thinks you run the show here and since most people believe you're going to get through the Wall sooner or later, he believes making nice with you is a good idea. He thinks if you are not talking to him you are talking to his competition at Feiss industries. So he sent me to you."

Elena watches his eyes and steps back. "Can you prove that?"

"You work for Feiss." Ewalt watches the believing eyes of an untrusting woman. He wonders why she does not like him. Ewalt is used to being liked--at least on a physical level--by most women. "Jack and I went to grammar school together. He's a prick, but I trust him on this. Only because he wants something and he knows he needs me. If he didn't, then I don't think I'd be here. How do I get you two together?"

She does not see the eyes of a coward. They show no fear, just intent. "Commander, would you kill me if you could?"

He blinks at the directness of the question. "If it would keep my country safe from your hordes and end this mess, hell yes, without hesitation."

The valor shocks her. "And if killing me didn't help your efforts? Or I had the same goals as you?"

"I would not. Ms. Etu, you are my key to getting through this mess." He stares at her and wonders how her skin could be so soft and smooth.

She grins and he grimaces. "Commander, do you really believe that the people who run your life are any better or worse than we?"

Ewalt watches the old man place his glass back on the table and wait. *That must be the brains of the outfit.* "I have no opinions. I am a soldier. I am here to defend my country. And if I cannot do that--there are those I care about who will be in danger when the Columbia Wall is breached by your forces. I am trying to protect them. That's the second reason I am here. I will cut a deal with you if that will protect them."

Her face breaks into a broad smile. *Coward.* Her eyes also lose all their light. "We are not in the deal-making business, Commander."

He sees he is now both excrement and a tool.

Elena refills Ewalt's glass. "So you are an intelligent man, working to save your life and the life of those you care about."

Baylor watches Ewalt's every move with darting eyes. His face pivots back and forth measuring the responses of Elena Etu. He cannot believe this gift. The crazy man believes he sees release at last.

"What would you say if I told you we can be trusted to take care of those you care about? Not as a deal, but because our society is based on mutual support--regardless of your checking account." She stands in front of him holding the pitcher of water.

This isn't just a discussion about talking with Jack Porter. There is something more. "So you are going to tell me you are the good guys?" Ewalt asks incredulously.

The Priestess Elena Etu puts the pitcher down and turns away from him. She speaks quietly. "Don't be absurd, Commander. Your leaders and I are the same, right?" She faces him.

He now considers Elena Etu the brains of the outfit, not Phillip. Envious of her gifts, the ones he measures today: Her beauty, the loyalty of these people, intelligence, and her charm, he finds her ways are beginning to make him angry. *Why did she get so much?* He looks at Phillip. "You want me to help you do what?"

Phillip, who has been watching the discourse, takes his cue marveling at how men always react the same in a first meeting with her: They make believe her beauty doesn't impact them. He has a theory and decides to run his gambit. "Commander, leaders use the respect generated by icons to support their power. That then turns into the shared view of a harmonious society. Or to put it another way, leaders manipulate people. And insofar as 'good' is concerned: The 'good' is who wins, the 'bad' is who loses. As a result, good is always considered stronger. If we win, we will be the good ones and his-tory will report the old power structure born of corporate feudalism was too myopic to succeed. If your friends on the other side of the Wall win then we will remain the Dirties--an evil threat to progress that was thwarted by good. On the other hand, we control the board and all the major pieces of this game. Does good matter to you?"

"Yes it matters to me. It also seems to me you're pretty far from keeping control once you win. If you win."

"We'll win," Baylor says.

"Do you believe the planet should be ruled by white society?" Phillip asks.

Ewalt wants to laugh while wondering if the job of assistant to the beautiful woman requires a racist bent; instead, he takes another sip of water. "You have a race thing going here, Priestess? You claim to help the people of color. Is that your game? Your advisor here is so white he could do a bleach commercial. So is Blondy over there."

Elena sits in a chair, crossing her legs. "How were you going to get back through the Wall?"

Ewalt finishes his water, then puts down the glass. *So that's it.* "When I am ready. We can talk about that. I know you need a safe way through the Wall. First we will come to some agreement that says you will work with Jack and I."

Phillip laughs and Ewalt knows he has overplayed his hand. "You're a pawn in a big seat, Commander. Do you really expect to hold sway at the end of this? You have a chance here to do yourself some good. Once events move along, your worth diminishes rather quickly."

"I am a soldier of the United States of America. All I want is to solve this mess and take care of those I care about--and yes I don't matter."

"Ah, could be so, or not," says Baylor.

The look in Elena Etu's eyes is more than embarrassment. "The people you serve helped me get to power. They don't like what we have achieved and so they are trying to destabilize us. As a result, I either defend my place and the society we have built--or we disappear back into chaos for a few years and then win. Your friends on the other side of the Wall have done nothing more than build a prison here in the Northwest. Their resources are finite. Ours are unlimited. Either way, we will win. You know that. That's why you agreed to do this mission of yours. If you help us then you can help yourself. If you do not help us. I cannot help you once I will lose track of you."

"And trust me. She doesn't want that," says Baylor following it with a wolf whistle.

Phillip who was about to speak, pauses, looks at Elena Etu and sees what he believes is intense anger in her eyes. He looks at Baylor and sees a placid man. He closes his eyes wondering about the truth he sees. Baylor looks relieved.

The Priestess Elena Etu speaks: "The Wall has created a barrier of fear and envy but it has also acted as a system to focus the efforts of people like us. There is nothing left of the old world order, soldier," she says. "Can you understand the depth of those words? It is over and we are in a period of change. The Patrician Order cannot rebuild because it cannot adjust. That is the flaw of a society built on commerce. The profit motive has no flexibility. Someone will rebuild. I hope it us. So we may not be perfect, but we are better than chaos or unbridled profiteering." She stares at him. Ewalt births a theory.

Phillip speaks: "We will not agree to any negotiations until we are talking to the decision-makers."

Ewalt turns bright red, then decides to try for the home run. "Do you work for us, Priestess?" He watches the old man in his chair fidget, apparently confused.

"Who is us?" Elena asks.

"The United States Government."

"As in indivisible, with liberty and justice for all, that government?" Elena says, trying to conceal her shock at this man's correct assumption. "Commander, the world has been one big corporate entity for decades." She pauses adjusting her notion of him, then sees what has gotten through to Baylor--he is perfect. She looks at Baylor and he winks at her. Her eyes widen then she looks back to Ewalt. "Nations have been replaced by feudalism. I don't know what it will look like when we win."

Ewalt watches her. "It's a good thing you have this old guy to play your poker for you." He smiles, not so much out of a sense of control or certainty, but from a sense of place. "I used to wonder why so much of the country went to the Dirties so quickly and why so little of it was held by civilization. At the Wall in Redding, I saw gaffes any grunt would laugh at. It didn't make sense. Jack told me you worked for Feiss. But that's a cover. Isn't it? I can see it on your pretty eyes. God, they're beautiful. Mr. Bleach over there doesn't know you work for the government. Does he?" Ewalt stops for a second pleased at the shock in the old man's eyes. "Now this mess finally makes sense. The intelligence mistakes, the lack of follow through on the battle field, all of it. The government, a government run by people--again owns most of the country. It's not big, bright, and glossy anymore. But it and its people are free. The government has beaten the corporatists into a small corner of the country. That's really what has happened here isn't it, Ms. Etu? Your food, the helicopters, the advances, that data on what you guys were doing, the mountain of mistakes," he looks at Phillip. "And you never really saw it. You just hate--something."

"I guess you can't believe everything you see," Phillip says. His leg begins to hurt.

"Commander, thank you for the nice compliment of thinking I am a patriot. From you, that is high praise. I am not sure how I will answer you."

"Other than that, babe, how'd I do?"

Baylor strides over to Ewalt, pulls him to his feet, and slaps Ewalt across the mouth. "You will respect her. Please." He tosses him back down and turns away. He winks at Elena again. She is horrified at what Baylor has done but she is even more horrified that the soldier has taken the abuse. "Take him downstairs, without damage," she says to Baylor.

When Baylor and the Commander are gone she sips water. "Okay, what?" She knows it is time for the light of facts.

"I'm sick. I'm tired. My legs hurt and I think I've been had-- by you." He glares at her. "Luckily for you, I am an idiot. So how the heck did I miss it?"

"Rage," she says.

"Our friend the soldier is one smart cowboy. You," he watches her placid face. "I could deal with the shill thing for Feiss. I could deal with the power hungry model. I could deal with the Baylor thing, even though I kept asking myself how you could have sacrificed him for Feiss. Then this--a patriot--you?"

"Why do you find that so distasteful?"

"Elena, you've made me a patriot. I'll be god-damned if I am going to help the country that killed my family. And if you think you can co-opt me into it you can forget it. One more question: Are you as nutty as Baylor? Why would you carry their banner?"

"You know those soldiers who killed your family were under the control of those behind the Wall, not the government," she says quietly.

"I do not."

"Liar. Soldiers fight for a country, its ideals, and its people. Once those thugs were soldiers. Once they were people. They gave up their souls for fear of losing their belongings to became perfect consumers. Then they morphed into the consumer's logical next step: killers. Those mercenaries who arranged for your family's death were weapons platforms with no conscience or understanding. They were children of the corporate state: assets."

"I'll be leaving with Commander Gung-Ho-Not when he crosses the border with your messages. I have a score to settle with Mrs. Feiss. You can stay here and play President."

Elena Etu looks at her friend. "Margrete Feiss is in control of her company. Jack Porter is in control of his company. They and their friends control the Northwest. They must be defeated. Their removal will free the last part of our country that the citizens of this country do not control. Game over. Unless we do this incorrectly."

"Porter is a toady. Feiss tried to kill her daughter for control of a company. Porter is an animal. Feiss is an animal. They are all animals. I haven't had time to tell you, but our intelligence reports say young Ms. Feiss was supposed to be flying one of the supply drops. We had the exact coordinates of her drop. She's only alive because she was tossed into Salem Hospital for that wound she received and couldn't fly. Once we present her with the truth, she will take us to Mummy to clear things up. If we make sure Mr. Porter is there, then he can talk turkey with the young--and clearly upset--Ms. Feiss. After that, I think you will have the solution. Then I kill them all. Then you can call it happily ever after and talk turkey with the remaining animals. I don't care about your country."

"Because you let them beat you. Phillip, what really happened to your family?"

"I don't do his-tory."

She angers. "Do you really think they will keep us alive for a second longer than they need to without real support, Feiss, Porter, or anyone else?' Elena asks.

"Then what the hell are you doing?" Phillip shakes his head back and forth. "Are you saying that as soon as you have an agreement, the Marines are going to drop through the roof and we are protected? I should believe in that?"

"I have been told to expect a helicopter assault."

"You're nuts, Elena. The Republic no longer functions."

"And you have forgotten what it means to live not focused on revenge, or commerce. In any case, you understand my point. You stay here, Phillip."

"No. I go in as the negotiator with the Commander. I check out and take them all with me. That leaves a vacuum and the rest is up to you and Dr. Vaz."

She is horrified. "No."

"I am not going to let you add hero to my list of terms for you by taking a bullet for me."

Elena Etu calms. "Fine, come up with a better plan. In the mean time when the battle of Portland is about done, I am going across the Wall. I talked to Joe about that tank and convinced him that he needs to stay here--with you. Commander Rader, or some other tanker, is going to drive me across the river as part of their retreat."

Phillip lies to her quietly: "Once they are behind the Wall, we wait. There is no reason to risk your life."

Elena stares out into the battle-worn night. "Those bad hoses on their tanks and helicopters will get solved quicker than we want. At that point if we haven't breached the Wall it will be years maybe decades before we breach it. We have a window of opportunity and I am going to use it." She points to his leg. "You have limits."

He takes in a deep breathe. "Perhaps we should both go." He

gets to his feet and hobbles down the hallway. Phillip had not seen this possibility of nationalism and needs time to think. The strategist was expecting a foolishly bold move with no chance of success. Government support means it might work. He already agrees those on the other side of the Wall will be blind-sided if she is a government operative. Continuing down the hallway, he mumbles curse after curse at his stupidity and her duplicity.

Elena Etu faces the battle of Portland. *We are not going to mess this up now.* Her thoughts then drift to Baylor's comments about the Commander. She wonders about a report she dismissed earlier that said Commander Rader goes into battle without the support of drugs. She finds that she admires the trait and cannot reconcile her view of him as a coward. Elena sits down in the chair in which he had sat. Her eyes close.

CHAPTER THIRTY SIX

As the battle for Portland enters the end of its first week, the planet's newest environmental dilettantes, the Patricians--realizing that their resources are finite--employ every strategy to slow the advance and secure resources. The retreating troops strip a section of the city for resources, then give up that small part of Portland by destroying it with fire bombs and explosives. In the seventy-two hours since Ewalt met with Elena Etu, her troops have only advanced two miles, moving into the south waterfront approaching downtown. Ahead of them are the remains of the high rise buildings. The Columbia River and its Wall are still eight miles away. In that eight miles is the heart of the city. The Columbia River bridges are still standing--a testament to the desperation of the retreating troops. In the past, the troops destroyed everything as the Dirties approached. Then they let the hoards do the rest of the damage. Here in Portland, they dig in, allow for more materials to be removed, and then destroy the rest. The battle of Portland is a murderer's dream.

Joe Vaz wanders the remains of the OHSU hospital on the hillside, staring at the carnage and bloodshed below, amazed at how even awareness breeds destruction from this retreating order. He knows that if the PO had originally seen the problem as resource allocation, not as a threat to their power, none of this would have happened. *The Patricians, to this day, see everything through an economic lens, rather than the lens of an ecosystem, branding effective allocation of resources--or effective tactics--in terms of cost or profit.* Were it not so sad, Joe might laugh at their stupidity.

The burning buildings blow smoke through the rubble of what was once the most advanced medical facility on the planet. Efforts to save it were marginally effective. Some medicine and machines have been retained, due to early teams that entered the city ahead of the main force, but the majority is ash, concrete, and twisted metal. Joe had originally come up here to see if there was anything to salvage but his anger at the destruction has forced him to work harder on ending this insane battle. Not ten minutes ago he argued with Phillip that Priestess Etu's troops should just dig in and wait for the retreat across the river to be complete--that Phillip's stalled blitzkrieg was costing too many lives. Phillip would have no part of it.

Joe stares, watching the well-defined battle line of burning buildings, poisonous yellow gas, and tracer fire. He continues to stare at the dynamic. Trying to understand the system--figuring that if he understands the system--he can break it. After an hour, he concludes it is already broken, and that there is only chaos.

As the light fades, he turns to the only building that remains standing, an old parking structure where the charges had failed to ignite properly. The building now looks like a fortress. Sandbags block the windows. Exterior gun ports are manned. Guards wait on all the high spots around it and a platoon of men and women march from the underground area carrying shovels and picks to dig trenches and latrines. Huge trucks with armed soldiers wait at every intersection of the hilltop fortress. Wondering about Elena moving her headquarters from the offices, he smirks at her insistence of keeping those huge plastic panes of her image with her at all times. Thinking how mad humans are most times, Joe stops on the long concrete steps that form the perimeter of her headquarters and sits. A squad of twenty men form a circle--a respectful distance away. No one gets near him when he is problem-solving. They know he is engaged in this process because he mutters to himself.

Phillip approaches him, his limp slightly better. Joe hopes this conversation is not about the tank again. Both men expect the tank to be a gate through the Wall if they can time its retreat correctly. Neither is willing to support Elena's plan to go herself. Phillip speaks as he gets closer. "Elena wants to discuss how to get teams across the Wall. She is now considering my suggestion for a helicopter flight with Ms. Feiss at the controls. Except she is going to fly in, not me. I'd like to discuss this alternative with you as well."

"Ms. Feiss flying? That's a good idea. She wears a Feiss corporate transponder under her skin. It should allow her safe passage. She'll be safe. Don't you think so?" Joe gets up from the concrete, his badly cramped hip stabbing him with every step.

"We have two or three people who flew helicopters working on it now. Any of them can do it if she says no."

"They don't have that Feiss security transponder," Joe replies. "And that's the answer." The two men cross under the exit sign and descend the ramp to the lowest level. "Are you thinking of the tank as an escape back here or just a diversion for Elena? I don't see any way it could ever get back across the river." Torches appear ahead as they enter the darkness.

"We need to first formulate a plan of what we are trying to get from the other side. You are to be Elena's second-in-command when I go through the Wall," Phillip says.

"So you are you planning on scuttling Elena's plan?" Joe asks already knowing the answer. "I could support that--but I think I should be making the key points in the negotiations, not you."

Phillip continues forward towards a set of people sitting around an open fire that burns in the center of a large empty space. The smoke billows up and out of the building through a pre-arranged set of flues. Some consider it stealth. Phillip considers it a camp out. "Joe, you are the key to this. We cannot risk you. Just like we cannot risk Elena."

Joe reaches out to stop him. "I don't see that she will let you go and negotiate. She thinks you will improvise--or just kill people. I should go."

Phillip nods as he begins to walk again. "I know--but they will kill her or they will kill you. I don't matter. It's best to send an unimportant person rather than a leader."

"Phillip, what's to stop them from killing her here?" Joe asks. "There have been no attacks on her. Her life is charmed. We must admit that. Her string of luck impresses me. We cannot ignore her karma." They enter the firelight.

"It's not luck, Joe."

"I didn't say that. I said karma." Joe Vaz sighs as he sits. The discussion around the fire begins with an overview of the day's events. Joe is too tired to listen to items that do not concern him. *How many people exist now? Eight billion, ten billion? The end-game is certain for Feiss and that cadre of locusts. Sooner or later their food will cease, or some other link in their prison system will break. Panic and death then sets in. Rather than sue for peace, it will be over: Civilization flambe'. We should wait. Then go in. What's the problem here? What is it that don't I understand?*

He considers his life one long futile warning. Those days in the committee meetings were the worst of his life--hearing leaders who cared for nothing but their own pleasure calling on moralistic terms to support their avarice. As if morality and ethics were tarts in an intellectual bordello. The politicians spent days proving that the enemy was Socialism. He can still see the lobbyists snacking on the last remaining Beluga eggs during the hearing. To this day, he cannot understand how the Senators scattered around the table could allow themselves to be so humiliated--*as their masters snacked from a fruit plates and drank orange juice.*

Joe's memory finds him sitting in that fishy-smelling room, listening to a think-tank-hack finish a cost estimate analysis on feeding and caring for the population of Earth. Her conclusion: "The cost to the United States was less, in dollar terms, for defense, than the cost of allocating resources to the masses. Defense is a money-maker. Social programs are a drain." That had led to an oratory by a North Texas Senator named Alec on how Darwin and God were in concert on population reduction through starvation. Joe still remembers the phrases: "Extended population controls through aggressive policies." "Sequestering emergency resources for a true emergency." "The pointlessness of wasting revenues on a population component with no expectation of ROI given the current financial circumstances." And Joe's personal favorite: "The need to avoid governmental concern over morality issues that had no cost-effective components."

He remembers being reprimanded by a chairwoman of a corporate committee for his lack of regard and the "...Sizeable dent that unemployed, welfare sucking, non-revenue generating masses might make in the budget and the GNP." A lobbyist then questioned Joe's "hypothesis" of recycling trash to feed people calling his theory "unproven crackpot science." The lobbyist produced three reports from industry sponsored think-tanks claiming Joe's proposal was junk science and a waste of valuable resources.

Then, when Joe exhibited the first crude cakes made of garbage and asserted: "There is nothing so immoral as a talented leadership that claims to serve its people, but in fact does not." Then the gunfire. It were as if someone had punched him. The force tossing him from the wooden chair onto the floor. His head swimming in pain and embarrassment, Joe had tried to stand. Slipping on his own blood, he fell into the lap of a screaming woman from the oil and gas lobby. Joe remembers her pushing him off her lap--then kicking him over and over--as if he were vermin that had crawled up from the sewer. Then there was the put, put, put, of automatic weapons. Amanda Feiss appearing, firing a pistol, and hauling Joe behind a table, guarding him until the police arrived. She took him to the hospital and then three hours later pushed him into a jet that flew him south. A year later he began his first factory in Brazil.

Joe watches the smoke--then stares at the people around the fire. They are now arguing whether it is appropriate take prisoners or not. *It never changes*, he tells himself.

Elena stands and demands that all the prisoners be treated well. It squashes the discussion. Joe marvels at how her insistence on following certain ideals garners respect from the men and women speaking with her. The faces of those around the fire appear relieved they have not been asked to abandon their fellow humans. *She is unstoppable.*

The men and women begin discussing how to get small teams across the Wall. Four plans are under consideration. One, is to wait out those on the other side of the Wall. Two, is to get across via helicopter after opening a hole in the surveillance systems. Three, somehow getting through the Wall with the tank, or four, the one most people dislike: continued assault of the Wall. The meeting ends with the Priestess Elena Etu declaring that she will be crossing the Wall via helicopter to conduct negotiations and that Joe Vaz will be in command while she is gone. No mention has been made of the tank. A decision has been made by the leader of the Dirties. Joe looks at Phillip and sees the discussion is over.

Ewalt, tied to an I-beam, feels the hemp rope tight around his chest and hands. He leans over and sips from an old water pipe that hangs just overhead. Outside, soldiers stack sand bags, others run back and forth assembling weapons and munitions. Bright flashes and the rumbles of weapons echo through the small space. Then the windows blow inward. Smoke fills the room. Soldiers run to the exits, grabbing their weapons. Ewalt is alone listening to battle.

A few minutes later, the explosions stop. He hears shouting and cheers. Three men enter his prison and cut the bonds. They push him passed the sand bags and up several flights of stairs until he finds himself out on the roof of the parking structure. It is early morning and down below he sees three burning SWAT tanks. Any kind of a counter attack impresses him--given what he has seen over the last days--though he wonders about the waste of equipment until he figures out that he is at the command post. When he turns, he sees that he has been left alone.

Scanning around, he notes a thin fog mixes with black smoke--there is no fire fighting equipment and several buildings in the city below still burn. Scattered gunfire in the distance sounds like nervous troops to Ewalt. The battles haven't started for the day.

On the far end of the roof, Elena Etu appears with Baylor, three guards, and a set of lieutenants. Everyone wears body armor except for Ewalt. They walk while surveying the battle lines. By the time she reaches him, only Baylor is left at her side. The others have gone to their tasks. A boat explodes in the Willamette river and the battle lines erupt into the mayhem of the day. A set of buildings by the Hawthorne Bridge bursts into flames--as does the bridge. The hills across the way sit in a silent shadowy white. With a flight of mortar rounds, the day's blood river begins there as well.

Elena Etu faces Ewalt. The chilling mist gathers on her black shawl. "Last night large parts of the city center were dynamited. Your comrades are setting the fires to cause chaos and fear--all so the Patricians can claim dominion for another day. Is that what you were running from? Or did you just have enough?" She looks at him from dark eyes, drenched, but holding back tears. The battle losses though less than expected, still number in the tens of thousands.

"If I was you. I'd just dig in and let them get their supplies and skedaddle across the river." He stands in front of her--wanting to get across the river as well.

"Commander, do you know anything about Feiss Industries?"

Ewalt looks at Baylor. "I know enough." He wonders for a moment about Amanda Feiss. It is the first time he has thought of her in days.

"Mr. Feiss placed me here because he thought I was the perfect person to lead the Dirties towards him. I was public, beautiful, and passed my prime."

"I wouldn't say that," Ewalt mumbles.

"That was kind," she says smiling.

"I didn't meant that...I mean. I think you are doing a good job here. That is not passed-your-prime." He scratches his head not all happy to be here talking to this woman, alone. He does not consider the madman, Baylor, present. He knows that taking her prisoner is his way out. He just can't bring himself to do it.

"My job was to promote chaos, desperation, fear, and weaken of their resolve. Of course that is not what Mr. Feiss told me. In effect, they expected failure from anyone who went in. I am a female African-American. Luke Feiss said my gender and heritage fed certain agendas and so there was no problem with approval. Others thought my capabilities were limited. Everyone eventually agreed and here I am."

"So they thought you were a clown?" He asks.

She points down the hillside. "These people are citizens of the United States of America. Once they refused to leave their comfort to retain their freedom. They thought they could hide from the horrors to come. When it was all taken from them, they rediscovered themselves. You know that was the supposed intent for removal of the social support systems--an attempt to put some sinew back in us."

"People take the easy route. It's what we are."

"I have done the best I could." She watches him, looking for that streak of cowardice. She is annoyed she cannot find it. "We will soon breach the Wall and take over the rest of the country. If I am still alive at the end of it. I will work to rebuild our country."

He doesn't like the confusion inside him. "Haven't we had this discussion? What do you want from me?"

"Your cooperation. Follow me." She walks him down a set of stairs. They enter that tent with the boudoir smell. Baylor is left outside. He sees the bizarre maze of hanging advertisements that contain her pictures. "Lady, you are something else." He laughs staring at the pictures. She walks to a picture of her younger self. Ewalt stares at the figure in front of the World Trade Center Memorial, wind blowing her hair, a bottle of perfume in her hand. "You really are a beautiful woman."

She pulls a torch from its holder and walks around back. "Come on. I won't bite you." As he gets closer. She cuts his bonds. Ewalt cannot believe her stupidity and looks around for how he will escape--once he knocks out the woman. Then he stands there. "Here, take this knife and cut along the bottom of that plastic pane. You'll see a glue line there." She hands him the knife and points to the bottom edge of the plastic panel.

"How do you know I will not kill you?" Ewalt says as he deftly cuts into the glue and then feels a second flat sheet of rigid plastic.

"You may, but you will wait to see what I am doing. Feel that sheet inside. Look at it, Commander."

He pulls a flat sheet out slowly. "Oh fuck me. Of course. What else? Or is this a fake?" He stares at her, a mix of confusion and pride. "This was burned. I know it was burned. It was all over the news."

"Wrong again, Commander. It was given to me as a way of validating my words." She sees hope in him. "There are some, like you and I, who still believe in the ideals that founded this country. Those same people will help me once I get across the river and we depose people like Feiss."

"And Jack Porter?"

"If need be." She smiles at him and puts her hand out asking for the knife. He does not comply but he does not assault her either.

"Why should I believe this is real?" Ewalt asks. He stares at the document.

She already knows he believes it because he is still here. "Why else would I have sacrificed my lover? Or do you think I am that evil?"

"For your country?" He watches her nod. Then he sighs. "Do you want me to put this back?"

"If you would. Commander, I need your help."

"Ma'am?" He says returning the Constitution to its hiding place. "Are there other documents like this in the rest of these posters?"

"A few, including the Bill of Rights and the Declaration of Independence." She watches him. *He is genuinely moved. I counted on his cowardice to embrace the country for his own protection. All I see is heroism and honor. Bay was right about him. God, another hero. Why all these riches?*

"You want me to help you get across the Wall--in a tank?"

"Commander, forgive me if I am speak plainly. I know you are not a brave man. I believed you when you said that you planned to help those you love on the other side of the Wall--and that was the reason for your surrender and subsequent story about being an envoy."

His brow wrinkles at the assertion, again, that he is a coward. *She still thinks I am a coward? Or she is yanking my chain?* He smiles and she sees the reason for the sly smile. Elena Etu hides her grin. "Jack Porter wants you to help him. I am to conduct you to him. So getting you across the Wall is okay with me."

She shakes her head no. "That's not what I meant. I met Jack Porter when I first began to model. He's pragmatic. The man he'd pick for this assignment would be...A deadly killer with no propriety. It would be a person with an insane single minded desire to stay alive." Her face is stone. "So why you?" She also wants to ask him why he fights without drugs to quell the horrors.

Ewalt Rader sees her feint but doesn't quite understand it. "So my cowardice and the rest of it is why you told me all this, and released me from my bonds. You think I am stupid?" It is his turn to smile at her. He has no plans to hide his intentions. Ewalt knows how to communicate with women. "What do you want from me--given I am so careful about staying alive? By the way, you have it all wrong about me being a coward."

She watches his eyes. "I mean no offense." Now sure she understands the lever, she continues: "If you will help me by allowing yourself to be repatriated you can serve two purposes. You can get yourself to the other side of the Wall where you can help those you care about--and you can help your country. I want you to get Mr. Bleach, Phillip, to the other side of the Wall in a tank."

"Okay, what then?"

"We have a pilot, the daughter of Luke Feiss, in our custody." She halts seeing shock in the man's eyes. "You know her?"

"We were once lovers," he says with a little too much pride.

Elena Etu hides her pique at the comment. "Why you?"

Ewalt hears the angry edge to her question and he tempers his response not trusting his observation. "I am not sure. We didn't get along well. I do know that she doesn't take rejection well."

She smiles. "Please, the story?"

"She cares for nothing. The world is her amusement park. The people are simply props. She also killed someone I cared about to get her out of the way and she knows she is on my shit-list. Sorry."

Elena Etu measures the story. *He is handsome enough to attract a woman like that, I guess. Maybe she didn't know he was an equal--and vice-versa. Why would he take her on by playing with her heart? He would never trust her.* "Well I am going to have to look into that. Will you help me?"

"She will fly you across the Wall and I am diversion?"

"Not quite. I need Phillip on the other side of the Wall to help me. I don't want to put all my eggs in one basket."

"Your plan fulfills my mission. You can count on me."

"Of course. Thank you." She puts out her hand. He pockets the knife, staring at her. *Some coward.* "Baylor take this man downstairs and feed him. He has decided to help us."

Baylor pulls Ewalt down the stairs. Ewalt soon hears the Earth's Voice echoing through the building.

Tap
Tap-Tap
Tap-Tap-Tap
Tap-Tap-Tap-Tap
Tap-Tap-Tap-Tap-Tap

He is surprised no one will give him a pair of stones to use. By the end of the ceremony he feels naked.

CHAPTER THIRTY SEVEN

The guards place Amanda on a stone bench by the wrecked hospital. She stares at the ruins, seeing that her mother has made good on her plan to destroy everything in the hospital. *Why couldn't we have just helped them? How does our need for power excuse all this horror? This will not be the way Feiss is run when I am in control.* Her gaze fogs as she sees Joe Vaz approach her. Ready to bathe in his goodness, happy in her confusion, and warmed by the truth of Joe's smile, she greets him. "I wondered where you had gone." *All these people are fed and healthy because of Joe's work. I did that. He is my tool for goodness. I am their savior. I must be gentle with them after I take control.*

"Good afternoon, Captain Feiss." Doctor Joseph Vaz stares at her. This man's ways are, on many levels, foreign to her. The purity and care of his intentions sets Amanda to stare. She notices his tidy clothes, his slicked down gray hair, and the trimmed mustache. *He looks like a teen ready for his first date. What would he have done without me? I am his savior as well.* Amanda Feiss is going mad.

"Are you alright?" He asks, seeing a blank stare come from her.

"I am fine, thank you, Dr. Vaz. We've done a great deal for these people haven't we?" The void for these two people is the gulf between heaven and hell: selfless service and servitude.

"I think the others are almost done destroying the city down there. I believe they will want you to pilot a helicopter so someone may negotiate with your mother. Will you do that?"

Amanda has been approached on this. She wears a bright school-girl smile. "Do we have to talk about that? Please tell me how you have been."Amanda Feiss has been preparing for this scene for hours. Her game of love with him is about who controls the party.

Joe Vaz blushes. Amanda looks at the ground. Again in awe of how this person ever lasted this long in a world of horror and death, she smiles up at him. Her eyes warm to the sight of him: a slight tilt to her face, hair strategically tossed over one eye.

Joe watches her seek him, feeling her love, as if he were dreaming. His eyes wander over Amanda's calm smile and confident eyes. His breathing becomes labored. His mind screeches to a halt. The suspicion he had felt before, blows away like smoke on the wind. He thinks Amanda Feiss has gotten prettier.

"Tell me, Dr. Vaz. Can you really feed all of them?" Amanda asks, missing the approach of Baylor and Elena from the side.

"Will you help us?" He asks.

She blinks. "Of course." Joe takes in a breath; afraid he might fall over at any moment.

"I thought you'd be happy to see her. I'm glad." Watching Joe's face, Elena is almost jealous to see such feelings coming from him. A soft glow comes from Amanda's eyes as well. *The bitch. But Doctor Vaz looks happier than I've ever seen him.* Elena knows Amanda sees Joe as a tool and she fears Amanda might also see him as a target. For just a moment, the Priestess looks inward and wonders about her own motives. Even so, she sees Joe's brittleness has fallen away like an outgrown carapace; while Amanda's belligerence has dissolved into her myth of love.

"We were like that once," Baylor says loudly to Elena. "Some can resist your charms and stay human." His eyes pause on Elena's pained face. "I'm sorry. I didn't say that right, Priestess. I was trying to let you know that the Commander is already mad. You cannot harm him." He bows formally at the waist and backs up.

Joe nods kindly at Baylor. "She has agreed to fly whomever we choose back across the Wall."

"So you know how to get us safely across?" Elena asks looking back at Amanda. "The last time we spoke of this you said there was some doubt."

The woman grins at Elena. "Us?" Amanda then speaks quickly, surprised she has accomplished her mission. "They will be killing until the last of the supplies are across the Columbia River bridges. Once the bridge is destroyed, we will have a small window of time as they check for wounded aircraft--and I have Feiss clearance for all travel. If we can slide by the first response--they always screw-up--we should be fine."

Elena notes the quick response; still, a feeling of hope rises in her. She looks back to Baylor. Elena Etu does not expect to live through the week so she will not mourn anymore. "All right." *So long as Joe Vaz stays here the mission will succeed. From that point forward the results are guaranteed as soon as remaining elements of the US government remove the last of the Patrician Order by force--if necessary.* "Doctor Vaz, I am counting on you to stay behind and keep order."

Amanda scowls. Losing control of Joe Vaz was not in her plan.

Joe nods--staring at Amanda--all sense of logic gone. He believes every word she says, having misunderstood the earlier comment by Elena Etu, that Amanda already knew of the plan for her to pilot the helicopter.

Amanda speaks again. "If you can explain to my mother how the Dirties are no longer a threat, I think she will listen."

"They probably wouldn't believe us," Joe Vaz says. "They didn't before." Elena keeps her smiles inside. "We would make a treaty," Joe says quickly.

Amanda nods kindly, knowing she has to keep Elena Etu's trust until she gets her to the other side of the Wall. "My mother will veto any treaty with the government. She will only approve a deal with Feiss Industries--and then we will negotiate with the government. The government wants California back--at any price. They figure once they have it, they can work from a position of strength with the corporations. Pathetic isn't it? But here is your one strength: The people on this side of the Wall do listen to you. All you need to do is convince my mother that you will listen to her."

"We can reduce the population. I can cut back on the population by adding a birth control drug to the food," Joe says. He notices a smile comes over Elena's lips and feels suddenly stupid. In truth--there is no reproach--just admiration for his open ways. He is a rare friend.

Amanda's eyes take on a patina of mirth, but she tilts her gaze to caring--as Elena looks back at her. "Priestess, let me be clear. I'd never believe you if you told me you were going to do as I say."

"Because I was responsible for the death of your father?" Elena waits for the affect of the words.

Amanda had not expected the connection and so she takes the words at face value. She again believes Elena Etu is a dilettante in the world of politics--as her father had told her. "It is all the more reason to make you a puppet, Elena. If we kill you then the game is over. Keeping you alive is far more fun. Though we will not give you the option of betrayal again."

"You paint a dreary picture, dearie," Elena says, unsure if she believes Amanda Feiss is this mad.

"Controlling you is the key, Priestess."

Amanda seems to prepare for her next comment. Elena fears for Joseph Vaz and considers all the efforts that must be made to protect him.

Amanda speaks: "Regardless, your position could be tenuous. The step after controlling you is to find someone--as quickly as possible--to replace you in the hearts and minds of your secondary leadership. At least that is my mother's plan."

"Elena," Joe says, "I think her point is by working with Ms. Feiss here, and not her mother, our leverage increases dramatically." He sees he has made a mistake but he does not understand what has happened.

"Miss Feiss," Elena says. "Why are you doing this? I would expect your family loyalty to preclude this remarkable suggestion."

"My mother tried to kill me." Amanda thinks she is lying to Elena Etu. The statement startles Elena Etu. "My copilot and crew were killed making a milk-run supply drop. She arranged their demise." Amanda gives herself a point for smart negotiating. It is about to backfire on her.

Elena Etu nods. "We know. We tracked those coordinates we received on the supply drop that killed your crew back to your mother." As Elena speaks, she can feel a sense of confidence, but she doesn't know why. "I don't think she thought we'd discover--or care--who was flying the mission."

Amanda Feiss loses control and begins to redden with anger. Elena immediately figures the lie and waits for the next comment. She hopes it will betray Amanda's plans. Amanda speaks: "My parents' plan was to negotiate a peace then take over. It relies on control of the food supply. That means if Dr. Vaz dies, I've destroyed the one event of my life that I am genuinely proud of." She takes in a deep breath, her eyes on Joe Vaz. "Maybe we three can do something else I can be proud of. Dr. Vaz, you must stay here. You are her insurance and our future."

The comment surprises Joe Vaz. He stares, amazed at her concerns, with an open mouth. "I am safety for both of you. You can tell your mother if anything happens to either of you, I will ruin her."

Elena tries to hide her panic. *Amanda plans to control or kill Joe Vaz.* She watches Amanda, seeing that Amanda Feiss plans to betray both her and her mother--using Joe Vaz as her plan's keystone. She cannot figure how Amanda plans to control Joe Vaz. *He is incorruptible.*

"I think we understand each other," Elena says. Elena weighs her options, sure that Amanda Feiss has no real leverage with her mother. On the other hand, task one is getting across the Wall. "Ms. Feiss, do you think can fly by stick instead of wire? Our helicopters are primitive."

"I can fly it with a little practice," Amanda says carefully. She does not want to show her glee.

"Joe, please have our people escort her to Salem airport and have a two seat helicopter available for her. Put a guard in the other seat who knows how to fly. If she heads north beyond the airport have her stopped. Can you make sure that will happen?" She stares into the eyes of the lovesick man sure Amanda Feiss will not try to escape.

"I can," Joe says.

Amanda Feiss says, "I am your servant."

Elena sees the dart of confusion on the face of Joe Vaz. She raises a hand and three guards trot over along with Baylor. "Guards, follow the orders of Doctor Vaz and then report to me. Station your people on site with Ms. Feiss and I want reports every four hours."

Joe and Amanda are escorted to transportation. "Doctor, I still need to speak to you."

Baylor nods knowingly. "She is as trustworthy as snake. I bet she tries to kill him and you. Don't worry; I will stay by your side." Elena watches Amanda speak to Joe Vaz. "I guess it just makes sense. The Food Man and the pilot are in love."

Elena turns to him knowing this good man will soon not matter. Her heart is in the future, lost to him. "It's nice to see, isn't it?"

"There is a great deal at stake here. You and I don't love each other anymore. I just don't understand why you rejected me for being so noble." He reaches down and picks up a few stones. He tosses them. "I cannot wait to leave this hell."

Elena's heart seems to stop beating, then it bubbles in her chest. "I won't leave you."

"I'm going to die soon anyway. I just wanted you to know that I knew we are over. I have no place in a civilized world. I have become an animal. But I did what I said I would do. I protected you and those dumb pieces of paper you love so much--more than me. It's okay." He beams that beautiful smile over sharpened teeth.

"We came here together. We'll leave together." She speaks the words even though she has no idea how she might fulfill them. She is no longer a woman lost in sentiment. "We will have so much to do when I return. I will need your strength."

"My strength died years ago. I am nothing more than your last line of loyalty. You know that you can count on me always." He moves his hand slowly and touches her cheek. Then he inches forward to kiss her. She will not pull back. He stops seeing her resolve to remain still for his kiss. "Why do you detest me for doing as I said I would do? Do you think I wanted to kill so many?" He asks. "I knew that I couldn't do it. I thought I was much weaker than I am. I also thought I was more a person and less of an animal. Amazing the things we learn about ourselves." He watches the resolve in her eyes.

"Maybe you'll change again when order is restored." She leans forward to kiss him.

"This isn't right." Baylor steps back and bows. He starts to leave then he stops. "I'm insane, Eli. I am not an idiot. I can see the truth. I just can't cope with it. Respect that please. Don't treat me like a child or a coward. I cannot share the rest of your life, Priestess. You serve only your beliefs, not our love--as you have demanded from me." He shakes his head like a dog trying to clear its ears. "Want to hear my farewell speech? Madness is my country. Brutality is my castle and love is my keep. And I will not give up my keep to a false kiss. That is an insanity I will not wear." For the last time in this life, she sees the spark she fell in love with. "I practiced that for almost a year." He stares into her eyes. "Do you really think I would let you return to the other side of the Wall without me? Please make sure I am there. You owe me the task of my life. I am to protect you." He takes another step backward. "Next life, Eli," he pauses and smiles at her. "I'll be the Priestess and you can be the warrior, okay?" The crazy man takes her hand, and kisses it. Then he marches backwards from her, crosses his arms across his chest, and watches Amanda and Joe speak. "I will make sure that woman does not harm him. And don't worry I will not hurt her. I know you need her to get home."

She turns to leave. "Have the Doctor come see me when she leaves. And Bay, I'll make sure you are with the Commander and Phillip in the tank." She leaves him.

CHAPTER THIRTY EIGHT

Four poles support a canvas canopy that keeps the rain off of her. The sounds of the battle mixes again with the tapping of rain. Elena Etu puts on a flak jacket over her rag wool sweater. It is almost time to leave. Phillip, dressed in khaki coveralls approaches her. She notes he sports a side arm. *Perhaps because Commander Rader is in tow.* "Priestess?" It is Phillip's voice. "We are almost ready to go." She follows him towards a truck that will take Elena Etu over to the waiting helicopter and Amanda Feiss. The rains continues in buckets. "Apparently, there is a communications system called WeatherEye in those tanks. We knew nothing about it--some kind of battle management system. As soon as it is activated the tank has 30 seconds to identify itself. Tanks that are not linked in as they approach the Wall are immediately targets. Your luck has helped again."

She nods politely. "And so you and the plucky Commander will cross over with the last troops. What about Baylor?"

"I have done as you instructed. He will be with us. He's waiting at the tank."

She looks over to Ewalt who stands in the rain, waiting for Phillip to finish. *He looks a bit bruised.* "And you have a plan to find me?"

"We still believe you'll meet with mother and daughter in Seattle. We have only two teams that have made it to the other side of the Wall. That's four people, but I am told we have support in other areas." He scratches his chin. "I hope you are right. Then there is Jack Porter who has the same objective as us, keeping you safe. I will try to meet up with him along with a couple of our people and their supporters to provide some level of protection once you meet with Feiss. Commander Rader will be kept under guard until we secure the situation and then he will be let go--per your orders." The truck door creaks as he opens it for her. "Our troops are less than two miles from the remaining bridge."

"Joe will remain here?" She asks not getting in the truck. "You've made the security arrangements I asked for?"

"He understands that he is the key to keeping you and Amanda Feiss alive." Before she can ask the next question he says, "And he will be well-guarded. I am also expecting an attempt on his life. Once the Wall is sealed he is going to a secure location. He knows there will be no order in the city for weeks. Security teams are already in place working the ongoing problem of his safety."

"So Joe will be safe while I am gone?"

"Elena."

"Phillip, I am ordering you and Baylor to stay here. I want you to send your most trusted people in the tank." She climbs into the truck.

He loves her at that moment. "Your choice is this: I can lie to you or I can tell you the truth. Which is it?"

She slams the truck door behind her but the truck doesn't move. "Please be careful. Commander Rader may not be a coward--but we do not know that." Without a bodyguard, Phillip is dead. That's her real plan for Ewalt Rader: Death before dishonor in service for his country--and she believes he will honor that. *But you can't be too careful.* "If he needs to, he might sell you out and run like a scared rabbit."

"And you're a coward." The old man smiles at her. "Don't get mad at me. It had to be said. So are you leaving or not?"

She gets out of the truck and walks passed him. Ewalt shifts back and forth on the muddy grass watching her approach.

"What happened to your eyes?" Elena asks.

"Mr. Baylor decided I needed some obedience training. I think Mr. Bleach put him up to it to see if I was to be trusted. Your doggy will be okay. He's just a little busted up."

Elena is furious with Phillip for not telling her. "You probably cannot be trusted. Or are you crazy?"

"I'm not crazy. That's because I'm not in love with you like the rest of them." He stares at her.

"You are not my type."

"I know it wasn't in your plan to sacrifice that man."

She pulls in a breath and holds it.

Ewalt finds himself pained. "I'm not a coward, lady. Deal with it. You can trust me. And I am sorry about what happened to your man. Battle scars up here," he points to his skull, "are the worst."

"Phillip believes you are helping us because of your dad." She waits, watching him shift his feet.

"Cold feet." He smiles at her. "I want to help you."

She stands snuggling into her sweater. "You care about your dad?"

"That, and the story about you being the real government. I believe that." He considers that he has been given a warm coat and that she seems to be cold in the storm around her. "Please take my coat."

She shakes her head. "I want your loyalty."

"A beautiful woman grows up with lies and learns their taste. Especially when they are used to couch something that a man wants from her. My wants are clear. I want to protect my family. That you count on."

"You can't guarantee Phillip's safety. I understand your limitations." Now she smiles. "But how do I make sure that you will not betray him the moment you get to the other side of the Wall?"

"I need to get my family to safety. That means I need all the friends I can get. You run the show here and in these last few days I have come to believe the others guys are dead meat. If things do go bad then Jack Porter can help me instead. Once I am on the other side of the Wall--I think the plan is to put me in chains--but look for me. I need you to know I am something more than a pretty face and a good line." He winks.

Elena Etu sees he is trying to calm her. She studies his eyes and the lines of sadness around them. "Don't ever try to take care of me. Just do your job, soldier."

"You fed them fish, sent out by a submarine's torpedo tubes." He grins. "That's the stupidest thing ever--masquerading as a plan."

She interrupts him. "I would have danced naked down the street selling cigarettes to children if I'd thought it would have stopped the madness, Commander."

His eyes glow for a moment but he keeps his comment silent. "You have an agenda. I happen to agree with it. But don't ask me to be a fool. If it turns out that you are going to support the ideals in those pieces of paper then you can give me a job. If not--I don't care. You're just another one of them. But I suggest you keep an eye on Miss Feiss. She's a case."

"She is heir to a powerful empire behind the Wall."

He shakes his head slowly. "I don't have your talents, beauty, or grace, Ms. Etu. I'm good at knowing who to keep an eye on--especially when the going gets rough--on either side. And so far as I can tell, she's a snake. She wants to cut your throat. She killed my lover because it suited her--and you're next."

She pauses. "So get to the other side of the Wall and protect us all. You obviously don't like her." Elena waits.

Ewalt considers her. "Sorry, that's what Blond-Dog is for. I'll do my job and get your friend Phillip across so that he can come rescue you. I'll take him to where he needs to go. I'll arrange for you and Jack to get together. I will be there as a soldier of the Republic to protect you and your ideals if need be." He pauses. "Then I'm out. Unless you speak the truth. Which I doubt."

Elena Etu smiles at him, satisfied she has done everything she can to protect Phillip. "Good luck, Commander."

"You too, Priestess. One more thing." He walks her to the truck. "You have got guts. I like that."

"I bet," she says and gets in the truck.

Ewalt understands the subtext and scowls."You're a recruiting poster with legs, aren't you?" He yells over the rain.

She faces him taking this opportunity to draw him in to her. "I'm glad you like my legs." She winks, then tells the driver to go. The truck rolls away.

Ewalt walks over to Phillip--who stands wearing a blank look. "All this bullshit just so I will protect you guys?"

"Nope. All this bullshit because she is afraid she might like you. Or worse, that you might like her." Phillip wears with a slight smile. "I could have told her not to worry."

Ewalt measures the man again. "You are a conniving son of a bitch. All right. Let's go."

CHAPTER THIRTY NINE

Ewalt guides the tank along Columbia Boulevard listening to the small arms fire fade away. The sound of another explosion. He fires the remainder of the weaponry behind him, keeping the tank ahead of the guided mortar rounds from the military river barges destroying the road behind them. Looking out from the driver's blister he thinks he is looking at hell. Flames rise from the city to his left. Other tanks roll along firing comet-tails of fire burning everything in their wake.

A loud horn begins to wail. Rader pushes the tank faster hoping the compressor running the tracks keeps working. He wonders how Baylor is doing in the gunners pod above. They loaded him into the tank unconscious. "This is WeatherEye. Commander Rader, are you out of fire?"

"WeatherEye, I boosted a tank from those mother-fuckers. I know it's no big deal. Problem is when I tried to get them to re-arm me so I could burn their friends to death--for some reason--they said fuck you. I am out of everything except for spit. I'm just heading home."

"Fuckin' Rader," someone says laughing through the telecom link. Ewalt wonders why the air support is nonexistent. Other tankers have said nothing so he stay's quiet. Truth is the crews are mostly safe at this point. A barrier of flames and mortar rounds separate them from the Dirties who have stopped about a quarter mile behind them and dug in waiting for the last of the retreating soldiers to disappear behind the Wall.

A bright yellow spark arches from another tank to a large machine that looks like a huge ice cream cone. It buckles, then collapses, falling to the roadway. Spilling a soupy gray liquid that immediately explodes into a ball of flames, the flaming liquid rolls onto a set of industrial buildings near the Columbia slough and lights them up as well in a series of timed explosions "This is WeatherEye. We confirm detonation. Runt One, Carpet Two, and Rabbit One, you have fifteen minutes to get across the river. It should take you three. Your count, is four by four. With the indomitable Commander Rader useless as tits on a bull--as always. Keep him safe Runts--we wouldn't want to inconvenience our local celebrity. Link going down. ID systems set on fifteen. Fail-safe locked. Interlocks in place. Self destruct on. Just get across the bridge. Good luck. WeatherEye, final-out." Ewalt watches all the lights on the communication system go red. It's a race to the I-5 bridge. The other SWATS engage full forward drive. He does so as well and the tanks speed onto the old freeway ramp heading north. Ewalt pulls his helmet off. The only tanker sure the tanks will receive no enemy fire.

"We are almost there," he calls to the old man crammed behind the driver's seat in the empty ammunition store. Baylor lies in the gunner's perch watching the show. "When we are across the bridge they will guide us to the staging area. I guess we bivouac ten or so klicks in from the Wall--unless SOP has changed. You make sure our friend Mr. Baylor keeps his mouth shut, old man, or we are both dead. No fuckin' howling and no scalps until we say so. He's battle damage and that will be easy for them to see--but he has to keep his mouth shut. I'll get you both to an ambulance and then we are done--until I can get a hold of Jack Porter and link up with the Priestess. At that point I'll collect you two and my druthers."

"We understand the rules. Just make sure you understand the needs of your country." Phillip watches the man as he drives the tanks scanning the area around him. The notion of a hound dog looking for prey comes to his mind.

Baylor, wearing the uniform of a tank commander sports a set of wounds from his battle with Ewalt and bloody bandages that hide a pair of pistols and his Bowie knife. Despite it all, Phillip is glad Baylor is with him as his protector and Elena's weapon. He is her best chance at getting home alive though Phillip wonders about Commander Ewalt Rader. From the one-sided conversation he has heard, it appears the others have a high regard for the Commander and his tenacity. Besides, the beating Baylor took was so one sided, Phillip wonders if he were dreaming the fight.

The three men were in the cafeteria getting ready to leave when

Phillip asked Baylor if he was sure Ewalt was good enough for Elena. Ewalt was reclining on a table, and Baylor tried to slug him in face. Ready as always, Ewalt slid the punch as best he could, grabbed the hand, and tossed Baylor over the table like he was a recruit. Then, knowing Baylor would grab for his knife, Ewalt tossed it away and clamped Baylor's windpipe shut. After he went unconscious, Ewalt pummeled him so he would know who was the boss. Then he walked out the door to the tank. Baylor was still recovering fifteen minutes later when they spoke to Elena.

Up ahead, Ewalt sees the spires of the remaining 1-5 bridge. The southbound bridge lies in the Columbia, a shattered mess. Scanning around, he sees another set of tanks rolling up from Hayden Island. Spinning to the rear he sees a third set, then a fourth set of SWAT. Nobody wants to be left behind. The twenty-one tanks form up and roar across the bridge. As soon as they motor into the huge concrete tunnel in the Columbia Wall a set of explosions echo through the short passage.

They emerge from the shaft into Vancouver seeing construction crews staged for closing the Wall and a line of semis with what appear to be sets of steel doors. Ewalt cannot believe his eyes. Last he had heard, there was no plan to allow egress except by air. The doors mean that everything he has heard from both Porter and the others may be true. For a moment, he allows himself to think about an end to the war. There may be a peace after all. *Nah, bullshit. There is no way Porter and the rest of them are going to give up power. It's all a scam for them--but not for her. Damn it all anyway.*

Joe Vaz turns west, his heart thumping madly as the small craft lifts up and darts toward the Wall. The moment it breaches the shore, weapons open up from the Wall. Black smoke erupts from the craft but it still races towards the Wall. He hopes the smoke will deter the weapons. As the ship gets to the Wall it feints west then goes east. The weapons cease. A moment later, trailing smoke, it is over the Wall and out of his sight. He picks up his radio. "Ms. Feiss, Elena?"

"We're okay. We're about to land in a mess." It is Elena Etu's voice. "They know who is flying the ship now, the transponder in her neck. I think we're okay. Make sure to get that message to Phillip. He'll know what to do."

"Every fifteen minutes, three red flares. Repeat it twice, Yes dear." He hears laughter.

"Dr. Vaz, you take care of yourself."

"You t--" the radio is dead. "Damn." Joe Vaz stands on a small hill watching the smoldering bridge as a second set of charges explode all along the structural steel above water. The metal heaves once, then the entire structure drops below the Columbia. Joe looks around the hill at the officers and soldiers surrounding him. He feels like a sardine in a can. "Tell the others that they all made it. Now could I please have some space?" He drops his field glasses against the Kevlar vest and begins walking down the hillside. He feels a powerful sting against his chest knocking him backwards and against the ground. *Not again.* Seconds later, soldiers jump on top of him to protect him and the rest fan out to return fire. A war erupts around him. He can feel sets of bullets impact the bodies above him and a wash of blood rolling out covering his face. Spitting trying to get up, the others hold him down. Unaware that he could drown in the blood of the dead soldiers on top of him. He begins to cough and choke. The gunfire intensifies. He can hear explosions and feel screams of pain.

The tank rolls along the freeway, passing looted machinery and equipment dumped on the Vancouver side of the Columbia River. Guards stand by the cache of materials so huge it overflows onto the freeway shoulders. A line of semis and rail trailers stretches as far as the eye can see. It is output from the truck factory that had been based in Portland. The line of tanks continues up the freeway eventually passing the clean, demure landscape of shopping malls and restaurants. Were it not for the equipment and machinery stored along the sides of the roadway--and everywhere else he can see--this could be anywhere suburbia.

"This TopCat, Rabbit One, we will guide you in. You're about two klicks away from out locale."

"TopCat, I need a shower. I stink and I am hungry."

"That's a no-go, Commander. Apparently, there were very few who made it back and you have a set of VIPs on their way down to meet you. Your GPS will be functional as well as limited communication. But you'll be under the command of N-MI-OPS. This is TopCat out. Welcome back, Rabbit One."

The tank lurches for a moment as the communications and control protocols shift to Northwest Military Intelligence. The forward motion adjusts to a slightly quicker speed as Ewalt's tank falls in closer to the other tanks. He watches the tanks take up protective positions around his tank. Then they all speed up passing the rest of the convoy. He checks his controls. They are non-functional. His tank is being driven remotely. "Gentlemen, I think we have a problem. We are now being escorted by three tanks. One behind us, one in front, and one on the side. We are on our way to a debriefing with military intelligence. If I had to guess, I'd say they know you are here and they are a little more than curious as what is going on. We will be scanned when we are let out of this can. Assuming they don't gas us first."

"And our options?" Phillip asks. He isn't overly surprised by the turn of events but he does need to know if Elena made it through the wall. "Have you seen any flares yet?"

"No."

"Did you know they might do this, Commander?"

Ewalt thinks for a moment before answering. He decides the truth is best. "I didn't think they had the capacity to monitor you two if you weren't hooked into the systems. I thought they would just recognize a dead load and assume it is loot."

"Then let me make a suggestion that might keep all of us alive. Tell them you are working for Porter Industries and you have information just for Jack Porter," Phillip says glancing at Baylor who now checks his meager weapons.

"You want me to tell MI that they will just have wait until I talk to Jack Porter? You're kidding?"

"Commander, it will keep us safe a little longer--until they talk to your friend Porter. Otherwise, we are dead bodies and you are a traitor. The sooner you do this the better."

The tank slows for the exit ramp, then heads west passed the artichoke fields. They are on their way to nowhere. He notes the other tanks remain close so he doesn't yet expect the tank to self destruct. "N-MI-OPS this is Rabbit One. Be advised I am on a mission for Porter Industries and I will have to speak with Jack Porter before debrief. Can you arrange this?" Silence greets him. "N-MI, do you copy?" There is no verbal response, but the tank begins to slow. Ewalt scans around and sees the other tanks falling away. Up ahead is an abandoned shopping mall. The tanks pulls in and stops. The back door lowers and the cool clean scent of cut grass enters the tank.

Joe Vaz is pulled from under the bodies. The guards continue firing as he tries to figure out if this is chaos or a planned assault. The locations of the snipers and the explosions tell him it is not just someone deciding they want control. This is a trap. They pull him along into a ditch and throw him to the mud. More soldiers appear and the battle intensifies for a minute or so. They grab him again and soon he waits in a small revetment of broken concrete as the soldiers surrounding him call in other troops. A truck pulls up full of soldiers; he is hauled into it and sped down the roadway to the ruins of an apartment complex that now looks like a fortress. All the buildings surround a central courtyard. The roof contains gun emplacements and troops fan out to what were once garages. The roadways around the central courtyard are sealed. Escorted from the truck, he is shown into a first floor apartment. The wood floors are pristine and his desk sits in the corner. He turns to a soldier beside him."What happened?"

"An ambush. We've got it handled. Where do you want the flares set up?"

"Where is Lloyd Center?"

"About five-hundred yards north from here."

"Over by the corner. Then we'll begin staging for the factory." He checks his watch. "Okay light the first set of flares." He steps into a large bedroom. By a hammock sits a small cage. Inside, a mouse eats a piece of lettuce.

Ewalt watches the flares. "Three flares--Ms. Feiss and Ms. Etu are two of the luckiest people I have even known. They made it across the Wall."

"Of course they'd make it." Phillip looks back at the tank door then out the driver's blister at the three tanks that had escorted them. They are a good two-hundred yards away. The tanks have fanned out surrounding them. Escape is impossible.

"General, I am sure we can take Iwo Jima." Baylor now wears only body armor covering his chest. He has removed the rest of his clothing.

"Baylor, get dressed please." Phillip faces Ewalt who stares, shaking his head. "Baylor, you are a wounded soldier in friendly territory." Ewalt notes that isn't too far from the truth. One eye on Baylor, Phillip continually scans the area and comforts himself with the notion Elena made it across the river. He expects to be in prison soon and that angers him. He has a score to settle with Margrete Feiss.

Ewalt stares out the back door, down the street, hoping for that big black limousine of Jack Porter's to motor up the roadway. Occasionally he looks at Baylor who is slowly dressing. *That is one cuckoo SOB,* he says to himself. He knows that in this situation Baylor is a ticking bomb. And he could get them all killed without any warning. Ewalt sees Phillip watching him. "If they were going to kill us they would have already."

The old man exits and circles the tank. Ewalt watches the tanks react as weapons are trained on the old man.

"Mr. Baylor, why don't you take a walk and scout the area?" Ewalt says stepping onto the daylight. He quickly puts distance between himself and Baylor who exits the tank and scans the area like a General.

"They'll kill you if you go too far, Baylor," Phillip says, understanding Ewalt's concerns but unwilling to sacrifice Baylor at this point. "In fact, please sit quietly. That might keep us all safe."

Baylor looks at the two men. "It's not worth the atom bomb." Sittings crossed-legged, arms at his sides, he rocks slowly back and forth trying to calm himself.

"Baylor," Phillip says. "She is safe. We saw the flares."

He smiles. "Then I am dead."

Elena Etu stands in the breeze, staring at the tanks and soldiers surrounding her. She has already heard her name mentioned by the soldiers who do not approach. Amanda Feiss stands beside her. Her face is smudged with soot from the crash. Behind them sits the flattened remains of the helicopter. "You're a pretty good pilot."

Amanda wears the eyes of Brutus and says nothing. She believes she has won. A jeep approaches with two uniformed men and a pair of men in suits. They stop a few feet away and one of the suits exits the jeep. She is not surprised the soldiers in the jeep wait like chauffeurs for the executives. She recognizes both suited-men and frowns. Then the jeep backs up. The taller man approaches, scans the two women, and then smiles at Amanda. "Ms. Feiss, Ms. Etu, I am Jack Porter." He sticks out his hand and shakes Elena's hand. The coarseness of her grip surprises him. The rest of her is so soft. "Ms. Feiss, your mother believes you are dead. Welcome back. And I believe you might remember me. Ms. Etu. Can you tell me about Ewalt?"

Both Jack Porter and Elena Etu see the surety of Amanda Feiss crumble with these words. Amanda recovers quickly. "Mr. Porter, why yes I remember you. I had been expecting someone from the Feiss staff to greet me. Is that my boy standing over there--waiting for you?"

"He is one of your executives--yes. Where is Ewalt Rader, Ms. Etu?" He asks.

Amanda Feiss blinks; her face red. She immediately turns to Elena Etu and waits for her response.

"I think he made it across," Elena says. "He was in one of their tanks."

Jack Porter nods. "They just captured a rogue tank."

"For some reason I am out of the loop on that part of it," she says. "Ewalt?" She is asking Jack Porter.

"Yes."

"Like a bad penny, that one."

He faces Amanda Feiss. "Apparently your mother has Ewalt and whomever he was transporting under her protection. I guess she figured the tank was the likely transport for the Priestess here and the helicopter was the decoy. That's why I'm here to greet you two. " For a moment, he considers who might be in the tank with Ewalt. He hopes it is Doctor Joseph Vaz. Tales of his food system have finally reached the Corporate Council--thanks to Colonel Cavanaugh. Jack decides to go for the win. "You might want to consider who your allies are and who stands to gain by your demise, Ms. Feiss." He brushes back his blond hair.

Amanda tries to regain her composure but fails wondering how Ewalt Rader made it through all this without her knowledge. "I know just whom I can trust."

Jack nods looking at Elena Etu. His eyes wander her face and figure, taking in the partially open tan flak jacket. "Only you could make that look good. Let me introduce myself: I am the man that sent Ewalt Rader to speak with you. I am hoping that his conversation with you has something to do with the reason why you are here. I would like to form an alliance with both of you." Elena Etu measures this man surprised that the Commander really does know him so well and would be so trusted. Jack Porter, like so many of his kind, has little trust in anyone or anything. She concludes he trusts a boyhood friendship, but not the man. "So then you know who I work for?" She says to Jack Porter. Elena wants to know just how much Porter knows, if anything.

He nods at Amanda Feiss. "You were working for them. You quit a few weeks ago with a rather pointed letter of resignation that resulted in the demise of her father." He pauses for a moment, sees that Amanda Feiss seeks no revenge, and begins to calculate the dynamics of these two. "Now I suspect you are here to state the obvious. The

end is near and you hold the cards for how ugly it gets. That means--
for people like me--that you are a prize that has high value, but little
respect. A long term loser in this negotiation who has every reason to
seek friends. You need people you can trust." He stares at Amanda
Feiss. "She and I are interested in power and we have impact on power
for this side of the Wall. We need your support for the other side of
the Wall. Shall we all work together?"

Elena Etu watches the smile on Amanda's face.

Elena speaks: "We are missing two key players in this: Margrete
Feiss and the Government. Once we are all sitting down at the table
we can work this out. Saying more than that makes me a fool. But I
have reason to support your efforts if they are congruent with mine."

Amanda looks at Jack Porter wondering if he is as fit and able as
his friend Ewalt. Killing Porter would be a win. Wounding him would
be a mess. And, not knowing the fullness of Ewalt's involvement she
worries that the wrong move could lead to worse trouble if this man
has control over Ewalt's father. She decides to play it low key until she
can account for all the players. "I agree with Elena. We all need to sit
and chat. Will that include your friend, Phillip? He is a loose cannon."
Amanda has an idea that his anger may be some help. "He is in the
tank," She says providing a piece of information she is certain Jack
Porter wants. Amanda Feiss plans to build an alliance with both of
these people--before she has them killed.

Elena nods. "Mr. Porter, Dr. Vaz has remained on the other
side of the Wall--as insurance."

"Sorry about that, Elena. Joe Vaz is dead. You are alone."
Amanda smiles. "The remainder of my team had orders to kill him as
soon as I was over the Wall."

"We'll see." Elena wonders about the flares, then assumes it is
possible he made contingency plans in case he died. That would be like
him, but she does not believe him dead. Phillip is far too thorough and
they both saw it coming.

"I think we have accommodations in Seattle at the Mark
Hopkins. I have a flight waiting for us at the airbase though I am
unable to contact your mother, Ms. Feiss. She seems to be ignoring me
at this point."

"May I call her?" Amanda asks. "I am sure she will attend once
she hears I am okay." Jack Porter smiles and hands her the phone. This
is exactly what he wants.

Amanda dials the family number and waits.

"Scout, oh my God, you're alive?" Her mother's voice is frantic.
It startles her daughter. "You were in that helicopter? Are you okay?"

"I am fine, Mother. I am here in Vancouver. I have Ms. Etu
with me, and Jack Porter. I believe he has been trying to set up a
meeting in Seattle at the hotel. Looks like it is time to end this mess
and get civilization back on track." Both Jack and Elena note she does
not report the death of Joe Vaz to her mother. Now neither of them
believes her words of support.

"Of course, dear. What about those men in the tank they have down there? One of them is that horrible Rader fellow."

"The old man is a brilliant tactician. He is responsible for much of what they have achieved. He is the key to understanding their logistics and plans. He should be kept alive at all costs." Amanda looks at Jack Porter amazed at how clean he looks. "The third man is just dangerous."

"I see. Well tell me more when you get into town. Will you fly up?"

Amanda holds her breathe for just a moment. "Of course. We should be there in an hour or two, once we collect everyone and make use of Mr. Porter's aircraft."

"Oh don't bother about those men in the tank. I'll take care of them, Scout. I love you. Be careful for God's sake."

"You too." Amanda closes the cell phone and hands it to Jack Porter. Elena and Jack both look at her waiting to see if she knows what they now know. Amanda speaks, "Mr. Porter, I believe you will be able to count on my support on the following condition: We drive north, but you send your plane anyway." Her lips close tightly at the end of the sentence and she waits. "If the plane makes it then we may have to make other arrangements."

"We will need to drive to the hanger to make a good show of it. I believe we will be able to work together, Ms. Feiss. And you, Ms. Etu, are you in agreement on this?"

Elena Etu stares at these two people wondering how she is ever going to get out of the meeting alive. Her next thought is for Joe Vaz. "Mr. Porter, you and Ms. Feiss are interested in the retention of power, even though you believe there is no future for the Patrician Order. I will not support the Patricians. I will support peace, trade, and normalization."

"Then we are agreed," says Amanda Feiss.

Elena stares at her madness. Jack Porter nods.

A Rapier gunship appears overhead. Ewalt hopes Amanda Feiss isn't flying it. The gunship hovers overhead, banked so that its armaments are set on the three men. A sun-white light bathes them in a sea of blindness. "Nobody move," booms a loudspeaker. "Hands over your head. Palms out."

"Only one gunship. Things are looking up," Phillip says with a smile. *This might mean they have begun to address the hose problem. That isn't good.* A set of five cars enters the parking lot. The two front cars are security as is the last car. The two vehicles in the center are armored limousines. *Well, we make to the end of the drive. Wherever the hell that is.*

The vehicles come to halt as a pair of four-person security teams emerge from the front vehicles. A set of four snipers emerge from the last vehicle. All the soldiers are heavily armed.

"Lie face down on the ground, hands and legs out. And don't

move."

Ewalt speaks quietly. "Mr. Baylor you need to drop all of your weapons. Those gunships know what weapons you are carrying because they are scanning all of us right now."

Baylor looks at Phillip who nods. Baylor places his two handguns and the Bowie knife on the ground. They all lie down and wait. A rush of boots thunder towards them as men and women swarm all over them. Soldiers with scanners and dogs circle them. Ewalt gets hauled to his feet blinded by lights from every direction.

A second later the men are told to advance slowly towards the third car. Its door opens and Margrete Feiss exits. "She's got balls that one," Ewalt says to the others. He watches her watch them.

When she sees Phillip she appears startled. A smile breaks out on her face. "I had heard it was a brilliant tactician, Phil. Who else could it have been?" She walks towards him and shakes his hand.

Phillip smiles hello and for a moment, Ewalt wonders if they have been betrayed.

"Your strategy, right?" Says Margrete Feiss with a smile.

He nods.

"I hate you." And she laughs. "We have a meeting in Seattle with your Ms. Etu, Jack Porter, and my daughter. There is food and refreshment in the car. We can neighbor afterwards." Her eyes drift to Baylor and his mad eyes. Then she examines Ewalt Rader as if he were a bug. She doesn't even acknowledge him other than to point at the two men and turn away. Just as she gets in her car two darts strike the two soldiers. They fall unconscious. She turns back around and looks at Phillip. "You'll ride with them. People might talk." She winks.

"That was always your concern." He grins, hiding his anger. "You are still too predicable, Margrete," Phillip says loudly.

"Then you still love me. I am warmed." She waves, gets in the car, and drives off.

CHAPTER FORTY

Jack Porter, on a secure cell phone, speaks to the female pilot of the aircraft telling her to take her time flying to Seattle. The pilot responds in the affirmative and he kills the link, smiling. "They will delay takeoff for an hour."

During the drive north, he has an unceasing set of questions for Elena Etu; Amanda Feiss tries to make sure his questions are answered in a way that will not weaken her position. The only piece of conversation that goes anywhere is the discussion on Ewalt Rader. And in that discussion, Jack is pleased to hear that between Amanda Feiss' debutante whining and Elena Etu's misconception about Ewalt's spine, they know almost nothing about him. Most importantly, Amanda has no idea Ewalt's father has been sequestered on the family farm near Everett. That means he is safe. Jack Porter genuinely fears Ewalt Rader.

As the small convoy passes the last hill and approaches Seattle, a plume of smoke from Boeing airfield catches their attention. Jack, having just answered a call from one of his subordinates, instructs the driver to take the exit and drive down to the airport.

Amanda Feiss, fearing the worst, tries to remain calm, but

Elena and Jack see her concerns. When they pass the security guards and approach the crash site, she sees for herself that a Porter Industries jet has crashed on approach. The limo stops at the crash site. There is a set of investigators by the fuselage section. Amanda exits the car and hurries towards them. Elena sees the body of the Feiss Industries executive who had been in the jeep, dead under a makeshift shroud. Jack Porter stares at the body of the female pilot and wonders if Susan has been alerted yet to the death of her lover.

Elena stretches her legs, waiting for the inevitable pitch from Jack Porter; it doesn't take a moment to begin: "Ms. Etu, I have just lost staff who were impersonating us. That, as I am sure you know, was our flight. It seems there was an explosion just before landing. My people tell me it was a missile--supposedly a terrorist act. I have never lost a jet in this airspace and I do not believe this was coincidental. There are no survivors." His matter-of-fact attitude chills Elena but she understands the theatrics. "Margrete Feiss is an unreasonable woman who will stop at nothing to control her world. You are in her way, as is her daughter. I may be minor in this but I seek sanity. This makes me similar to you." He pauses, sees no response, then continues. From the corner of his eye he sees Amanda Feiss turn from the investigators, recognize her mistake of leaving the two of them alone, and start to walk back. "Killing my own progeny is just outside my league. If you will help me I will protect you in any way I can. And until you say different--I will do this. If only to prove my metal."

Elena watches his eyes. He appears sincere, in the way a minor player will be sincere. Later on is another story but she is willing to deal with that challenge at another time. The common enemy is Margrete Feiss. She knows at this point this is true for Amanda Feiss as well.

"The people from the FAA say it was a terrorist missile. Idiots." Her eyes are pure rage as she approaches them. "I am impressed that you rate a visit from FAA, Mr. Porter."

"We are far more important a player than you might imagine."

They both ignore Elena who is a bit surer of her position, upon hearing that representatives of the federal government are on site. Jack Porter looks at her and mistakenly assumes it is the result of his offer, not the arrival of federal officials. Jack speaks: "Anyone care to speculate on why we were targeted?" He fronts a sad countenance. He believes he has won.

Amanda will have no more of his game. "With my mother alive, I have no support inside Feiss. With her death, I will assume the chair person's role. Can we stop the nonsense and get this done?" She opens the door of the car and gets in. Elena and Jack trade glances. She nods to Jack. "You have my support." The vehicle leaves the crash site, heading north. "How trustworthy is your friend, Phillip?" Amanda asks thoughtfully.

Elena nods. "I trust him. Though I suspect the first chance he gets he will kill your mother. He sees her as a prime mover in all this." Elena Etu has become a pragmatist in the last few minutes. "We should find out where your mother is as soon as possible. That's how we will find Phillip and Commander Rader--that bit player who seems to be right in the middle of everything. That's an event I don't like. It seems odd to me that this supposed warrior just gave up when the going got tough. I don't trust him." In truth she does trust him. She believes that he and Baylor are the only two people she can trust at this point--though she thinks that Baylor is, in fact, dead. Elena also believes that if nothing else, the Commander will know his chain of command and that is her next step--if she can stay alive.

Jack stares out the window wondering about this Phillip person. There are rumors Margrete Feiss had a lover many years ago. His name was Phillip also. The coincidence scares him. "According to the reports, your mother waits for us at the Seattle Mark Hopkins. Presumably she will be duly informed of our demise and then inform Ms. Etu's people whom she has prisoner. She will then conclude she controls the game. It seems to me she may kill them if they are not cooperative--but she will worry about Dr. Vaz. How smart is this fellow, Phillip?" He asks Elena.

"Quite, but I suspect that with the report of my death he will just assume the hell with it all. So far as he knows, Dr. Vaz will solidify our position and wait out the end of your resources and defenses here. What about your friend, the Commander?"

Jack Porter shakes his head. "I don't know. Ewalt is far smarter than I gave him credit. You know him well, Amanda. What will he do?" He sees confusion in Elena's eyes. "They were lovers."

Amanda is surprised to see no real shock in the eyes of Elena Etu. "Seriously?" Elena asks Amanda. "You slum?"

"Now why would that matter to you?" Amanda grins. "My mother will take any lever she can find and use it. Presumable she would mourn my death and suggest Ewalt help her get to Dr. Vaz-- and then kill him to destroy the food factory. She does not know he is already dead." They crest the hill and enter the glow of light and activity that is Seattle. "She would use the doctor as leverage when she speaks to the corporate council. Too bad for her he is dead."

"You don't know he is dead," Elena says.

"That's true. Don't you love a good mystery?" Amanda knows she has scored a point when Elena Etu looks back at the city.

The multicolored lights of the flashy cars on the crowded freeway, the airships overhead with their glowing signs, the tall buildings surrounding the rush of commerce, Elena stares at well-dressed Seattle with awe in her eyes. The population of the Seattle Metropolitan area is now well over ten million. She watches it as if she were fresh off the farm.

The atmosphere inside the vehicle has become confusing for Jack Porter. All three people think they have won. Amanda Feiss because of her connections and her belief that Joe Vaz is dead. Jack Porter because he sees Amanda Feiss as naive and Elena Etu as needing his help; Elena Etu because she is now sure the federal government knows where she is and where she is going. As Elena looks outside she continually checks the sky. Not seeing any helicopters or other surveillance, she focuses on the opulence and blindness of those in the streets and speaks quietly to the others "My, what's wrong with you people? How much is enough for you?"

Jack Porter looks away suppressing a smile. "There is never enough to fill the maw of pain we create. It is the key to the system. You know that." This time he smiles at Amanda. "Ms. Feiss, your mother will have those men brought to her--at the hotel? Presumably to gather information?"

Amanda nods her agreement. "She will be in the Feiss suites on the 23rd floor. Three floors below and three above will be Feiss employees." She watches Jack Porter. "Of course you knew this already."

"You need a strong ally on this side of the Wall because you don't want any of the myths about your family destroyed. You need Elena's support on the other side of the Wall because it makes everything that much smoother. Ms. Etu needs us to keep her alive. We don't need your mother's support. When she is neutralized we can work towards peace and the ascendency of our corporations during process. Porter Industries will be happy to work under Feiss. But I want three board seats, including Vice Chair--which I will take. In exchange you can have three seats on the Porter Industries board including Vice Chair. Is that acceptable?"

"Done." Amanda would have agreed to elect the Easter Bunny CEO of Feiss at this point. "Tell the driver to take us to the old monorail station downtown. There is a way to get onto the 23rd floor from there. We can't take weapons, because of the sensors. But the three of us should be able to get to the office suite undetected. With any luck, we can toss the old bitch out a window."

His eyes widen at the comment but he says nothing other than to direct the vehicle downtown. Elena speaks as she watches the city. "So when we get there, the plan is to remove your mother from power. Then what?"

Jack likes this woman. He says: "We will get you back to your side of the Wall and begin making peace by providing resources."

"We can return some of the items we took from Portland and allow some low level manufacturing to begin--as well as provide advisors--to restore services in Portland," Amanda says quickly.

"And you want?" Elena asks.

"No more assaults against us," Amanda says looking at Jack. "Okay with you, Jack?"

"Fine." He appears pleased with Amanda, even though he has no faith in her words.

"What about the Wall?" Elena asks.

"It remains shut until we see that there is no danger. The first major step to opening the Wall is the reestablishment of order in Portland through the use of a joint police force. Once order is established, we will allow entrepreneurs to cross the Wall and continue development. We will arrange a tightly controlled visa system to allow family member to find each other. Feiss Industries will assume control of that process."

"Okay by me," Jack says.

Carefully Elena Etu says: "And what about on this side of the Wall--what kind of changes will be made?"

Jack and Amanda look at each other as if Elena were speaking a foreign language. "No changes. We will integrate the ravaged lands back into America. Socialism has no place in America," Jack Porter says.

"So the status quo, and everything that has happened is a vague memory of some madness that took over the poor deranged Dirties." Elena speaks calmly and follows it up with: "And what is in it for me?" She speaks the language that shows she is no fool. Without this question, she knows the other people in the car will not trust her.

"Now we are getting somewhere. What do you want?" Amanda says taking the lead role and letting Jack Porter understand where his place is in the Amanda-World-Order.

Elena notes he has no problem with her tone or disrespect. It gives her some modicum of hope. "I run the show on the other side of the Wall--board seats on both corporation--support for my economic policies by this side of the Wall."

"Meaning?" Jack asks.

"There is a great big wonderful world out there. You want parts of it. If the price is right I am selling my support. I get fifteen per cent of everything that crosses the Wall. Once the Wall is down, I will retain ownership of some key commodities."

"Which ones?" Amanda asks amusing herself.

"The ones which are most valuable," Elena replies, not missing a beat.

"You drive a hard bargain, but okay," says Amanda.

Elena wonders why Amanda does not see her own ineptitude. Her plans are as clear as the buildings around them: Betrayal. Elena smiles at Jack Porter who seems to understand that he is being relegated to a minor player stuck between two power bases. It is a position he is used to and he feels somewhat better seeing what he thinks is clarity in the dynamic of those in the car: Amanda is a snake and Elena is an idealist.

"Okay," Amanda says. "I think we can work together. Jack, do you agree?"

He nods. "There are some minor details but I think we can handle those in due time." The car rolls to a stop in an underground parking garage beneath the monorail station. "I have long coats for you both--I had a sense we might be needing some level of stealth." He walks over to a waiting car, nods at the driver, then hands the two women leather coats of the finest calfskin. Jack remains clothed only in his blue suit. He removes a hand gun from his shoulder holster, thinks better of it then removes the holster. By the time he has put the jacket back on, the women are ready.

The damp smell of the parking garage mixes with the smell of ozone from the charging stations. The host of parked cars shine as if there were no such thing as dirt. "We go this way," Amanda says pointing to an elevator. They cross through twin glass doors just as an elevator opens. A pair of well-dressed couples holding shopping bags exit, ignoring the three people. Amanda gets in first and hits the 3rd floor key twice. Then she holds down the door-close key and pushes the 3rd floor button three times. The elevator door closes.

"How Bond," Elena says. *Amanda really believes that we can arrive unannounced now. How could Feiss security not monitor that code?* She feels sad for the little girl playing queen.

A few moments later, the doors open and they are looking at what appears to be a narrow construction hallway lit by mold-covered skylights. The trio hurries down the hallway crossing over the street to enter the hotel. Directly in front of them is a ladder. Beyond it is a service elevator. "We climb the ladder. The elevator alerts security. I found that out when I was a kid." She smiles and grabs onto the ladder. Hoops of steel provide some level of safety for their climb. "There's twenty stories of climb. Let's go." She leads the way.

"Can you see anything?" Jack says.

"When I was a child this was one of my favorite places in the city. You can get off the ladder at each floor and spy on almost any room. I can get us to the 23rd floor with my eyes closed."

"What about that leg?" Elena asks.

"I'll be fine. Thank you for your concern." They continue climbing.

Ewalt sits at a table in the luxurious apartment overlooking Seattle. He eats another a ham and yellow cheese sandwich. Phillip, who has just changed into the first clean clothes in over a decade, cannot help but wonder about Elena Etu and considers that Margrete Feiss' was there to greet them rather than the government forces. He marvels at the impotence of government and fears Elena's idealism. *The documents inside those pieces of plastic are nothing but an embarrassment anyway. She never thought of it that way.* He crosses over to Ewalt looking for Baylor. "Where is Baylor?"

"In the next room, still drugged, still tied up. I think they figured the guy was a looney tune and they're just waiting for the right time to off-him. He has no idea where he is. They're just not sure what he knows. Good sandwich--this is great ham. You might want something to eat before we get to the big show. "

"Meaning?" Phillip asks.

"This is where we find out just how fucked we are and what they want."

"No, this is where we find out how to save our asses. What do you want to do?"

Ewalt is certain the room is bugged and he wonders what the old man means. "Let's find out just how fucked we are first." He takes another bite of his sandwich. He can't remember the last time he had a ham and cheese sandwich on toast. "This is really good."

A heavily armed dark-suited guard enters the room "Chairperson Feiss would like to see you all." He points to the door and three more guards. Ewalt stuffs a piece of ham into his mouth and smiles seeing that there are only four guards.

They walk down an opulent hallway of fine hardwoods and paintings. Baylor is roused and dragged after them. The thick deep blue carpets caresses their gait and seems to propel them forward as they walk.

On their right is a pair of double doors leading to a large front office full of administrative people. "Go right in," says one of the lithe secretaries who stands at the door. Ewalt winks at the woman as he walks by and notes the four guards follow them inside--but there are no others. He assumes a team of heavily armed guards are located behind a fake wall somewhere in the opulent office. Baylor is dropped in an elegant chair off to the side. His hands pat the leather. "Nice, very soft. I had gloves like this." He looks around for Elena Etu, then closes his eyes. Baylor has had enough.

In front of a wall of windows sits Margrete Feiss. Two of her male executives stand alongside the chair. One of them speaks to Ewalt and Phillip. "You gentlemen please sit down on the couch. A long deeply cushioned oxblood leather couch faces the desk. As he passes Baylor to sit, Ewalt notices an odd calm and pities the drugged soldier. He licks the salt off his fingers from the ham.

The men sit on the couch facing Margrete Feiss. "Can I get you anything?" She asks, the soul of congeniality.

"I'm thirsty, coffee?" Says Ewalt. Phillip looks at him considering him an idiot; he assumes anything will be drugged to lower inhibitions. Then he remembers the ham sandwich and smiles.

"You remember our traditions." Margrete raises her right hand. "Amanda speaks of you often." A small woman immediately enters with a tea caddy. She pours Ewalt a cup of coffee. Offers him cream and sugar, which he greedily takes then hands him the absurdly small cup of finest porcelain, trimmed in gold leaf.

He can barely hold the cup it is so dainty. "I can't remember the last time I had coffee. Oh wait. I do remember. You served it to me."

She nods ignoring him. "So Phillip, how have you been? I lost track of you after our last meeting in the Hunt's Point Hotel. Did your wife ever divorce you and take the kids? Did she ever forgive us? Whatever happened to her?"

He angers. "Can we get down to it?" Phillip asks. "What do you want?"

"We have some more guests. We should wait." Margrete Feiss stands up and circles the desk to lean back against it. Ewalt sips his coffee quietly. Margrete looks at one of the guards who watches a small video screen in his palm.

"Any moment," the guard says. "They just entered the family

quarters and they are heading this way. About five seconds." She nods then looks to her right at a wooden panel. The door swings out and Amanda Feiss walks in with Elena Etu and Jack Porter. Everyone but Margrete Feiss is surprised. When Elena sees Baylor drugged in the chair, she looks at Phillip angrily. She knows he is dead if he is in this room. Baylor stirs--and winks at her--a happy man.

"Please sit down on the couch," Margrete says.

As soon as they sit, two of the four guards approach Baylor. One of them pulls out a pistol and shoots him through the temple killing him instantly. The men pull him backwards on the floor. As expected, Elena cannot function. This is exactly what Margrete Feiss wants.

Amanda looks over to Ewalt noting the coffee cup. Her eyes are pools of worry. "I hope you like the coffee. It's our special blend."

"I know."

Her eyes brighten into a full moon's glow. "Good."

For the first time in his life, he understands Amanda's tragedy. She calms knowing he will be safe, looking at her mother. The gaze startles Margrete Feiss.

"Okay now that we are over that, and you all know I mean business, I want you all to know there is a place for all of you: Either on my team or with that Baylor fellow. Who'd like to start? Scout, I am guessing you are seething with rage. By the way, did you really think I'd allow you unfettered access to my office? I thought you were smarter than that. So?" She watches a child's anger.

"We'll see," Amanda replies.

"I understand." She lifts an index finger and the other two guards grab Amanda Feiss by the hair pulling her backwards off the couch. The guard puts a bullet in her skull and tosses her over onto the pile that was once Baylor. "None of you held her in very high regard anyway so shall we continue? I want your support on the other side of the wall. Do I have it?"

Ewalt sips his coffee. Phillip calms himself waiting for his opening.

Elena Etu looks over to the two dead bodies guessing either the Commander or Phillip is next. Jack Porter is decoration. "What do we get in exchange for our support?"

Margrete Feiss lifts her index finger again and a guard grabs Ewalt Rader. The moment he does, Ewalt takes the coffee cup and drives into the hand of the man, spinning out with surprising speed. He flips sideways missing a round fired at him and pulls the weapon from the wounded man. He then sprays the room killing three guards and turns. What he sees surprises him.

Elena Etu has bolted from her seat and now stands behind Margrete Feiss her hand clenched on her windpipe. The other guard and the two executives stand stunned for a moment. So Ewalt kills them. He slams the main door shut, locking it and then steps away from the doorway--scanning the dead for movement.

Margrete Feiss snarls: "You have control of the room but nothing else. Let me go, you animal."

Seeing Jack Porter and Phillip grab weapons, Elena pulls the older women across the room by her throat, away from the window.

"Are you fucking nuts?" Ewalt asks. He levels his weapon at Margrete Feiss. "Kill that bitch."

"Fuckin' Ewalt," Jack Porter says. "Hang on, dude." He faces Elena Etu. "We can get out of this if you will agree to work with me. I have people on the way."

The phone beeps three time. Elena picks it up and steps back to the side of the office. Ewalt notes her movement and moves closer to her and the side wall. Jack sees their motion and does the same.

"This is Feiss security. We want to speak to Chairperson Feiss. You are surrounded. You will never get out alive."

Elena looks at the others. "Five minutes more of negotiation and we will give ourselves up." She places the phone down on the receiver. She looks at Baylor. Her heart stops for just a moment.

"Mind telling me the plan?" Jack Porter asks.

Ewalt speaks: "Let's take that exit you came in and get the hell out of here." He looks around and picks up another weapon.

Jack Porter barricades the door. "Ewalt, we have a problem. There's lots of them out there."

"No shit, Jacko."

"Do you really trust this man?" Elena points to Ewalt. She is asking Jack Porter.

"You wouldn't know a hero if he walked up to you and saved your life," Jack says, checking the windows. "He is too dumb to cheat."

Phillip walks over to Elena. "Are the good guys on the way?" He is within a foot of Margrete Feiss.

"Madam Chairperson was nice enough to alert them to my arrival by trying to kill me in a plane crash. The FAA was doing an investigation when I arrived in a limo. So I sure hope so." With her words a Rapier helicopter appears outside. Everyone but Elena scatters to get out of sight. She walks to the window and stares out at it. Her hand still on the throat of Margrete Feiss. The helicopter tilts back and forth and the phone rings. She walks over and picks it.

"Ma'am, please have your team step to the side of the room. There is about to be a frontal assault. We will take care of it. And please let Ms. Feiss know that Colonel Cavanaugh sends his regards."

She puts the phone down and looks at Margrete Feiss. "A Colonel Cavanaugh, sends his regards."

Margrete's face is ash.

Elena explains to everyone that they need to move to the side of the room. She drags the woman by the neck to stand by them.

The door and barricade explodes in splinters knocking them against the wall and then to the ground. A team of ten heavily armed men and women rush through the smoke. They are immediately met by the Rapier's twin Gatling guns which shred everything, including them, the far end of the room, the next room, the hallway, across the hallway, the sleeping quarters, and the other exterior wall of the building. When the firing ceases, there is a hole in the building running from wall to wall, with nothing in between except debris and small body parts.

Phillip stands up and hurries over to Margrete Feiss, apparently helping her to her feet. She takes his hand and grins malevolently. She screams.

"Phillip, don't," Elena pleads.

Tightening his grip, the old man hauls Margrete through the shattered window into the night and down to their death.

From the hidden side doorway, four men rush forward firing their weapons. Jack Porter dives behind the couch. Ewalt dives at Elena Etu knocking her back to the ground. Firing his weapon, protecting her with his body, bullets rip into his arm and chest. He keeps shooting, killing two men. His weapon coughs empty. The Rapier reacts: It opens another hole in the building.

When the smoke clears, Jack sees Elena tending to Ewalt's wounds. She will hover over Ewalt's hospital bed tonight, and then be there tomorrow when he opens his eyes.

AMENDMENT

CHAPTER FORTY ONE

The verdant surroundings mean nothing to him. The large pond at the end of the walkway, the maples and elms that form a corridor, the roses and the sport court, the tea garden off to the side, the large garage made to look like a coach house, even the six glistening autos are all lost on Ewalt. He has no sense of now as he walks passed guards, their dogs, the defense berms, and the gun emplacements. *Is this the way they live in their homes? Surrounded by guns and strangers?* He thinks back to his recent conversation with Joe Vaz about how neighbors had protected him for years. *This is power? It looks like another prison. They really are crazy.* Circling a hedge built into a concrete wall that could protect a platoon against a division, he approaches the house. It's done in the grand Tudor style with heavy brickwork and gargoyles. The diamond-shaped windows hold glistening leaded glass lights.

Ten teams of two patrol the area. Ewalt follows the circular path around a central patch of juniper and approaches the front door. It is set back in a four-column wooden portico to protect entrants from the rain. The twin oak doors open and Jack Porter waits dressed in a black sweatshirt, blue jeans and a homburg hat. His hands are on his hips and he's smiling, shaking his head back and forth. "If you aren't

the toughest son of a bitch I ever met, I'm a dog. Come on in, Walt."
He waits all smiles and bright white teeth. Jack closes the door behind
him and puts the hat on a table.

"Jack, I saw my dad. He said you've been by a few times, even
while I was in the hospital. He also said he has an exclusive contract
with Porter Industries for bagels. He's going to open a commercial
bakery just for you guys. Oh, he also says a store opened across the
street selling hardware. The guys running it are the biggest toughest
men he has ever seen. Your men?"

"I knew if you came out of the hospital and anything had
happened to him, well, it would have all been a waste. You'd have
slit me open and tossed in a bed of ants. I told you. You are the only
person I am really afraid of. Let's go talk." He leads Ewalt through the
doors and down a short hallway They pass through a security scanner
and enter a small dark atrium with plush green foliage growing from
the walls. They cross through a single door leading into a greenhouse.
"Do you want any food? Something to drink?" He speaks into a small
intercom that blinks green on the metal frame. "Please bring in a tray."

"Just tell me what you want." Ewalt speaks the words exactly
as he had been instructed to, with just a hint of impatience. The wire
listening device he wears just under his skin itches but he dare not
scratch his arm. The door to the room opens. Ewalt sees a man and
woman enter with twin carts. One cart has food and the other holds
various bottles of drink. They roll the carts to the center of the room.

Okay." Before Ewalt can say another word, the woman places
an automatic pistol to his head. The man who brought in the other
cart puts his index finger to his lips meaning Ewalt needs to be silent.
Jack Porter continues speaking. "So I heard you had a hell of a time in
the hospital."

The man rolls up Ewalt's sleeve, deftly locates the transponder
and quickly injects him. The arm goes immediately numb. "So what
was it like following those crazies up through Oregon? You look ill.
Hang on a minute. I'll get you a napkin." A moment later and the
microphone is gone and a recording of someone coughing erupts from
a small audio device. Then he hears Jack's voice on the audio device.
"Ewalt? Get me a doctor. He's passed out. Damn hero." The two
people leave the room carrying the microphone and playback device
while Jack Porter holds his finger up to silence Ewalt. The doors close.

"That was nicely done," Ewalt says. "But I can't help you."

Jack Porter stares at him. "Ewalt, just who the hell do you
think you work for?" Jack Porter stares at him. The jovial false smile
has faded into a look of determination. "And why would you set me
up? I thought we were friends?"

"Elena Etu works for the US Government. She has for a
generation or so. Joe Vaz has their support for new factories in Seattle
and Chicago. Portland has power." Ewalt glances at a desk clock.
He has been told it is bugged as well. "Jack, Dr. Vaz's food factory
miraculously remained in tact for almost eight years even though they

bombed everything around it into hell. Feiss Industries is in chaos. Lippman's a joke, and Porter Industries can be dissolved. You have a choice. You work with the government or they are going to cut your nuts off. The days of the corporate state are over. And fuck-you, I am your friend. You only get this choice because of me. Because you watched over my dad. I am here to save your ass."

"You?" He laughs. "You're telling me that people like you are going to run things?"

"No me, Jacko. But I am going to support the people who run this nation. You or your group of corporate thugs are now history. Your days have ended."

Jack laughs. "Ewalt, you are a good man and you are an asshole. Wait. Okay, so I say yes and play nice. Then over the next few years new companies set lobbying teams to work against your idealist notion of a national state--and the result? The corporate state regains power. You can't stop us. You are a person, but people like me represent a corporation--a unified power base generating obscene amounts of money. Ewalt, those who do not remember the past are going to do it again. Get it? Forget the national fantasy. It is over. One way or the other we will win. You cannot stop corporations from bending government policy to our will. We have the cash, the motive, and the lack of ethics to win. Work with me. The corporate system is unstoppable. The national state is a dinosaur."

Ewalt smiles. "The peace settlement with the Dirties has an amendment, a clause that was insisted upon by the Dirties. I think Dr. Vaz was behind it. In fact, negotiations broke down until it was agreed upon by all parties. But everything was agreed upon and the amendment was signed."

"A clause? In a contract?' Jack takes a bottle of water opens the top and sips it. "Dude, you are a dope. There is no way to keep my lobbyists from waltzing into the halls of power and taking it over again--contract or not."

"Don't be so foolish, Jacko." Ewalt grins. "I didn't say a contract. I said an amendment--to the Constitution. An amendment that strips corporations of all citizen's rights. You guys can't lobby anymore. And you can't impact laws or alter policy by your actions. You can't alter legislation. You can't even speak to a politician, either in person or through lobbyists. Corporations are now only a tax structure. You are a non-event focused only on the commerce that develops as a result of national policies that are exclusive of corporate desires--by law."

Jack Porter stops drinking and stares at him. "Bullshit. You are saying corporations in the United States of America no longer have the right to petition or influence government policy for any reason?" The white-face and open-mouth of Jack Porter tell Ewalt he has a kill.

Ewalt winks. "That includes contributions for election. A corporation is once again only a legal structure for the production of capital--no more. I've gotta' say, Jacko. I memorized that line. And to be honest, I don't really see why it is such a big deal, but I can tell by the look on your face that you and your friends are now well-screwed. Elena told me I would enjoy this show."

"She fucked us." Jack speaks: "We'll challenge it in court." He sees Ewalt doesn't even consider his words and Jack begins to recognize his world has changed forever. "Damn, son of a bitch. Well I guess that explains why the Generals are in town. They're taking land around here like drugs in a battle." Jack lifts his water in toast to Ewalt. "You really should come work for me, Ewalt. I'm going to be big. By the way, I am your boy. Death to the corporate state!"

"Jacko, I'm going to work for Elena Etu on the other side of the Wall."

Jack's arm freezes. The bottle tips to the point of spilling liquid. "Really?" He straightens up and leans forward. "What are you going to do for her?" He asks as casually as he can.

Ewalt's eyes bore into Jack's. "She needs a killer to protect her."

"Oh bullshit." He laughs.

"She wants me on staff--whatever the hell that means."

"What the heck? Are you serious?" When Ewalt looks at him, Jack unconsciously takes a step back. He knows the look of power. "So the corporate hegemony have been done in by the Dirties, a beautiful woman, and a nut-case academic?" Jack scowls one last time. "And you are in the cat-bird seat?"

"Yup."

"Damn, how did I let that happen?" Jack is laughing.

"With a little help from the Government." Ewalt scans the greenhouse and decides Elena might like a space like this. "Elena made all the difference. She's amazing."

His worst fears bubble out. "Walt, are you in love with Ms. Etu?" Jack finds and lifts the bottle of vodka to his lips. "She'll never go for you. She'll use you like she used that guy, Baylor. They were lovers you know." He picks up a small napkin and wipes his face. Then he follows with, "And that's too bad. You deserve to settle down." He shakes his head in apparent concern. "But I hope she falls for you, Walt. I really do." Jack watches Ewalt, a look of fear in his eyes. This is a look that Ewalt understands and he feels a bit of remorse for his old friend.

"Don't worry, Jack. She'll never fall for me. That woman will die alone at an old age."

"So then maybe I have a chance?" He says in an absurd show of bravado. "Can you get us together? Susan and I are divorcing."

"That's what I always liked about you, Jacko. You never give up. By the way, I am going to stand for you and say you are going to support the plan. If I find out you don't; I am going to come back and kill you. That's really what I wanted you to know. You support the plan or else. I can be your friend or your enemy. Are we clear?"

"Okay, hero, you win. Can you get me into to see her?"

"No problem. She and I are going to see my dad tonight. I'll ask her if she wants to date you."

Jack stares at him unable to think. "Did you just fib to me, Walt?"

"Me? Never. We're buddies. What was that you said in the office at Feiss, that I was too dumb to lie?"

Jack Porter shakes his head no. He has no doubt the world he knew has disappeared. "I said you were to dumb to cheat. You can count on my support."

"Then welcome to the United States, Jacko. I'll put in a good word for you with Elena. Did you know she likes to sail?"

"No, Ewalt, that is news to me."

"Oh, and don't screw it up. I hear the new laws regarding corporate connivance make the military laws look like grade-school detention. In the case of conviction on any level there is a mandatory life sentence for the CEO and destruction of corporate assets--at minimum--and that assumes the Dirties running the trial are feeling benevolent. Execution is an option. You know Elena said there was never any doubt for the demise of the PO. I wonder how she knew?"

"We were never a match for the government?" Jack says with a smile.

"Could be, Jacko. Could be."

www.ingramcontent.com/pod-product-compliance
Lightning Source LLC
Chambersburg PA
CBHW030918260626
47169CB00002B/306